Swim Season

Swim Season

MARIANNE SCIUCCO

Published by Bunky Press

978–0–9895592-4-9

Cover design by Heather McCorkle at McCorkle Creations

Cover Images ©danchooalex/ThinkStock

Formatting by: Perry Elisabeth Design | perryelisabethdesign.com

Bunky Press artwork © patrimonio designs ltd/ Shutterstock

Interior swimmer graphics ©Andrey7777777/AdobeStock

Author Photo © Lou Sciucco

Dedicated to Allison Rose Sciucco, my very own swim champion, who introduced me to the world of swimming and made me love it.

In memory of my friend and fellow Swim Mom
Linda Wiley-Small
Save me a seat.

WEEK ONE:
Walk-ons, Winners, and Wannabes

Chapter 1

Aunt Mags didn't say a word on the way to the high school and neither did I. We were up and out too early for anything more than, "Got everything?" "Uh huh," and "Let's go." We'd left the house before her first cup of coffee and she was not in a talkative mood.

It was just after dawn, the moon still visible as the sun peeked out over the horizon. A chill in the air hinted at summer's end. I regretted leaving my sweatshirt behind, although after swim practice the sun would be shining and we'd be back to the mid-August heat.

We arrived at the school and a deserted parking lot. Mags parked her minivan at the athletics entrance.

"Are you sure it starts at 6:45?" she asked.

"Positive," I said.

She yawned. "Looks like you're the first one here."

"I doubt it."

Today was the first day of swim season. Tryouts started at 7 a.m. The coach had instructed all wannabe swimmers to be on the pool deck no later than 6:45. My experience as a varsity athlete told me that anyone with any degree of competitiveness had already arrived. I had five minutes to spare.

"Want me to walk in with you?" Mags asked.

My horror at her suggestion must have been all over my face, because she said, "Sorry. Having a teenager is new to me. My girls would beg me to walk them into that big, scary building." We looked at the three-story hodgepodge put together to house Two Rivers High School.

"I can take it from here." I was sure I'd remember the meandering route to the pool area from the tour we took when we registered for my senior year.

She still looked anxious. "Sure you're all right?"

"Don't worry. I've got this routine down pat." Two Rivers would be my third high school. I played the role of new girl so well I deserved an Oscar.

I opened the door and hopped out. "Don't hang around waiting for me to call for a ride home," I said, reaching back to grab my bag. "I'm not sure when I'll get out, and I don't want to mess up your day. I'm okay to walk."

Aunt Mags nodded, and I shut the door.

"Don't forget we're going back-to-school shopping later on," she said through the open window.

"Got it."

"Go get 'em, Aerin." She gave me a thumbs-up.

I shot her a grin, hoisted my bag over my shoulder, and went off to join the Two Rivers High School Girls Varsity Swim and Dive Team.

Minutes later, I stood on the pool deck with an odd blend of girls vying to earn a place on the team. I spotted the usual huddle of newbies benched together at the far end of the bleachers, glancing at each other nervously and at the seasoned swimmers with something like awe. On the opposite end were the members of last year's championship team, all wearing team T-shirts and chatting like old pals, ignoring everyone else. In the middle was a bunch who looked like they wanted to go back to bed, the ones whose parents pushed them into a sport and who chose swimming because we did it indoors and it looked easy. Most of them wouldn't make it.

I found a place to stand against the wall and blocked out the curious glances shot my way, using the time before practice began to check out my surroundings. Aunt Mags had said the natatorium, built just a few years ago, was state-of-the-art.

Banners hung from the rafters and on clean white walls, touting the team's success, and an enormous leaderboard listed all of their champions and their accomplishments.

A wall of windows on the farthest side and a ceiling loaded with skylights filled the room with light.

The six-lane pool had blue and white flags and lane lines, and the Trailblazers logo – a torch - was laid out in blue tiles on the bottom.

The floor tiles were a mosaic of white and three shades of blue.

The air was thick with the smell of chlorine.

I checked my expression, not wanting anyone to catch me gaping over the finest natatorium of any team I'd joined. The thought of swimming in it, of calling it "home" for the next few months caused a thrill of excitement in my belly. Around me, the other girls talked and laughed, none of them seeming to appreciate the beauty of the pool and the privilege to use it.

"Good morning girls." A man's voice cut through the chatter, and each girl sat up at attention. "Let's get started."

The voice belonged to an older man, with bushy white hair and bifocals, dressed in the school's colors: navy blue shorts and a white polo shirt. Coach Steven Dudash. I hadn't met him yet – he was out of the building when my father and I visited the high school – but Maggie and her husband, Pat, gave him high praise. He'd coached the Two Rivers boys and girls swim teams for more than twenty years, and they were both winning teams.

He pulled a chair behind him, positioned it in front of the bleachers, sat down, and organized the pile of paperwork on his clipboard. "Good morning," he said again, studying us over the rim of his bifocals. "I'm happy to see last year's team back for another year. And welcome to those of you here for the first time. I'm glad you decided to give us a try."

He took a swig from an extra tall cup of coffee before continuing. "For those of you new to the team, meet Coach Denise." He gestured toward the young woman who accompanied him. "She's my daughter. I coached her for six years when she swam for Two Rivers and got her name on the leaderboard."

I checked out the leaderboard and saw she held the record in the 200 IM and the 100 breaststroke. Good creds.

"This is her second year as assistant coach," he said. "She did a terrific job last year so I invited her back."

The young blonde smiled at him and the swimmers cheered.

"Yay Coach D!" a few seniors shouted.

"It's great to be back," she said. "Ready to win another championship?"

The shouts and applause were deafening.

"During the next two weeks," Coach said when the noise died down, "you'll all be working hard, doing drills both in the pool and in the weight room, four hours a day, six days a week. During the season, you'll be practicing from after school until five or six every weekday, and four hours on Saturday. Sunday is a resting day. And, of course, you will compete in swim meets at least twice a week. So, if you don't think you can make it through the first two weeks, you might as well leave now." He paused, waiting for anyone to opt out before we even got started. No one moved.

"Okay," he continued. "Most of you know that Two Rivers won the Division Championship last year, and the two years before. I plan to win again. When we do, and I say when, not if, we will be the first team in the division to ever win four consecutive division titles."

Last year's team broke out in wild applause and cheers. Coach waited for the outburst to die down before he continued.

"I need performers," he said, "swimmers who aren't afraid to push themselves, to try new things and discover where they best support the team. So, in practice you're all going to swim every stroke, you're all going to swim distance, and you're all going to swim sprints. Each person will do all she can to defend our title."

Silence filled the pool deck as the girls looked each other over, wondering where each would fit in.

"That's the good news." He paused for effect. No worries. He had everyone's riveted attention. "But I've got some bad news. For years, the school board has been supportive of our team, and we've reciprocated by working as serious athletes and turning in winning records. Most years, the team can support as many as thirty-eight swimmers. This year, due to a budget crisis in our school district, our funds have been cut, and I can only put twenty-eight girls on the team."

Raised eyebrows and shocked inhalations followed this bit of news. I counted bodies: thirty-six.

"Yeah, eight of you will be cut, either at the end of this week or the end of next. Anyone want to leave now?"

Again, no one moved.

Coach Dudash smiled. "I like your level of commitment. Let's see if you can keep it under pressure."

He spent the next half hour reviewing team policies and the season's schedule. I'd heard such talks before from other coaches and tuned him out while I studied the other girls, trying to figure out what their positions might be.

Most of them focused on Coach's every word, but last year's champs ignored him and whispered among themselves. One of them, a lanky girl with sun-bleached hair and a killer tan, looked over the group of wannabes and held up her fingers one to five, scoring them, I guess, on whether or not they had a chance. Her friends snickered, trying to act as if they were paying attention to Coach instead of fooling around.

At last, the lanky girl's frosty blue eyes rested on me, and I met her gaze straight on. We stared at each other for a few seconds before she looked away first, then held up three fingers. It seemed she was ambivalent. I could go either way.

I was ambivalent too. I joined this crowd as a walk-on, someone with no history with the team and questionable ability. In their eyes, I was no better than a wannabe who needed to prove herself to gain a spot on the team and the other girls' respect.

I showed up because it's what I did at the start of every school year. Swimming was my only sport, and I was good at it. Really good. Still, I almost skipped tryouts today. The truth was, I didn't have the energy to join a new team, in a new school, for the third time. If anyone found out I'd won championship titles in club and varsity last year they'd expect great things from me, and I didn't want the pressure. Swimming was no longer the focus of my life. It was my therapy, and I wouldn't let anyone mess that up.

The glimmer of challenge in the way the lanky girl looked at me caused a stirring in my gut, and I shot it down. I didn't come here to get involved in any personal challenges. I came here to swim, and not make any waves. My plan was to get through the senior year and go away to college, away from my troubles, and on to a new life that I could control.

I turned away from the girls judging the rest of us and focused on what Coach had to say. At last, he stopped talking and let us get in the pool.

I got behind the wannabes and dived into lane six, the slow lane. I started stroking freestyle, breathing on the third stroke, taking my time. I came into my rhythm and swam lap after lap, gliding through the water like an eel, oblivious to the other girls around me. I focused on the black line on the pool's floor, kicked off the walls with a light push, and kept pace with the swimmer in front of me.

After I had finished the set – 1,000 yards - I stopped for a break and pulled off my goggles. I checked out the other swimmers while catching my breath. In the two middle lanes were last year's champs, moving through the water in flawless formation, making perfect turns. In the other lanes, the wannabes and the slackers struggled to make it from end to end, splashing needlessly, their arms and legs out of sync.

"Hey." A swimmer popped up in lane five. She pulled down her goggles and peered at me with the most exquisite blue-green eyes, like robins' eggs, the lashes dark and thick and not from mascara. "You're new here, aren't you?" she asked, a little breathless.

I nodded, still wondering about those eyes.

"I'm Mel."

"Aerin."

"Senior?"

"Yeah."

"Where are you from?"

"Manhattan."

"The city?" Her eyes lit up.

"That's the place."

"What are you doing here?" she asked, then said, "Sorry. I mean, Two Rivers is such a small town. We almost didn't make it on the map."

"No problem." I liked the way she looked, her face open and honest as though she were genuinely interested in me. "I needed a change."

"Change? In senior year? That's weird."

I raised my eyebrows.

"I don't mean *you're* weird," she was quick to clarify. "I just think it's weird someone would want to change schools in senior year."

"Well, it wasn't like I had a choice."

A whistle blasted right behind us.

"Cut the chit-chat, girls," Coach Dudash said. "No time for talking. Now start over."

Mel and I groaned, pulled on our goggles, and pushed off the wall.

Forty minutes later, we sat on the pool deck as Coach wrapped up practice. "Great first day, girls. Now go home and get some rest. First cuts are on Friday."

A lot of grumbling combined with excited chatter. The lanky

bleached blonde who had been judging us all earlier raised her hand. "Hey Coach," she said, "what's up with the Allison Singer scholarship?"

"Thank you for asking that important question, Jordan." Coach waited for us to stop talking.

Mel sat across from me and I mouthed, "What?"

She smiled back and mouthed, "Listen."

"Allison Singer called me the other day," Coach said. "She is very disappointed that no one has broken her record."

"So does the challenge still stand?" Jordan asked.

"Oh yes." Coach tried not to smile but failed. "And she tells me she's had such an excellent year business-wise she's increasing the scholarship."

All around me, the girls sat in silence, some wearing expressions that showed they had no idea what Coach was talking about. Others leaned toward him, waiting on his every word. I was clueless and studied my nails. Whatever he was saying, it didn't have anything to do with me.

"The scholarship is now at fifty thousand dollars."

Last year's champs broke out in a collective whoop. The rest of us looked at each other like dopes. What was going on?

The lanky blonde, Jordan, was the loudest. "No way!" she shouted. "Hear that Tati? Fifty grand."

The tiny brunette sitting next to her ducked her head. "Wow, that's a lot of money."

"And you're gonna get it," Jordan said, "Right, Coach? I mean, she's four and a half seconds from breaking the record. She'll do it this year, won't she?"

All eyes were on Tati, who blushed and shook her head. "Swimmers faster than me have tried and failed. I probably won't make it either."

"What kind of an attitude is that?" asked Jordan. "You've got to think positive, Tati."

Coach stared at Tati. "She's right," he told her. "Be positive,

Tatiana. You're the best distance swimmer I've had in years. If anyone has a shot at breaking Allison Singer's record, it's you."

Her teammates erupted in cheers.

"Go home, now," Coach said, rising. "We start again early tomorrow morning."

Chapter 2

We adjourned to the locker room, showered, and changed. I took my time, lagging behind the others. Mel was in no hurry too, and we ended up leaving together.

"So, what do you think?" she asked as we headed out the door.

"It's okay," I said. "Like any other practice."

"You swam in the city?"

"Well, yeah, I didn't just start today. Why, do I look like a wannabe?"

I'd started competitive swimming at age eight for a big club in the city. Most years I swam eleven months out of twelve. When life as I knew it came to a dead stop after my parent's divorce, I moved out of the city to live with my dad in the suburbs. I quit my club and left my awesome coach. I wasn't done with swimming though, and joined the varsity team in my new high school because it was the only team in town.

Over the last four years, I went back and forth from one parent to another, from the city to the suburbs, and from club swimming to varsity. It was a complicated system. I tried to meet my goals and potential, but after what happened to my mother last spring, I quit. There seemed little point in going on. I hadn't been in the pool for months. Still, I doubted I was so out of shape I'd be mistaken for a wannabe.

"You've got a good stroke," she said. "What are your best events?"

"The 200 and 500 free. You?"

"Sprinter, short and fast. Ever win any titles?"

That would be my first lie. "Nope."

"Me neither. I'm a fill-in."

"A what?"

"I fill in second, third and fourth place. I don't win much."

I must have looked shocked at her admission because she said, "It's okay. A team can't win a meet with first place finishes alone. It needs to pick up points in second, third, and fourth. That's what I do. My goal this season is to crack 25 seconds in the 50."

"Are you close?"

"Very."

I changed the subject. "What were they talking about back there? What's with the fifty grand? Who is Allison Singer?" We left the building and started walking across the parking lot.

"Allison Singer holds the school record for the 500 freestyle. She made it way back in 1989."

"That's more than 20 years ago. What is it?"

"4:52.50."

"Wow! She's a jet ski!"

"She held some other records too," Mel went on. "The 100 and 200 free, and she was on all the relays, but they were broken a few times since. No one has broken the 500, but many have tried. For the last ten years, she's offered a scholarship to the swimmer who does. Every year the amount goes up."

"Where does she get the money?"

"She's brilliant. She created that video game *Snakes and Dragons*. You know it. Everybody plays it."

I did know that game; I played it myself. No wonder she could give away fifty thousand dollars.

"She's good to the team, too," Mel went on. "She sponsors our pasta party the night before the Spartans meet and comes to the Division Championships."

"Who's gonna break that record?"

"Who do you think? Tatiana Reese."

"The little girl with the curly hair?"

She nodded.

"She's four seconds off?"

"Four and a half."

"That's pretty close." She'd most likely succeed.

"She holds the school records in the 100 and 200 free, and was on the relay teams that set the latest records in the 200 and 400 free relays," said Mel. "Everyone thought she'd break the 500 last year, but she got hurt during our last home meet – shoulder injury – and couldn't get up to speed before the season ended. We were all disappointed."

"What's her best time?"

"4:57.20."

"She's a rocket."

"Yeah. Her father sent her to some big swim camp this summer in California where she trained with a bunch of Olympians, so I bet she's faster than ever."

"Lucky her."

"What's your best time in the 500?"

"Not as fast as Tati's." I dodged the question. It was most likely true – I hadn't been to any elite swim camps this summer. Or ever.

"Good, because if anyone else breaks the record Jordan Hastings will have a fit."

"What's up with her?" I already disliked the lanky blonde.

"She's Tati's best friend."

"Is she any good?"

"She's all right. She made the Division Championships last year but not the finals. Her biggest achievement is running a blog for the team. It's part gossip column, part sports page. She thinks she's going to be some big-time news reporter at a major network." She rolled her eyes.

"How many teams are in the division?"

"Fourteen."

"Not bad."

"Coach thinks this year's team will be even better, but I'm not so sure if we drop to twenty-eight girls."

"Are you worried?"

"No. This will be my sixth year on the team. I'm solid."

"Do you plan to swim in college?"

"Of course. Don't you?"

I shrugged. "I'm not thinking that far ahead."

"So, you never did tell me. What brings you to Two Rivers?"

Everybody asked that question, and I'd perfected an answer weeks before I moved here, lie number two. "My mom's a nurse in the Army Reserve. She deployed to Afghanistan, and I chose to stay with her best friend Maggie Flynn and her family and finish school here."

I hated lying, but I couldn't tell anyone the real story. Last year, my mom had returned from a tour of duty in Afghanistan a wounded warrior, with shrapnel implanted in her hip, chronic pain, an opiate addiction, and Post-Traumatic Stress Disorder. She stole drugs from her employer, from her *patients,* and a coworker turned her in. Given her situation, the judge was lenient, but sentenced her to six months in a correctional facility where she would also receive treatment for her addiction. It was a long, sad story, and not one to share with the kids at Two Rivers High School. They'd never understand that Mom was more victim than criminal.

"What about your dad?" Mel asked.

"Not an option. My parents are divorced. He's remarried and has a couple of bratty step kids. I stayed with them while my mom did her first tour of duty in Afghanistan, and I hated every minute.

And my grandparents moved to some senior citizen condo in Florida last year so I couldn't stay with them. When Maggie offered to let me stay here, I jumped at it."

"Starting at a new school must be hard."

I shrugged. "This is my third high school. It's a piece of cake."

Mel came to an abrupt halt. "Three high schools?"

"Keep walking, and yeah, three different schools in three different places." I counted off on my left hand. "Freshman year I lived with my mom and went to school in Manhattan. Sophomore year I stayed with my dad because my mother was in Afghanistan. He lives in Westchester, so I had to go to school in his town. Last year, I was back in the city with my mom and went to my old school. Now I'm here."

"That sounds tough."

What an understatement, but I never revealed my weaknesses to anyone, especially someone I just met. "It was okay."

"So three different swim teams," she said.

I nodded. "I swim for myself. I'm not into the whole team bonding thing."

She looked at me with reproach. "Coach is big on team bonding. He wants all of us to be friends and support each other. He says that's the foundation of our success. Everyone cares."

"Well, that might work for you guys, but I just do my thing and don't get too involved with everything else." Indifference was my suit of armor. It kept me from exposing the multitude of hurts that dwelled within my head and heart. I hid them well, not wanting to be the recipient of pity, or worse, too many questions.

We'd walked for almost twenty minutes before Mags' house came into view. "Where do you live?" I asked.

"Just a few blocks from the high school."

"So why are you walking all this way with me?"

"I wanted to get to know you."

"You're crazy," I said, but I was happy she went out of her way to talk to me. I loved Mags, her husband Pat, and their kids, but I needed a friend my age to hang out with. It *was* my senior year, and, although I was the new girl, I still wanted it to be special.

"There's Aunt Maggie's house," I pointed to the white colonial with the blue hydrangeas draped over the picket fence that bordered the front yard.

"Pretty house. Don't the Flynn's have a bunch of kids?"

"Five. Paige is twelve, Danny is ten, Timmy is seven, and the twins, Mary and Sarah, are five."

"So you've gained a whole family."

I smiled. "I did. It gets a little chaotic, but most of the time it's great always having someone around. My mom works twelve-hour shifts and tons of overtime when she's home, so I'm on my own a lot."

"Do you have to share a room?"

"No. I lucked out," I said. "Aunt Mags and Uncle Pat planned to turn their attic into a bedroom for their daughter Paige in another year or so. They'd already moved all their junk out, put up the walls, installed AC, and laid down carpet. When I agreed to live with them, they moved me in instead. Do you want to see it?"

She pulled her phone out of her pocket and checked the time. "Not today. I need to get home. We have company coming for dinner and I promised to help my mother get ready. Maybe next time." She repositioned her backpack across her shoulders. "I've got to run. I'll see you tomorrow."

"Yeah, and thanks for walking with me."

She grinned and turned around, heading back the way we came.

I entered the house, and seconds later the twins and Salty, their old yellow lab who still barked at me like I was an intruder every time I entered, rushed at me. Their enthusiasm at my appearance was still a novelty and made coming home a happy time. I dropped my bag to the floor and gave each one a pat on the head.

Aunt Mags sat in the living room by the window with a dog-eared Dr. Seuss book on her lap. "You made a friend already," she said, smiling. She was a pretty woman, dark Irish with intense blue eyes and overlapping front teeth.

"I did."

"Is that Melanie Ford?"

"Her name's Mel. I don't know her last name."

"Her mother's Dr. Ford, our pediatrician. She's in the Lenten Sewing Club with me." Even with five young children at her feet, Mags always found time to serve in community groups. "The Fords are a nice family. Melanie and her brother, Justin, are both swimmers."

"Brother?"

"They're twins."

"She didn't say anything about a twin brother."

"I'm sure you'll run into him. He helps at all the girls' meets. He's the announcer, among other things."

"So I guess I'll run into him. What's to eat? I'm starving."

"I made waffles. Pop a few in the toaster."

I went off to the kitchen in search of carbs, and within minutes devoured the rest of Aunt Mags' delicious waffles, a bowl of cereal, a banana, and a tall glass of OJ. Swimmer's diet.

Chapter 3

The first week of tryouts flew by, each morning a blast of drills and skills. We put in almost 4,000 yards each day, practiced our starts and turns, and listened to Coach Dudash and Coach D lecture us about proper meet behavior, their expectations regarding our academics, breaking team records, upcoming fundraisers, and everything else associated with the season. All I needed was a schedule so I could show up when and where I was supposed to. I didn't have a parent to help with the Boosters, the team's parents' club, and I wasn't going to take the lead in organizing any activities. I was a worker bee, not a queen bee. I'd do my part and go home.

On Friday morning, Coach made the first cuts. No surprises - four of the original slackers were let go, much to their relief. Two of them couldn't complete four laps without stopping to rest, and another one whined the whole time. Good riddance.

I looked at the others who remained. One, a girl named Charlie, rose above the rest, and managed to keep up with the girls in my lane, not complaining, and asking smart questions. She had a chance. In the wannabe section were two others with potential. Another was hopelessly uncoordinated, and although the coaches might be able to work with her to improve her stroke, with the team limited to twenty-eight, I was sure she'd be next on the cut list.

I figured all of the girls on the previous year's team would keep their spots; they won last season's championship.

As for myself, I kept my head down, my mouth shut, and followed directions. Coach watched me with a critical eye, but I wasn't worried he'd cut me. In spite of my pretense at being an average performer, I was strong enough to be a benefit to the team, and the only senior among the wannabes and slackers. I figured he'd give me a chance.

After practice, Mel and I walked to her house to have lunch and hang out. As soon as we walked through the front door, I shook off a chill.

"Justin," Mel called. "Turn the AC down. It's like a refrigerator in here." She turned to me. "I'm sorry. He always keeps it this cold. I swear he's an Eskimo in disguise."

Footsteps pounded down a staircase and a tall, gangling boy with arms and legs like a windmill barreled into the kitchen. He almost plowed into me and stopped short, grabbing on to the doorframe.

"Whoa! Who's this?" he asked.

"This is my friend, Aerin. She's new on the swim team."

"Hey, Aerin. I'm Justin." He held out his hand for a handshake, and I took it. His grip was strong, and a little charge passed between us.

"Hey," I said looking up into robins' egg blue eyes just like Mel's, complete with the thick, dark lashes. After that, no resemblance. He was blond, his hair almost down to his shoulders and parted on the left, his bangs falling over the right side of his face. He had the clearest complexion and a most contagious smile. I worked at keeping a straight face and failed. I broke eye contact, dropped his hand, and stuffed both of mine in my pockets.

"He's my big bother," Mel explained.

"Don't you mean big brother, baby sister?" he asked.

"No, I mean big *bother*," Mel said as she dropped two pieces of bread in the toaster.

"I thought you guys were twins," I asked, confused.

"We are," Mel said, "but he was born five minutes before me and claims the title 'Big Bother.'"

Justin tapped out an innocuous rhythm on the kitchen counter. "That and the fact I'm so much bigger than she is."

He towered over her by at least half a foot. His shoulders were almost as wide as the door frame and padded with muscle. He wore a raggedy old T-shirt that read, "Win or Die," and a pair of silky basketball shorts, his long legs with thick, ropy muscles ending in feet like flippers.

"And, Big Bother," Mel went on, "I thought I asked you to keep the AC at a minimum in the morning. I don't want to come home to a freezing house after being in the pool for four hours. You wouldn't like it if I turned the heat down when you're in season, and you came home to a Frigidaire."

"Sorry," he said. "I forgot. I'll reprogram the thermostat, okay? I'll keep everything at a cool 68 degrees."

"Try 70," Mel said.

He left the room and came back seconds later. "Done," he said. "So, how was practice?"

"It was practice," she said, opening the refrigerator and pulling out some eggs and a carton of milk. "You know how Coach is."

"You're making eggs?" he asked. "I'll take mine over easy."

Mel snorted. "Make your own."

He pouted and turned to me. "So, where are you from, Aerin?"

"She's from Manhattan," Mel said as she placed a frying pan on the stove and lit the flame below it.

"A city girl, huh?" He gave me an appraising glance and I squirmed under his attention. "Well, you're a long way from the Big Apple."

"All right by me," I said.

"How do you like the swim team?"

"It's okay."

"Just 'okay'? They're the best girls' team around here," he said. "You'll be lucky if you don't get cut, being the new girl and all."

"Justin!" Mel spun away from the stove, spatula raised. "What a dumb thing to say. And how would you know, anyway? Aerin is an awesome swimmer."

"Yeah? What do you do?" He crossed his arms over his chest and gave me a hard stare.

"Distance," I said, meeting the challenge in his eyes. I'd met his type before.

"500? 800? 1500?"

"We don't even swim the long events at the high school," Mel said as she flipped an egg.

"All of them," I said.

"You swim club?"

I nodded.

"What's your best time?" he asked.

"Gosh, Justin, leave her alone, why don't you?" Mel asked. "Drop the third degree. Don't listen to him, Aerin. He thinks he's the next Michael Phelps."

"Do not," Justin retorted.

"Do too," Mel said, eyes narrowing, "and besides, Coach Dudash likes her. I doubt she'll get cut, although, I'm not too sure about a few others." She lifted two eggs out of the pan and placed them on a plate. "Here," she said, handing it to me. "Eat them before they get cold."

I took the plate and sat down at the table, digging in. I hadn't had much breakfast, and it was almost noon.

Justin took the seat across from me. Mel cracked two more eggs in the pan and they started sizzling.

"So, who do you think is getting cut next?" Justin asked.

"Well," Mel said, her back to us as she tended the eggs. "I wouldn't be too surprised if Jordan Hastings finds herself on the outside looking in."

"No way," Justin cried. "Coach can't cut Jordan. Her father's on the school board."

"I'm not too sure that matters anymore. I heard Coach talking to her after practice. He told her to change her attitude, to lighten up on the younger girls. She had two of them in tears yesterday."

"She's one mean girl, but I don't think she'll get cut. Coach needs a breaststroker. She's not great, but she's the best he's got."

"Not anymore," Mel said. "This new girl, Charlie, looks pretty good for a middle-schooler. She's been keeping up with Jordan, although she's in lane six and Jordan's in lane five."

The faster swimmers swam in the middle lanes, and the slower swimmers swam out toward the edges. Two Rivers had a six-lane pool, so the slower swimmers were in lanes one and six.

"Jordan doesn't know because she doesn't pay attention to the slower swimmers," Mel went on. "But I noticed, and so did Coach. He's been spending a lot of time with Charlie. She's working hard to make the team. She comes to practice on time and does what Coach tells her to do. She never complains. Jordan's always the last in the pool and the first one out, a big-time slacker. Don't be surprised if he lets her go."

All of this was news to me. I didn't waste time on team politics and drama. I didn't care who was on the team, as long as I made it.

"That would make headlines," Justin said.

"Tell me about it," Mel said, a smug smile on her lips. She placed a plate with four eggs, over easy, and four pieces of buttered toast on the table in front of her brother.

"Thanks, Mel, you're the best," he said before stuffing his mouth with a whole egg.

Mel made her breakfast and joined us at the table.

"Oh," she said, "I almost forgot. Did you hear about the Allison Singer scholarship? It's up to fifty thousand dollars."

Justin raised his eyebrows and whistled. "You girls are so lucky.

We don't have anything like that challenging our team. Think Mighty Mouse will do it this year?"

"Mighty Mouse?" I asked.

"He means Tatiana," Mel explained. "Everyone calls her Mighty Mouse because she's small and strong. I hope so," she said to Justin. "I'd love to see someone break that old record while I'm on the team. I wish I had a shot."

"What about you, Apple?" Justin asked, his eyes on me.

"Apple?"

"Yeah, I'm going to call you Apple because you come from the Big Apple."

"Please don't."

"Everyone on the team has a nickname. Consider it an initiation rite."

"Oh yeah? What's your nickname?"

"Tonka," Mel answered for him, "like the toy truck. Everyone calls me Bunny because I'm like the Energizer Bunny – I keep going, and going and – "

"Going." Justin finished for her.

"So," I said, "everyone has a nickname. What's Jordan's?"

Mel and Justin exchanged glances and burst out laughing.

"Viper," he said.

"No way!" I laughed. "She lets you get away with that?"

"Of course not," said Mel. "That's what *we* call her. Everyone else calls her Ariel, you know, the Little Mermaid?" She smirked.

"I like Viper better," I said, and we laughed again.

Mel pushed her chair away from the table and started stacking our dirty dishes.

"Let me help," I said, springing up. Together we loaded the dishwasher and cleaned up the rest of our mess.

"What's your agenda this afternoon?" Justin asked.

"Floating," Mel said.

In the afternoons, Mel liked to float on an air mattress in their pool and snooze. She'd invited me to join her.

"I'm off to the Y," said Justin. "Dozens of little kids are waiting for me to teach them how to swim, and then I'm guarding until six o'clock." He went to the sink and washed his hands.

"Have a good shift," Mel said. She also worked as a lifeguard and swim instructor at the YMCA, and had promised she'd put in a good word for me so I could get a job, too, after swim season ended.

Justin pulled a set of car keys out of his front pocket and jingled them. "Nice to meet, you, Apple," he said. "I'm sure I'll be seeing you around."

The intensity in his blue eyes as he stared deep into mine unnerved me. "Yeah," I stammered. "I'll be around."

"Come on," Mel said, grabbing my arm. "Let's put on our suits and get outside."

I allowed her to pull me along as she headed to her room. A few minutes later, a car sputtered to life outside. I peeked out of Mel's bedroom window just in time to see Justin speed away in a beat-up Jeep Wrangler.

"Yeah," I muttered. "I'll be around."

Week Two:

Cuts & Captains

Chapter 4

Tryouts ground on for the second week with more skills and drills. The new girls were getting tired, and the moaning and whining from the slackers grew louder and longer. The seasoned swimmers prepared for another three months of lengthier and harder practices, while the wannabes struggled to keep up and hide their tears.

Varsity swimming is a six-year sport, but sometimes the younger girls are a little *too* young to compete with high schoolers. They complained about everything: practice was too early, the water was too cold, they couldn't keep up with the sets, and they felt dwarfed by the upperclassman.

It took courage and determination to pull off varsity swimming as a middle-schooler. I knew; I'd done it. Girls not ready to make a total commitment were better to wait another year or so. Most of them figured that out and drifted away. Charlie, the eighth grader with the killer breaststroke, was not one of them.

With one day of tryouts left to go, I ended up in the locker room with her after practice. She stood in front of the mirror combing her long, wet hair.

"How are you doing, Charlie?" I asked as I put on my sneakers.

"I'm good," she said, glancing back at me in the mirror.

"Are you a club swimmer?"

"Yup," she said. "I started swimming with the Marlins when I was eight."

"No wonder you're so good."

She shrugged. "You're pretty good too," she said, as she tied her hair into a ponytail.

"You're better than I was when I was your age. Keep it up."

"I hope I don't get cut," she said, a glimmer of worry in her eyes, her bottom lip trembling. "Everyone else in my age group is already gone."

"You're not going to get cut. Coach needs you."

Her sad eyes brightened. "Really?"

"You're the best breaststroker he has right now."

"What about Jordan?"

"She's no competition for you, trust me. You just keep doing what Coach tells you to do, and you'll beat her all the way to the Division Championships."

She finished packing her swim bag and we left the locker room together. I walked her out to the parking lot where her mother waited to pick her up. "See you tomorrow, kid."

She smiled and waved back at me as she got into the car.

"Who was that?" I heard her mother ask as the door closed.

I looked around for Mel. She'd left ahead of me with Erica Duczeminski to go to her car and get the sweatshirt she'd left at Erica's the night before. They leaned against Erica's Honda and called me over.

"Getting chummy with the youngster?" Erica asked. She was the biggest girl on the team and a top butterflyer. Everyone called her "Duke," short for her last name, but also because of her size. She was like a mastiff, tall, big-boned, and full-bodied. I would not want to crash into her in practice. It would be like hitting a wall.

"She's a cute kid. And fast," I said, dropping my swim gear onto the asphalt.

"She's going to give Jordan some tough competition," Erica

said.

"Good," said Mel. "Jordan thought she would be top breaststroker now that she's a senior. I'm going to love watching a middle schooler knock her off her throne."

We laughed.

"Maybe you can adopt Charlie as your Little Sister," Mel said to me.

"Little Sister?" I asked.

"We have a Big Sister-Little Sister program. The upperclassmen adopt the younger girls and act like their big sisters, showing them the ropes, providing support, all that," Mel explained. "Once Coach announces the team, we'll pick our Little Sisters."

"I'll take Charlie," I said.

"You're new to the team," Erica said. "Coach might not let you be a Big Sister."

"Aerin is an experienced swimmer," Mel said on my behalf. "Coach will be glad to have her help. She might teach all of us a little something."

The following morning, Coach sat us down in the bleachers before we changed into our swim gear.

"Say hello to your team," he said. "You've all made it."

I looked for Charlie and found her sitting in the front row, a triumphant smile on her face. I checked out the other girls and saw no one I didn't expect to see. The slackers had all disappeared, and the wannabes had pared down to two: Charlie and me, the only new girls on the team. She looked back at me sitting at the top of the bleachers next to Mel and Erica and waved. My sense of bonding with her intensified.

Coach gave us a few minutes to congratulate each other.

"Now you vote for team captains," he said.

Coach D handed out little slips of paper and pencils.

We'd been talking about our captains for the last week. All of the seniors except for me were in the running as well as a couple of juniors. We would each vote for one girl and the top two would win the honors.

I quickly wrote Mel's name on my ballot and handed it to Coach D. She collected the others and stepped off to the side to count the votes. A few of the girls made some small talk but hushed after Jordan sent them dirty looks. She nibbled at her fingernails, face in a grimace, while Coach D counted. No doubt she was hoping to be named captain, alongside Tatiana.

At last Coach D broke our suspense. "The captains are Tatiana and Mel."

Mel beamed.

"I'm glad that's over," Erica whispered to me. "We wouldn't be able to live with her if she lost to Jordan."

Jordan scowled, but perked up when Tati gave her a triumphant hug.

"I'm happy for Mel," I said. "She deserves it."

Next we picked our Little Sisters. Mel and I had decided to share responsibilities for Charlie, who readily accepted, and Coach approved.

Coach ordered us into the water, no slacking, 5,000 yards today and get used to it. No one complained, relieved to have the stress of tryouts behind us and happy to have pushed through.

I dove into my lane and started moving forward, losing all sense of time as I entered my zone. It was a peaceful place, with no noise except for the splashing of the water as I glided through it. My arms arced overhead and plunged under the surface - left, then right, now breathe on the third stroke - while my feet made efficient flutter kicks. My mind was free of worry. I experienced a sense of comfort and control here that I found nowhere else.

A sudden tug on my left foot jerked me out of my zone. I stopped and sputtered upright.

"Hey," said Mel. "We're done."

Half of the girls had already exited the pool, and the rest were cooling down. Coach stood at the deep end, his clipboard in his hand, watching me over the rim of his bifocals. I didn't make eye contact and let Mel lead me to the shallow end. We did some stretching and climbed out.

Before letting us shower and change, Coach ordered us all in the bleachers again to review plans for the next three days, which was Labor Day weekend.

"Tomorrow morning we have a shortened practice so we can get to our car wash on time," he said. "It's our biggest fundraiser. You'll all be assigned jobs, which will rotate throughout the day. Wear shorts and a t-shirt, no bikinis or bikini tops. Bring a towel and plenty of sunscreen. Jordan's father has organized this event, and he will provide supplies, snacks, and plenty of ice-cold water.

"After the car wash, we'll meet at Tatiana's house where her parents are hosting a barbecue and backyard campout. These are team-bonding activities, and I expect everyone to attend."

After answering a few questions, he sent us home.

Two Rivers Trailblazers Girls' Varsity Swim and Dive Team Roster

Swimmer	Year
Jamie Di Benedetto	Senior
Erica Duczeminski	Senior
Melanie Ford	Senior
Jordan Hastings	Senior
Aerin Keane	Senior
Cassandra Kramer	Senior
Taylor Maddox	Senior
Tatiana Reese	Senior
Franky Brown	Junior
Jess Elliott	Junior
Maria Gomez	Junior
Ava Mallory	Junior
Kris Noorman	Junior
Ashley Pearl	Junior
Chelle Pennington	Junior
Eliza Tilton	Junior
Kira Adler	Sophomore
Jessica Daigle	Sophomore
Alexis Rivera	Sophomore
Jazmin Vidals	Sophomore
Regina Zeoli	Sophomore
Janet Beam	Freshman
Amanda Bocekci	Freshman
Marissa Catania	Freshman
Kimberly Fox	Freshman
Danielle Hughes	Freshman
Allison Sciucco	Freshman
Charlotte Donovan	8th

Chapter 5

Halfway through the car wash, I stopped for a quick break, guzzling a bottle of water and drying off with a damp towel.

"Why does it have to be so hot?" Mel asked as she joined me. "I can't remember a car wash day as scorching as this."

"Yeah, but washing the cars is fun," I said.

"You've never done a car wash?"

"My swim teams raised money other ways."

"We'll raise money other ways too," Mel said, reminding me we had meals to serve at a pancake breakfast in a few weeks, and poinsettias to sell in October.

"Whatever."

A hook and ladder from the fire station drove in and broke the monotony of washing car after car in the blistering heat. Two firefighters hopped down from the cab and ordered a wash, handing us a one hundred dollar bill. All of us fought over who would spray the massive red truck and who would wash it, some of us climbing onto the top with sponges and hoses. We posed for a team picture with the firefighters and their rig, and by the time they drove off in their clean, shiny truck with a blast of the siren, our spirits had lifted. We were ready for three more hours of washing cars.

"That was fun," I said as Mel and I took a water break.

"They come every year," she said. "Oh, look who's here. More excitement. It's my big bother and his best buds. Watch Tati and Jordan go nuts."

Justin's battered Jeep cruised through the parking lot and he pulled into line for a wash. He had two other guys with him. They hopped out and put the top back on, finishing just seconds before Tati turned the hose on them.

"Hey! Watch it," the blond one said while Tati laughed and blasted him with the spray. He wrestled her for the hose.

"Knock it off, you two," shouted Mr. Hastings, Jordan's father. "Get out of the way, Sean."

"What's that all about?" I asked Mel.

"That's Tati's boyfriend, Sean Hines. He plays football."

"That figures."

"Oh yeah, they're the perfect couple. See the other guy with him and Justin? That's Travis Hoyt. He goes out with Jordan. He's also on the football team."

I checked out Jordan's guy - husky build, dark hair, pimply face. Jordan sauntered over to him and wrapped her arms around him. He picked her up off her feet and they kissed.

"I'm going to be sick," I said.

"That's nothing," Mel said. "Jordan's big on PDA. She's all over him all the time."

"Why am I not surprised?"

"Knock it off, Jordan," said her father. "Get back to work."

The girls were ready to wash Justin's Jeep. He pulled it to the head of the line and got out. The girls with the hoses started blasting the Wrangler.

"Hey, Apple," he called out to me as he dodged the hoses. "Get back to work. Break's over."

Jordan stood between us, and mouthed the word "Apple" right after he said it. The nickname was sure to stick now.

Justin joined Mel and me on the sidelines. "How's it going?" he asked.

"We're doing great," Mel said. "I think we'll break a thousand bucks."

"Awesome," he said. "I wish the guys could do a car wash. Our season is in winter. Who wants to go out and wash cars then?"

"Aerin's never done a car wash," said Mel.

"It's fun," I said.

"I guess so," said Justin. "You're all wet."

My shorts were soaked right through, and my waterlogged sneakers made sucking sounds with every step I took. "Oh well," I said. "I'm used to being wet."

"So, what's up with tonight? Everybody's going to Tati's house?" Justin asked.

"Yeah, the Reese's are hosting," Mel said. "It's a campout. We have a bunch of tents, and we're sleeping outside. We're having a campfire, too."

"What time?" he asked.

"What difference does it make? No guys allowed."

"Oh, come on," he said. "Of course we're going to crash the party."

"You better not. Coach said no more campouts if we give him any headaches tonight."

"Why do you care? You won't be on the team next year."

"I'm a captain! And I don't want to mess it up for the other girls."

"Yeah," I said. "You guys stay away. Don't mess it up for us."

Justin laughed. "Who says we're going to mess anything up? We just want to drop by and say hello."

"Say hello now and be done with it," I said. "It's a girls' thing. We don't want guys hanging around."

"Well, we'll just have to see about that," he said. "I bet if you asked Jordan and Tati they'd have a different take on it."

"Jordan can spend one night without Travis," Mel said.

"Why don't you guys do your own thing? Have your own guys' night out?" I asked.

"That's a good idea, Apple. Why didn't I think of that?"

"You should have," said Mel. "Look, they're drying off your car. It's time to go."

"They better not scratch the finish," he said.

"As if you could tell on that old piece of junk," Mel said.

"Hey! That's my old piece of junk," he said. "You don't complain when you need a ride." He walked back to the Wrangler, climbed into the front seat, and gestured for his friends to follow. Sean and Travis disentangled themselves from their girlfriends and climbed in. A moment later, the three of them were gone with a screech of tires.

"Think they'll crash the party?" I asked Mel.

"Oh, he's all talk," she said. "Coach will kick their butts if they show up tonight. We don't have to worry about them."

~

After the car wash, we all stopped off at home to clean up and get ready for the rest of the day's festivities. When I got to Aunt Mags, I found everyone in the kitchen.

"How'd it go?" she asked.

"Great," I said. "You wouldn't believe how many people came by to let us wash their cars. We made more than a thousand dollars."

"Wow," said Uncle Pat. "What's the team going to do with all that money?"

"We need it to pay for our trip to the Long Island invitational."

Every season the team made an overnight trip to a big swim meet outside of the division. This year it was on Long Island.

"Sounds like fun," Mags said. "By the way, you got a letter from your mother. I left it on your dresser."

"Thanks," I said. Mom didn't have access to the internet or a phone and used snail mail to communicate with the rest of the world.

"Let me know when you're ready and I'll drive you to Tati's," Mags said.

"Thanks. I'm tired and don't feel like walking to her house."

Upstairs in my room, I went right to my dresser, picked up the letter, and held it in my hands. My mother's elegant cursive filled the envelope's white center. I opened it and extracted the single sheet of paper inside. I unfolded it and read.

"My darling Aerin, another week has passed, and I am closer to coming home to you. These last weeks have been hard. I'm making progress, but it's a long road. I have a lot to come to terms with, a lot of hurts I need to deal with, and not just my hurt but the hurt I've caused others, especially you. You're the best thing in my life. I hope I haven't screwed us up.

Enough about me. What's up with you? How are things at Maggie's? How's swimming? I hope you're doing well and having a good time. Make some new friends and enjoy your last year of high school. Write back and tell me about everything. *I have my first visitation day coming up in two weeks. Please come. I want to see you. I* need *to see you. I love you. Mom."*

I read the letter three times before putting it away with the others I'd received from her over the last five years, ever since our world had changed and separated us for months at a time. The letters brought me some comfort, but they also documented our troubles.

I took a quick shower, dried and straightened my hair, packed my duffle bag for the night, and went downstairs to find Mags. She was in the kitchen peeling potatoes for dinner. The twins sat at the table playing with some Legos.

"Ready when you are," I said.

She finished slicing the potatoes, rinsed them off in the sink, and placed them in a pot of water on the stove. "Okay," she said. "I'll boil these when I get back. Come on kids. Let's give Aerin a ride to Tatiana's house."

Chapter 6

The Reese family lived all the way across town, in an upscale neighborhood with huge houses, big yards, and at least two expensive cars in their driveways. Mags pulled up in front of the grandest and stopped her minivan.

"Some house," I said, peering out at the immaculate lawn and thriving garden.

"Calvin Reese owns several businesses in town," Aunt Mags explained, "an insurance agency, a hardware store, and a couple of laundromats. He also owns a number of office buildings. He's done very well for himself. Calvin and I go way back, all the way to grammar school. To be honest, I don't like him. He's a braggart, self-centered, and snobbish. His wife, though, is a lovely woman. We work together on several committees, including the PTA and a church board."

While we sat talking, a few more cars pulled up in front of the house, and my teammates piled out of them with stuffed backpacks, pillows, and sleeping bags. They said goodbye to their parents and grouped at the end of the long driveway. I hopped out of Mag's minivan with my gear and joined them.

The party had already started in the backyard. Several girls splashed around in the enormous swimming pool, playing Marco

Polo. Others sprawled out on chaise lounges. A few sat at a table loaded with munchies, chips, dips, and salsa. A buzz of contentment and laughter filled the air. I searched the crowd for Mel and found her sitting by the pool, her legs dangling in the deep end. I slipped out of my sneakers and joined her.

"Hey," she said. "You made it."

"Yeah," I said. "This is quite a place."

"Tati's father is rich. This is their new house. The one they used to live in was a lot smaller, but still very nice. Mr. Reese has an appetite for bigger and better."

"Funny, I never got the impression that Tatiana comes from money. She seems so down to earth."

"She is, and so is her mother. They don't let all their money go to their heads."

"So, what are we doing tonight?"

"Mr. Reese hired caterers. They'll put on a big feast, chicken, and ribs, potato salad, corn on the cob, all that good stuff. Then we'll play some games and have a campfire. Oh, we have to set up our tents, too. I guess we'll do that after dinner before it gets dark."

Little groups had formed in all areas of the yard. One boisterous crowd played a game of Ladderball. A quieter bunch sat in a circle on the grass with their phones in hand, staring at their screens. The pool crowd grew more boisterous. After being splashed a few times, we retreated to a picnic table under a maple tree.

Erica joined us and pulled a deck of cards out of her back pocket. "How about some Rummy 500?"

She turned out to be a Rummy 500 whiz, racking up points and beating Mel and me at every hand. While we played, we did what Coach referred to as "bonding," which started with Erica questioning me about my background.

"So, Aerin," she said, "I hear you're from New York City."

I nodded, concentrating on my hand, which was pitiful. I held twenty cards with no more than two of them in line to make a play.

"She's from Manhattan," Mel said, throwing down three queens.

"I've never been to Manhattan," Erica said, studying her cards before throwing down a royal straight.

"Get out," Mel said. "Everyone's been to the city."

"Not me. My parents are busy running the farm. We don't have time to go to the city. But someday, I plan to go to a Broadway show and have some pastrami at a Jewish deli."

"Your parents own a farm?" I asked.

"Yeah, we got a few hundred acres. My father supplies most of New York with onions."

"I've never known anyone who owns a farm."

"See?" Mel said. "Duke can show you her farm, and you can show her the city. We'll take a road trip."

I hadn't thought of going into the city anytime soon, but it seemed like a fun idea. "I can get cheap tickets for the theater, not front row, but decent, and I know the best deli a few blocks from Times Square. We can take the train."

"I can't go until after the harvest. My father needs my help," Erica said.

"You say when," Mel said. She laid a four-card run of hearts on the table. "I'm out." She handed me the cards. My deal.

"So, what are you doing here?" Erica asked while I shuffled. "Senior year and all, I'd think you'd be finishing up at your high school in the city."

Mel answered for me. "Her mother's a soldier. She went to Afghanistan. Aerin's staying with the Flynn's because she doesn't like to stay with her father and his new family."

"It must be tough knowing your mother's in a war zone," said Erica, her eyes wide.

"Geez, Erica," Mel said, "do you have to bring that up?"

"No, it's all right," I said. I heard the question all the time. "I'm used to it."

Our card game had stopped. They looked at me with a mixture

of curiosity and pity.

"You've been through a lot," Mel said.

"Tough breaks," Erica said.

"What tough breaks?" Jordan's strident voice interrupted our conversation. She and Tati had found us under the maple tree.

"Aerin was just telling us about her mom," Erica started, but I interrupted.

"It's nothing," I said. "What's up?"

"Just making the rounds," Tati said, "How are you guys doing? Having a good time?" She had a high-pitched, little girl's voice, sweet and funny.

"Great party, Tati," Mel said. "Thanks for having us."

"No problem. My father wanted to do it," Tati said, "since it's my senior year and all."

"Nice place you've got here," Erica said.

"It's okay," said Tati. "A little too big. I kind of like our old house better."

I looked at her as if she were a freak. Who wouldn't want to live in that house?

"So, Apple," Jordan said, "how do you like Two Rivers? Is it big enough for you?"

Justin's nickname had caught on like wildfire after the car wash. Although I found it cute when he said it, Jordan's take on it offended me.

"Sure," I said, considering my words, wary of falling into a trap. She had a talent for making people say the wrong thing and look foolish. "I've been here before. I've known the Flynn's all my life."

"Isn't it boring, though, after living in the city?" Jordan asked.

"How boring can it be with five other kids in the house?" Mel asked.

"I love Manhattan," Jordan went on. "I'm going to New York University to study journalism, and then I'm going to get a high profile job at CBS and have my own show."

"Well, good luck with that," Erica said, shuffling the cards.

Jordan's eyes narrowed. "You're just jealous Erica because you're never going to leave that stinking farm."

"Hey," said Mel, rising from the table, her face pink with indignation. "You take that back."

"So, is everyone having a good time?" Tati asked again in an apparent attempt to cut the tension.

"Everything is just great," Erica said, glowering at Jordan. "Sit down, Mel."

Mel sat, arms crossed as she glared at Jordan.

"Okay," said Tati. "Dinner's in a few minutes. You might want to wrap up your game." She took Jordan by the arm and the two of them walked off.

We played another hand of Rummy 500. When the rest of the team crowded around the grill, we joined the line to fill our plates.

Once we finished dinner, we went to work setting up our tents all over the backyard. Mel and I shared a tent with Charlie in a back corner. We placed our sleeping bags inside with a few flashlights and a couple of bags of chips then joined the rest of the girls. Tati divided us into two teams, and we played a quick game of softball while Mr. Reese and a few of the other dads set the campfire. Once they had it roaring, we tugged on sweatshirts, wrapped ourselves in blankets, and settled around it in a large circle. Tati pulled out bags of marshmallows and chocolate bars and a box of graham crackers. We passed the makings of the S'mores around and took turns roasting marshmallows over the flames.

"How about some music?" asked Jess, a junior with a fast fly. She pulled out a guitar and started tuning it up. "Any requests?"

We spread out on the lawn in small groups or pairs, forming alliances, singing along to Jess' skillful guitar playing. The fire in the pit burned low, and some of the girls fell asleep. The chaperoning adults hung in the background, talking among themselves.

The Two Rivers girls were unlike any other swimmers I'd

known. They were a good bunch, a nice mix of ages, personalities, and abilities. While I could live without some, or, at least, one, of them, I found myself growing attached to Mel, Erica, and Charlie. The truth? I needed them more than they needed me.

I even liked Tatiana, a big surprise, because given the facts of who she was – rich girl in town, daughter of a big shot, star swimmer – I thought she'd be stuck up and snotty. Instead, she was friendly, sweet, and welcoming. Even with the scholarship challenge hanging over her, she wanted to have fun and make friends. She didn't need the money. Her father could pay her way at any college she wanted to attend. She didn't seem like the competitive type, either. I wondered what motivated her to beat that old record.

As I dozed off to the sounds of Jess's strumming, I wondered what would happen if I broke the record and won the scholarship. It could change my life, and my life needed changing.

When I woke, the fire was out, and the backyard was dark. The girls, roused from their languor, drifted towards their tents. One by one, their door flaps closed and the yard became silent. Mel, Charlie, and I climbed into our sleeping bags.

Mel yawned. "Did you have fun?"

"Yeah," I said, fighting sleep. I didn't want the evening to end.

"I had fun," Charlie said.

"Well, the party's over," Mel said. "School starts on Wednesday and we have our first meet."

We digested that fact, which meant something different to all of us. For Charlie, it was her first high school meet, competing with older, bigger, more experienced girls. For Mel, it was the start of her last season with the Blazers; anything she had left to prove as a high school swimmer was now or never. For me, it was the start of another varsity season, one I was determined to glide through, marking time, and putting in my yardage while the water helped me forget all the reasons I was swimming in Two Rivers.

Chapter 7

We must have fallen asleep because next thing I knew footsteps and stifled giggles outside the tent startled me awake. A beam of light bounced off the walls.

"What the –?" I sat up and unzipped the door flap. Three figures crept through the yard, a flashlight illuminating their path. One was Jordan. The other two looked like males.

"What's going on?" a drowsy Mel asked.

"It's Jordan and a couple of guys. I think one of them is Travis, and the other one looks like your brother."

"Justin?" Mel asked, crawling up behind me and sticking her head out of the opening. "What are they doing here? If Coach finds out, he'll kill us."

"Is everything okay?" a sleepy Charlie asked.

"Yeah, Charlie, everything's fine," Mel said. "Go back to sleep."

Charlie put her head down and snuggled deep into her sleeping bag, asleep in no time.

"Come on," Mel said. She unzipped the door and we crawled out of the tent, zipping it shut behind us. We followed Jordan, Justin, and Travis as they crept around the house to the driveway, heading for Justin's Wrangler parked across the street.

"I don't believe it," Mel whispered.

Tatiana and her boyfriend Sean leaned against the Wrangler, lip locked, holding on to each other as if it were their last night on Earth.

Jordan and Travis, holding hands, strolled up to the Jeep and got into the back. Justin hung in the background, suddenly the odd man out. He ran his fingers through his hair and spun around almost crashing into Mel, who jumped in his face.

"What are you doing here?" she hissed. "Do you know what time it is? Coach will bench us if he finds out you guys were here, and we've got a big meet coming up."

"Hey," he said, holding his hands up in surrender. "I'm just the driver."

"Then get back in your car and drive away," Mel said, "and take your buddies with you."

"Come on, Mel, lighten up. They're not staying long. They just want to say goodnight to their girls."

"I don't care. I want them out of here. You heard what Coach said: no boys. We're supposed to be setting an example, and look at those two, Tati and Jordan, all over those guys. They make me sick."

"You're just jealous because Matt Kendrick's not here."

"Get out," she said, slapping him on the arm. "Matt's nothing to me."

"I see how you look at him," Justin teased.

"Get real," she said. "You see nothing."

I stood in the shadows, listening to their argument undetected, but Justin took a step back and saw me. "Hey, Apple," he said. "You nosy, too? Why don't you two go back to bed and leave them alone? We'll be taking off in a few minutes."

"I mean it, Justin," Mel said. "Get out of here *now*. If Mr. Reese wakes up, we're all in trouble."

"Can you believe her, Apple? Standing in the way of true love. Just last night she was making out with old Matt."

"I was not!" Mel said, slapping him again, but, this time, she meant it.

"Weren't you parked in his car behind the Tasty Cone?" he asked, rubbing his arm where she'd hit him.

"Troublemaker," she said. "Stop making up stories."

Suddenly the front yard lit up like mid-day.

Mr. Reese stood on the front steps in basketball shorts and a T-shirt. "What's going on out here?" he shouted. "Is that you, Justin Ford?"

"Thanks a lot, Justin, now you've got us all in trouble," Mel whispered.

I looked over at the Jeep. Tati, Jordan, and their boyfriends were nowhere in sight.

"Oh, hi, Mr. Reese. It's me, Justin. Mel forgot her pillow, so I stopped by to bring her one. I'm leaving right now."

Mr. Reese stared at the three of us for a moment, looked at the Wrangler, and then gazed back to us. "Are you alone?" he asked.

"Yes, sir," Justin said. "It's just me, Mel, and Aerin."

"You know the rules, Justin. If Mel needed a pillow she should have asked me for one. Now, get out of here before I call Coach. Don't make me report the three of you."

"No sir, please don't do that. I'm sorry I disturbed you. Get your pillow, Mel."

Mel and I walked him back to the Jeep. Where was everyone else?

Justin reached into the back of the Jeep and pulled out a pillow. I heard a stifled laugh and peered in, meeting Jordan's eyes. Travis was beside her, and Tati and Sean popped up in the back seat.

"Get out of here," Jordan hissed. "If Mr. Reese sees us with these two we'll be toast."

I backed away from the Wrangler. Mel grabbed the pillow from her brother. Justin gave us a wink and then hopped into the driver's seat. He started the vehicle and slowly pulled away from the curb.

"Go to bed, girls," Mr. Reese said. He waited until we

disappeared from the front yard and then turned out the lights. We were again in darkness.

Mel clutched the pillow her brother had handed her.

"Does Justin always drive around with a pillow?" I asked.

Mel shrugged. "Yeah, he and his buddies pull a lot of all-nighters. He's got a sleeping bag back there, too. They camp out at each other's houses or sleep in the Jeep."

"What are they going to do now?" I asked.

"Not my business," Mel said. "But if Tati and Jordan get caught with those guys we're all going to get in trouble."

"They'll sneak back after Tati's father goes to sleep."

"Like he doesn't know what's going on. Believe me, if it were you or me in that Jeep with a couple of boys, he'd speed dial Coach *and* our parents in two seconds flat."

"He knows Tati and Jordan took off in the Jeep?"

"Of course he knows! Tati's no angel, and when she's with Jordan it's like she's possessed. But no way will Mr. Reese let on that *his* daughter isn't 'Little Miss Perfect.' He lets her get away with everything."

It was getting juicier by the minute.

"Tati and Jordan will come back in a little while and climb into their tent, no one the wiser," Mel went on. "That's why it's just the two of them in there, get it? They planned the whole thing."

We were outside our tent. The back yard was eerily silent, cloaked in darkness. I looked up at the house – no lights, not a sound. I checked the clock on my phone: 1:17 a.m.

"We need to get to sleep," Mel said as she unzipped the door flaps to our tent. "Get in."

I ducked in and she followed close behind, closing us in for the night. I stumbled over Charlie in her sleeping bag and dropped onto and then into my own. Mel climbed into hers and we lay quiet in the dark.

"Just once," Mel whispered, "just once, I wish Jordan and Tati would get theirs."

"Why do you dislike them so much?" I whispered so I wouldn't wake Charlie.

"Tati's all right," Mel said after a few seconds, "but I can't stand Jordan. She thinks she's better than everyone, always has, and she's not. Her family's not rich, like Tati's, and she's not a great student or a winning athlete. She latched on to Tati back in seventh grade and thinks she's right up there with her and her other big shot friends. She's a fake. I can't stand people who pretend to be something they're not."

I bit my lip, not knowing what to say. If Mel knew I wasn't entirely what I claimed to be she'd hate me, too. I couldn't let that happen. She was the best friend I had in Two Rivers, and I liked her a lot.

"Forget about them," I said. "Who's Matt Kendricks? And what were you doing with him behind the Tasty Cone?"

Mel snorted. "Matt is someone I've known since I was two. What do you think we were doing behind the Tasty Cone? Eating ice cream."

"Justin doesn't think so," I teased.

"Justin doesn't know everything," she said. "But Matt *is* one of the hottest guys in school. You'll meet him next week. He'll be at the meet."

"Is he a swimmer?"

"No, he just likes to help out at the meets."

"Boys *and* girls meets?"

"No, just girls."

"Oh, so you guys *are* an item."

"Not yet," she said. "But I'm working on it. It *is* senior year, after all, and doesn't every girl want to share it with someone special? Football games, homecoming dance, senior trip, the prom. It would be a lot of fun to hang out with Matt. He's funny, and we know each other so well."

A lump had formed in my throat. I'd never had a boyfriend, never had anyone special, because I moved around so much. By the time I set down any roots, I'd be packing up to leave again. Realizing that filled me with a sense of loss and longing I hadn't allowed myself to feel before. I shrugged it off. This year would be no different. Might as well forget about it right now.

"Hey," Mel said as if she'd just had a brilliant idea. "We'll have to find someone for you."

Not so brilliant idea.

"Don't bother," I said. "I've got other priorities. I need to focus on my studies, raise my GPA, ace the SATs, and write a great college admission essay. I'm determined to get into a good school."

"All work and no fun make Aerin a dull girl," she said. "Don't worry. We'll find you someone. I can't wait for you to meet all the great guys at Two Rivers. I'm sure someone will catch your eye the first day."

Justin's lanky frame and long blond hair popped into my head. "We'll see," I said, wanting to end the conversation. "We need to get some sleep. Morning comes early."

Mel turned over and punched her pillow into shape. "Good night, Aerin. Thanks for listening. I'm happy you're here."

I smiled in the darkness. "Me too."

Chapter 8

After a breakfast of bagels, fresh fruit salad, and orange juice, Mel's mom dropped me off at Aunt Mags. Everyone was up, and Uncle Pat was at the stove flipping pancakes.

"Hey, Aerin, how was your night?" he asked.

"I had a good time," I said, taking a seat at the table.

Aunt Mags cradled a cup of coffee, the twins crowding her lap. "Did you get any sleep?" she asked.

"Some," I said. "We had a little drama after the lights went out."

"Do tell," she said, a mischievous gleam in her eye.

"Jordan and Tati took off with their boyfriends. Mr. Reese almost caught them, but they came back sometime during the night. They were there when we woke up, but looked like they hadn't gotten any sleep."

Aunt Mags shook her head. "That Jordan Hastings is a piece of work. Tatiana had better watch herself around her. She's always been a good kid, but her mother's concerned about her friendship with Jordan. Since her parents' divorce, that girl's been a little wild."

"I didn't know Jordan's parents were divorced."

"It's been a while. Her mom and dad both remarried. They play a tug of war with that poor kid."

I could understand that, as I was often the rope in a tug of war too.

"Hungry?" Uncle Pat asked.

I shook my head. "We ate at the Reese's. I think I'll go to my room and try to catch some sleep."

Aunt Mags put down her coffee cup. "We're going to church, Aerin. I was hoping you'd join us."

Aunt Mags and Uncle Pat were regular churchgoers and belonged to a small Catholic church in town. I hadn't been to mass in months. I used to go every week with my parents, but ever since Mom's troubles began a year ago, I stayed away. My prayers hadn't stopped my family from breaking up, or the judge from sending my mother to that awful place.

"I'm exhausted," I said, feeling sheepish. The Flynn kids didn't always want to go to church, but their parents made them. Five pairs of eyes stared back at me. I was setting a bad example.

"I promised your mother," Mags murmured so the kids wouldn't hear.

I thought of Mom, trapped in a place she didn't want to be, far from home and everything familiar. If she were here, she'd go to church. "All right," I said. "I'll go. I wouldn't want to disappoint Mom." I looked at the clock. "Do I have time to shower?"

Mags smiled and nodded. "We've got about an hour."

Getting a family with five kids plus one more ready for church on time was a challenge, but Aunt Mags managed to pull us all together. We arrived with moments to spare and filed into a center pew, Mags in the middle with a twin on each side, Uncle Pat and I on either end with the other kids between us. As soon as we settled in, an organ began playing, and the voices of a choir brought everyone to attention. We stood for the processional. Once everyone was in place, the mass began. I read along in the missal, the words and structure of the service familiar and comforting.

I knelt and bowed when necessary, and sang along with the hymns, setting a good example for Paige and Danny standing beside me. After Communion, the choir sang one hymn, and then the organist played a solo, which led into another hymn. The melody sounded familiar and I hummed along. Seconds later, a voice like an angel's filled the church, soaring in its spirit, rich in its youth and innocence. Its sweetness captivated me, and I turned to look up at the choir loft, wondering who possessed such a beautiful voice.

My jaw dropped as I set eyes on the vocalist: Mel, dressed in a white choir robe and singing with devotion and purity I'd never witnessed before. A lump formed in my throat as I watched her, her face radiant, her voice perfect. At the close of the hymn, she looked down at the congregation, and our eyes met. I gave her a little wave, and she smiled down at me before disappearing to the rear of the choir loft.

When mass ended, we stood outside in the sunshine, mingling with the other parishioners. I felt a tug on my arm and turned to see Mel, a huge grin splashed across her face.

"Hey," she said. "Surprised to see you here."

I shrugged. "Aunt Mags made me come."

"So you're not a churchgoer?"

"Not lately," I said. "Too much moving around and not getting settled any place, I guess."

"I've been coming here my whole life, and singing in the choir since I was in fifth grade."

"Hey, Apple." Justin had sidled up beside us without my radar giving me an alert. He was dressed for church in a shirt and tie. He even had dress shoes on. "I didn't know you came to our church."

"I don't," I said. "I came with the Flynn's."

"Well, welcome anyway."

"What are you doing now?" Mel asked.

"Going home to get some sleep. I'm wiped out."

"We've got youth group this afternoon at three. We're planning a missionary trip to Haiti next spring. Think you might be interested?"

I'd had enough of missionary trips and helping out in disasters to last me a lifetime. "Not today," I said. "I need to get some sleep."

"So take a nap," Mel said. "Justin and I will pick you up. Father Mancini is so cool. You'll love him. And we need a few more people to sign up for the trip or we won't be able to go."

Aunt Mags overheard our conversation and spoke up. "Go ahead, Aerin. These trips are a life-changing experience."

The last thing I needed was another life-changing experience, but I figured I'd look like a jerk if I kept protesting. I'd find out what it was all about and then find a way to bow out.

"All right," I said. "Pick me up."

Chapter 9

The youth group met in the basement of the church, a room reserved for parish meetings with hard metal chairs and rickety tables that had seen better days. The smell of old coffee permeated the air. A projector sat on a small table in the center of the room, aimed at a projection screen.

I took a seat next to Mel and watched Justin flow through the crowd, greeting his friends with ease and familiarity. It had been a long time since I'd had that kind of closeness with a group of kids, the kind that grows over a lifetime of knowing one another and sharing the same experiences.

In the past, that didn't bother me, but since joining the Blazers I found myself dwelling on what I'd lost these last few years. Stifled emotions resurfaced and made me uncomfortable. Accompanying Mel to the church meeting may not have been the best idea. The other kids laughed and joked together, and I realized I didn't fit in. I wasn't one of them. I'd endure the meeting and go right home.

"Here comes Tati," Mel said.

Tatiana walked in carrying a tray full of cookies. In seconds, a small crowd surrounded her. She put the cookie tray on the table, pulled off the plastic wrap, and within moments the crowd had devoured half.

"The cookies are always a hit," Mel said. "She bakes them herself."

"Does that mean Jordan will grace us with her presence?"

"Nope," Mel said. "Lucky for us Jordan doesn't belong to our church."

The priest from that morning's mass entered, and the crowd hushed. He strode to the head of the room, placed a laptop on the table next to the projector, and addressed us.

"Good afternoon, everyone, I'm glad you're all here on such a beautiful day. I know you want to get back to your pools and whatever else you do on a summer Sunday afternoon, so I promise I'll make the meeting quick. Even though our trip isn't until April, it's important we meet today to start planning. But first, let us pray."

He led us in a short prayer. His robust voice carried well in the church but was soft and comforting in the smaller space. He was young, much younger than the priests from my home parish, and handsome, with light brown hair, blue eyes, and a dimpled chin. He seemed approachable, someone you could walk up to and talk to anywhere. The white collar around his neck and his black pants and shirt were all that gave him away as a man of God.

The prayer ended, and Father Mancini took a seat. "I've been on the phone with Father St. Jean in Port Au Prince," he said. "He and the children are very excited about your visit to help them with some important projects. We thought it might be a good idea to visit this afternoon, and we've set up a Skype chat." He gestured toward the equipment on the table. An excited murmur coursed through the crowd.

"He's talking about the orphanage in Haiti," Mel whispered.

"In a few moments we'll place the call, but what I first need to know is how many of you intend to take the trip."

"When are we going?" a girl to his left asked.

"We leave Easter week, early Monday morning, and come home the following Saturday. We will have five full days of work on the island," the priest answered.

"Where will we stay?" a guy at the rear of the room asked.

"We will sleep at the orphanage, with the children, but I must remind you conditions there are very different from conditions at home. There is little electricity, only during certain parts of the day, and poor access to TV and the internet. There is no fast food, no snacks, no soda. We will have limited transportation. Our purpose is to work, to help the people. We will eat with them, sleep amongst them, play with the children, and help them with their studies. You'll get little rest, and you'll be worn out when you return. However," and his eyes twinkled as his lips spread into an irresistible smile, "you'll take home memories you'll never forget. It will be a life-changing adventure."

A buzz spread through the room as everyone discussed if they wanted in. Father Mancini busied himself with the laptop and projector, preparing for the Skype talk.

"I'm in," Mel said. "Last year we went to Appalachia, and it was incredible, but this time we're leaving the country. It's a completely different culture. Most of the children don't even speak English."

"Father Mancini," asked a cute girl with blonde curls from across my table. "Who pays for the trip?"

"We do," he said as he plugged a cord into the projector. "We'll hold fundraisers, as many as necessary, between now and our departure to raise the needed money. You may also contribute funds or ask your parents to make a donation, but part of the commitment is to participate in the fundraisers so everyone who wants to can make the trip regardless of their financial situation."

"What kind of fundraisers?" Mel asked. "Same as last year?"

"Yes," Father Mancini said. "The dance we held last year to fund our trip was very successful, and the Women's Group has agreed to help us do another one. We can hold a Thanksgiving bake sale and sell Christmas trees again, and have a few coin drops at the supermarkets. You kids are smart and experienced fundraisers. I'm sure you'll come up with plenty of ideas."

"Aren't we already doing fundraising for the swim team?" I whispered to Mel.

She nodded. "Yeah, but most of the fundraisers will happen after swim season ends so that won't interfere. Remember, we have until April."

"So," Father Mancini said, as the screen lit up with the Windows logo and our Skype session was about to begin. "Who's coming with me?"

Just about every hand went up.

"Well?" Mel mouthed at me.

I shrugged, uncommitted. I didn't come to Two Rivers to go on a mission to a foreign country. "I'm not sure," I said. "My mother is coming home in February, almost half a year from now, and I can't make any commitments."

She stared at me, compassion in her eyes. "It's okay," she said. "I forgot. Maybe it's not the right time for you to join us."

I nodded, grateful for her understanding.

Father Mancini had set up the Skype call, and the room became quiet as we made our connection. In seconds, the screen filled with the faces of many Haitian children huddled around a smiling priest.

"Hello, St. Joseph's Youth Group," he said in a booming voice.

"Father St. Jean," said Father Mancini, "it's wonderful to speak with you once again."

"It is our honor and privilege to speak to you and your beautiful young people in Two Rivers. My children," he said, gesturing toward the kids clustered around him, "say hello to our friends in America."

The children waved, a few venturing to say hello. I stared, transfixed, at the screen. They were all smiling, full of life, dressed in shorts and t-shirts. They did not look desperate, starving, or hopeless. They looked like children I saw everywhere, and their beauty and grace captivated me.

"Hello Jeannette," Mel said, and a little girl with her hair in braids held together with colorful barrettes waved at her, her face shining with joy at being recognized in the crowd.

"You know her?" I asked Mel.

"We Skyped a few weeks ago, and I read her a story."

I sat back and watched as the children interacted with the kids in our room from hundreds of miles away. Father St. Jean acted as interpreter. Their conversations were personal and caring. They had a history, shared a world, held a connection.

I looked beyond them into the room from where they called. It was a simple classroom, not unlike the one we were in, with modest furnishings and concrete walls adorned with colorful children's paintings. There were no electronics, no computers, and very few books. Its simplicity moved me. The joy on the children's faces opened up a swell of happiness within me. I was drawn to them, as though we were kindred souls.

"They're amazing," I whispered to Mel.

She nodded. "Jeannette's my favorite," she said.

"How old is she?"

"Six."

I remained silent, an observer, as the conversations went on around me, spellbound. When it ended, and we had all said our goodbyes, Father Mancini disconnected the Skype call. Everyone continued to talk, unwilling to end the experience. Justin sat on the other side of the room in conversation with the guy sitting next to him. He had spoken with a small boy named Philippe, who said he wanted to learn how to swim. Justin had promised to teach him.

"What do you think?" asked Mel. "Changed your mind?"

"I had no idea the children would be so adorable," I said.

"I'm in love," Mel sighed, "with Jeannette."

"I'm in love with all of them."

Father Mancini got up from his seat, and the chatter stopped. "So," he said, "who's with me?"

Every hand in the room shot up, including my own.

Week Three:

A Flurry of Firsts

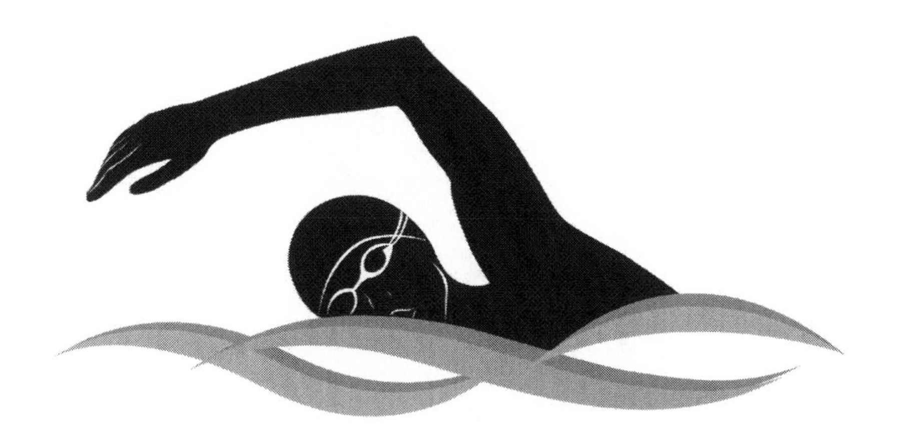

Chapter 10

The first day at a new school is tough. I got lost in the labyrinth of corridors, mistook one building for another, backtracked to classrooms I'd passed minutes before, and bumped into a few people who didn't appreciate it. I'd played the role of "new girl in school" enough times to know I needed to keep my eyes and ears open, ask for directions and follow instructions. I kept an eye out for Mel, Justin, Erica, or anyone I recognized to give me a wave or a smile to get through the day.

One of the reasons my parents agreed I could go to school in Two Rivers' was the high school's solid reputation and excellent programs. I was enrolled in three college level classes – English, Math, and History – and was taking Gym, Physics, Digital Photography, and French III. The teachers seemed all right, the other kids not too dumb, and the school had all the latest in high-tech resources: computers in every classroom, smart boards, and high-speed internet.

I had the late lunch, an advantage because I'd be able to eat before practice and meets. I entered the cafeteria, searching for a familiar face. In the rear, Mel and Erica sat with another girl and I hurried to their table.

"Hey!" Mel said, her face lighting up. "We all have the same lunch period."

"Lucky break," I said, sliding in beside her. "What are we eating? I'm starved."

"Meet Kelsey," Mel said, introducing me to the girl with a thick head of curly blonde hair, braces, and glasses who sat across from us.

"Hey," I said. "I'm Aerin. Nice to meet you. Awesome hair."

She reached up to pat her hair, smoothing it down. "Thanks," she said and took a bite of the peanut butter and jelly sandwich she'd brought from home.

"Who's getting lunch?" I asked.

Mel slid out of the booth and stood up. "I am. Follow me."

We moved to the front of the cafeteria where food stations were set up as a buffet, offering deli selections, a salad bar, pizza, and a hot meal. I got behind Mel in the deli line and waited.

"So who's Kelsey?" I asked.

"My cousin, and manager of the swim teams. She's a real brain, never forgets a number, keeps track of everyone's times, and watches the competition for us."

"Senior?"

"Yeah. How's your day going?"

I shrugged. "Okay, I guess. I'm taking Digital Photography, which is cool. I like the teacher."

"What's up next?"

"Physics," I said, my stomach tying itself into knots of anxiety.

"Me too. Mr. Ferrara?"

"I think that's his name."

"We're in the same class," she said. "Perfect. We can study together. Justin took it last year. Nerd. He got an 'A'. We can pick his brain."

I felt better already. The line moved along, and minutes later we returned to our table, rejoining Erica, who munched on a slice of pizza, and Kelsey, who popped grapes into her mouth one at a time.

"Ready for the meet?" Erica asked me.

"I guess so. What should I expect?"

"A win. We always beat the Hawks. They're a smaller team, not much depth, and they haven't beaten us in ages."

"The only teams we have to worry about are the Boxers and the Bears," Mel said.

"And we beat both of them last year," Erica said. She and Mel high fived each other. "How'd your other teams do? Did you win a lot?"

"Some," I said, finishing my turkey sandwich. "We went 8-4 last year."

"Not too shabby," said Mel.

I opened a carton of milk and took a swig. "Not as good as you guys."

"Two Rivers' teams dominate in almost every sport," Mel said. "Our teams have won more division titles than any other team in our division."

"All those farmers' kids," Erica said and laughed.

"Speak for yourself," Mel said. "I'm no farmer's kid. My mom's a doctor."

"What does that have to do with anything?" I asked.

"You know," Erica said, "the old farmer's work ethic: early to bed, early to rise. We tend to work a little harder than the rest of you."

"Can it," Mel said. "You have no proof of that."

"Just kidding," Erica said, smiling. "You're so easy to tease."

"Well, knock it off," Mel said.

Kelsey listened with no comments, her lunch finished, the remains packed up in their little paper bag.

"Do you swim, Kelsey?" I asked.

"Kelsey's an excellent swimmer," Mel said. "She was on the team in seventh, eighth, and ninth grades."

"Why'd you quit?" I asked.

"Long story," Kelsey said.

"She had an accident, broke both legs," Mel explained.

"That's awful," I said.

"I put on forty pounds while recovering and haven't been able to take them off."

"Swimming will help," Mel said.

"I'm not getting into that two-sizes-too-small swimsuit again. I'll stay on the sidelines and keep the books."

"You're in enough books," Mel said. "You need to take a break."

"I like to read," Kelsey said.

"Reading isn't everything," Mel said.

"What was the last book you read, Mel?" Erica asked.

Mel thought for a moment. "I read 'Wuthering Heights' for English last term."

Kelsey looked aghast. "You didn't read over the summer?"

"Who has time?" Mel asked.

"I read twenty books this summer," Kelsey said.

"I wouldn't let that get around," said Mel.

"I think it's great you read a lot," I said. "I'm a bit of a bookworm too." My books were another way for me to escape, and I devoured mysteries and sci-fi.

Mel jumped up from the table. "The bell's about to ring. We have to get moving."

We collected our things, threw out our trash, and went to class.

Chapter 11

As soon as classes ended for the day, the team assembled on the pool deck dressed in our warm-up suits, swimsuits underneath. The chatter was at a feverish pitch as the girls drifted into their tiny groups, watching as Coach and a few members of the boys' team, including Justin, set up equipment for the first of our dual meets, one team against another. Some of the girls looked terrified, including Charlie, who gave me a weak smile when I said hello. It was her first meet with the big girls, and she'd been talking about nothing else the last two days. She was afraid she'd make a mistake and get disqualified. No matter how much Mel and I tried to convince her she had nothing to worry about, she continued to bite her nails to the nubs and fear the worst.

The seniors staked out their spot in the bleachers, talking, joking, and much more relaxed than the underclassmen. All of them had been on the team for several years. For some, it was their sixth. I sat with Mel and Erica, waiting for Coach to give us our pre-meet pep talk and plan of action. Our opponents had not yet arrived.

Coach joined us with his clipboard in hand. "Come here, girls," he said, bringing us in close. "This is our first meet, and we're lucky it's against the Hawks. We beat them most every time, and this year they're looking thin. They lost their powerhouse senior and haven't replaced her with anyone as dynamic that we know of today. So, feel confident we'll win again, but not too confident because they've got a couple of Chinese exchange students they're keeping under wraps. We don't know too much about them, and they could surprise us. It's happened before. They swim distance and butterfly, so Tatiana and Erica, pay attention to what's going on in the next lane, ok?"

He turned toward the younger swimmers. "I want you all to take a few breaths." He demonstrated some relaxation breathing. "You're going to do fine. You'll each swim one event, and some of you will swim two and a relay." He looked at Charlie. "Just get in the water and do what you know how to do."

An audible sigh of relief passed between them.

"Now, here's the lineup," Coach said. "I had to mix it up a little bit to cover all our bases." He went through the order of events, announcing who would compete in each one. A few moans and a couple of groans came from swimmers unhappy with their events. No one liked to race out of her comfort zone and many preferred to do what she did best. Only a few girls excelled in more than one stroke. I was not one of them. Coach had me in the 200 and the 500 freestyles, plus on the "B" team for the 200 and 400 free relays. No surprises. I figured I'd pace myself to a third or fourth place finish. No way I'd come in last. That never happened.

"Now, everybody in the pool for warm up," Coach ordered.

We jumped into our assigned lanes and started easy laps, warming up our muscles, preparing our bodies for the upcoming races. I moved through the water languidly, stretching my arms and legs as far as possible, taking easy breaths on the third stroke. I shared my lane with four other swimmers, and we stayed out of each other's way. I executed smooth flip turns, not losing any speed, and glided from wall to wall. After about twenty turns, I stopped in the shallow end to catch my breath. Mel was in the next lane.

"Here they are," she said, out of breath, her face red. Our opponents emerged from the visitors' locker room in their red and white warm-up suits. In seconds, they stripped to their swimsuits. "They're pretty big," I said.

"The biggest ones are seniors, and they didn't do much last year," Mel said. "They didn't even make the championship finals. That small one with the long, blonde hair is their best swimmer. She almost beat Tati in the 200 and 500 free last year. Other than that, no real threat."

"If you girls are done with your warm-up get out and head to the locker room for final instructions," Coach said from the sidelines.

Mel ducked under and swam for the ladder.

"You're looking good, Aerin," Coach said. "I hope you show me something special today."

I nodded. It was the first time he'd given me any praise or laid any expectations on me. A tiny thrill was followed by a huge sense of foreboding. Part of me was proud to be recognized, but another part of me longed to remain anonymous. My intention to stay under the radar was still a top priority. Gaining Coach's attention threatened that, and made me a little uneasy.

"I'll do my best," I said.

Swim Meet Order of Events

200-yard Medley Relay
200-yard Freestyle
200-yard Individual Medley
50-yard Freestyle
Diving
100-yard Butterfly
100-yard Freestyle
500-yard Freestyle
200-yard Freestyle Relay
100-yard Backstroke
100-yard Breaststroke
400-yard Freestyle Relay

By the time the meet started the stands were full of spectators. I looked up to find Aunt Mags and the twins in that maddening crowd and spotted them in the center of the action. Aunt Mags caught my eye and waved. She directed the twins' attention toward me and they waved. I smiled back and gave them a thumbs-up.

"Go Aerin!" Mags called, and the twins echoed her, yelling out my name with a five-year old's exuberance.

The meet progressed as expected. We won the first relay, and then I competed in the 200 free with Tatiana as the top seed in lane four, and a freshman named Kim in lane six. It was an easy 200, and I stayed just behind Tati for the first half before easing up to come in a solid fourth. The Hawks Chinese exchange student took second, and another Hawk took third. Kim came in fifth. I climbed out of the pool, removed my goggles and cap, and squeezed the water out of my hair while I caught my breath. I joined Tati and Kim for a post-event chat with Coach, who gave Tati a high five for her win and patted Kim on the back for not finishing last. He looked at me over his bifocals.

"I expected a little more today, Aerin," he said. "Something tells me you haven't hit your stride."

I met his gaze and shrugged. "I did my best, Coach."

We maintained eye contact for a moment, and he was the first to look away. "Get ready for your next event," he said, dismissing me.

Erica won the IM, and we took third and fourth. In the 50 free a Chinese swimmer touched out Mel in two one hundredths of a second, a pitiful loss.

"Next time," I told her.

We had a few divers on our team, and they were good, all qualifying for the championship meet last season where two of them placed in the finals. The rest of us put on our warm up suits and cheered them on. Coach was strict about the no talking rule during diving. The divers needed silence to concentrate on their moves.

After they hit the water we could clap and cheer. Our divers took the lead, placing first, second, and fourth. The score was now 49-29, our lead.

Erica won the fly, and our swimmers took third and fourth place. Next, we took second, third, and fifth in the 100 free. By the time I went on deck for the 500 free, we had a nice cushion, 67-43.

"Listen, girls, I want you to keep it steady," Coach said as Tati, Kim and I huddled together by the blocks. "Tati, you've got this, and Aerin, you should be able to come in second. Kim, if you focus on your turns and do what we did at practice, you could come in third. Their distance swimmers aren't that great, and they're starting to look tired. You girls have the advantage. Now get out there and show them how it's done."

We took our places in our lanes, and I did some last-minute warm-ups, stretching my arms overhead and doing lunges to loosen my legs. I took a few deep breaths and fastened my goggles and cap, making sure they fit right and wouldn't slip off. The starter blew his whistle and we took our places on the blocks. I was in lane two. Tati was two lanes over in lane four. Kim was at the other end of the pool in lane six. I looked at the swimmer to my left, a scrawny little thing, a middle schooler. She didn't look at me but stared straight down into the water, knees knocking. I turned to my right. The swimmer was about my size and stared back at me, her gaze challenging, her body poised on the block, ready to hit the water. She was Tati's competition, the same Chinese student who had come in second in the 200 free.

The starter asked for silence, announced the event, and the buzzer pierced the air. I flew off the block, my body a perfect streamline as I glided halfway across the pool before coming up for air. I took a big breath and started churning through the water, no longer hearing the sounds from the pool deck, the cheering crowds, or my teammates at the pool's edge urging me on. All I heard was the sound of my arms slicing through the water and my legs kicking up a small wake behind me. I hit the wall, did a perfect flip turn, and started back. I did it again and again, focused only on my breathing and the execution of perfect turns. I lost sight of the swimmers on either side of me. I did not know who was in the lead or who was behind. I counted the laps – 5 – 8 – 10 – 12 – 15 – 18. A clanging bell signaled that the lead swimmer approached her final lap. I was not far behind. Was I in second place? Did I want to be in second place? No, I decided. If I came in second, Coach would start putting on the pressure for me to strive for first, taking away the joy I got from swimming. I slowed down a bit to take a couple of extra breaths, and the swimmer in lane three raced past.

My final turn was sloppy. I tried to make it look like I'd run out of steam. I pushed toward the finish and punched the wall: fourth place. Tati had won. The Chinese swimmer in lane three came in second, and Kim came in fifth.

Short of breath but not winded, I pulled myself out of the pool and joined my 200 free relay team, again in lane two. Coach had placed Tati, Kim, and I in the event as a cool down.

"What happened to you?" Tati asked. She was the lead swimmer, followed by me, Kim, and Mel as anchor. "You were right behind me. You had it nailed."

"I don't know," I said. "Guess I miscalculated my energy."

"Guess so," she said turning away to prepare for the race.

We came in first. After the relay, I went with the other girls to hear what Coach had to say, dreading the conversation. He congratulated Tati on her win in the 500, then said, "Nice relay, girls. You looked solid."

All smiles, Tati, Kim, and Mel walked away to join the rest of the team. I followed, but Coach stopped me.

"What was that all about?" he asked. "You had second place in the bag. Did I miss something?"

I shrugged, unwilling to meet his eyes. "I guess I lost my steam. Maybe I started out too fast. I tried to keep up with Tati, but she was flying."

"You did an excellent job keeping up with Tati, and if you can pull that off meet after meet we can take first and second in the 500 every time. The only person who comes close to Tatiana just lost to her, so the field is wide open. I want you to concentrate a little harder on your pace and your turns in the second half. Got that?"

I nodded, my heart sinking. So much for keeping under the radar. He'd already spotted I was a close second to Tati, and now the pressure was on. He wouldn't let up until I proved him right, or lost big-time. He was counting on my pride and drive to win to motivate me. Little did he know I was determined to lay low. The pool was my sanctuary. I would not have it turn into a battleground.

"I'll do my best," I said to placate him, but he had already moved on to the next event.

Back on the bench, I dried off and put on my warm-up suit. I had one race left, the 400 free relay. I wanted to rest a while, clear my head, and watch the other events.

"What happened to you, Apple, can't keep up with the big girls?" Jordan had sidled up beside me.

"Quiet, I'm watching the race." I motioned toward the start of the 100 back, Taylor's top event. The official started the countdown and the buzzer went off. Taylor sprung away from the pool wall in a graceful arc and disappeared under water.

Jordan came closer. "You can't beat Tati," she said.

I ignored her, focusing on Taylor. She broke through the water's surface and started backstroking in long, flowing movements, her torso twisting left and right in perfect synchrony. In seconds, she was in the lead.

"No one can beat Tati," Jordan said. "She's going to win the scholarship. I just know it."

Taylor made her first turn, and I stopped watching to look at Jordan. "So? I don't care if she wins it or not. I don't care about it at all."

"Didn't look that way," she said. She twisted a piece of her bleached blonde hair between her fingers. "You stayed tight with Tati, almost to the end, like you wanted to win."

"I don't care how it looked," I said, turning my attention back to Taylor and her race. She made her second turn, still in the lead. "I just want to swim. I don't care about winning."

"You don't care about winning? Give me a break. Everyone cares about winning. That's what brings us here every day."

I looked her straight in the eye. "I don't," I said. "You've got nothing to worry about."

"Oh, I'm not worried," she said, rising. "I'm just telling you not to waste your energy trying to beat Tati."

"Okay, Jordan, whatever you say," I said. Taylor was in her final turn and heading back on the last 25 yards, still in the lead. "Tati can win all the races, the championships, and the scholarship. I don't care. I just want to swim."

"I'm glad we have an understanding."

"Why do you care so much, anyway? What's in it for you?" I asked.

"Tati's my best friend. I'm not going to let some outsider come in and steal her place on that leaderboard." She pointed up at it. Allison Singer's record seemed lit from behind, dominating the board. It was just my imagination, but the numbers 4:52.50 almost blinded me.

"Like I said, I'm not here to win."

At that moment, Taylor reached the finish, and the crowd erupted in shouts and applause. She took first, and two of our swimmers placed third and fourth. We racked up eleven more points and knew we'd won the meet with two events left.

"Don't you have a race in a minute?" I asked Jordan.

She slipped out of her warm-up suit and grabbed her cap and goggles off the bench. "Remember what I said," she whispered, and sauntered off to the starting blocks.

I leaned my head back against the wall and closed my eyes. What was with this team? Why was everyone on my back? Didn't they see I just wanted to be left alone?

"Hey," Mel said, and I opened my eyes. "Where's Charlie? She's in this race."

"She was here a minute ago," I said, getting up to look for our Little Sister.

"She better get on the block or they'll start the race without her," Mel said.

I headed toward the locker room thinking she might have gone in there, but before I was halfway she walked out and met me.

"Ugh, you look awful," I said. "What's wrong?" Her face was a nasty shade of green, and she looked like she'd been crying.

"I threw up," she said, her eyes glossy with tears. "I'm afraid, Aerin. I don't want to do the race. I want to go home."

"Get a hold of yourself, Charlie. It's just a race. You can do it in your sleep. No problem."

"I don't want to race Jordan," she said.

"Jordan? She should be worried about you."

I kept her walking toward the starting blocks, Coach watching our every step. He gestured for me to hurry and I quickened our pace. "Now, get in there and do what you know how to do. You can beat Jordan. You may even beat the girls on the other team."

"But Jordan said I'm toast. She told me I'd sink before the second fifty. She said I had no business trying to swim against her because she's a senior and I'm just an eighth grader."

I clenched my fists. Jordan tried to intimidate everyone, but picking on Charlie was the last straw. Charlie was the best breaststroker on our team, and Jordan had never been in first place. Just because the previous top breaststroker had graduated didn't mean Jordan nabbed the top spot. You had to *earn* that spot, and Charlie had already proved she was stronger and faster than Jordan.

"Charlie, Jordan's a bully, and she's afraid you're going to make her look bad. She doesn't want to lose to an eighth grader, but she's about to, so she'd better get used to it. Now, get on that block, take your place, and swim as fast as you can, okay? I'll be cheering for you. Listen for my voice and don't listen to anything Jordan says ever again. Got that?"

She looked up at me with the biggest brown eyes I'd ever seen and nodded, her chin trembling.

"Now go!" I said.

Less than two minutes later, Mel and I had her wrapped in our arms as our teammates rushed to congratulate her on taking second place. Jordan had come in fifth, and after throwing her cap and goggles onto the pool deck plopped down on the bench next to Tatiana, her head buried in her hands.

"So much for the Little Mermaid," Erica snickered.

Mel glared at her from over Charlie's shoulder. "Be nice, Duke," she said. "It hurts all of us when someone doesn't perform at her best."

"She's not as good as she thinks she is," Erica said.

"Let her have her moment," Mel said.

I gazed at Mel in admiration. As our captain, she showed great leadership. As much as we disliked Jordan, we didn't want her to lose because it hurt the team. Still, as a senior Jordan should have been able to brush off her loss.

The final event was the 400 freestyle relay. We'd already clinched the win, so Coach went easy on the Hawks and put our slower swimmers in the lineup. The Hawks won with much cheering from the stands, and the meet was over.

Chapter 12

We finished the week with another meet on Friday against the Colts, a lackluster team the Blazers had a long history of beating. No one had much to worry about, and the Blazers finished first in each event, winning the meet. Our stiff competition was weeks away, when we'd face the Boxers and the Bears. In the meantime, the team was gaining confidence and pulling together. Mel and I left the locker room that evening a little euphoric from our two easy wins.

"So, what are your plans for the weekend?" Mel asked as we exited the building.

"I have to spend the weekend with my father," I said.

"I forgot you had a father. You never talk about him."

"There isn't much to say. He lives in Westchester with his new wife and her two kids. We don't have much in common anymore."

"That sounds so weird," she said.

"You're lucky. Your parents are still together, and they seem happy, and you have a twin brother, even though he's a big bother."

"Yeah, I guess you're right. I shouldn't take them for granted."

"Don't. Everything can change in a heartbeat. One day you're in a happy little family, comfortable and secure, and the next day you're on the outside, wondering where you belong."

"That's sad."

I shrugged. "It is sad, but I deal with it. I don't have a choice, do I?" I changed the subject. "What's up for your weekend?"

"Homework, for the most part. On Sunday, we have another meeting to talk about the Haiti trip. Too bad you'll miss it."

"You can fill me in on Monday." I was almost sorry I'd committed to the trip, but couldn't tell her that, seeing as how she was one of the leaders and ecstatic about my joining them. I still had to raise the money to pay my way. I'd have to discuss that with my father, not a conversation I looked forward to.

My dad coached his stepdaughters' soccer team on Saturday mornings and couldn't drive to Two Rivers to pick me up, so Aunt Mags brought me to the train station after swim practice. I didn't mind. The 90-minute ride gave me time to prepare for the visit.

Dad and Dawn had a home in the suburbs with a big yard, inground swimming pool, and a tennis court, courtesy of Dawn's huge divorce settlement. The two of them had disrupted many lives so they could be together. Dawn's ex-husband was my father's boss, which made things even more complicated. He fired him for breaking up his marriage. Dad was a lawyer and landed on his feet, starting his own one-man firm and working as a consultant for some big name clients in Manhattan.

Dawn worked as a tennis instructor at the local country club and taught private lessons at the house. She'd played tennis throughout high school and college and won a few titles. Her greatest achievement was losing to the Williams sisters. She was the picture of fitness, with short blonde hair, and phenomenal legs. She had a lot of energy and always tried to make me feel at home, but I was so much the outsider there I could never feel at home, even if I did have my own room in their McMansion of a house.

Her daughters, Emily and Avery, were ten and eight years old and spoiled brats. I found nothing likable about either of them. They were mini Dawns: petite, pert, and pretty. They followed me around the whole time I was there, asking me to play with them, read to them, and help them take their baths, like a real big sister. I was an only child and not used to having little kids at home. I didn't want to read to them, or give them a bath, or do anything with them.

My father, on the other hand, played with them all the time, board games like Clue and Pictionary. And they watched movies, all the Disney pictures, including my favorites *Aladdin* and *Cinderella.* I had few memories of him doing those things with me. When we lived together, he was always working and came home late at night, sometimes long after I was in bed. The most time we spent together was on the weekends, and even then he had a briefcase full of paperwork and spent a lot of time on the phone and at his computer. As for my swim team, he'd had little time to help out, claiming client commitments, paperwork, and research. His new law practice allowed him to work from home, and he ventured into the city just once or twice a week. He had a lot of time to spend with his new family.

He was waiting for me when I got off the train.

"How was the trip?" he asked as we walked toward the parking lot.

The September day was sunny, hot, the sky blue and cloudless. A pleasant breeze moved the air. I had on shorts and a T-shirt and felt overdressed. Although I'd swam 5,000 yards at practice earlier, I couldn't wait to get into the pool to cool off.

"It was okay," I said.

"Congratulations on this week's wins."

"We did okay."

"The team did great," he said, "but what happened to you?"

"I did okay," I said, on the defense.

We were at his car, a shiny new BMW. He didn't own a car when we lived in the city, but now that he was a hotshot attorney in Westchester he owned a top of the line luxury vehicle but still took the train into the city. The BMW got more use chauffeuring Emily and Avery to their activities. He popped open the trunk and placed my bags inside.

"You can do more than okay," he said, banging the trunk shut. "You're my little champion, remember?"

I bristled. "Not this time."

"What's that mean?" he asked as he backed out of his parking spot.

"It means I'm not swimming to win. I'm swimming to keep my head straight. That's it."

"What are you talking about? What's wrong with your head?"

"I need to keep my head straight with all that's been happening in my life."

"I don't follow. What's going on in your life?"

"Are you serious? What's going on in my life? How about Mom? How about what's going on with her? And what about you and your new family? I've been through a lot, and I don't need any more pressure. It's my senior year. I need to focus on my grades, on getting into a good college. I have a lot on my plate."

"What's going on with your mother has nothing to do with you," he said. "She'll be home before you know it. And what about my new family? You're part of that too, you know, although you could try a little harder."

I sighed. He never got it. "I try as hard as I can, but I'm not comfortable with your new family. I'm an outsider."

"You're not an outsider, Aerin," he said. "Dawn and I have done everything we can to help you fit in."

"That's just it," I said. "Why do *I* need to 'fit in'? I feel like it's all about them and I'm just your every other weekend obligation."

"Don't say that," he said. "You're my daughter, not an obligation. I love you. I want you to be a part of this new family."

"What was wrong with our old family?"

"I don't want to discuss it now," he said. "We'll talk about it later."

"If at all," I said, because he tended to delay these conversations to the point where they never happened.

"We have a lot to talk about this weekend," he said.

Ugh. Whenever he said those words I knew he was going to tell me something that probably wouldn't be good for me. I tabled the discussion, wondering what news he'd deliver once we got back to the house. Maybe Dawn had news. She always had something going on, like a tennis tournament she wanted me to enter. She didn't consider swimming a serious sport and urged me to switch to tennis. I wasn't interested in tennis. I wasn't interested in anything that would bring me closer to her.

Or, maybe something was going on with one of the girls. They went to a private school chock full of extracurricular activities to keep my father and Dawn nonstop busy. Perhaps they were in a play, or a piano or ballet recital, and I needed to switch my weekend or clear my schedule to attend. If so, I hoped the event fell on the same day as a swim meet, giving me an airtight excuse to skip it.

Chapter 13

When we got to their house, Dawn was giving a tennis lesson to some old lady, the thwack of the ball greeting us as we got out of the car. Inside, Emily and Avery were eating lunch in the kitchen with the au pair, a funny girl from Belgium named Geneviève. She was one of the few perks at my father's house.

"Bonjour," she said as Dad and I came in.

"Bonjour," I said. "Comment vas-tu?" I made sure to practice my French on her every chance I could.

"Très bien, merci," she said, smiling. "Et toi?"

"Mieux maintenant que je vois que tu es là."

She laughed, understanding what I meant when I said I was better now that I knew she was there. Some weekends she was off-duty and went to the city to spend time with some other Belgian girls who worked as au pairs. She was two years older than me, and made the perfect buffer between my stepsisters and me. As long as the girls were cared for, occupied, or, even better, sleeping, she and I could hang out, watch TV (she loved American reality shows), listen to music, or shop online.

"Aerin!" a tiny voice squeaked and Avery crashed into me, her arms wrapping around my waist as she buried her head into my belly. I looked down at her, hoping she hadn't smeared jelly on my shirt.

Great. Now I needed to change.

"Hey, Avery," I said, giving her a pat on the head. "What's up?"

"I got a goal in my soccer game," she said, looking up at me with bright blue eyes framed by long, dark lashes. I had to concede both she and her sister had the same incredible blue eyes, like their mother. Their baby fine blonde hair was like Dawn's, too. I ran my fingers through Avery's silky strands and wished my own were as soft and fine.

"Way to go, kid, that's great," I said.

"So what?" asked Emily, the older sister. "It's a stupid game. Who cares?" She took the butter knife used to spread peanut butter on their sandwiches and licked it clean.

"She's just mad because she was the goalie and her team lost," Avery whispered to me.

"Shut up, Avery," her sister said, "and stop bragging about scoring a goal. It's not like you score in every game."

"Watch your mouth, Emily," my father said. He poured two glasses of water and offered me one. "Don't talk to your sister like that. She had a good game. You should be proud of her."

Oh, my, I thought. What had I walked into? Emily was in a foul mood because she'd lost her game and Avery had scored in hers. Even when things were going her way, Emily was a disagreeable girl, but when things didn't go her way, she was horrible. Was that a preview of the rest of the weekend?

"Come on, girls," said Geneviève, lightening the mood. "Finish your sandwiches and put on your swimsuits. The last one in the pool is a rotten egg!"

The two girls jumped down from their stools, leaving their sandwiches behind with their milk.

"Come on, Gordon," Avery said to my father. At least they didn't call him "Dad." "Put on your suit and swim with us."

"I'll be out in a few minutes," he said.

They ran off, their footsteps sounding like thunder on the stairs leading up to their rooms.

"Hungry?" my father asked.

"I'll have PB and J," I said, reaching for the loaf of bread. He handed me a clean butter knife. I made my sandwich while Geneviève cleaned up after the girls. She offered me a glass of milk, and I accepted.

The girls were soon back wearing their swimsuits. Geneviève ushered them outside, and within moments they were splashing and shrieking in the heated pool.

My father and I ate lunch without talking. The house was quiet other than for the hum of the air conditioning and the on-again-off-again buzz of the refrigerator.

"Have you heard from your mother?" He had finished his sandwich and downed his milk. The glass left a milky white ring on the table.

I swallowed the last of my sandwich and crumpled my napkin. "Yeah," I said. "She writes to me once a week."

"How is she?"

I shrugged. "Okay, I guess." He always made a point to ask about my mother. I don't know why he cared. He didn't want to be married to her, so why bother pretending she meant anything to him?

"When will you visit her?"

"In a couple of weeks."

"She doesn't get to call or email or anything?"

"No."

"Aerin, I know her incarceration is hard on you, but she's getting the help she needs. She'll come home soon and everything will be okay."

I understood what he was saying, but I didn't want to hear it. He was her lawyer now, not her husband, and didn't have the right to talk about her or make comments about her life. Before I could change the subject, the door to the mudroom opened, and Dawn walked in.

"Hey," she said, her face and hair damp from exertion, her arms and legs glistening. The old lady must have given her some workout. "Have you guys had lunch?"

"Just peanut butter and jelly," my dad said. "Should I make you one?"

"No thanks," she said. "There's a salad in the fridge. I'll eat that. How are you Aerin? It's good to see you again." She gave me a big smile. Dawn tried hard to make me like her, but her efforts were wasted. How could I ever like the woman responsible for breaking up my family? Nothing she did would change that little fact.

She was waiting for an answer, so I said, "I'm okay."

"How's school going?"

"It's okay."

"And swimming?"

"Swimming is okay."

"Okay is right," my father said. "That coach must be working her hard in practice. Her race times stink."

I stiffened. Why couldn't he let it be? "I thought we talked about this already."

"Yeah, I know, it's all about your head. Did you know she has something wrong with her head?" he asked Dawn.

"What are you talking about?" she asked. "Are you having headaches, honey?"

I sighed. "No, I don't have headaches, at least, not until I got here. I was just saying that I have a lot of stuff going on and I need to take a break. I don't want to swim to win. I just want to swim to stay balanced. When I'm in the water, I don't worry about things."

"What kind of things?" Dawn asked

"Well, my mom, for one," I explained. "And school. I didn't do great last year, and I need to get my grades up." The last quarter of my junior year was a disgrace. My mother's troubles came to a head in the middle of it, and I could focus on little else, causing my grades to plummet. High marks the first three marking quarters saved my overall GPA, but if I hoped to get into a good college, I needed to concentrate on my grades. "I need to study a lot, especially physics," I told them. "I might need a tutor. And I have to take the SATs again. I completely bungled them last time."

"If you need a tutor, I'll take care of it," my father said.

"Thanks. That's a help."

"When is the SAT, anyway?" he asked.

"In a couple of weeks. I've been studying with some kids from school. I think I'll do okay. If I don't, I'll go to one of those prep classes and retake it again."

"Have you looked at any colleges yet?" Dawn asked.

"Not really."

"Have you given up on swimming in college?" my father asked.

I shrugged.

"If you have, I need to know because that changes the financial picture. Your mother and I socked away money for your education but most likely not enough. Scholarships will make a huge difference in your choices."

"I've been to the career center at the high school and talked with a counselor. I'm not sure where I want to go or what I want to study. She thought a community college would be a good idea."

"A community college?" my father asked. "No. You're going to a four-year school. You're getting a bachelor's degree, and then you're getting a master's."

"Some of these community colleges are good, Gordon," Dawn said. "The tuition's reasonable and you can save a lot of money. She can transfer to a four-year school after graduation."

"That's what the counselor told me," I said.

"I don't care about the money. That's not the issue," my father said.

"Gordon, we have three children to send to college," Dawn said.

"Your ex-husband will take care of your children's expenses. I'm not worried about them."

"Still," Dawn said, "there are many other expenses involved, and we'll have to manage them ourselves for all the girls."

"Don't worry about it," he said. "Right now we have to worry about Aerin getting her grades up and getting into a good school. As a matter of fact, if you're serious about giving up on college swimming, Dawn and I investigated a few colleges for you." He and Dawn glanced at each other, and she gave me a sheepish smile

"What did you say?" I asked, now on hyperalert.

"Did you know there are some excellent schools right here in Westchester? I called a few and asked them to send us some brochures. I thought we could look at them together over the weekend." He turned to Dawn. "Honey, get the brochures, please."

Dawn got up from the table, went to her desk in the corner, and came back with a colorful stack of college admissions brochures she placed before me.

"Why Westchester?" I asked, starting to pick through the pile, seeing which schools they were considering.

"Westchester's perfect," my father said. "You could live with us and go to school nearby. Some of the schools have swim teams, if you change your mind."

"Live with you?" I was starting to get the picture.

"You can commute to schools that aren't too far from here. I'll spring for a car, whatever you want, within reason. And you can stay here with us. You can help with the girls."

"Oh, I get it. I can be the new *au pair*."

"*Au pair*?" Dawn looked confused. "Oh, you misunderstand. Geneviève will leave at the end of the year, but we've already arranged for somebody else to take her place. We don't need you to be an *au pair*."

"Then what do you need me for?"

"You can help out by driving the girls to their activities, for example, their piano and tennis lessons," Dad said.

"Won't I be studying?" I asked.

"Well, I assume you'll have some downtime."

"Won't that be *my* downtime?"

"Well, if you're living here," he said, "we'd expect you to help in some way."

"What about the *au pair*? Won't she be driving them around? Isn't that her job?"

"I think we have a misunderstanding," Dawn said. "We've left something out." She and my father exchanged a glance taut with tension.

My radar amped up. Something else was going on here, and I suspected I wasn't going to like it.

"We need to back up," my father said. "I'm sorry, we left out an important detail." Again, he and Dawn glanced at each other.

My hands were in my lap, fingers entwined as I flexed them, trying to release the tension.

"We've got some news. Good news. Dawn's pregnant. You're going to have a little brother or sister."

I didn't know what I expected to hear, but it certainly wasn't that. My jaw almost fell into my lap. They were having a baby? Weren't they a little old for that? After all, I'd be heading off to college in a few months. That's some age gap. I got the whole picture now.

"Congratulations," I said. "But what does that have to do with me? You won't need me to help take care of a new baby."

"No, we won't need you to take care of the baby," Dad said. "Dawn will be here, and she'll have the *au pair*. The *au pair* will help with the girls, too, but we thought that if you went to school here and stayed with us you would be available to help, too. It would be an opportunity to get to know your stepsisters better and to bond with your new brother or sister," he said.

"Sounds like a great plan," I said, "except for one thing: I don't want to go to school in Westchester. And, another thing: I don't want to live with you. I could be living with you right now, but I'm not, I'm staying with Maggie and Pat because I can't stay here. I don't care to know my stepsisters better, and I don't plan to take care of your new baby."

Dawn stiffened. "We thought you'd be happy for us."

I gaped at her, astounded by her arrogance, her lack of understanding. Why would I be happy for them?

I wasn't happy she'd met my father.

I wasn't happy he left my mother.

I wasn't happy they got married.

I wasn't happy to have two stepsisters.

And, I wasn't happy to be a big sister to their child, their new family coming full circle, completion.

I would be no better than an *au pair*. They had no obligation, no commitment, to these foreign girls who came and stayed with their family a year at a time to help them with the care, feeding, bathing, and driving around of their little monsters. I wasn't sticking around. I was going to college, a college far away so I wouldn't have to stay with them or help them with their children.

"You know," I said trying to be as calm as possible, "the two of you act as though you're the only two people in the world. You're oblivious to how you've hurt my mother and me. You've hurt Emily and Avery, too. You've turned our lives upside-down so you could be together.

"I can't forgive you," I said looking at my father, "for leaving Mom and me at such a critical time. If you want to go on as if no one's been hurt by your selfish actions, that's fine. I can't do anything about that. But don't ask me to pretend everything's okay and we're one big happy family, because we're not."

Chapter 14

They stared at me in silence for a moment, the girls' splashes and screeches in the pool punctuating the tension.

"Well, Aerin," my father finally said, "you've made your feelings clear. We've talked about this umpteen times. I can't help it that my marriage to your mother failed. She chose to join the military. She knew she'd be deployed. I did my best as a single parent, but I was lonely, and Dawn filled that void. I'm not going to apologize for falling in love with her, and I'm not going to apologize for building a family with her. Your mother made her choice, and I made mine."

He sugarcoated everything so he wouldn't look like the bad guy. What he failed to mention was that my mother was *compelled* to serve our country in a time of war. She put aside *everything* - her comfort, her security, her marriage, her *child* - to administer to our soldiers in a foreign land, many of them wounded in ways only imaginable. While she was altruistic and patriotic, my father thought only of himself and found another woman. When my mother came back after her first tour of duty, he greeted her with divorce papers.

"You think you've done nothing wrong," I said, "but from my point of view, you cheated on Mom while she was in the middle of a combat zone, working around the clock to save lives, putting her own life at risk. I think she's brave and unselfish, the best woman I have ever known. She may not work out four hours a day," I looked at Dawn, "or get her nails done every week, but she's beautiful. She didn't deserve what you did."

"Well," Dawn said, finding her voice. "This conversation has gone a little off track. We hoped you'd be excited for us. I've done all I can to welcome you into our home. I treat you like a daughter. Yet you've made it quite clear you don't want to be a part of our family."

"Now, honey," my father said, "that's not what she means. She's still angry with me, with us, for the changes in her life. But Aerin," he said looking at me, "you're a big girl now, and there are a few things about your mother and I that we haven't told you. It's time you know the whole story.

"Long before September 11th and your mother's enlistment, our lives were about to change. Your mother is a good woman, an excellent nurse, and always puts others first, qualities I admired when we first met. I started my career as a public defender, and in that way she and I were alike - we wanted to serve others - but it was impossible to support our family in the city on a public defender's salary. When I had the opportunity to join a corporate practice I jumped at it, but your mom was not pleased. She liked the money, but her worldview is about service, and she had a hard time justifying my job in business law.

"When September 11th happened, your mother and I were already at a standstill. She enlisted in the Reserve against my wishes. How were we supposed to save our marriage when she was on the other side of the world? I didn't go out looking for another woman, but Dawn came into my life when I needed someone, and provided me with comfort."

These revelations stunned me. "I don't believe you," I said. "I would've known if you were on the verge of splitting up."

"Your mother and I made sure you didn't know," my father said. "It was our trouble. The last thing we wanted was to upset you. We went to counseling, but that didn't help. Then the towers fell, and your mother became consumed with that, with the recovery effort, and then enlisting once the war started. After that, we didn't have a chance."

As a lawyer, he was well-trained at circumventing the truth, at making arguments to support his point of view. I wanted to close my ears to what he was saying, but had to wonder if any of it were true. From the outset, I'd blamed him and Dawn for breaking up our family, but if what he said was true, my mother had played her own part.

"I'm asking Mom," I said. We had a visit coming up, and in her fragile condition it might not be the best time to bring up this subject, but I had to know.

"Ask her," he said. "She'll tell you the same thing. Our marriage was over whether Dawn entered my life or not."

The sliding door that led to the patio opened, and Emily and Avery came into the kitchen wrapped in towels, shivering as they encountered the air-conditioned room. Geneviève came right behind them.

Their entrance could not have come at a better time. I was still reeling from my father's disclosure, still disbelieving, my thoughts and emotions in chaos.

Dawn got up off her stool and went to her daughters, entering mother mode, towel drying them and asking if they wanted a drink. My father grabbed the milk from the fridge and a box of cookies from a cabinet. Geneviève excused herself to go to her room and change.

I stayed seated, once again feeling like an outsider. I suppose I would always feel like an outsider, regardless of the circumstances that had led to this new family and my role in it.

Without saying a word, I went up to my room, grabbed my bags, and went back downstairs.

"Where are you going?" my father asked.

"I'm going back to Maggie's. I need some time to think."

"But what about our weekend? We have plans. We're going to a movie this afternoon, and then dinner. We were looking forward to your joining us."

"I'll take a rain check. I'm not feeling too great."

"Please don't go," he said. "We spend so little time together and you're already here."

"I'm sorry, Dad, but you just dropped a bombshell on me, and I already have a lot on my mind. I'll see you in two weeks."

He sighed. "Well, I wish you'd change your mind. And you'll see us next week, remember? We're coming to your big swim meet on Saturday."

I remembered. Most of my meets were during the week, but because of his work schedule and the distance between us he was unable to come. The few held on weekends gave him an opportunity to watch me swim. He said he made his best effort, but something always came up, and he usually missed half of them.

"So I'll see you then." I moved toward the door.

"Let me drive you to the train station," he said.

"No thanks, I'd rather walk."

"But it's three miles!" Dawn exclaimed.

"No problem. I'm a competitive swimmer, remember? I can walk three miles."

"If you insist," Dad said. "But call me when you get to Maggie's."

I agreed, and as I walked by he grabbed me and pulled me close, giving me a hug and a kiss on the top my head.

Emily and Avery sat at the counter with their milk and cookies, watching and chewing. I walked past them toward the door.

"You're leaving?" Avery asked.

"Yeah, but I'll see you soon," I said. They didn't seem too perturbed at my departure.

"Take it easy, Aerin," Dawn said. She knew better than to try to give me a hug.

I nodded and slipped out the door, sliding it closed behind me.

Minutes later my dad's BMW pulled up alongside me with Geneviève at the wheel.

"You left without saying goodbye," she said.

I'd forgotten all about her and mentally kicked myself. "Sorry," I said. "I just had to get out of there."

"Everything okay?"

"No, but there's nothing I can do about it right now. I'm going back to Maggie's. They're away for the weekend, so I'll have plenty of peace and quiet. I just want to be alone."

"Let me give you a ride to the train station. It's hot out, and it's a long walk."

She had a point. I was already soaked with sweat and had almost two miles to go. I walked around to the passenger side of the car and got in, grateful for the AC's frigid blast. We drove to the train station without much conversation. Geneviève was skilled at knowing when to speak and when to remain silent, especially when personal matters were concerned.

"You're lucky," I said, after she parked. "You leave home and live with another family with no strings attached. What's it like?"

"It's okay," she said. "It's a way to get into the country, to get my bearings before I decide whether or not I want to come back and stay."

"I guess it's kind of like my living with Aunt Maggie and her family, except they don't expect anything from me. I don't have to help with the kids, drive them around, or anything like that. I'm grateful they let me stay with them. Otherwise, I'd have to stay with my father and Dawn, and that would be a disaster."

"I would welcome the opportunity for us to get to know each other better, to become friends," she said, which made me regret the inevitable loss of our deepening friendship. She was the only bright spot in my visits with my father and Dawn.

We sat in the car and waited for the next train to pull in, talking about her experiences as an *au pair*, her family, her plans for college, and what we could do the next time I visited my father.

"I'll make sure not to be in the city with my Belgian friends, ne c'est pa?" she said.

"Sounds great," I said. The train pulled in, and I collected my belongings.

"This too shall pass, Aerin," Geneviève said. "Trust me."

I gave a nod and got out of the BMW. I grabbed a seat on the train just seconds before it pulled out of the station.

Maggie's house was family-free. I hadn't spent much alone time there and welcomed the silence and freedom to do as I pleased. I made two grilled cheese sandwiches and poured a glass of milk. I polished that off with the last piece of chocolate cake Mags had made the day before. I camped out in the living room in front of the TV, tuned to the Cartoon Network, and tried to focus on my physics homework. It failed to interest me, and my mind wandered back to the events earlier that day. I thought about Dawn having another baby, and about my father having another child. It had never occurred to me, but as my initial shock wore off I realized I'd been naïve not to anticipate a pregnancy. I guess it was only natural, yet I felt a bit displaced, more than I had these last four years. I wondered if Emily and Avery also felt displaced, or perhaps they were excited to have a new baby in the house.

My father's revelations about my mother and their marriage still pained me. If what my father said turned out to be true, what I'd believed about my life was wrong. For the last five years, he'd been a good scapegoat for our problems. After all, *he left*. Now it seemed my mom also played a role in their breakup. She could have chosen not to enlist, or not to reenlist when she had the chance to get out. Two tours of duty had taken considerable time away from our family and left irreparable harm. When I thought of my father during that time, when she was on the other side of the world and we didn't know what was going on with her, I remembered him being tense and anxious. He did his best to maintain the normalcy of our days, but things at home seemed off no matter what he did. We missed her. Neither of us managed well without her. I guess he wasn't able to recover, and I'd had no choice. When I could, I'd ask her about these things and find out if they were true, and if so I'd have to forgive my father. I didn't know if that was what I wanted, but it was only fair.

The physics text acted like a sedative and put me to sleep. I drifted off, the book sliding onto the floor. When I awoke, the room was dark, lit only by the glow of the TV. Outside, the crickets sang their evening serenade. I didn't even bother going up to my room, just pulled an afghan over myself and went back to sleep.

Chapter 15

The next morning, I got up early, made breakfast, and got ready to go to church. Mel thought I was away for the weekend and I wanted to surprise her. I'd promised I'd sit up in the choir loft with her some Sunday. She had some crazy idea I could sing. Little did she know I had no pitch.

As soon as she saw me she rushed over. "What happened? I thought you were at your dad's. Is everything ok?"

"I left. Too much tension. I'll tell you about it later."

The choir was a mixed group of adults and kids, and everyone went out of their way to welcome me. I stayed in the back and sang along with the hymns, as usual trying to attract no attention, but this time I had no talent for anyone to discover. Mel again sang like an angel. When services ended, we went to the coffee hour in the parish hall to have a snack.

"You sounded good," Mel said.

"Yeah, right." I snickered. "I can't even carry a tune."

"Yes, you can. Our voices always sound different to our own ears. You have a pretty voice. If you worked with our choir director I'm sure he'd have you singing solos in no time."

I almost choked on my orange juice. "No way, Mel," I said. "You'll never get me up there to sing a solo."

"Don't worry about it," she said. "I'm kidding. I've been singing for eight years, and I just started solos."

Justin joined us, balancing a plate of powdered donuts.

"Don't tell me you're going to eat all of those," Mel said in a reproachful tone.

"Why wouldn't I?" He bit into one, powdered sugar coating his lips. I looked away, not wanting to focus on that part of his face. "It's not like I'm in training or anything," he said, his mouth full.

"It's gross," Mel said. "I mean, one is enough, but five is just gross."

"You want one?"

"No."

"How about you?" He looked at me and pointed to the plate with a powdery finger.

"No thanks," I said. "*I'm* in training." I nibbled on the blueberry muffin on my plate.

A moment later, Father Mancini stopped at our table. "Melanie," he said as he pulled up a chair and sat beside her. "I have terrific news. The Women's Group has set a date for the dance."

Mel's face lit up. "That's great," she said. "When?"

"Third Saturday in October," he said.

"That's perfect," Mel said. "We have an overnight meet the day of the Homecoming Dance, and the girls on the team are disappointed we won't be back in time to make it. We'll have our dance the following week. When's our next meeting?"

"How about next Sunday afternoon?" the priest asked. "We can Skype again with Father St. Jean and the children."

"Sounds good to me," Mel said. She and Father Mancini began making plans, discussing which DJ they should hire and what type of snacks they should offer.

Justin and I listened to their conversation but made no suggestions. He sat to my left and leaned over to whisper, "How do you feel about dances?"

I felt a flutter in my belly as his breath grazed my cheek. "They're okay," I said, noncommittal.

"The dances here are a big deal," he said. "Everyone gets dressed up. Most people bring a date."

My face flushed and I hoped my cheeks didn't turn scarlet. "And who's your date?" As far as I knew he didn't have a girlfriend, but the subject hadn't come up and I wasn't one hundred percent sure.

"I don't usually bring a date, but this time, I might make an exception."

"Anyone in particular?"

"Someone special," he said. "Someone with a killer front crawl and a sick start. Someone like a girl I know from the city."

I gulped. "Are you talking about me?"

He gave me a tiny smile, his eyes crinkling. "Does anyone else fit that description?"

"You're asking me to be your date?" No one had ever asked me out, and my lack of finesse with the invitation must have unnerved him because he started to look a little worried, as though preparing himself for a letdown.

"And what if I am?" he asked, his voice losing the easy confidence he'd had when he started the discussion.

"Come on you guys," Mel interrupted. "Time to go."

I forced myself to look away from him and realized the parish hall had cleared out, except for a few people cleaning up after the refreshments. I caught my breath, still feeling flushed, my stomach doing flip-flops. Was Justin really asking me to be his date? *Yes!* I wanted to shout, but the moment had passed. As I got ready to follow Mel out of the hall, I sensed Justin behind me.

"Think about it, Apple," he said, before speeding up and passing me, the first of us out the door.

WEEK FOUR:

School, Swim, Study, Sleep

Chapter 16

With the first week of school and our first two meets behind us, we settled into our rhythm, a predictable schedule of school, swim, study, and sleep punctuated once or twice a week with a dual meet. Coach had us in the pool right after school, working on skills and drills, putting in as much as 6,000 yards each day. As each practice ended, the less experienced girls grew stronger, their whines dwindling to an occasional peep. Their muscles started to look more defined, and their strokes resembled something that might earn them a few points. The seasoned swimmers built upon their strengths, improved their times, and perfected their starts, turns, and finishes.

On Tuesday, we went up against the Titans and won, 96-88. On Thursday, we clobbered the Lions, 112-74. We were now 4-0, and everyone was confident. In six weeks, we'd face our biggest challenges – the Boxers and the Bears – and if we beat them, we'd be well on our way to another undefeated season. I imagined the headlines: *Blazers Take Fourth Consecutive Division Title.*

The swim team at Two Rivers got a lot of respect, something I hadn't experienced at my other schools. When we wore our team shirts on meet days, students and teachers stopped us in the halls to wish us luck. On mornings after a win our victories were announced over the loudspeakers, and the school website posted detailed accounts of our meets. Sometimes I felt like a celebrity.

At first, I hadn't wanted any attention at all, content to swim under the radar, keeping my head clear, using the water as my therapy. But as the season progressed, I was proud to be part of this team and proud of our accomplishments. Of course, I hadn't done anything spectacular, coming in third and fourth in most events, but I was pleased with my contributions. Not much was expected from me, so everything was cool.

That Saturday we had our first big meet, the Boxer's Country Swim & Dive Open, when all the teams in the division came out to show their stuff. Mel said it was a fun meet, and gave us a chance to check out the other teams' talent. My father, Dawn, and the girls planned to attend, as did Aunt Maggie, Uncle Pat, and their kids.

The Boxers' natatorium was the biggest, newest, and most up-to-date in the division. Coach liked our team to be the first to arrive at any big meet and we walked on to an empty pool deck, settling ourselves on the bleachers assigned to us, and getting ready for warm-up. Coach reviewed the order of events and told us our lane assignments. The complaints that followed were loud and long. Some of the girls still had to find their niche and swam events they had no feel for, but some of us had no complaints. Once again, I was swimming the 200 free, 500 free, and the 200 and 400 free relays. These events had become my usual routine, and I was comfortable. Mel swam the 50 and 100 free and anchored the 200 and 400 free relays. Charlie and Jordan claimed the breaststroke, Erica owned the 200 IM and butterfly, and Tatiana shared the distance events with me.

Tati's season was under the microscope as talk of her most likely breaking Allison Singer's 500 free record spread throughout the division and made the local news. It was all anyone talked about at the meets. No other school had ever had such a challenge. I couldn't imagine the pressure, but Tati handled it with poise. She won every event, her swimming graceful, appearing effortless. She had yet to come close to last year's best time, but she'd hit it soon, and then it was do or die as she got closer to that 4:52.50 record.

The other teams arrived and the pool deck grew crowded. The chatter and laughter of more than 300 girls filled the natatorium, creating a dull roar. Swimmers dove into the pool one after the other, practiced their starts, and then glided through the water like schools of fish, each team in their own lane, the girls moving in head to toe formation, careful not to collide with one another. Mel, Erica, Charlie, and I finished our warm up – two hundred yards – and sat on yoga mats on the pool deck to stretch out.

"The Boxers are there," Mel said, giving a nod to the team across the pool from us. They had a bigger team – thirty-six girls to our twenty-eight – and most of them upperclassmen. They also had a pair of Chinese exchange students we'd heard were more competitive than the two we went up against with the Hawks. Like us, they were 4-0, and Coach said they expected to come in first today.

"And the Bears are there," she said, pointing toward the only other team with the potential to beat us. They were the largest in the division - forty swimmers. Like the Boxers, most of the girls were juniors and seniors, but I'd heard they had a couple of freshman dynamos who could make trouble for Tati and me.

"No problem," said Erica as she did a hamstring stretch. "As long as we don't get injured or sick we can take all of them. It's my last season, and I don't plan to leave this team a loser. Just let them try to take our title. We'll show them who's boss, right?"

"Oh yeah!" said Mel, her competitive streak kicking in.

"Go Blazers!" cheered Charlie.

Their enthusiasm was infectious, and I rallied around them. "Starting today," I said, "they won't know what hit them."

"And we don't even have any Chinese exchange students," Mel said, a wicked gleam in her eye. Next to the Singer challenge, the Chinese students were the talk of the season on the pool decks, the division website, and the local papers. They came from the same province, champion swimmers who had graduated high school last year and were now having the "American experience" before going on to college. The four exchange students who had come to Two Rivers didn't swim, so we didn't have that advantage.

"Who needs them?" Erica asked.

"A couple of them could pose some trouble for Tati," Mel said. "One on the Boxers' team comes close to her best 500 time."

"You're so fixated on Tati's breaking the record," I said. "Not a day goes by without you bringing it up."

"Well, yeah," Mel said, giving me an incredulous look. "That record's been solid for more than twenty years. Tati's the only one who's come close in at least ten. Lots of people want to see it fall, including Allison Singer. That's why she started the challenge - to motivate people. I'd hate it if a Chinese exchange student broke it."

"So?" Erica asked. "They can't win the scholarship. Only a Two Rivers student can win that prize."

"That's not the point," Mel said. "It's not about the money. If anyone other than Tatiana breaks that record, it will embarrass all of us."

"I don't get it," Charlie said, looking puzzled. "You lost me at the Chinese exchange students breaking the record."

"Okay, here's how it works," Mel said, taking a deep breath. The three of us stopped moving and focused on her words. "There are two records. The first is the school record, which Allison Singer owns – 4:52.50 set at the 1989 New York State Championship meet. That time broke the state record, too, but someone broke *that* in the 90's, so it's not hers anymore. Next, we have the division record, which is also Singer's state record from '89. Follow me?"

"Yeah," said Erica "So, anyone can break the division record, right?"

Mel nodded.

"But only a Two Rivers student can break the school record and win the scholarship," Erica said.

"You've got it," Mel said, smiling. "And we don't want anyone but Tati to get near these records. It's a matter of Blazers' Pride."

"We need to keep Tati pumped up," Erica said.

I looked at Tati, who sat next to Jordan on the bleachers looking like she didn't have a care in the world, talking and laughing while her fingers worked Jordan's bleached blonde hair into a French braid.

"She doesn't seem to be too concerned," I said.

"It's all an act," Mel said. "Tati knows better than anyone what's expected of her. She's been struggling with it for more than a year. Her father pushes her harder than anyone else. If he could pay to put Tati's name up on that leaderboard, I bet he'd write a check right now."

"It's not like they need the scholarship money, either," Erica said. "Calvin Reese just wants his daughter's name on that board in all of her events. And he wants her to win the division title in the 500."

"And she missed it by four and a half seconds last year," Mel said. "I thought Mr. Reese was going to have a heart attack."

The talk about winning and titles and records made my head hurt. What happened to the joy of swimming? Of doing your best? Good thing my father was too preoccupied with his new family to worry about my performance in the pool.

I looked up into the stands and picked out Aunt Maggie, Uncle Pat, and the kids in the throng of spectators and caught Mags' eye. She waved at me and grabbed hold of one of the twins, who picked up something from the floor and then raised her arms over her head. "Go Aerin!" was painted on a piece of poster board in a kindergartner's script. The twins' handiwork filled me with an indescribable sense of belonging and support. I waved back and shouted, "Thank you!"

Mel turned to see what all the fuss was about. "Great poster," she said. "Cute kids."

"Look," I said to her, "isn't that your mom next to Aunt Mags?"

"Yep," she said and waved to her mother.

"My folks are over there," Erica said, pointing to the other end of the stands. She was the youngest of six, and her parents were a few years older than the rest of ours. They looked worn by their life on the farm, but happy. Her father gave her a huge smile and a thumbs-up while her mother waved like she was trying to flag down a cab in the rain.

I scanned the stands, looking for my dad, Dawn, and the girls. No sign of them. The meet was about to start. Maybe they were stuck in traffic.

Chapter 17

We finished our stretching and joined the rest of the team on the bleachers. Coach gave last minute instructions, the announcer made his opening statements, the national anthem played on the loudspeaker, and the meet was on.

All fourteen division teams attended, which meant several heats in each event. We weren't going anywhere for a long time. When we weren't preparing to race, in a race, or recovering from a race, Coach expected us to cheer for our teammates in the pool. The first event was the medley relay. I took up a spot on the back wall and cheered for our "B" team, which won its heat, and then for Taylor, Charlie, Erica, and Mel's team who were in the final heat and came in second to the Boxers by a fraction of a second. After speaking with Coach, they came back to the bleachers to catch their breath.

"Good job," I said, as I tugged on my cap. The 200 free was coming up, and I was in the next to last heat.

"We stunk," Mel said, panting. "We should have won. I was touched out."

"You did your best. That Chinese girl was smoking."

"I'm getting the feeling they're going to be a force to contend with all season. There's one in every event."

"I've got a couple in mine too," I said.

"Tati will clobber them," Erica said.

"So will you," Charlie said.

I gave her a grateful smile. "Thanks for the vote of confidence, Charlie."

"You're a lot stronger than you think, Aerin," she said.

I studied her face, wondering what she knew. Her big brown eyes betrayed no suspicion or hidden knowledge. "Maybe," I said.

I adjusted my suit and headed for the starting blocks. While I waited for my heat, I scanned the spectators again, looking for my father. Still no sign of him. I hoped nothing was wrong. We'd spoken that morning, and he said there was no way he'd miss my meet.

The heats moved with coordination and efficiency, and soon I was on the block, poised for the start. The buzzer buzzed and I launched, hitting the water in a perfect streamline. I kicked my way to the surface and started my stroke, my arms moving in a perfect rhythm as I glided through the water, breathing on the third stroke, flutter kicking my feet. My flip turns were powerful. I kicked off the wall as hard as I could, maintaining a steady pace. I didn't bother to look to my left or my right, not concerned about the competition. I didn't care. I was one with the water, letting my concern over my father's tardiness wash out of me, letting the water absorb it. He'd be here soon. He'd promised. But it would have been nice if he'd caught my first race.

I counted each turn, and when I'd finished three laps slowed down. Winning this race was not my goal. I wanted a respectable finish, but no glory. A Chinese swimmer had entered the pool alongside me, and was half a body length away. I held back enough to give her the lead. When I reached the finish, I looked up at the clock. Third place, my time hovering around the best I'd done all season - 2:05.12. Satisfied, I hauled myself out of the pool, pulled off my cap and goggles, and went to see Coach. He peered at me over the top of his bifocals and shook his head.

"I thought you might break out today and rise to the

competition," he said. "I can't shake off the feeling you're holding back on me."

I shrugged, still catching my breath. "I did my best. What more do you want?"

He stared at me, then gestured for me to move on, looking back down at his clipboard.

I plopped down on the bleachers next to Mel and Charlie, who each gave me a high five.

While I recovered from the race, I searched for my father in the stands. Still no sign of him.

I turned my attention to the pool. For the first time, I was able to watch Tati swim an event. We always competed together, so I hadn't yet seen her technique. She approached the block full of confidence, not looking at the other swimmers. She waited until she got the go ahead to climb onto the block and jumped on, doing a few final stretches while she waited for the official to announce the start. She got into starting position.

When the buzzer buzzed, she dove off the block like a crackerjack. Within seconds, she dominated the event, three or four strokes ahead of the next swimmer. She had textbook technique, feet flutter kicking non-stop, arms arcing overhead in perfect form, breaths timed to every third stroke. Her expert turns kept her in the lead. Mel, Charlie and I watched, cheering her on until we were hoarse. Coach followed her progress from the sidelines, bellowing out orders, his arms waving wildly.

But halfway through the race the swimmer to her right started to catch up, and the two of them swam side by side for one full lap. We watched in disbelief when her opponent got the advantage and slipped ahead of her on the final turn, moving faster, her arms cycling through the water.

When it looked as if Tati might lose her first event of the season we stopped shouting and waited, stunned.

"No way," Mel whispered.

Tati tried to catch up, but the other swimmer was too fast and hit the wall with an emphatic slap. She won, touching Tati out by only a few hundredths of a second.

Tati looked up at the clock, her chest heaving, disbelieving. She turned to the girl who'd beaten her and offered her hand. The other swimmer took it, and they shook hands. Then the swimmer removed her goggles. She was the same Chinese exchange student Tati had beaten just a week before.

Tati pulled herself out of the pool, still breathless, and yanked off her cap and goggles. She stood catching her breath for a few moments before reporting to Coach, who had thrown his clipboard across the pool deck when it looked like Tati would lose. He glowered at anyone who tried to approach him. I felt sorry for her, knowing that no matter how many races she'd won in the past, Coach was sure to chew her out for losing this one.

"Don't watch," I said and turned Mel and Charlie's attention to the next event queuing up on the blocks, the 200 IM, Erica's race. She finished fourth, a strong effort.

Next was the 50 free, Mel's race, and she left us to get in line for her heat. We stood on the sidelines cheering on our teammates. It was a fast race, and the swimmers took off from the blocks just seconds after each heat. Mel was in the second to last heat, seeded seventh, and swimming in lane one, right next to where we were. We followed her along the deck, screaming at her to "Go!" "Move!" "Kick, Mel, kick!" urging her on. It worked, because she sped up at the turn, gave a mighty push off the wall, and pulled ahead of three other swimmers in the last twenty-five yards. We chased her along the deck, cheering her on, and she finished in third place. She looked up at the scoreboard, saw she'd finished with her best time of the season and gave us a triumphant wave.

The meet went on, the Blazers finishing near the top in each event and racking up points. We were in second place behind the Boxers. The Bears trailed us in third.

Tati and I lined up for the 500, both of us top seed in our heats, which put us in lane four. I stood ahead of her waiting for my turn. She seemed subdued, disengaged, not speaking to anyone and not watching the other swimmers, still shaken by her loss in the 200 and Coach's tongue-lashing.

"Hang on, Tati," I said, trying to cheer her up.

She gave me a thin smile and said, "Thanks."

I glanced up into the stands, searching for my father, but saw no sign of him, Dawn, or the girls. The meet was almost half over and I figured they bailed on me. Again. It seemed they never had time to fit one of my swim meets into their busy schedules, even though they claimed "Supporting Aerin is a top priority." What crap.

My muscles tensed and my stomach tied itself in knots. My face burned and I wondered if my cheeks were pink, the giveaway that I was upset. I wouldn't want anyone swimming against me to get the idea I was worried. I had to get hold of myself, and quick. My heat was about to start, and I had to clear my head before hitting the water. I concentrated on erasing my father and Dawn from my mind, and focused on the race in progress, the sound of swimmers thrashing through the water, and the crowd cheering. In just moments, the tension receded and the knots in my stomach untangled.

A few minutes later, my heat came up and I dove in, maintaining an easy pace, timing myself to finish a respectable third at 5:10.42. Tati was right behind me, and off the block before I had a chance to wish her luck. I squeezed the water from my hair while I watched her set her rhythm, establishing an early lead and keeping a full body length ahead of the next swimmer. Lap after lap, she stayed in first place, an efficient underwater machine, her swimming a skillful mix of incessant kicking and cycling arms. No wonder they called her "Mighty Mouse." Her diminutive size was no indicator of her power in the water. She was a tough competitor, and I pondered what would happen if I let loose and took her on as an equal in an event. A shot of adrenaline raced through me, the thrill of a challenge sparking something deep inside I'd put to rest months ago. No, I remembered, I was not here for that. The water was my sanctuary, my therapy, and I wouldn't give that up for anything, not even a chance to beat Tatiana in her own event.

After losing the 200 and enduring Coach's tongue-lashing, Tati wouldn't come close to losing the race, and she didn't, finishing at 4:58:18, one second off her all-time best and a full four seconds before the next swimmer. She shook hands with the swimmers beside her and climbed out of the pool last, taking a moment to catch her breath before heading to Coach for a quick high five.

Seconds later we were again behind the blocks for the 200 free relay. Mel and I were on the "B" team and Tati anchored the "A" team. Each team won their heat. Charlie finished eighth in the breaststroke, a super finish for an eighth grader. The meet ended with the 400-yard freestyle. We won, putting us in first place for the meet with the Bears in second and the Boxers in third. As promised, Coach jumped into the pool, clothes and all, after the officials announced our win. We all jumped in behind him, celebrating our victory. For the first time, I felt like a real team member. The fact that my father didn't show up didn't spoil my happiness.

After cooling down with a few laps, Coach told us to hit the showers. The Boosters were taking us all out for pizza to celebrate our win. We hit the locker room bursting with excitement. Fifteen minutes later, twenty-eight girls were showered and dressed, heading for our bus. While we waited to climb on board, I saw Tati and her parents talking to a couple of men I'd never seen before. One looked about my father's age, the other much younger. He addressed Tati, who seemed a little impatient, glancing at the bus every other second and tapping her toe on the pavement. The older guy focused on her parents, who smiled and nodded their heads.

I nudged Mel. "Recruiters?"

"Yeah, but they're wasting their time. I'll bet Tati's going to one of the big Division I schools, like Stanford or Cal Berkeley. Her father thinks she's bound for the Olympics, and he'll do anything to position her for it."

"Too bad he can't buy her a spot on the Olympic team."

"He would if he could."

We took our seats on the bus.

"Is that what she wants?"

"I don't think what she wants matters," Mel said, settling into her seat.

Tati said goodbye to the recruiters and her parents and hurried to the bus, the driver waiting for her. Jordan held a seat for her, but she passed it up and took one by herself a row ahead of me on the opposite side. She pulled a set of ear buds and her iPhone out of her pocket and plugged herself in. I often felt that way after a big meet, and didn't miss it.

Chapter 18

I'd been in bed just a few minutes when my father called. I didn't even bother saying hello. "What happened to you? You missed my meet."

"Hi honey," he said. "That's the reason I'm calling. How'd it go?"

"You didn't check the results online? That's a first."

"I'm sorry. I haven't had time to look online." He sounded tired.

"I'll save you the trouble. We won the meet."

"How'd you do?"

"I did great: 2:05.12 and 5:10.42."

He was silent for a moment and then said, "Aerin, what are you trying to prove?"

"I'm not trying to prove anything. I told you – I'm not winning any titles this year. I just want to swim and be happy."

"You can do better than that, you *have* done better than that. Don't you want to see how much farther you can go?"

"You're starting to sound like Tati's father," I said, anger getting the best of me.

"Who's Tati?"

"Never mind, just some girl on my team."

"You need to think about your future. You qualify for a swimming scholarship at a Division I school. Wasn't that the plan all along? You need to get a scholarship because I'm not sure I can swing your college expenses on my own. I have a lot of responsibilities here."

"Forget it," I said. Once again, he placed the needs of his new family above mine. "I'll get an academic scholarship. I'll go to a state school."

"Honey, you're eligible for so much more. Don't cheat yourself out of a top-notch education because you're angry with me. Don't mess this up. You'll regret it later on."

I was sick and tired of listening to him advise me about my future, about shortchanging myself and regretting it for the rest of my life. He was such a doom-and-gloomer. Besides, it was *my* life. He'd opted out when he married Dawn and moved out of the city, moved away from me. He was just an every other weekend dad, who paid his child support on time, free from my daily difficulties and dramas.

"Hey, you forgot something," I said. "Where were you today?"

Several seconds elapsed before he answered. "That's something we have to talk about." His tone put me on high alert.

"Is it Mom?" I whispered, afraid to ask, afraid to know.

"No, it's not your mother. It's Dawn. She's having some difficulties with the pregnancy. We were at the hospital all day and night. We just got home. That's why I didn't make the meet, and I forgot to call. I apologize."

I felt instant relief because my mother was okay, but my father sounded like he was on the edge of tears, and that was not okay, not even when I was angry at him. My father never cried, not when my mother left us to go to Afghanistan, nor when he moved out of our apartment and I clung to him in the open doorway of our home and begged him not to go. He was tough, stoic, and never showed a weak side.

"She's going to be all right? Isn't she?"

"I don't know," he said, his voice sounding small. "The doctor said it's one day at a time. He wants her on bed rest for a while, maybe until the baby's born."

I knew nothing about having babies, but it sounded serious. I couldn't imagine pert, perky Dawn on bed rest, couldn't see her not swinging a tennis racket or driving her girls all over creation in pursuit of the perfect activity. "When will that be?"

"She's due February 14, Valentine's Day. Five months to go," he said. "She has an appointment with the doctor on Wednesday. We'll know more then."

I didn't know what to say. Dawn wasn't my favorite person in the world, but he sounded so sad, and I realized this baby meant a lot to him.

"I'm sorry, Dad," I said, and to my surprise, I meant it. "I'll say a prayer that everything will be all right."

"Thank you," he said. "We appreciate that."

"Call me on Wednesday after the doctor appointment."

"Okay," he said. "And I'm sorry I missed the meet and didn't call. You know I wanted to be there."

"Yeah," I said, unconvinced.

"You've got another one next month, right? Long Island?"

"Yes," I said.

"I promise I won't miss it," he said.

"Okay."

"How's school going?"

"It's good," I said.

"Any grades in yet?" He was such a stickler for the numbers.

"Yeah, I'm high 80's, low 90's. I'm doing okay."

"You need to do great. If you don't swim, you'll need an academic scholarship."

Again with the money. He never used to talk about it before Dawn and her girls entered the picture.

"Things are tight here," he continued. "And with the new baby coming….."

"I know," I said. "Every dollar counts."

"I hate to have to mention it, but, yeah, it's true. And with your mother not working, it's all on me."

"I get it," I said. "Don't worry. I'll raise my GPA. I'll apply for every scholarship out there."

"You're working hard. You'll do great."

We said nothing for a moment, and then he asked, "How is your mother? Have you heard from her?"

Her latest letter rested on top of my physics text. "Yeah," I said, "I got a letter today. She's doing okay. She's got a visiting day coming up and wants me to come."

"Ask Maggie to bring you," he said. "That's part of our agreement."

"She said she'd bring me," I said.

Silence ensued. We had nothing more to say to each other and I prepared to hang up, but before I could say good-bye, he said, "Tomorrow's September 11th."

A knot formed in the pit of my stomach. I nodded, but realized he couldn't see me and whispered, "Yes."

"You're going to be okay?"

"I have to be," I said.

"It's always a tough day for you, and I want you to call me if you have any difficulties at all. I don't care what time it is or what I'm doing. I'll drop anything if you need to talk."

My dad. He always pulled through in the tough times. I couldn't always count on him for the small stuff, like a swim meet, but when September 11th rolled around he knew I'd be a basket case.

The day brought back harsh memories, not just of the towers falling or the chaos that consumed the city, it was all that and more. For me, September 11th was the day life as we knew it ended. If it had been just an ordinary day, perhaps my mother would never have joined the Army Reserve, and my parents would have figured out their marriage and stayed together. We'd still be living in our little apartment in the city. Happy. A family.

A lot of people, no, *thousands* of people, had suffered a *million* times more than I did because of that day, but it was the only family I had, and it was broken beyond repair, and it all happened because of that day.

I brushed aside the memories, resentment, and sadness that threatened to overwhelm me and thanked my father for his concern. He meant what he said because I'd called him in tears, an emotional wreck, every year on that day and he'd put me back together.

"I think I'll be okay." I didn't sound convincing to my own ears and covered it up by changing the subject. "I got an 'A' on my history test."

"That's great," he said. "Keep it up. Have you got any plans for the rest of the weekend?"

"Nope, just church in the morning – I promised Aunt Maggie - and then homework. I've got an English paper due Monday and a math test on Tuesday."

"Great. You'll be busy, your mind occupied."

"Yeah, it's good."

"I'll call during the week to update you on Dawn."

"Tell her I'm sorry she's not doing well with the pregnancy and everything, and I hope she'll be okay." That sounded lame but I was clueless on how to address these kinds of issues.

"She's resting now, but when she gets up I'll tell her," he said. "You have a good night. And call me tomorrow if you need me."

I said my goodbyes and disconnected. I wasn't tired anymore and figured I'd get some homework done. I sat down at my desk, picked up my mother's letter and studied her handwriting on the envelope. She had a perfect cursive, taught by the nuns in parochial school. My name, Aerin, flowed across the white paper in flowing blue ink. She'd dotted the "i" with a little bubble and finished the "n" with a flourish. I brought the envelope to my nose and inhaled, hoping to catch just a whiff of her scent, her lavender shampoo, her rose-scented skin cream. All I smelled was paper and glue. It seemed so impersonal. But she'd addressed the envelope in her own script, she'd held the letter in her own hands, and even though I couldn't smell even a hint of her I could feel her energy, her love, through the paper. I reopened the envelope and slid the thin sheet of paper out.

"My darling Aerin, it's been too long. I miss your sweet smile and wish I could hold you in my arms, could see your beautiful face in person and not just in the photographs I've got on my nightstand. I look at them every night before I go to sleep, and pray for you, asking God to give you courage and understanding through this difficult time. I wake each morning and gaze upon your face, wishing you a wonderful day, kissing the cold, glass frame, imagining it's your warm, soft cheek.

"The days here are long and boring. I attend my therapy, and meetings, but in the hours between there's not much to do. I read some books from what passes for a library here – dog-eared romance novels, out of date women's magazines - and watch game shows and the Lifetime Channel with the other women, most of whom I would never encounter, unless, of course, they were my patients in the hospital. We have little in common, except that we're here and expected to help each other. Some of them are sweet, but most of them are hardened, and some are scary. But I didn't come here to make friends. My doctors and caseworkers say I'm making progress, and I'm feeling so much better. I've put on weight, and the pain in my back and hip is now manageable because of the physical therapy I do three times a week. If I didn't miss you so much, the situation would almost be tolerable.

"But enough about me. I hear you're doing well. Maggie said your swim team wins all the time and you're one of their best distance swimmers. That's great. So many good things can come from swimming. Have you heard from any recruiters? I wouldn't be surprised if several offer you a scholarship. Three of them did last year, and you were just a junior! Be sure to keep your grades up, they'll be looking at that, too, but that's not something I have to tell you.

"Anyway, Saturday is the big day, VISITING DAY. *Mags said you'll*

be leaving right after practice. Visiting starts at two and ends at four. I can't wait to see you. I have a big surprise. You're not going to believe what I did, but it turned out great and is so me *you're going to love it. And don't waste time trying to guess what it is because you won't. It's a huge surprise, something even* I *didn't see coming.*

I wish you an awesome week, full of fun with friends, straight A's in all your classes, wins at every meet, and your personal best in all your events. See you in 234 hours. I'm counting the minutes, too - 14,040. Love, Mom."

She'd signed off with a smiley face.

I stared at the letter, absorbing her words. I detected a hint of my old Mom in her excitement about her "surprise" (I couldn't imagine what she was talking about), and her anticipation for our visit. I folded the letter and placed it back in its envelope. I missed her more than I ever had, even more than when she was in Afghanistan and I worried she'd never come home. Before we left town on Saturday, I'd ask Aunt Maggie to bring me to the used bookstore so I could stock up on some books Mom would enjoy, then go to the grocery store and get her some good, dark chocolate and the biggest bag of Cool Ranch Doritos I could find. I tucked the letter away with the others in the bottom drawer and settled in for some late night physics.

Chapter 19

On Sunday, I sat in the choir loft behind Mel, listening to her angelic voice as she sang the hymns. Looking down at the congregation and the altar from up here gave me a different perspective. The sun streamed through the stained glass windows and filled the church with a rainbow of light, settling on dust motes as they floated in streams of color only visible from up high. I followed in my prayer book and sang along with the choir, careful not to allow anyone to hear my voice. I was no singer, but singing the hymns filled me with a sense of peace I only got from swimming. "She who sings prays twice," Mom always said, and now I understood what she meant. I'd stopped praying a while back when I realized God wasn't answering my prayers, but now I thought maybe He'd hear me better from up here. I said a quick prayer for my mother, asking for her to recover and to be safe in that place. I also prayed that Dawn's pregnancy would continue without further complications. I figured that was enough to pray for at one time.

After church, I waited while Mel hung up her robe and said goodbye to the other choir members.

"That was fun," she said as we made our way down the stairs toward the vestibule.

"You sounded great," I said. "Are you planning to study

music?"

"I've thought about it," she said, "but I'm not sure. It's tough to get into a music program, and then tougher to find a job, but my parents want me to consider a music major paired with a degree in education so I can teach. They think it's a way for me to continue with my love of music and earn a living. They might be right, but I haven't heard back from any programs, so I don't know what I'm going to do."

"Well, it will be a shame if you don't. You would be an awesome singer and teacher."

"Thanks," she said, bowing her head to my praise. "If not, I'll go into business or something. What are you going to do?"

"I don't know," I said, avoiding an answer. The only thing that lit a fire in my belly was swimming. When I really thought about it I wondered if a career as a coach was in my future. I could run a kids' swim team, teach them how to swim, how to win, organize meets. I hadn't mentioned the idea to my parents, not sure if they'd shoot it down or not, but I dreamed about it at least once a day, especially at swim practice.

"Hey," Mel said, chasing away my dreams of being a swim coach. "What are you doing this afternoon?"

"Homework. I've got a ton."

"Today's September 11th," she said, giving me a sideways glance. We were outside in the parking lot waiting for her parents to drive up with the car. Aunt Maggie and Uncle Pat were a few rows over, stuffing their children into their minivan.

"I know," I said. It was my first thought that morning and I'd been trying not to think of it since.

"It's a tough day for us, and I figured it's a tough day for you, seeing as you lived in the city. Justin and I need to get away for a while. We're taking a ride out to Minnewaska. We're going on a hike and bringing along a picnic. We'd like you to join us."

I had one question. "What's Minnewaska?"

"It's a state park in the Shawangunk Mountains. Lots of trails, a pristine lake, rock climbing. We go there all the time. It's about forty-five minutes from here. A little piece of heaven on earth."

Heaven appealed to me right now. It was a beautiful September day, the sky blue and cloudless, the temperature climbing. My homework could wait, even if I had to stay up all night to do it.

"What time will you pick me up?"

Mel and Justin pulled up in his Wrangler minutes after I got home from church and changed. I hopped into the back seat. He had the hard top off, and as we drove away the wind rustled through my hair and the sun beamed down on my head. I took a deep breath of the warm air and sighed with contentment.

"Gorgeous day, huh?" Mel asked, turning around.

"The best."

"Wait till you see Lake Minnewaska. It's beautiful."

Justin had the radio on but I couldn't hear much because of the traffic and the wind. We traveled back roads, driving past horse farms, apple orchards, and acres of corn fields, majestic mountains in the distance.

I started drifting off - not to sleep, I was too excited for that - but into a sort of somnolence, a deep sense of satisfaction and comfort I hadn't experienced in a while. Out here in the country, breathing in the fresh air, my eyes feasting on the green grass, the lush trees, the farms and ranches, all of my worries, resentments, and disappointments started to melt away. It felt like sweet freedom. I was intoxicated with the sights, scents, and sounds of the rolling landscape, and could almost taste the apples ripe for picking on their branches, could almost feel the flanks of the horses as I imagined straddling them and riding off into the wind. I was a city girl at heart, but that glimpse into country life filled my senses and set off a need for simple things and quiet places. It was a balm to the dark spaces inside me that I kept hidden where no one, not even I, could see them.

I sat behind Mel, catching bits of her chatter as she narrated our journey. She pointed out sights along the way, and commented on the ice cream shacks and pizza parlors we passed, reminiscing about horse farms where she took riding lessons and parks where she'd played Little League softball years ago.

I studied Justin in his reflection in the rearview mirror, admiring his chiseled looks, the strong jawline, his incredible blue eyes, their long lashes brushing the delicate area underneath. He was the kind of guy who had no clue about his good looks. He was comfortable in his body and moved with ease, not self-conscious of his six foot two frame or his flipper-sized feet. He caught me staring at him in the mirror a couple of times and smiled back, his perfect teeth flashing in the sunlight.

I looked away, embarrassed to be caught, but couldn't keep my eyes off him and went back to staring moments later. He held on to the steering wheel with one hand, the other on the stick shift, and maneuvered the Jeep around the twists and turns that led to Minnewaska. I was comfortable with him in the driver's seat.

Everything about the day was perfect.

As we entered the state park, Mel grew more animated, turning around in her seat to play tour guide, making sure I took in all of the beauty surrounding us. We made a hairpin turn and a gigantic rock face loomed in front of us, rising hundreds of feet with dangling climbers on its surface reaching for the clouds. My jaw dropped, revealing my awe and wonder, but I didn't care.

"Ever go rock climbing?" Justin asked, meeting my eyes in the mirror.

"No," I said, the thought of it sending shivers of fear through my belly. I was afraid of heights and couldn't imagine hanging from a rope so high above the ground.

"Justin's done it," Mel said, "but I prefer to be on terra firma."

"Me too," I said.

Minutes later, we pulled off the road at an entry to the park and stopped at a gatehouse. Justin paid the entrance fee, got a map of the area, and we drove in. The road to the parking lot was uphill all the way over a fern and tree-lined road that became a deep forest, the boughs of the tallest trees forming a canopy of leaves overhead, blocking out the sun. At the top, the lot was crowded but we managed to find a spot. I hopped out and waited for Justin and Mel to gather their gear. They each carried backpacks that looked heavy.

"What are you carrying? Rocks?" I asked.

"Lunch," Mel said.

"That's a lot of lunch."

"Hey, we're all swimmers," she said. "I've got heroes stuffed with roast beef and cheese, apples, carrots and dressing, a bag of chips and a bag of Oreos."

"What have you got?" I asked Justin.

"Water, two bottles each, a can of sunscreen and a first aid kit."

"So prepared," I joked. "Like a Boy Scout."

"Don't laugh," he said, smiling. "I *was* a Boy Scout."

"Until he got kicked out for sneaking out on a Jamboree to stargaze," Mel said.

"Hey, don't give away all my secrets," he said.

"I've got to hear that story," I said.

"Well," Mel said as we started on a path out of the parking lot, "it goes like this. Big Bother was the senior camper in his tent, in charge of all the younger boys, and supposed to maintain law and order. But he's never been one to follow the rules, and one of the rules was to stay in your tent after lights out. He convinced the boys to take a midnight walk."

"In my defense, there was a meteor shower that night," Justin interjected. "I had a purpose. I was teaching them astronomy."

"He took all the boys on a walk in the pitch black darkness."

"We didn't go that far," he said, "only about 200 feet."

"Yeah, but on the way back one of the kids tripped over a tree root, fell, and broke his arm."

"It wasn't my fault he didn't watch where he was going."

"They had to take him to the Emergency Room at, like, two in the morning. His parents were *not* pleased, and demanded the troop leader expel Justin."

"He suspended me," he said, "but I got busy swimming and preparing for Junior Olympics, and didn't go back."

I couldn't help laughing, imagining Justin leading the group of innocent boys through the night forest, stargazing, and then getting into trouble. "What happened to the kid with the broken arm?"

"Nothing," he said. "He had a cast all the way up to his elbow. Everyone thought he was cool, and covered it with doodles and autographs. He was fine."

We talked while we walked, and when the story ended stopped at a split rail fence.

"Look at that," Mel said.

I followed her gaze and looked down upon the most beautiful body of water I'd ever seen, the color of jade, shimmering in the sunlight, surrounded by cliffs of white rock. Specks of red and gold graced the trees, but for the most part an endless wreath of green bordered the lake.

"Lake Minnewaska," Mel said.

"Wow," I said, almost speechless. "Can we swim?"

"Yeah," she said. "We swim all the time, but not now. The season's over."

"I want to go," I said. "How do we get down there?"

"We can go down there, but we can't swim," Justin said. "No lifeguards. And if the Rangers catch us they'll kick us out."

"You're a lifeguard," I reminded him.

"And as a lifeguard I say we're going to follow the rules."

"You're no fun." I pouted.

"Don't worry," Mel said. "We'll swim next summer."

"Let me take a picture," I said, snapping a few shots with my phone, knowing my mother would love to see them. When she came home, I'd bring her here.

We resumed our hike, walking downhill, venturing into the shaded pathway. A band of bicyclists passed us, giving us a heads up as they approached.

"We should've brought bikes," I said.

"You have a bike?" Mel asked.

"Aunt Maggie lets me borrow hers."

"Then next time we'll bring bikes." She grinned and I grinned back.

I enjoyed the talk about "next time" and "next summer." It promised a future together, plans to make, fun to share. I hadn't talked about a future with friends in months. I'd lost contact with my Manhattan friends the year I lived with my dad and Dawn. When I returned the following year, I didn't fit in anymore. Kids can be cruel, and I found myself left out of my own group. I tried to find a new one, but my hours spent in the pool left little time for socializing so I spent most of my time alone. When my mom started having her troubles, I stayed home to care for her, and became further isolated. I'd forgotten how good it was to spend time with someone my own age, someone I liked, who accepted me for who I am, no questions asked.

Chapter 20

We resumed walking, rounded a curve, and started down a slope, stones scattering beneath our feet. I caught a glimpse of water up ahead - the jade lake! – and broke into a run, Mel and Justin right behind me. I raced ahead to the shoreline and stopped at the water's edge. The sun shimmered on its surface. I kicked off my sneakers, pulled off my socks, and dipped my toe in. Not too bad. I turned to give Mel a challenging look and then whipped off my T-shirt, revealing a bikini top, followed by my shorts, exposing its bottom. Before either of them could stop me, I took three quick steps and dove in, cruising a few feet before popping up for air, shocked by the cold, speechless with exhilaration.

"Woo hoo!" I shouted in triumph.

Mel and Justin still stood at the water's edge, laughing at me.

"I should have known you were wearing a bathing suit under that outfit," Mel said.

"Come on in," I said. "It's great." I floated on my back, gazing up at the sky, watching the cottony clouds pass overhead.

Justin ran into the water and swam toward me, stopping when he was just inches away.

"Yikes!" he shouted. "This water's cold." He splashed me, spraying my face.

I splashed him back and ducked under, swimming away. He came after me and grabbed my foot, bringing me to a sudden halt.

"I thought I told you swimming season was over," he said.

"Not for me."

"You disobeyed the lifeguard. Now you have to pay." He grabbed my waist and tried to pull me under. I was too fast for him and ducked away, swimming back to shore. I beat him and joined Mel at the water's edge.

"You guys are crazy," she said, shaking her head.

Shivering, my teeth chattering, I grabbed my backpack, pulled out a towel, and wrapped it around me. Justin, wearing swim trunks, sprinted out of the water and seized his backpack. He yanked out a towel and started drying off.

"Great minds think alike," I said.

"You know me. I'm no Boy Scout."

We dried off and put our shorts and T-shirts back on.

"Are you two ready to go?" Mel asked.

We packed up our stuff and got back on the trail.

"You guys better hope the Rangers don't come looking for you," Mel said.

"What Rangers?" Justin asked. "Do you see any Rangers, Apple?"

Mel slapped him on the arm. "Knock it off," she said. "I don't want to get into any trouble."

"You hear that, Apple? Mel doesn't want to get into any trouble."

"No trouble," I said. "Just good times."

We walked another twenty minutes around the periphery of the lake, climbing higher with each step, a good hike, steep, but not too challenging. The paths were clearly marked and easy to follow. Mel and Justin knew the way and while we walked, we talked about school, swimming, some of the other girls on the team, and whether or not Tatiana would beat the 500 record. Mel was sure of it; Justin not so sure. I remained neutral. I didn't know enough about it or Tatiana to offer an opinion, but if pushed, my guess was she would. If I were in her place, I would too.

We came to a clearing, a large, grassy picnic area.

"Can we stop here?" I asked. "I'm starving."

"I know a better spot up ahead," Justin said, leading the way. We continued a few hundred feet, ducking under some low hanging branches and up a small incline that led to a cliff overlooking the lake. We stood on an enormous rock, nothing holding us back from the edge except our own common sense. The lake below us was a mirror image of the sky. The reflections of clouds floated across its surface. It was so beautiful my eyes filled with tears.

"It's all right, Apple," Justin said. "Everyone cries the first time they come up here."

"It's incredible," I said, wiping away my tears. "Thanks for bringing me."

"What can I say? I'm a show-off," he said. "I love to show off my favorite places."

Mel had gotten comfortable, sitting cross-legged on the flat surface of the rock, taking our lunch out of her backpack and setting out sandwiches and chips. Justin dropped down across from her and got out the bottles of water, still cold because he'd brought an ice pack.

"So prepared," I said, accepting the bottle from him.

"I know what I'm doing," he said.

I sat beside Mel where I had a great view of Justin and the magnificent lake behind him. We each picked up a sandwich and began eating, all conversation on hold. I'd never had a more delicious lunch. The roll was fresh, stuffed with lean roast beef, red ripe tomatoes, and leafy greens. I'm sure the fact that I was famished contributed to its tastiness. We didn't come up for air until we'd each devoured half. I took a long swig of water and leaned back.

"Awesome sandwich, Mel," I said.

She smiled between bites and gave me a thumbs-up.

Justin looked like he was inhaling his sandwich. In between bites, he fished chips out of the bag and stuffed them in his mouth. When he finished chewing, he said, "I made the sandwiches."

"Get out of here," I said.

"It's true," Mel said, wiping her mouth with a napkin. "He makes a great hero."

"Seems your talents have no end," I said.

He shrugged. "Hey, a guy has to eat. I know my way around the kitchen."

Mel said, "Our mom works a lot, tons of overtime, so we have to fend for ourselves sometimes."

I knew that routine. My mom wasn't home much either, dedicated to a job that put her at the mercy of other people, picking up extra shifts, filling in when other nurses needed time off or didn't show up. She didn't mind. She loved the hospital, her patients, the work. I learned long ago not to resent it; it's who she was. Only recently did I realize the toll it took on her, on all of us, and how it was no longer good for her but unhealthy, even dangerous.

"What about your father?" I asked.

"He runs an online business and spends a lot of time on his computers," Justin said.

We finished our sandwiches and polished off the chips. Mel collected all the wrappings and stuffed them into a plastic bag, which she stuffed into her backpack.

"Minnewaska is a carry-in-carry-out park," she explained. "No trash cans. We have to take out what we bring in."

I sipped my water and stretched out on the rock, shifting around until I got comfortable, basking in the warmth of the mid-afternoon sun. Now that my belly was full and I'd rehydrated, I was ready for a nap.

Mel and Justin also stretched out and we fell quiet. I listened to the breeze as it rustled through the trees, and the singing of birds hidden in their boughs. Every few seconds I caught an occasional voice or trill of laughter from nearby hikers passing by. It was a lazy Sunday afternoon and I was miles away from the troubles I'd expected the day to bring.

"Thanks for bringing me out here," I said again. "It means a lot to me."

"I figured you could use a getaway," said Mel. "Today is such a hard day. We wanted to go somewhere where we wouldn't have to hear about it on the news or read about it in the papers. It opens up old wounds."

"You lost someone?"

Mel nodded, her face still. "My Uncle Mike," she murmured. "He was FDNY, one of the first to head into the North Tower, one of the first lost."

"Of course, we didn't know that for weeks, but my mom and dad lost hope after a few days," Justin said. "He was my father's youngest brother."

"We were only eight, but we remember him so well," Mel went on, gazing up at the sky. "He was always around. He wasn't married, didn't have any kids of his own, so he hung out with us, brought us places - the park, the movies, for ice cream and pizza. He came with us on vacations to Disney World and the Jersey Shore. He stayed over some nights when my parents were both working, and took care of us."

"He was a funny guy," Justin said. He turned on his side and looked at me. "He was always telling jokes and fooling around. We played pretend a lot. He'd act like a big scary monster and chase us around the house, remember Mel?"

Mel smiled. "Yup. Uncle Mike was a great guy. His passing left a huge hole in our lives. That's why we came here today - to remember him, to visit a place he loved. He brought us here all the time. We'd hike these paths, sit out here on this rock, and have a picnic. He'd be glad to know we're here now."

I felt a lump in my throat. Once again, I was reminded that many people, too many people, had lost a lot more than I had on September 11th.

Chapter 21

"So, Apple, what's your September 11th story?" Justin asked. "Does it have anything to do with your mom being in Afghanistan?"

Mel rolled over and slapped him. "Geez, Justin, have some tact. We came here to get away from all that. Maybe Aerin doesn't want to talk about it."

"No," I said. "It's okay." I sat up, crossed my legs, and took a sip of my now warm water. "I don't talk about it too much because no one ever asks me about it. Touchy subject, I guess. I didn't lose anyone, I mean, no one I loved died, or was injured, or is missing, so I'm better off than most people who lost someone that day. September 11th affected my family in a different way.

"My mother worked at St. Vincent's Hospital, in the ER. That's where they brought all the injured from the towers. She'd worked there for years, long before I was born, and was on duty that day. It was supposed to be her day off, but someone asked her to switch and my mother never said no, so she was there from the first moment. I'd been in school for less than an hour when it happened. The principal came to my classroom and asked my teacher to go out into the hall, and when she came back, she was crying. She didn't say why, but I knew something was wrong.

"A little while later, parents started coming to the school and taking their children out. My father showed up around eleven o'clock. He came to my classroom, helped me pack up my books, and we left. We walked home because the subways had stopped running and we couldn't get a cab. It took hours.

"After we made it home, my father turned on the TV in his bedroom and watched the news nonstop. My grandmother came to stay with me. She was angry with my father for watching TV all day. She said it wasn't healthy. No one told me what had happened, but I knew it was bad.

"When my mother didn't come home from work I was scared. I thought something awful had happened to her. I started crying, I was hysterical, and my father finally came out of his room and told me what happened. I couldn't believe it. I mean, I was only eight. None of it made any sense."

I stopped talking and took a long sip of my warm water, finishing it. Justin reached into his backpack and handed me a fresh bottle.

"I couldn't believe it either," said Mel. "Who dreamed such evil existed in the world? In our world?"

"Our parents were worried about Uncle Mike, on duty that day. My father called his cell phone every five minutes but never got an answer," Justin said.

"It was the worst day of my life," I said, "but I was too young to know it. Anyway, my mother didn't come home until the next day. She was exhausted and slept almost twenty-four hours. When she woke up, she returned to the hospital and did back-to-back shifts every other day. They were still looking for survivors but not finding too many. At that point, it started to sink in that most of the missing people had died. The recovery workers, the police and fire people, came to the ER around the clock for injuries and my mom wanted to care for them. It went on for weeks, and she didn't let up, working sixteen hours a day, two or three days in a row. When she was home, she slept and left in the morning before I woke up. My grandmother moved in with us for a while and helped my dad keep it together.

"When it started to slow down at the hospital, my mother took some time off. She went back to her usual work schedule and things returned to normal. When our country went to war with Afghanistan, she wanted to do something to support the troops, so she joined the Army Reserve. My father was mad. He didn't want her to go, but my mother was always doing things to help people. That's why she's a nurse. She wants to make a difference. She was deployed right away and gone for nine months. When she came home, my father told her he'd met someone else and wanted a divorce."

"Man, that's cold," Justin said.

"Shush, Justin, let her talk," Mel said.

I uncrossed my legs and stretched out on the smooth surface of the rock. The sun beamed down, bathing us in warmth. A bird squawked overhead and I looked up in time to witness a hawk swoop down from the top of a tree and soar across the lake, its wings a perfect expression of art and physics. I looked at Justin.

"Yeah, it *was* cold. My mother had no idea. She came home from Afghanistan broken, depleted, and he moved out. Rough times. She went back to work and I continued with school."

"How old were you?" asked Mel.

"Twelve, so sixth grade. We thought she was finished with active duty, but a year or so later, they called her up again, sent her back to Afghanistan. She served another nine months. When she got home, she was a mess."

"What happened to her?" Mel asked.

"One month before her deployment ended, she was with a group of medics on a mercy mission to a nearby village to help the Afghans. They had little to no medical care, and the doctors and nurses often went to help them. During their visit, someone set off a bomb. My mom was a little too close and took some shrapnel in her right hip. She had surgery, her wound became infected, and it was one medical problem another, so they sent her home."

"And then what happened? She got better, right?" Justin asked.

"Somewhat," I said, not sure how much I wanted to tell them.

"Well, she must be okay; they sent her back to Afghanistan, right? Isn't she there now?" Mel asked.

I bit my lip. That was the part of the story I hadn't shared with anyone, and although I liked Mel and Justin, I hadn't known them that long and wasn't sure I could trust them. I had two choices: continue with the lie that my mother was serving in Afghanistan, or tell them the truth.

I studied Mel, focusing on her pretty blue eyes. She was so sweet, helpful, and concerned. She'd gone out of her way to be my friend when I was new in town and knew no one. I turned to Justin, who tried to give off an air of indifference that I saw straight through. He attempted to hide it but he was caring and open. They were the best friends I'd had in a long time, and kind enough to include me in their special plans today. If I couldn't trust them, I couldn't trust anyone, and I was tired of carrying this secret.

"Okay," I said. "Here's the story." They both nodded, arranging themselves on the rock to get more comfortable. "What I'm about to tell you is private, so please don't tell anyone else." The sun had traveled a little west of where we were and the air had turned cooler. I wrapped my arms around myself, keeping warm.

"Everything I just said about my mom is true," I said, "but when I first came to Two Rivers I told everyone that the reason I was here is that she's serving in Afghanistan right now. She's not. I only said that because I didn't want to tell people what's really going on."

Telling Mom's story was harder than I thought it would be and I stopped to catch my breath.

"Go on, Aerin," Mel said. "You can trust us."

Justin nodded. He hadn't taken his eyes off me since I started speaking, which also unnerved me. I never liked being the center of attention, and I didn't like being the center of *his* attention. After a deep breath, I resumed my story.

"The truth is that after my mom returned from her last tour of duty with her hip injury, she didn't do too well. She has post-traumatic stress disorder because of the blast. Her hip didn't heal properly, so she has a lot of pain. The doctors had her on all kinds of medications, including oxycodone, and she got hooked on it. She got a job at another hospital in Manhattan because St. Vincent's had closed, and she worked just a couple of twelve hour shifts a week, but even that proved to be too much for her. The pain was awful and she became depressed.

"What they say about addiction to pain pills is right on. My mom couldn't control it, and when the doctors stopped prescribing the pills she had to get them somewhere else, so she started taking them from the hospital. She got caught and was arrested."

I paused to gauge their reactions. They both looked at me with the same incredulous expression. What was I doing? Kids like Mel and Justin didn't live in a world of drugs and addiction. How could they possibly understand? No one looked kindly on drug addicts, and few would understand how my mother had become one. They didn't know her. They didn't know how hard she worked, how much she cared about others, how much my father had hurt her, how much pain she endured. Even if they did, they wouldn't care.

"People say drug addicts have only themselves to blame," I continued, "and the world doesn't offer them much pity. And they say people who steal drugs are thieves, criminals. My mother isn't a criminal – she's a victim – but what I learned from the court system and from the court of public opinion showed me I'm one of the few who thinks that way."

They hung on my words and I finished the story, talking double time, rushing to get it out. "She didn't want to put us through a trial, so she took a plea deal. The judge sentenced her to six months. He sent her to a place upstate for convicts addicted to drugs." I wrapped it up without looking at them, afraid of their reactions. They were silent, their expressions unreadable.

"That's some story, Apple," Justin said, breaking the silence.

I shrugged, still wary of their responses. I wouldn't be surprised if they wanted to leave right that minute and take me home, moving on with the day and their lives as though I didn't exist.

"Your poor mom," Mel said, her voice small. "That's just awful. I mean, she has a problem. She doesn't belong in jail."

My spirits lifted.

"After everything that happened to her, I'm not surprised she got hooked on pain pills," Justin said. "I learned all about that in health class. They make that oxycodone so you can't help getting addicted, and the doctors prescribe it like crazy. It's a huge problem. She needs help, rehab or something, not a prison sentence."

Their solidarity comforted me, but I couldn't let them overlook what she'd done. "She stole drugs from her employer, from the patients she served. It's a crime. That's why she's incarcerated." Oh, how I hated that word.

"Yeah," said Justin, "but she wouldn't have taken the drugs if she wasn't addicted, right? The addiction made her do it. It's not like she's a bad person, right?"

I wanted to cry with relief. "No," I said. "She's not a bad person. She tried to help herself, but everything was coming down on her, and she couldn't cope anymore."

"Well, how's she doing now?" Mel asked. "Is she okay?"

I nodded. "She says she's doing great, making progress, and feels good. I'm visiting her next weekend. She's allowed a visit after she completes thirty days, which are almost up."

"That's good," Mel said, smiling. "When will she be released?"

"In February."

"And then what happens? She goes home?"

"Yes."

"And do you go home, too, Apple?" asked Justin as he peeled the wrapper off his now empty bottle of water.

That was something we hadn't figured out yet. The plan was I'd finish the school year and graduate from Two Rivers. But if my mother needed me upon her release, I wanted to be home with her. I'd transfer back to my old school and finish there, no regrets.

"You need to stay here, with us," Mel said. "Sounds like your mother could use a fresh start. Maybe she could move to Two Rivers too, and you can both live here."

I laughed. "My mother's a city girl. I can't picture her living in Two Rivers."

"Her best friend Maggie lives here. Maybe she'll change her mind," Mel said.

I thought about that. Maggie and Pat had always been helpful and supportive, and my mother would need their friendship upon her release. Perhaps staying in Two Rivers wasn't such a bad idea.

"We'll have to wait and see," I said. "It's several months away. Anything can happen. Plus, I'll be going off to college in the fall, and she'll be on her own."

"You don't have to worry about it today," Justin said, stretching out to his full six-foot-two length with a groan. "I'm starting to stiffen up. We should get going."

I helped them pack up the wrappings from our lunch. We put on our backpacks and stood looking out over the cliff, at the lake and the beach far below. The voices of other hikers strayed toward us, and I turned to lead the way out. Mel and Justin followed in single file. When we reached the path that led to the main road, Mel pulled up alongside me and grabbed my hand.

"Don't worry," she said. "Your secret's safe with us, right Justin?"

He came up on my other side and took hold of my other hand. He gave me that cocky grin of his and said, "No worries, Apple. Mum's the word."

We headed for the car, the two of them jabbering on about what's for dinner and would they make it home in time. I half-listened, almost lost in my thoughts, a deep sense of relief and satisfaction washing over me. I'd revealed the worst about me, and they hadn't flinched. Instead, they rallied around me with support and friendship. I had a place here with them, in Two Rivers, no longer the outsider. With their friendship, I was sure I could do anything.

Week Five:

Mom

Chapter 22

On Wednesday, we had a meet against the Ravens. The local newspaper reported the results:

Girls Swimming and Diving – Trailblazers vs. Ravens

The Two Rivers Trailblazers blew past the Ravens in a dual meet at Two Rivers High School 106-75. The 200 medley relay team of Taylor Maddox, Jordan Hastings, Erica Duczeminski, and Melanie Ford won with a time of 1:51:06, their season best. Senior Tatiana Reese won both the 200 freestyle (2:00.20) and the 500 freestyle (4:55.55). Reese is the team's latest contender for the Allison Singer Scholarship Challenge and has a better chance than anyone in recent years to break Singer's longstanding 500 freestyle record of 4:52.50. Ford took second in the 50 freestyle (26:22). Duczeminski won the 100 butterfly (1:05.18). The Blazers won the 200 freestyle relay (1:49.25) and the 400 freestyle relay (3:47.48). Divers Jamie Benedetto and Cassandra Cramer took first and second place. Blazers are now 5-0.

A photo of Tatiana pounding the water accompanied the story.

We won Thursday's meet too, and the school's website posted the highlights:

Blazers Girls Swim and Dive Team Wins Again

The Blazers Girls Swim and Dive team remains undefeated midway through their season's dual meet schedule after a win against the Giants, 116-70. Once again, senior Tatiana Reese took first in both of her signature events, the 200 freestyle (2:00.25) and the 500 freestyle (4:54.54). Reese is inching closer to beating the 21-year-old record (4:52.50) set by former distance state champion Allison Singer, class of '89, who now offers a hefty scholarship to the swimmer who knocks her name off the leaderboard. Other meet highlights include a win in the 200 individual medley by senior Erica Duczeminski (2:19.59) and Duczeminski's close finish in the 100 butterfly, victorious at 1:06.87. Senior Melanie Ford had a second place finish in the 50 freestyle (26:25.) The Blazers took first in all relays. Divers Jamie Benedetto and Cassandra Cramer finished first and third. Blazers are now 6-0.

Once again, a photo of Tatiana accompanied the story.

It didn't take long for me to see she was somewhat of a celebrity. The newspaper and the school website covered all of her events. She couldn't walk the corridors without someone giving her a high five or making some comment about the scholarship race. She seemed to take it all in stride, but I wondered what she was thinking. It's hard enough to compete at your best without additional stress. I empathized with her, but at the same time I was relieved the pressure was not on me. I had enough on my mind.

Chapter 23

On Saturday, I left practice early so I could head upstate with Maggie to visit my mother. We passed the time on the two-hour ride spinning through the radio stations, switching from country to pop to Christian as the miles sped past. We'd stopped at the store on our way out of town and picked up a few things for my mom: the shampoo and conditioner she liked, a couple of bags of Doritos Cool Ranch and a bag of Hershey's Dark Kisses. We also had a bag of books for her that included several titles from her favorite authors.

I tracked our progress on the GPS, counting the minutes and the miles. When we turned off the highway, we were just five minutes away, and my stomach started doing flip turns.

"How are you doing?" Mags asked, glancing at me. She had a sixth sense about these things.

I kept my eyes on the road and said, "I'm okay."

"It's not too late to turn back."

I wouldn't dream of it. "I'm good," I said.

We traveled along winding country roads, the trees on the brink of their autumn brilliance, fields of corn picked clean, and rolls of hay dotting the hills in the distance. It reminded me of the trip to Minnewaska with Mel and Justin, and the thought of them filled me with peace.

When we entered the grounds of the correctional facility we stopped at a guardhouse, and Mags checked us in. The guard sent us on our way with directions to the building where the state held my mother. Even here, the landscape was clean and beautiful, and I felt more at ease knowing she was able to enjoy the views and breathe the fresh air.

Aunt Mags found the building and parked. We entered a three-story brick structure that looked cold and institutional. The flip turns started in my belly again but I put a smile on my face and tried to act as if visiting my mother in this place was no big deal.

The guard on duty asked for identification and verified we were on the day's visitor list. He examined the contents of the bags we brought in and made us empty our pockets and place everything, including Maggie's purse and the stuff we brought to my mom, through an x-ray machine. We went through a metal detector. The process seemed to drag on, prolonging my anxiety. I grew queasy, and worried I'd need to find a restroom or throw up on the floor. A swarm of people lined up on the other side of the check-in, waiting to see their loved ones. Finally, a guard cleared Mags and me to join them.

Another fifteen minutes passed before a female guard escorted us into the building's interior, leading us down whitewashed corridors with closed doors on either side. At the end of one corridor she used her keys to open a door, and ushered us into a large meeting room full of tables and chairs. Reunited families hugged each other. Couples held hands. A pair of little boys ran in circles, chasing each other as if on a playground. Spirits were high. It was easy to forget we were in a correctional facility.

I looked for my mother and the nervous knots in my stomach tightened when I didn't see her in the crowd. Mags, too, looked around, her head swiveling as she perused the scene. Moments later, a woman rose from a table in the back and walked toward us. Something about her seemed familiar, and I gasped. It was Mom, and she looked so different I hadn't recognized her.

"Oh!" she said, the voice unmistakably hers. "You're here." Two steps later, she stood before me, reaching out for me, her face alight with joy. I held back a moment, drinking her in, trying to figure out all that was different. "Get over here," she said, coming closer. "Give me a hug."

I let her enfold me in her embrace, inhaling her familiar scent as I buried my face in her hair. Her arms encircled me, holding me close. Her breath caressed my skin, and the wisp of her eyelashes brushed my cheek. I relaxed and sunk into her, all the fear and anxiety escaping.

Mom.

We stood for a moment and then she released me, still keeping her eyes on me. "Let me look at you," she said. She gave me a once-over and smiled. "You look great. Strong and healthy." She turned to Mags. "You're taking good care of her, Maggie." She reached for Maggie and they embraced. I gave her a once-over and noticed she'd put on weight, filling out her jeans in a way she hadn't in years.

"Let's sit," she said, gesturing toward the table in the back. We followed her and took our seats, staring at each other, at a sudden loss for words. My mother broke the awkwardness.

"So, how is everything?"

"What did you do to your hair?" I asked. No wonder I hadn't recognized her. She'd chopped off her long, chestnut locks, her trademark, the only hairstyle I'd ever seen her wear. It was a pixie cut, short around her face and ears, with a side part that led to soft bangs.

She reached up and tucked a stray piece behind her ear. "Do you like it?" she asked. "A hairdresser comes once a month. I hadn't planned on cutting off more than an inch, just a trim, but when I looked in the mirror, I didn't recognize the woman I saw. I decided to do something new, something different, now that I'm getting a second chance."

I studied her new look. She had a freshness about her, an unexpected youthfulness. Her face had filled out a bit, and her skin was clear and rosy, her eyes bright.

"I like it," said Mags. "It's very becoming. I don't think I've ever seen you with short hair."

"It's so easy to take care of," Mom said. "No blow dryer. Just wash and go. What do you think, Aerin?"

"I like it," I said. "It's time for a change."

"Oh, I'm so glad. I was afraid it might be too drastic."

"No," I said. "It's fine. You look beautiful."

"I feel great," she said. "I'm doing so well here. I've gained almost ten pounds, and I've been working out. This place has a pool, and I've started lap swimming. I haven't swum laps in years, but I'm getting my stride back. It's like riding a bicycle – once you learn you never forget."

We laughed. It was good to see her excited about something, especially swimming, because she'd once been a college champion and hadn't been in the pool for years, too busy working. Since she'd come home from Afghanistan she'd lost a lot of weight, and grew dangerously thin because of the pain and the pain pills. Her depression sucked the joy out of life, and she did little but work and sleep. Now she looked more like herself, in spite of the short hair, which was adorable, especially the way it spiked on top. Her enthusiasm was contagious and I smiled back, relieved she was happy, healthy, and on her way back to being my mom.

I handed her the bags we brought and she pulled everything out, exclaiming over each item. It was like Christmas.

"Tell me all about school, and swimming, and your new friends," Mom said, and I did. I told her about Mel, and Erica, and Charlie. I told her about the swim team and my coaches. I told her how well I was doing in school, raising my grades and prepping for the SATs.

"I'm proud of you," she said, holding my hand. "Sounds like

you're doing well."

"Enough about me. How about you?" I asked. I checked out the crowd in the visiting room, her fellow inmates and their families, a mixed bag of characters.

"I'm okay," she said squeezing my hand. "The people here aren't too bad. The guards are fair. The food's edible. I have an excellent counselor and sit in on some helpful group sessions. And, like I said, I've been swimming and focusing on getting back in shape, restoring my health."

"Well, whatever you're doing, it's working," Maggie said.

"I'm sorry Maggie," she said. "We're leaving you out."

"Don't worry about it," Maggie said. "You two have a lot to catch up on. In fact, I spotted a mall nearby and thought I'd leave you two alone while I did a little shopping."

"Are you sure?" Mom asked.

"Are you kidding? An hour of shopping with no kids?" Maggie rose to leave. "I'll meet you out front at four o'clock, Aerin," she said. I nodded, and she was gone.

Chapter 24

The room was noisy, a steady din underscored with sudden bursts of laughter, the chatter of children, and a few low voices locked in close, quiet conversations. Mom sat about three feet from me, our toes touching under the table. She hadn't let go of my hand since we'd sat down. She spoke in her usual tone of voice, no hint of anxiety or pain. Her face was relaxed, the skin around her eyes free of worry lines and dark circles. I couldn't remember the last time I'd seen her so at peace, at least not since September 11th, and not since she'd joined the Army Reserve.

"Are you having fun?" she asked. "I don't mean now. There's not much fun here. I mean back in Two Rivers, at the high school. I know swimming and studying take up most of your time, but I hope you're having fun, too."

"I went to an incredible place last weekend," I said, but stopped, unsure if I wanted to tell her about Minnewaska when she was locked up in this miserable place. She nodded, encouraging me to go on. "It's in the mountains with a beautiful lake. We went swimming, even though we weren't supposed to, and had a picnic on a gigantic rock that looked down on the lake. It was a beautiful day, and I loved it."

"Who's we?" Mom asked.

"Remember I told you about my friend Mel? I went with her and her brother, Justin. They're twins."

"That color in your cheeks tells me he's someone special," she said.

My cheeks burned. "He's just a friend," I mumbled.

"Looks like he's more than a friend to me. What's he like?"

I conjured up an image of Justin in my mind, not hard to do because I thought about him most of the time. "He's tall, very tall, like six-two, and he's got the most beautiful blue eyes, like robins' eggs, and long blond hair. And he's kind, and sweet, too, and he drives a Jeep, and he swims - " I realized I was rambling and clamped down.

"You do like him," she said.

I shrugged.

"That's great, honey, you've never had a crush on anyone before. Does he feel the same way?"

"I don't know," I whispered, wondering, but then I remembered the almost invitation to the dance. "I think he might ask me out." I told her all about the dance, Father Mancini, and the trip to Haiti.

"Wow, you are having a good time," she said.

All at once I felt mortified. How could I be having such a great time while she was in here?

My remorse must have shown on my face, because she said, "No, Aerin, it's all right. You deserve to have a good time. Don't worry about me. Tell me about swimming. They must be thrilled to have you on the team. What did they say the first time you won an event?"

I looked down at my lap in shame, not wanting to tell her the truth, but I had no other option.

"I haven't won any events," I said.

"What do you mean?" She looked puzzled. "You were the division champion last year in both of your events. You were going to work on your times, shoot for the state championship, try to get a scholarship. We talked about Division I schools, Stanford, Cal, Georgia. What's happening?"

She'd never understand. She was a star in high school, made it to States her last two seasons, and swam for a Division I team, a winner all around. Losing wasn't in her DNA.

"Aerin?"

I shook it off, leveling with her. "I'm not swimming to win. I've got too much on my mind and don't want any additional pressure. I swim to relax and forgot about everything else."

She looked taken aback, and I regretted my words. The last thing I wanted was for her to feel responsible for my choices. She was at the root of them, but I could have chosen to go the other way, to work off my stressors in competition, beating everyone, even Tatiana. It didn't seem worth it.

"Honey," she said, "don't let my circumstances change your course."

"It's not about you, Mom," I interrupted. "It's about me. I've lost interest in competing. I mean, I love to swim, but I lost my will to win. It's not important anymore. All the effort, all the preparation. It's pointless."

We sat in silence for a moment. A chain of emotions flashed across her face: sadness, worry, regret. She said, "That doesn't sound like you, Aerin. You were always a champion at heart, a fierce competitor. I always thought you'd do great things, be a better swimmer than I was."

"I did too," I admitted, "but after last season I started to realize there's more to life than winning, than being a champion. That sucked up all of my time, and I wasn't paying attention to other things, like you, and look what happened."

"Aerin, listen to me. You are not responsible for what happened to me. It's all my fault. Nothing you could have done would have stopped it."

I shook my head. "No, Mom. I was too wrapped up in my life and didn't see what was going on with you. If I had, I could have gotten you help."

"No, you were doing *exactly* what you needed to do: being a kid, going to school, swimming. We were counting on your getting an athletic scholarship, competing at the national level. Don't forget your dreams and goals. Giving up competition is not going to change anything that's happened, but it could change the future."

"Do you honestly believe I have a future in swimming? Come on, Mom. That was you."

"You're the best I've seen in years, and I'm not saying that because you're my daughter. Your coaches have told me you have a real shot at competing at the national level, maybe the Olympics."

I snorted. "You haven't seen me lately. And you haven't seen the kids I'm swimming against now. I'm not the fastest on my team and not even close to the fastest in the division."

"But you're not trying," she said. "You said that yourself."

She was right. I hadn't done any more than I'd needed to make the team and hold on to my spot in the lineup.

"And stiff competition never stopped you from winning before," she went on. "You were up against some strong swimmers last season, but you worked hard, and you believed, and you won when it counted. When you have that much talent, you can't hold it back. You have to take it as far as you can and see where it leads."

She knew what she was talking about. I'd heard her swim story a thousand times, from her, my father, and Aunt Maggie. She'd come from behind her last two seasons in high school, made a commitment to be her best, and won her division's title in the butterfly and the individual medley both years. Her success earned her a college scholarship and a shot at nationals and the Olympic trials. She finished fourth in both strokes, an incredible achievement, but not enough to win a spot on the Olympic team. Now she'd passed her dreams off to me. I'd been trying to fulfill them ever since

I started swimming competitively, but no longer responded to that urge, that desire. It cost too much, and I wasn't willing to pay the price anymore.

"Look at me," she said. I met her eyes. They were so bright and full of light. "Promise me you'll do your best. Don't let me or anyone else get in your way. Now is your chance to prove what you're capable of."

"I'm not making any promises," I said, looking down at the table, my index finger tracing the grooves on the table top. Around us, the crowd had thinned. Visiting hours were almost over. I had yet to bring up what my father told me about their marriage and the breakup, and I was determined not to leave without getting her side of the story.

"What does your father say?" she asked, almost reading my mind.

"He's on your page. He wants me to try harder. He wants me to win."

"He's only looking out for your best interests."

"I know," I sighed, slumping back in my chair. "He's got some crazy ideas about my going to college in Westchester, somewhere close to him and Dawn and the girls. He wants me to live with them and help out with the – " I suddenly realized she might not know about the baby.

"I know about the baby," she said. "He wrote me a letter."

"Yeah, they're having a baby."

"How do you feel about it?"

I shrugged. "At first, I was mad, I mean, it was such a surprise. Dawn's like forty-something and I thought she was done having kids. It wasn't something I thought would happen. But now that I'm getting used to the idea, I think it's okay. Although Dawn's having some difficulties and the doctor has her on bed rest."

"Really?" Mom asked, her nursing instincts kicking in. "Is everything all right?"

"I guess so. I don't know too much about it."

"You know, Aerin, it's not their first pregnancy. She's had two miscarriages."

Now *that* was a revelation. "That's sad," I said and meant it.

"I'm sure she'll be fine," Mom said. "She has an excellent doctor and a top notch hospital nearby. Plus, your father will take good care of her. So," she said, changing the subject, "are you considering schools in Westchester?"

"No, I'm not. I want to get away, far away, from the city, from everything that's happened."

"Any idea where?"

"No," I sighed. "I have no clue."

"California has some great college swimming, so does Georgia. Visit the school's career center, do some online investigation. You'll figure it out."

"I know," I said, glancing at the clock. Ten minutes left. "Mom, before I leave, I need to ask you something."

"Go ahead. I promised no more secrets. You can ask me anything."

"It's about Dad," I said, "and you."

She frowned, but remained steady. "Okay. Ask away."

Chapter 25

It was best to spit it out. "Dad said Dawn wasn't the reason he left. He said you two were having issues for a long time, and that he would have left even if Dawn wasn't in the picture. He said you were having problems and instead of working on them you joined the Reserve."

"Wow," she said. "He said all that?"

I nodded. "Is it true?"

She paused for a long moment, debating her response, then let out a long breath. "Most of it," she said. "I won't deny it. We were having problems for a while, long before I enlisted. He didn't want me to do it, but it was something I had to do. Our country was at war, and our soldiers needed my skills. I couldn't not go, even when he begged me to stay home. He told me about Dawn before I got back, and said he was leaving. Our marriage was over."

"How did I not know?" I asked. "Was I that oblivious? That wrapped up in my own little world?"

"Aerin, take it easy. You were twelve. You had your own concerns – school, swimming, your friends. Your father and I did our best not to disrupt your life until we were sure of what would happen."

"I never saw you argue," I said. "I had no idea we were in

trouble."

"Your father worked long hours, remember? He'd just started at the firm. I was doing 12-hour shifts in the ER and lots of overtime. Your grandmother stepped in to help after school and swim practice. She stayed with you until one of us came home."

As she spoke, I remembered our home life before she left for Afghanistan. Everyone was so busy we spent little time together. She left rather abruptly – the Reserve didn't give much warning when they shipped her out – and then it was just Dad and me, until my grandmother moved in to help because he worked so many late nights.

"Besides," Mom continued, "Gordon and I didn't fight. We tended to bury our feelings and ignore our differences." Her voice faded, almost to a whisper. She looked wistful as she said, "Sometimes I wish we had fought. Perhaps we could have stayed together."

A bell rang, and I jumped, thinking for a second I was at school. Then a guard announced that visiting hours were ending in five minutes. All around us, people packed up their belongings and said goodbye with lots of tears and even some hysterics as families prepared to separate. My stomach started doing flip turns as I realized I wouldn't see my mother for another month, and only if she earned enough credits to qualify for a visit. We'd discussed a lot of issues, and I'd have to sort them out on my own.

Mom stood, and I rose to meet her. She came around the table and held out her arms. I fell into them, holding onto her as tight as I could. She rocked me the way she had all my life, and we swayed together, silent. After a minute, she pulled away and looked at me.

"I don't want you to leave here feeling sad about anything. What happened between your father and I was our doing. It had nothing to do with you. People sometimes drift apart, and that's what happened to us. In spite of our divorce, we both love you as much as we ever did. Nothing you could have done would have stopped us from splitting up. So don't blame yourself, okay?"

I nodded, tears in my eyes.

"And make the most of your swim season," she continued. "Don't give up. You're too good; you can do great things. Please don't worry about me or think that somehow my troubles were the result of your focusing on your schoolwork and swimming. That's what you were supposed to do. I brought on my own troubles. I accept responsibility for them. I just want you to succeed. You will try, won't you?"

I was crying shamelessly, tears rolling down my face, my nose running and all stuffed up. I could do nothing but nod. Mom reached into her pocket and pulled out a packet of tissues. She offered me one and I wiped my face, blew my nose. I was a mess, just the way I didn't want to leave her.

"Time's up," the guard announced, and I scowled at him. Couldn't he see something serious was happening here?

Around me came the sound of chairs scraping against the floor as people stood to leave, more wailing and sad goodbyes.

Mom pulled me close to her again, burying her face in my hair.

"I love you, baby girl," she whispered. "Don't give up on yourself, or on me."

"I'll never give up on you," I sniffled.

"That's great, but don't give up on yourself, okay?"

"Okay," I said, holding on.

"Promise?"

I pulled back from her so I could meet her eyes. "I promise."

Chapter 26

I followed the guard who escorted the departing visitors through the maze of sterile white corridors until we emerged into the late afternoon sunshine. Shielding my eyes with my hand, I looked for Maggie in the parking lot and spied her minivan several rows over. She must have seen me because the minivan started moving and a minute later pulled up beside me. I got in and closed the doors, settling into my seat and adjusting my seatbelt. Maggie put the van in gear and we joined the parade of vehicles exiting the facility's grounds. Neither of us spoke until we hit the highway.

"Your mother looks good," Maggie said, glancing at me.

I slouched against the door, my head resting on the window. I was exhausted, like I'd just swam 1,000 yards nonstop. I took deep, long breaths, trying to release the tension that had built up inside me during our two-hour visit. I missed her already, and my heart hurt. "Yeah," I said not trusting my voice.

"I love her hair," Mags went on. "That short cut looks beautiful on her."

"Yeah."

She concentrated on the road for a minute and then turned to give me a quizzical look. "Are you all right?"

I sat up straight. "I'm okay."

"You don't look okay." She switched lanes.

"We had a lot to talk about," I said, not wanting to get into all the details, although she knew most of it or more than I ever did. After all, she was Mom's best friend long before my parents met. She was maid of honor at their wedding and took my mother on a girls' night out in the city right after the divorce was final. She was always there when we needed her. She was there now, although I wasn't up for sharing. She must have sensed that, because she turned away and kept her eyes on the road, silent. The beautiful upstate country rolled by as we cruised along, my mind churning over what my mother had told me.

My life was a big, fat lie. I'd been living in some fantasy where all was good, and everyone was happy. What a dope. My world was crumbling around me for *years,* and I had no clue. I was oblivious, underwater, swimming hundreds of thousands of laps, coming up for air only when necessary. How could I have been so blind? My life was a series of swim, school, swim, study, sleep for so long I didn't notice my parents were in trouble, or see that our life together was about to implode.

When it happened, it caught me off guard, and because my father was the one who left, I blamed him. He was the perfect scapegoat, especially when his relationship with Dawn went public. Dawn and her husband had a *huge* custody fight over their girls. She got everything she wanted, married my father ASAP, and moved into the house in Westchester with him and the girls. That's when I realized my parents would never get back together.

I was beyond anger. It wouldn't change anything. Dad had his new family with Dawn, my mother had her issues to work out, and I needed to graduate high school and figure out what to do next. I had some vague ideas but nothing concrete. I didn't want to live with my father's family in Westchester and go to school nearby – that was *not* going to happen. My mother seemed a little more open minded about the possibilities before me, and I thought I'd explore some of her suggestions. Georgia. Stanford. Cal.

The miles rolled on while I sorted out all the new info and what it meant to me. Before I expected, the exit for Two Rivers came in sight.

"Anything you want to talk about before we get home?" asked Maggie. "We can stop for ice cream."

It was so like Maggie to make sure everything was okay before we moved on, and I was anxious about leaving the comfortable cocoon of the minivan without verbalizing what was going on in my head.

"Good idea," I said.

Chapter 27

Maggie turned into The Tasty Cone and we got out of the minivan to stretch our legs after the two-hour ride. We lined up at the takeout window. Maggie ordered a kid-sized dish of strawberry ice cream, no frills. I got a hot fudge sundae with double scoops of vanilla because it was *that* kind of day.

Although late September, it was still warm, so we sat at a picnic table under a leafy maple tree with plenty of shade and privacy. Maggie ate half her ice cream before saying, "You've been quiet these last two hours. When that happens, I get worried."

I laughed. She knew me so well, almost as well as my mother did. I wiped my mouth with a napkin before answering. "Yeah, I'm a deep thinker," I said. "Mom and I talked a lot. She cleared up some things. I learned most of what I thought about my family wasn't true."

"How so?" she asked, scooping up another mouthful of ice cream.

I took a break from my sundae, stirring it around in its cup, mixing it all together. "I always thought my dad was the bad guy," I said, articulating the thoughts that had occupied me on the way back from the correctional facility. "You know, the way he skipped out on my mom while she was in Afghanistan. I thought he was a cheat and a liar, and I hated him. And that hurt, you know? Because I always loved my dad." I paused to eat a spoonful of my gooey sundae, which now looked more like a milkshake. "And now I find out they had troubles a long time before September 11th, the war, and Dawn, and I was oblivious."

"Children are not supposed to know about their parents' unhappiness or marital problems," Maggie said. "It's not fair to them unless the situation is irreparable and the marriage falls apart. Most couples have problems but manage to overcome them, and the children are better off not knowing about them."

I nodded. "We were all so busy, going about our days in our crazy routine that kept us glued together. When I think back on it now, I see that we were all living in a bubble, and the bubble had to burst."

Maggie's blue eyes were full of concern.

"I hated Dawn, too, but guess what? She's all right. I could have made out worse with a stepmother. And her girls, even if they are spoiled brats, are okay sometimes. I've been hard on them, and I shouldn't have been because the divorce and everything that happened after wasn't their fault. It wasn't anyone's *fault.* It just happened."

Maggie finished her ice cream and put the empty cup down. "Sometimes," she said, "when we don't have all the facts we make assumptions, and these can be painful. I'm glad you and Devon had the chance to clear up some of these issues. Your mother asked me to speak for her after your visit if you have any questions or just need to talk. I know the whole story so maybe I can help clarify any confusion."

Maggie always tried to be helpful. I don't know why I never went to her in the past with my concerns. Maybe I didn't want to be disloyal to my mother. But then, she hadn't been honest and let me go on blaming my father and Dawn, hating them at times, and acting like a real jerk whenever I had the chance.

"Why didn't my mother tell me the truth years ago?" I asked Maggie. "I deserved to know. It wasn't fair to me."

"No, it wasn't," she said, "but your parents wanted to downplay the fact that their marriage went sour to protect you along the way. Sometimes adults do dumb things for dumb reasons. Your father thought your hostility toward him and Dawn was a part of the process following the divorce and his remarriage, and you'd grow out of it. Your mother was wrapped up in her problems and not paying much attention to anything else. We lost her for a while. She did her best, but the pain and addiction were too powerful. I hate seeing her in that place, but getting caught stealing narcotics saved her. In a sense, we should be grateful."

I nodded. I'd had that thought too. "Too bad she went into the Army Reserve. None of that would have happened."

"*Some* of that wouldn't have happened," she corrected me. "You can't blame the Reserve for the marriage breaking up."

"Why did she go, anyway?" I asked. "She could have continued to work at St. Vincent's or some other ER and done the same thing."

"I don't have to tell you about your mother," Maggie said, smiling, her blue eyes crinkling at the corners. "Devon always wanted to save the world, even when we were kids. I admire her for it, but sometimes she goes too far. Becoming a soldier *was* over the top, I told her, but you know your mother. Once she gets an idea in her head you can't stop her. September 11th broke her heart, and she wanted to be part of the war effort. She was compelled to enlist, to serve the soldiers. She's a real patriot."

I knew all that, but hearing Maggie say it made it real. I felt a new pride for my mom, who had given up so much for others. I could never be mad at her, which made it easy for me to be angry at my father. But now, after hearing the whole story, I wasn't mad at him anymore.

"What do I do now?" I asked.

"You go on with school, swimming, your senior year. Life is too short to carry grudges. Next time you visit your father and Dawn, apologize for the way you've been acting, then change your act. It will be better for everyone if you all get along."

"But I was having so much fun hating Dawn and the girls," I joked.

We laughed.

"Resentment is a wasted emotion," Maggie said. "Focus on other things, such as graduating high school, getting into a good college, and winning a few races."

"I haven't won any races." The loss of those little triumphs suddenly filled me with sadness.

"Do you want to talk about that?"

I shook my head. "I haven't decided anything about competition. I kind of like being in the middle of the pack. There's less stress, no one's expecting any more from me. Besides, don't you think it will be strange if I take off, start winning? I mean, I can beat Tatiana, and that would shake things up."

"Sometimes things need to be shaken up. I'd love to see the look on Calvin's face if you were to beat Tatiana."

"She's lucky to hold her own with the Chinese swimmers."

"And Calvin is quite concerned about it. He's counting on her to break that record and win that prize. Knowing him, he's already written the press release."

"Maybe I shouldn't take that away from them," I said. "I *am* the new girl. I don't belong to Two Rivers. Tati's been working on breaking the record for years. Wouldn't I be stealing from her, from the team, from everyone, if I busted it first?" I finished the last of my sundae and wiped my mouth with my hand. "I could do it, too, you know. I could beat her. Hey, on paper I have beaten her. My time at the Division Championships last year was faster than her best time ever, and that wasn't even my fastest time."

Maggie reared back, her eyes big and round. "Really?"

I nodded, using a napkin to wipe the remnants from the sticky sundae off my hands.

"Looks like you have something to think about."

I nodded again, not meeting her eyes, my mind racing with the possibilities, imagining the thrill of the competition, the glory of winning, and knocking Allison Singer's name off the leaderboard.

"That scholarship would be a big help."

"I know." I couldn't even *think* about the scholarship without getting dizzy.

"You don't have much time. You have six more dual meets and the Long Island Invitational before the Division Championships."

"How do you know so much about my season?" I asked.

"I pay attention. I've got two kids who want to swim, and I need to know what I'm in for, right?"

I smiled. "Thanks for making the effort."

"No problem." She picked up our empty cups and used napkins. "Ready to go home?"

We got back into the minivan and Maggie merged into traffic on Main Street. I felt lighter than I had in months. I'd left behind years of resentment, displacement, and confusion. My head was clear.

I was ready to move on with my father, Dawn, the girls, and the new baby.

And I was willing to think about winning again.

Too much had happened today. Too many emotional revelations. Too many decisions. As we rounded the corner to Maggie's house, I put everything out of my mind, saving it for another day.

Week Six:

Slacker

Chapter 28

Midway through school on Monday, my English class went to the College and Career Center to meet with the counselors to discuss our "ambitions" and "plans for the future." The center was in a classroom at the back of the library. Pennants from colleges across the country decorated the walls. Brochures filled every rack in the place. A bank of computer stations were turned on and ready for us to log on to college websites for virtual tours. I'd visited once before but hadn't made much progress, overwhelmed by the whole ordeal. I stood in front of a rack of brochures and perused their covers.

"So, you're looking at a college nearby?" asked a voice to my right. I startled and turned, finding an older woman in a dark blue pantsuit. "I don't believe we've met," she said, holding out her right hand. "I'm Michelle Cashman, director of the center."

We shook hands. "Aerin Keane."

"You're new here?"

I nodded.

"Tough to change schools in your senior year," she said.

I shrugged. "It's okay."

"Where were you before?"

I told her the names of my former schools.

"Good schools," she said. "Did you do any career planning at either one of them?"

"A little," I said, "but I didn't get too far."

"You're looking at New York schools." She gestured to the brochures in front of me. "Are you looking for a state school or something private?"

"I'm not looking at New York schools," I said. "I want to get away, far away."

"Okay," she said, not surprised. "Any place in particular?"

"I don't know. California?"

"Northern? Southern? City? Mountains? You've got lots of choices."

"I'm not sure, but I want a Division I school with a swim team."

"You're a swimmer!" she said, her eyes brightening. "So was I, at New York University. It's a Division III school, but I had a great time. I did the fly and the IM. What's your stroke?"

"Distance," I said.

"Oh, so you're one of the girls trying to beat Allison Singer's record."

That statement caught me by surprise, but then I realized of course she knew about the contest. She worked in the school, and as a former swimmer probably followed our team. "No," I said. "Not me. I think Tatiana Reese has it all wrapped up."

"Tatiana's a great swimmer," she agreed, "but you shouldn't give up. What's your best time? Is it even close to a possibility?"

She was so nice I couldn't lie to her. "Not now," I said, fudging the truth.

"I'll have to make it to one of your meets," she said. "I'd love to see that old record get broken. Whoever wins it will be a lucky girl. That scholarship is enough to pay for a full year at most private schools, and at least two at a state school."

"Yeah," I said, "real lucky."

"So you're looking for a Division I school? Think you're a good enough swimmer?"

Her doubt about my abilities when she knew nothing about me was insulting, but I refused to react. "So I've been told."

"Okay," she said without batting an eye. "Do you have a career goal in mind? A course of study?"

"I'm not sure, but not medicine or nursing, and not law."

"So, business? Teaching? Computers?"

I shook my head. Nothing she said moved me.

"What about coaching or phys ed teacher? You love to swim, right? I always say, do what you love."

I smiled. Hearing the words ignited a spark. "Yeah, I said, "something like that, but not little kids, high school kids."

"Like Coach Dudash?"

I thought of Coach and how he pushed us, helping us to get the most from ourselves both in and out of the pool. I'd been fortunate to have good coaches throughout my swimming career. The thought of following them in their field seemed right and something I could do with pride. "Yes," I said.

"Well, that narrows things down to Division I schools not in New York, with swim teams and a phys ed and coaching program. Sound right?"

I nodded, surprised that a woman who had known me all of five minutes had figured me out.

"Okay, Aerin, let me show you the materials for the schools that meet your requirements." She walked me across the room. "Feel free to take what you like, look them over, and check the schools out online. You'll have to do your homework to determine which academic programs interest you. If you have any questions stop by or send me an email." She handed me a slip of paper with her contact information on it. "Let's talk again next week. You don't need an appointment, but you might want to make one so you'll have my undivided attention." She gave me a big smile and moved on to help one of my classmates.

Class time was running out, and I had just a few minutes to pick up the brochures for the schools Mom and I had talked about. I stuffed them into my book bag and headed out to my next class.

~

That afternoon, we had a meet against the Diamonds, a team we were expected to beat, and we did, 109-77. I came in third in both of my events, my time flat – no better, no worse than usual. In meets like that, we tended to slack off a little bit, not wanting to destroy our last place competitor. Coach mixed up our 400 free relay team, putting in some of our slower swimmers, so the Diamonds won. Tatiana sat that one out. I was the lead leg, and it was good to be out in front again, setting the pace. I put up a decent time and Coach gave me a pat on the back. The third string swimmers behind me gave the Diamonds one of their few victories, and we finished the meet now 7-0, and in first place in the division.

Once I'd finished helping Aunt Mags clean up the kitchen after dinner, I went up to my room and did my homework. I finished an English essay, solved twenty math problems, and read a chapter in my history book. Then I burrowed into my bed with the college brochures and my laptop. I read every pamphlet cover to cover, studied the pictures, and visited their virtual campuses. The possibilities were fantastic, and the colleges were outstanding. Everything looked full of promise and potential.

I lay awake long after I turned the light out, my mind in a whirl, replaying the images of the various schools, their descriptions, and wondering if I could get into any of them. I fell asleep with the brochures surrounding me, filling my dreams with visions of college life, in a city I'd never visited, on my own, swimming, and learning how to one day coach my own team.

Chapter 29

We were almost halfway through the season, and my days were an endless blur of school, swim, study, and sleep. I woke up at 6:30 each morning to catch the 7:15 bus, attended classes, then swim practice or a meet, followed by dinner, a shower, and homework before I crashed into bed around nine. I tried to stay up late enough to catch my favorite TV shows, but conked out before they were over, no big deal because once swim season ended I'd have plenty of time to play catch-up.

Most days I didn't bother to dress up for school, although some of the girls, Jordan and Tati in particular, managed to pull it all together that early in the morning, fixing their hair and makeup and coordinating cute little outfits. I was more the sweatpants and T-shirt type, my hair wrapped up in a messy bun on top of my head, my face clean of makeup; simple, comfortable, and I liked it.

On non-meet days, Coach scheduled morning practice at 5:40, but it wasn't mandatory, so I didn't bother going. In the past, I'd never skipped morning practice, knowing it separated me from the rest of the pack and gave me my edge. Gym class first period and no ride to school at 5:30 a.m. were two great reasons to skip it, and since I wasn't trying to stand out at Two Rivers anyway I slept in guilt-free, and listened to the other girls complain about jumping out of bed and into the pool.

"I'm starting to feel like a reptile," Mel said at lunch on Wednesday. She never missed morning practice. Coach allowed the boys to swim too, to stay in shape in their off-season, so Justin drove her to the pool and put in his own time. "My skin is so dry," she said. It was a common swimmer problem – the chlorine dried out our skin, turning it ashy and dull. No matter how much or what type of lotion we slathered on before and after swimming, we still felt tight and itchy.

"Well, if you're reptilian you're cold-blooded, so you can tolerate being in the pool longer," said Erica. She, too, was an early riser and made morning practice most days.

"I'm not cold-blooded," Mel said. "That water is freezing. I can't stand it if I'm not moving."

"That's the point," I said, taking a bite out of the second half of my turkey sandwich.

"At least your hair's not turning green," Erica said, gesturing toward Jordan, who sat at a table a few rows from us with Tati, Travis, and Sean. Jordan's overprocessed hair was a pukey shade of green, and the ends looked like straw. She picked at a salad while playing footsie with Travis, unaware that her head was starting to look like Kermit the Frog's.

"I'm a brunette. I don't worry about that," Mel said.

"What about redheads, Aerin?" Erica asked me. "Your hair doesn't turn green, does it?"

"No," I said, "but my sensitive skin takes a beating from all the pool chemicals." I stroked my cheek; it was a little tight, but softer than it usually was at this point in the season. Must be the excellent moisturizer Aunt Mags recommended and the decrease in pool time.

"I can't believe you guys get up so early to swim," said Kelsey.

"Don't remind me," said Erica. She looked like she was ready to fall asleep at the table.

"It's only three times a week," said Mel, "and it's not

mandatory, but anyone who's serious about swimming makes it."

"Not Aerin," said Erica, giving me a sidelong glance.

"Hey, I've got gym first period. I don't want to work out in the pool, dry off, and then hit the gym."

"A weak excuse," Erica said.

"And, unlike you two, I don't have a ride, remember?"

"You could walk," Erica suggested. "You only live a half mile from the school."

"At five-thirty in the morning? No thanks."

Mel finished the rest of her orange juice and crushed the carton in one hand before putting it down on the table. "Tatiana has gym first period, and she makes morning practice. And a few of the other girls walk to practice in the dark, so that's no big deal. Aerin doesn't come because Aerin is a slacker." She met my eyes straight on.

"Ooooh," said Erica, sitting upright. "This is getting interesting."

A flash of anger ran through me, starting at the top of my head. I swore I could feel it run through my entire body and exit somewhere from the bottom of my feet. The air between us bristled with tension. I rose to Mel's challenge. "You called me a slacker?"

No one had ever done that before. Other swimmers slacked off, not Aerin Keane, who gave every practice, every event, every heat, everything she had, and then some. I was the hardest working swimmer no matter what team I was on. Then I remembered I was no longer that swimmer.

"Yeah, you're a slacker," Mel said, leaning forward and staring right into my eyes. "You skip morning practice, you wimp out at the end of your races, and you don't push yourself in the weight room."

I didn't react. I was an *intentional* slacker, no doubt about it. I figured I could get away with it since no one had any idea of what I could do. Until now, I thought no one had noticed. Was she the only one? I had to stop this talk.

"What do you mean?" I asked. "I'm busting my butt. I never

miss practice. I'm always on time. I keep up with the rest of you, including Tatiana and Erica. I'm racking up points. I'm pulling my weight."

"She's right," Erica said, coming to my defense. I gave her a grateful smile. "Not everyone comes to morning practice, Mel, only the ones who want to do their best. I think Aerin's already doing her best."

Ouch! That hurt, but I kept my face neutral, not letting on that my temperature had risen five degrees. Where was that lunch bell? I had to get out of here.

"Something tells me you can do better," Mel said.

"And what is that?"

"You've got the best technique of anyone I've ever seen," she said. "Your starts are perfect, and your turns are powerful. I can't figure out why you always get bogged down in the middle of a race. You're in great shape. You don't appear to be winded. Something just doesn't click."

"Maybe she doesn't want to win," said Erica. "Not everybody does."

Mel rolled her eyes. "Please, Erica, really?"

"Just saying," Erica said.

Kelsey leaned forward. "I think Aerin's an excellent swimmer."

"You can't weigh in here, Kels, you're not a swimmer," Mel said.

"Hey," said Erica, "that's not nice."

"Only a swimmer can tell when another swimmer's slacking off, Erica. You know that."

I'd had enough. "You're lucky we're friends, Mel, or we'd be done after what you just said."

"Come on, Aerin, you know what I'm talking about. How'd you do last year? Where did you finish?"

She was getting too close for comfort. I had no clue how to answer, but I didn't have to because the lunch bell went off signaling we needed to move on to our next class. A wave of relief flowed over me as I got up and grabbed my book bag. "Later, Mel," I said.

She scooped up her stuff and followed. "We're not done, Aerin."

"Yes, we are." I pushed my way through the crowd and headed to College English.

Chapter 30

At practice that afternoon, I kept to myself, not making eye contact with Mel, or Erica, or anyone. I concentrated on making my intervals and let the water bear the brunt of my anger.

The irony of Mel's comments didn't escape me. I *was* slacking off, but her criticism stung. She was my best friend, someone I admired and whose opinion I respected.

I thought I'd been doing so well. I was right where I wanted to be: in the middle of the pack, not the best, but not the worst either. I brought in points and was keeping everyone happy, especially myself, because for the first time I actually *enjoyed* swim season. No one looked at me like I was some kind of freak because I was so much better than everyone else and headed places most would never go.

I was tired of everyone expecting me to do great things, like swim for a Division I school, win at Nationals, and go on to the Olympics. Now that I'd tasted what it meant to be just an okay swimmer, I kind of liked it. I wasn't as sore as I was in prior years, and I wasn't fatigued, which gave me time for other things, like my friends.

I was in a good place.

No way I'd let anyone take that from me.

Practice went by in a flash and I was the last swimmer out of the pool. While I toweled off, Coach D came over and said, "Great practice, Aerin. You made almost every interval. It's nice to see you hitting your stride."

I wrapped the towel around my dripping self and nodded. "The water felt good," I said, not wanting to give anything away. The last thing I'd intended was calling more attention to my performance.

"I've been watching you. You have a lot of potential, but I found a couple of areas we can improve on, streamline things a little bit. Come to morning practice on Friday and I'll work with you one on one."

Great. Now Coach D was on to me. "Sounds good," I said, "but I can't. First-period gym and no ride."

She nodded, looking thoughtful. "Maybe you can catch a ride with someone else. I'll ask around for you."

"No thanks," I said. "Morning practice is optional, right? Not mandatory? I kind of like things the way they are. I'm not a morning person."

She shrugged. "Okay," she said, "I'm just trying to help."

"I'll tell you if I need any help." I packed up my swim bag and went off to the locker room. The place was deserted; everyone else had already left. I decided to take a hot shower and stayed in until Coach D told me my time was up. It was almost six o'clock. I left the natatorium and walked out into the early evening.

The mid-September air was crisp. I stopped to pull on a sweatshirt. Heading off campus, I walked past athletic fields in full action. A soccer game was in progress, and the football team was running drills. The parking lot was crowded, as people attended the game or waited to pick up their kids from volleyball or tennis practice. I kept my head down, not wanting to run into anyone, my mind reeling from my conversations with Mel and Coach D.

I'd almost made it past the football field when someone called my name. My head whipped around, searching.

"Hey, Apple!"

I looked toward the football field. Justin leaned against the fence gesturing me to join him. I waved and continued on my way.

"Hey! Wait a minute," he called.

I stopped and waited.

"What's up?" he asked as soon as we were face to face.

"What's up? I'm going home. What's up with you?"

"I'm watching Sean and Travis get their butts kicked in practice."

"Don't you have anything better to do?"

"No," he said, that grin of his turning me to mush.

"Well, I do. I've got tons of homework. Physics quiz tomorrow."

"How are you doing in physics?"

"Could be better."

"I aced it, 98.9. Want me to help you study?"

"Are you serious?" His proposal was irresistible. Physics was the most difficult of my classes, and I was determined to ace it.

"Come on. I'll drive you home and then we can hit the books. I've got a couple of hours to spare."

"Okay," I said and followed him to his broken down Jeep. We settled in and he started the engine.

"Your Jeep sounds a lot better than it looks," I said as he backed out of his parking spot.

He shifted gears. "This Jeep is vintage," he said. "1991. I bought it at a junkyard and work on it in automotive shop. The engine's been totally rebuilt. I'm restoring the body next. In another year, this baby will look brand new."

"I didn't know you were a gearhead," I said, impressed. I didn't even have my driver's license.

"I've been into cars all of my life. My father was a mechanic before he went into business. He taught me all I know."

"My father never owned a car until he moved to the suburbs. He made up for it though, and bought a Beemer."

"Sweet," he said, then changed the subject. "You guys are having an awesome season. You're blowing away the competition."

"We're undefeated," I said. "And almost half the girls have made cut times for the Division Championships."

"What about you?"

"I'm in for both the 200 and the 500 free, and the two free relays."

"That it?" he asked.

"That's enough," I said.

I watched the scenery roll by as we entered Aunt Mags' neighborhood, her house just a block away, annoyed because I couldn't avoid talk of my performance today. First Mel, then Coach D, and now Justin.

"I can help with that," he said.

"With what?"

"With you making more cut times."

"You?"

"Yeah, me. I won the division title in the IM last year. Didn't Mel tell you?"

"No," I said. "We don't talk about you."

"Oh," he said, eyes downcast. Was that a hint of disappointment?

"I'm good," I said. "I'm happy where I am."

We pulled up in front of Aunt Mags house. He shut the car off. "Let me know if you change your mind," he said.

"Definitely." I didn't have the heart to shoot him down, but I had no intention of changing my mind.

He came around to my door, opened it and ushered me out. Such a gentleman. He grabbed my bags and we went into the house.

Everyone was in the kitchen. Aunt Mags stood at the stove stirring a pot. I smelled her homemade spaghetti sauce and my stomach rumbled. A pot of water for pasta was set to boil beside it.

"Yum," I said. "That smells delicious. I'm starving."

"What about your guest?" Mags asked. "Will you stay for dinner, Justin?"

"If you've got enough," he said.

"With this crowd? Don't worry, I make plenty."

"You know I eat a lot," he said, giving her one of his knockout grins. She was charmed, I could tell.

"I've heard that," she said. "I've already got one swimmer in the house. I've learned to accommodate her appetite. The rule around here these days is double the recipe."

I blushed, embarrassed. "I don't eat *that* much."

"We swimmers tend to eat everything in sight," Justin said. "My mom complains her grocery bill doubles during my swim season."

"Ours hasn't gone up that much," Mags said.

"We'll need to get used to it," Uncle Pat said. He sat at the kitchen table with Timmy and the twins, surrounded by their homework. "I've got at least two wannabe swimmers on my team. Aerin has inspired Paige and Danny to join the Marlins swim club."

"Awesome," said Justin. "I coach for the Marlins. I'll be glad to help them out."

"You coach?" I asked. More news to me.

"I've been with the Marlins since I was five, Aerin. I know a thing or two. The coach hired me last year as an assistant."

"Huh," I said. "And I thought you were just a gearhead lifeguard who aced physics and the IM."

I helped Mags put dinner on the table, and we all sat down to eat. Justin had two helpings of everything, and when we finished he helped me clear the table and load the dishwasher. It was after seven before we took over the dining room table with my physics book and notebook. He reviewed the test material with me, quizzing me until I was confident I knew it. He had an easy way about him, which made him an excellent tutor.

"You should be a teacher," I said as I packed up my books.

"No thanks," he said.

"Why not? You're good at it. I learned more from you tonight than I have in the last two weeks with Mr. Ferrara."

"I have no intention of teaching in a classroom. Now a pool, that's a different matter," he said.

"You want to coach?" I asked, surprised.

"Why is that a shock? I've been swimming all my life. I love it, and I can't think of a better way to earn a living and continue to enjoy the sport."

"I think that's great," I said. "That's what I was hoping to do, too." It was the first time I'd verbalized that to anyone other than my career counselor.

"Yeah?" he asked, his eyes lighting up. "Where do you want to go to school?"

"I'm looking at Cal, Stanford, and Georgia. What about you?"

"Coach thinks I have a shot at a Division I school, but I'm staying close to home. Maybe Penn State or Virginia. We'll see. I've got to improve my times."

"Me too," I said. Aunt Maggie was rounding up the kids for bed, signaling the end of our evening. "You need to get going. I still have math and history homework, and I'm sure you have work to do too."

We went into the living room, and Justin said good night and thanks to Maggie and Pat. I walked him to the door, and we stepped out onto the porch.

"Thanks for your help. It made a big difference," I said, suddenly shy.

"No problem. Call me if you need any other help." He started down the steps, pulling his keys out of his pocket.

"I'll see you tomorrow," I said, remaining on the porch as he walked backward toward his Jeep.

"That's right. You guys have a meet. Who is it this time?"

"The Dragons."

"Don't sweat it. You guys will crush them."

"That's what I hear. It's getting a little boring, winning all the time."

"You want to lose?"

"No, never, I love winning, but where's the competition?"

"Two Rivers has great coaches and resources," he said. "We have the best athletics in the division. But, you'll soon meet up with the Boxers and the Bears, and they are a challenge. And don't forget the Long Island meet. You'll come up against a lot of competition there. So don't feel too complacent."

"Thanks for the pep talk."

"You going to morning practice on Friday?"

"Me?" I asked. "No way. I need my beauty sleep."

"Good excuse," he said, "but you don't look like you need any beauty sleep to me."

My face grew hot, and my heart started pounding. Had I heard him right?

"I can pick you up if you change your mind," he said.

I remained speechless as he jumped into the Jeep, shut the door, and rolled down the window, waiting for my response.

I shook my head. "No, thanks. I'm good."

"Your call," he said, "but if you want to get into a Division I school, you better step up your game." He started the Jeep, rolled up the window, and drove off with a short blast of his horn.

I watched him disappear around the corner, stunned. For the third time that day, I'd been called a slacker. First, it was Mel, who made the accusation outright, then Coach D, and now, Justin. People were beginning to notice there was more to me than I had originally let on. I couldn't let that happen, not if I wanted to stay under the radar and continue to swim for the joy of it and nothing more. Once the truth was out everyone would be on my back, pushing me to win, to excel. I'd left that all behind, and although I sometimes felt a spark of competitiveness I managed to tamp it down and stay in control. If unleashed, I'd topple the status quo at Two Rivers, upset everything, and lose a few friends. For the first time in years, people liked me for myself and not because I was a winner and brought home lots of titles and trophies. I was happy and didn't want to risk losing that.

When all sight and sound of Justin and his Jeep had vanished, I pushed away my worries and went inside to tackle the rest of my homework.

Chapter 31

I was right about Justin's tutoring skills. I scored a 94 on the physics quiz. Mr. Ferrara beamed when he handed back my paper at the end of class. "Great job, Aerin. Keep it up."

The meet against the Dragons was a home meet. I went to the pool area right after my last class and was first on deck, dressed and ready to race. I spied Justin in the back corner setting up the sound system.

"Hey," I said, "guess what?"

"You aced the quiz."

"How did you know?" I asked, a little deflated that I didn't get to break the news.

"I tutored you, remember?" His smile had my stomach doing flutter kicks.

"Well, thanks," I said, smiling back. "It helped."

"No problem."

"Can I give you a hand?"

He handed me some cables and told me where to plug them in. Around us, the rest of the team assembled on the bleachers. Coach D started the pre-meet pep talk, and handed out the psych sheets. Seconds later, moaning and griping flooded the pool deck.

"Here you go, Aerin." Coach D handed me the psych sheet. I

scrolled over the events, noting who was swimming where. I zeroed in on what had caused the flurry of excitement. He'd mixed up the lineup. None of the swimmers were in their regular events. I was in the backstroke and the IM. The IM? I hated the IM!

"Is Coach crazy?" asked Jordan. "He put me in the 500. He knows I'll sink."

"I'm doing the breast," said Erica. "What's up with that?"

"Tati's doing the fly instead of the 500! What a waste," Jordan said. "She loses a shot at breaking the record. That's not fair."

"It's not a big deal, Jordan," Tati said.

"Hold on," Coach D said. "Coach Dudash said he was going to mix things up a little bit, and you guys can beat the Dragons without swimming your usual events. That makes it more challenging."

"The relays are the same," said Tati.

I double-checked the sheet. She was right. The relay teams hadn't changed.

"I think the whole thing's stupid," Jordan said and parked herself at the end of the bleachers to sulk. A few others sat beside her, studying the psych sheet and muttering amongst themselves. I looked at Mel, who sat with Erica and Charlie. None of them appeared happy. I looked back at my sheet and saw Mel was swimming in the 500 free and the breaststroke. No wonder she looked stressed; not the best events for her, a sprinter. Erica also had the 500 free and the breaststroke, and Charlie was doing the 50 free and the IM with me. It was going to be an interesting afternoon.

Coach was right – the Dragons were pitiful. They'd lost their starting lineup to graduation and were grooming a field of newbies. Shaking things up evened out the competition, so we didn't humiliate them with a crushing loss. I appreciated Coach's decision to let the Dragons save face and give us a chance to qualify for the Division Championships in other events. Erica made the cut in the breaststroke and Charlie did in the 50. In the IM, I finished two seconds away from the cut, but I made a division time in the backstroke.

"Little hustle today, Aerin," Mel said when we were back in the locker room getting ready to go home. "Maybe you're swimming in the wrong events."

I was still bristling from her comments at lunch the day before. "I could say the same about you. That breaststroke was smoking." Mel was turning out to be an all-around swimmer, excelling in several events: the sprints, the back, and now the breast.

"The breast was my best way back when, until I started going under 27 seconds in the 50 free and Coach made me a sprinter."

"It's always a plus to be good in more than one stroke," I said.

"Which is what makes a good IM'er. Somehow I'm not surprised you do well in the back, breast, *and* fly."

I shrugged. "Look, Mel, I've been swimming since I was eight. I've had a lot of coaching, and I've been in a lot of meets. Sometimes I win, sometimes I don't. That's not why I'm here. I love to swim, and the only thing I want to do right now is enjoy it."

She stopped brushing her hair, and we stood eye to eye, staring at each other. "I get that," she said. "I do, but I don't understand why you don't work a little harder to be the best you can be. I guess I see more in you than you see in yourself. Maybe I'm wrong," she shrugged and resumed her brushing, "but I can tell when someone's not living up to her potential."

Her words stung, but I accepted them, wanting to move on. "Truce?" I asked, extending my hand for a handshake.

"Truce," she said. "I'll get off your back. You've got enough to worry about with Coach nagging you."

"You've got that right." We laughed.

"Are you going to the football game?"

"Football game?" I asked. "Unlikely."

"Why not? It's fun. Everyone goes."

"Who's everyone?"

"Well, me, Erica, most of the girls on the team, and tons of other kids. Come with us. We need to cheer on our team. Blazers Pride and all that."

Blazers Pride was the school's motto, written on everything and concluding every announcement the principal made. "When is it?"

"Tomorrow night. Starts at seven. It's a big game. Our first at home. We've had two away, won both of them. We're up against the Boxers next. They're second in the division. We're first. Should be fierce. "

"I'm not much of a football fan," I said. I'd had zero exposure to the game. My parents and I followed swimming, baseball, and tennis.

"That's okay," Mel said, zipping up her swim bag. "You'll have a good time anyway. Just follow my lead. I'll tell you when to stand up and cheer and when to boo. Make sure you bring your loudest voice. We're going to tear it up."

I laughed. Her enthusiasm convinced me. "I'll need a ride," I said.

"No problem. Erica and I will pick you up."

"Okay. I just have to check with Aunt Mags, make sure she doesn't need me to babysit or anything."

"The Flynn's will be at the game. Pat Flynn used to be a tight end for the Blazers and Maggie was a cheerleader."

"I did not know that," I said, picturing Mags in a cheerleader get up and Uncle Pat in football gear. "But now that I think about it, it makes sense."

"Yeah, big rivalry tomorrow night. The stadium will be rocking."

Chapter 32

Mel and Erica picked me up just minutes after Aunt Mags and Uncle Pat drove off in the minivan packed with their very own cheering squad, all of them decked out in Blazers sweatshirts. Aunt Maggie wore Uncle Pat's old varsity jacket, and he sported a fleece pullover with the Blazers lightning bolt logo embroidered across its back. They also had stadium blankets in the school colors, a thermos of hot chocolate, and a basket of homemade cider donuts.

I got into the backseat of Erica's Honda and we took off.

"What's in the bag?" Mel asked.

"Aunt Maggie made cider donuts," I said, shaking it. "I've got about a dozen."

"Awesome," she said, reaching for it. She peeked in and inhaled. "Yum. We'll hang on to these for later." She handed them back.

Traffic heading into the parking lot was heavy. Fans dressed in the Blazers' blue and white school colors clogged the lanes, making their way to the football field. Erica cruised the lot, searching for a spot. Mel checked out the crowd, pointing out friends and teammates. "Look, there's Charlie."

"Who's she with?" I asked.

"Her mom."

I recognized Charlie's mom from seeing her at meets and

picking up Charlie after practice. We waved as we passed them and Charlie shouted, "I'll save you a seat."

Erica found a parking spot at the farthest end and we started walking to the field. We were at the tail end of Indian summer and the days were still warm, but since the sun had set, a chill descended on us and I stopped to put on my sweatshirt – not Blazers' wear but a red and white souvenir from a Cape Cod vacation. Mel and Erica stopped too, and pulled their team hoodies over their heads.

"Oh," I said, "I didn't even think about wearing my Blazers hoodie."

"I should have told you," Mel said. "All the athletes wear their team gear. I'm sorry."

We joined the stream of fans heading into the field, showed our student ID's at the gate to get free admission, and climbed into the stands, searching for the rest of the team. They were in the middle of the muddle, some of them holding signs they'd made to cheer the team on: "Go Blazers! Beat the Boxers!" "Blazers Pride!" and "TRHS Swimming Loves Blazers Football!" Jordan held that last one.

Charlie gestured to us to join her, and we slid into the bleachers right behind Jordan and Tati, both in varsity jackets with their swimming letters attached. Tati had a bullhorn. She turned as we settled in behind her.

"Hey," she said. "You guys made it."

Jordan turned to look at us.

"Nice sweatshirt, Apple," she said with a smirk.

"Like it?" I asked. "I got it on Cape Cod."

"No kidding."

Before I could respond, a roar ripped through the crowd. The game was about to start, and everyone jumped to their feet. What followed next was a type of mass hysteria I'd never seen before. A boom of applause exploded from their fans when the opposing team burst onto the field. Our team came out seconds later accompanied by a marching band and the rumble of the crowd stomping their feet on the metal bleachers. Caught up in the excitement, I stomped and screamed with everybody else. A minute later the crowd was seated, the opening preliminaries ended, and the game began.

I followed along as best as I could, counting on Mel and Erica to clue me in on what I was supposed to do. When a Blazers' player had the ball and started running, I stood up and cheered. When the Boxers' had the ball, I sat on the edge of my seat, tense and waiting for the play to end. At the end of the first quarter, we were ahead, 10-7.

Jordan and Tati were loudest of all - their boyfriends were on the field. Tati held a sign with the number 24 painted on it and Jordan had one with 56, their guys' numbers.

"What position does Travis play?" I shouted into Mel's ear.

"Quarterback," she shouted back. "He's not bad, either. "

The cheerleaders on the sidelines revved up the crowd with cheers, tumbling, dancing, and jumping. They looked like they were having a lot of fun, and for a minute I wondered if I would have preferred cheerleading over swimming. I quickly nixed the idea. I'd never be caught outdoors in a skimpy little skirt on a chilly fall evening. I gathered my sweatshirt tighter around me and refocused on the game.

"What's happening?" I asked Mel. The team was leaving the field.

"Half-time," she said. "We take a break. Time to go to the bathroom and get something to drink." The three of us joined the crowd streaming out of the bleachers, waited in line for the restroom, and waited in another line for hot chocolate. The hot cup warmed my cold hands. I was starting to wish I'd worn more than a sweatshirt.

"Let's have those donuts," Erica said. I pulled the bag out of my pocket, and she passed them out.

A familiar voice spoke from behind me. "What are you guys

eating?"

I didn't have to turn around to know it was Justin. A little chill ran through me, and it wasn't because of the colder temperature. I'd figured Justin would be at the game, but I'd tried to put him out of my mind while learning the fundamentals of football and spending time with my team.

"Aerin's aunt made cider donuts," Mel said.

"Can I have one?" he asked, looking at me with that irresistible grin of his.

"Of course," I said, and Erica handed him the bag.

"Just one," she said and supervised his helping himself.

He extracted one, took a big bite and closed his eyes, an expression of pure bliss on his face. "Maggie Flynn makes the best cider donuts."

"How do you know?" I asked

"She makes them for all the games, and if I'm lucky I manage to find her before she runs out."

"I didn't know you and Maggie were so chummy." More surprises, and why hadn't Maggie said anything?

"She's friends with my mom. I've known her all my life."

I remembered Maggie telling me that she and Mrs. Ford were in some club together. It made sense they knew each other's kids.

"We need to get back to our seats. The game's already started," Mel said.

"And we're ahead," Justin said, walking along with us. "Think we got this one, Apple?"

"Looks good to me," I said, although I didn't have a clue.

The third quarter was even more exciting than the first half. The Boxers scored two touchdowns and took the lead, 21-10. The crowd went wild, both parents and students screaming and stomping during every play, cheering and booing as if their very lives depended on the game. Even my teammates were wild with excitement, Tati shouting through her bullhorn, Jordan standing on the bleachers with her

"56" sign raised high and screeching like a lunatic. Mel and Erica screamed themselves hoarse. Charlie sat beside me almost as bewildered as I was but caught up in the excitement, shouting along with the others and clapping her hands raw. Justin sat almost motionless, watching the action on the field with narrowed eyes, muttering under his breath.

"Crazy crowd," I said, leaning into him so he'd hear me.

"Don't see that at a swim meet."

I nodded. He was right. Even in the most contentious of meets, attendance was limited, and the crowd controlled. "I don't think I could swim with that much noise."

"Yes, you could," he said. "That kind of response feeds them," he gestured toward the players on the field. Blazers had the ball. One of our players took it down to the Boxers' twenty-yard line. The crowd bellowed, on their feet. The air was ripe with expectation. On the next play, our player got clearance and entered the end zone. Touchdown! The noise from the crowd was thunderous. The score was now 21-17, Blazers trailing, and the third quarter finished.

"This crowd wants blood," Justin said.

"It's kind of scary," I said. "These players can get hurt."

"Someone always does," he said.

The players huddled to start the next quarter, Blazers kicking off. The ball went high and long and landed in number 24's - Sean Hines, Tati's boyfriend – beefy arms. He took it and ran, dodging players all the way up the field, the Boxers' closing in on him. At the last second, he handed the ball off to Travis, number 56, who veered to his right into a path free of any opposition. The stadium went wild – a touchdown could win the game – as Travis barreled down the field clutching the ball. From his left came a Boxer running just as fast, and with a leap he came down on Travis, knocking the ball out of his hands and slamming him into the ground. The two were soon lost in a pile of players while the referees blasted their whistles.

"Travis!" screamed Jordan, her face white. She grabbed on to

Tati's arm and clung to her.

The Blazers crowd roared, faces contorted in anger.

One by one, the players pulled out of the pile and joined their teammates, the Boxers backslapping each other in victory for having stopped the touchdown, the Blazers hovering over the last lone body on the field. Travis lay still on the ground, making no effort to get up, the coaches huddled around him.

"What's happening?" I asked. The crowd grew hushed as it sunk in that our player might be hurt.

"It doesn't look good," Justin said. "Look, my mom's on the field."

Dr. Ford had joined the huddle around Travis and took command of the situation, giving rapid fire orders and gesturing wildly with her hands.

A murmur rushed through the crowd as people took their seats, watching and waiting while Dr. Ford and the coaches attended to Travis.

"What's happening?" cried Jordan. She and Tati were the only members of the swim team still on their feet. "Get up, Travis!" Jordan shouted.

"He's going to be all right," Tati said, patting her on the back. "He just needs a minute."

Minutes passed while we waited for Travis to move, to do *something.* He lifted his head and then put it back down. He stretched his arms and legs, and the trainer tested his range of motion in all extremities, which looked okay. Still, our quarterback didn't get up on his own.

One of the coaches and the trainer each hooked him under an arm and sat him up. The crowd roared. Seconds later, they had him on his feet and escorted him off the field. From the bleachers on both sides, the fans clapped and cheered, applauding him as he left the field and the game.

Chapter 33

"Come on. We're going to the field house to find out what's happening," Jordan said, pulling Tati as she made her way through the crowd and exited the bleachers.

"Is he going to be all right?" I asked Justin.

He shook his head. "I don't know. He got slammed pretty bad. The ref should penalize that Boxer. He had no reason to jump on Travis so hard. He could have taken him down without landing on him like a ton of bricks." He stood up. "I'm going down to the field house."

The game continued, but without Travis and the uncertainty of his condition the Blazers lost their steam. The Boxers took full advantage, scoring two more touchdowns and winning the game 35-17.

Dejected Blazers fans remained in the bleachers, subdued after witnessing Travis' injury and losing the game. Even the crowd on the other side of the field was quiet, their victory tainted.

"I hope Travis is okay," Mel said.

"Did you see the way that guy flew out of the air and landed on his head?" Erica asked.

"I don't like football," Charlie said, her voice small.

Her mom joined us. "Time to go, Charlie."

"I can't go until I hear Travis is all right," she said, sniffling.

"You girls have an early practice in the morning," her mom reminded us.

We had a coin drop at the supermarket at 10:00. Coach scheduled practice for 7:00 so we could get a couple of hours in before we begged the town to give us money to pay for our team trip.

"You girls need to get some sleep," said Charlie's mom. "I'm sure Travis will be okay. He just got the wind knocked out of him."

"I'll text you as soon as I hear something," Mel told Charlie. "Don't worry. He'll be okay."

Charlie continued to look worried but collected her things and left with her mother.

"We should go, too," Erica said.

The field was clear of players, coaches, and officials, the lights illuminating it. The stands had dwindled to a few hangers on waiting for word on our player.

People moved on as the minutes passed, gathering their children and their game gear to head home. Cars lined up to leave the parking lot. From the distance came the wail of a siren, and we clambered to the top of the bleachers to look out over the parking lot to the street. In moments, an ambulance had turned onto the road leading to our school, its siren now muted. Exiting vehicles parted the way and in seconds, the ambulance entered the stadium.

"It looks bad," Mel said.

The remaining spectators began to stream out of the bleachers and made their way toward the exits. When we arrived at the field house, Travis was bundled on a stretcher and EMT's were loading him into the rear of the ambulance. The doors closed, the EMT's climbed on board, and the ambulance took off. As soon as it left the school grounds, its siren started blaring.

Mel's mom was talking to the coaches and trainer. When their conversation ended, she joined us.

"Is he going to be all right?" Mel asked.

Dr. Ford nodded. "I think so, but he may have sustained a concussion. We'll see what the CAT scan says."

Justin was standing next to his mom. "He could be out for the rest of the season," he said.

"That's a real possibility," Dr. Ford said. "He'll miss the next few games at the least."

"There goes our football season," Justin said.

"Oh, who cares about football?" Mel said. "Travis is hurt."

That hushed everybody up. After all, it was only a game.

"We'll know more in the morning," said Dr. Ford. "You girls need to go home and get to sleep. Big day tomorrow. I'm heading to the hospital. Travis is my patient. I'll see you in the morning."

"Can I come with you?" Justin asked.

"Sure, but we're going to be out late."

"That's okay." They left.

With Travis gone to the hospital, the night was over. School security guards ordered people to leave the field. As the last of the stragglers made for the parking lot, Mel, Erica, and I plodded along behind them, not saying much.

As soon as Erica started her Honda, Mel got a text message. She read it and said, "Tati and Jordan went to the hospital. Tati will text everyone when the test results come in."

They dropped me off. When I entered the house, Aunt Mags and Uncle Pat were sitting at the kitchen table drinking tea. The house was quiet, all the kids tucked in their beds.

"Any news about Travis?" Aunt Mags asked.

"They took him to the hospital. Dr. Ford thinks he has a concussion." I pulled up a chair and poured a cup of tea.

"Tough going," Uncle Pat said. "It's one of the dangers of football."

"And they're getting stricter about it these days," Mags said. "Even in the NFL. They say these concussions can cause brain injury and lead to dementia later in life."

"Sounds serious," I said, worried for Travis. He wasn't a friend – I knew him only as Jordan's boyfriend, a fellow athlete, and a classmate - but I felt bad for him and his family, and for Jordan too, because her reaction to his injury showed how much she cared for him. I thought about how I'd feel if I were in her shoes. I doubted she'd sleep tonight. I'd be surprised if she made practice or the coin drop in the morning.

I went up to bed. Before turning in, I readied for the next day, putting my practice bag together and setting out an outfit to wear to the coin drop. Coach wanted us in our swim gear: sweatpants and hoodies. Mine was fresh out of the laundry and smelled like the detergent Aunt Mags used, a flowery fragrance, not too strong. I buried my face in their softness. When I wore these articles of clothing, I felt like I belonged somewhere, like I fit in. This was new for me because I'd never connected with any other team like I had with the Blazers.

Coach was right. Everyone cared. I realized that after witnessing the evening's events. Everyone at the game cared, whether the team won or lost, and they cared when one of their own was hurt, sticking together to reassure each other everything would be okay. Waiting to find out what happened to Travis. Worrying that his season – his career – might be over. Staying up late to hear what the CAT scan showed and what the doctors said. Two Rivers was a tight knit community, and I was part of it.

I climbed into bed, exhausted, my alarm set for 6:30. I kept my phone by my hand, waiting for a text from Tati. It buzzed me awake at 1:00 am with bad news. Travis had a concussion. His football season was finished.

I turned the phone off and placed it in its cradle. I tried to fall back to sleep, but my mind was racing. I thought about Travis, forced out of his last high school season. I'm sure when he felt better he'd be angry and disappointed. I wondered how I'd feel if I got knocked out of my season by an injury. I'd been lucky – nothing but sore muscles and a mild shoulder strain had caused me any pain, and still I got in the water. Concussions were almost unheard of in swimming, although it did sometimes happen when a swimmer miscalculated and crashed into the wall, or another swimmer kicked her in the head. Forced out of swimming by injury? I guess that would be the worst that could happen.

Here was Travis, playing a sport he loved, excelling, counting on it to help him get into a good college and score a decent scholarship, knocked out of his game by an accident.

Here I was, strong, healthy, and uninjured, competing in a sport I loved, pretending to be an average swimmer, and cheating myself and my team out of what I could achieve.

In light of tonight's events, it seemed silly.

Maybe it was time to reexamine my motives.

Chapter 34

As I expected, Jordan did not make it to practice Saturday morning, but Tatiana was the first to arrive, looking a little beat up after her long night at the hospital waiting for word on Travis. Coach let us take the first few minutes to fill the team in on what happened at the football game, and then he blasted his whistle and herded us all into the pool.

Practice was short due to the coin drop scheduled for most of the day and we did a quick 5,000 yards before climbing out to shower and change into our team sweats.

Mel, Charlie, and I had the first two-hour shift at the Shop & Save. Asking total strangers for money was a bit awkward, but the way they readily reached into their pockets and dumped what they found into our buckets was encouraging.

One lady dropped a twenty dollar bill into Mel's bucket. "My daughter used to swim for Two Rivers," she said, smiling. "Have a great season."

"Whoa!" said Charlie. "Look at that!"

"Her daughter was a flyer," Mel said. "She was a senior my first year. Pretty good, too."

With Charlie's mom acting as chaperone we raked in the cash, filling our bucket halfway before the shift ended and Erica took over with a couple of the freshmen girls.

"That was fun," I said as Mel and I headed for her Mom's Volvo. Mel jangled the keys. It was her first solo trip after getting her driver's license the week before. She was supposed to drive me home and then meet her mother at the hospital where she had morning rounds.

"Are you going to check on Travis?" I asked, buckling in for the ride. Mel still hadn't gotten the hang of accelerating, and we jerked back and forth a few times before she swung into traffic.

"Yeah," she said, concentrating on making a right turn. "Want to come?"

"I can't," I said. "I'm heading down to my father's place. It's his weekend. Keep me posted on how Travis is doing."

"Mom said he's doing much better. He'll be released this afternoon."

"That's good news."

"It's too bad he'll miss the rest of the season. I don't know what I'd do if that happened to me. It messes things up for him."

"My mom would say it's a sign he should focus on other things," I said.

"Like what?"

"His grades. College."

"He needs a football scholarship."

"Maybe he needs to work on his grades instead. Maybe he shouldn't count on a football scholarship to get through college. It's not a sure thing."

"He's not a great student. He'll probably end up at the community college."

"Whatever," I said. Travis's options didn't concern me. If he thought football was his ticket to college without studying, he was a fool.

"When will you be back?" she asked, pulling up in front of Aunt Maggie's house.

"Tomorrow. I'm taking the two o'clock train. Look for me around four. You got something in mind?"

"Youth group meeting at 3:00. Guess you'll miss it."

"Keep me posted."

"We need the first installment for the Haiti trip. Three hundred bucks."

"No problem," I said. I'd decided to forgo asking my dad for the money. He'd probably say no, tell me to concentrate on my studies and swimming, maybe tie it to my performance. I'd dip into my savings - I had enough saved up to pay for the trip.

Mel parked in front of Maggie's house. I got out of her car and grabbed my swim gear from the back seat. "See you Monday." With a few jerks and some hard stops, she was on her way.

When I entered my father's house, it was unusually quiet. The kitchen was vacant; the only sound the drone of the refrigerator.

"Hey!" I called. "Is anyone home?"

"We're back here," Emily hollered from the other side of the house.

I followed her voice to the family room. She and Avery lay camped out on one sofa and Dawn lay on the other. A movie played on the home theater system, and the room was dark, blinds drawn, lights out.

I dropped my bags on the floor and collapsed into a recliner. "Movie time?" I asked.

"Momma's resting," Avery said.

Dawn was asleep, her eyelids fluttering, her face pale. She had dark circles under her eyes. An afghan covered her, and she had slipper socks on her feet. Her short blonde hair was uncombed and rising in peaks all over the top of her head. She must have sensed my presence because she opened her eyes. Adjusting to the low light, she focused and gave me a weak smile.

"Hey, Aerin," she said. She kicked her legs, letting the afghan fall to the floor, and sat up.

"Don't get up for me," I said, not sure if that was good for her or not. Dad said she needed full bed rest. Her rounded belly strained against her t-shirt.

"I need to move," she said and yawned. "What time is it?"

"After three."

"Oh my, they must be on the second viewing of this movie. Come on girls," she picked up the remote and stopped the movie.

"Mom!" Emily shrieked.

"Show time's over. I want you girls to go out and play, get some air. You can't stay in the house all day, especially when it's so gorgeous outside."

"*You're* staying in," Emily said, the usual pout on her face.

"I want to stay with you," Avery wailed.

"Where's Geneviève?" Dawn asked. "Ask her to take you outside. Time for tennis practice."

"Mommmmmm," Emily said, drawing out the word with exasperation. "The movie's not done yet, and I wanted to watch another one. We can practice tomorrow."

"No more movies," Dawn said. "That's all we've been doing all day. Time for tennis practice and then reading. Geneviève!" she called.

Emily and Avery continued to whine, but Dawn ignored them. Geneviève's footsteps sounded on the stairs and the Belgian *au pair* entered the family room.

"Yes, Mrs. Keane?" she asked. "You called?"

"It's time for the girls' tennis practice. Please take them outside and get them started. I need to speak with Aerin."

"Salut Aerin," Geneviève said, her face lighting up. "Ça va?"

"Ça va, et toi?"

"Comme ci comme ça. We'll talk later. Come on girls. Outside as Maman says." She took Avery by the arm and led her outside with

Emily trailing behind, continuing to plead for a missed practice and another movie.

Dawn sighed. "This bed rest is harder than I imagined. My girls expect me to organize their days and activities. They don't know what to do when I'm not leading them."

"Where's my dad?" I asked.

"He had to go into the city. Big client meeting, last minute. He sent his apologies and said he hopes to be home for dinner, but he warned me we might be on our own."

Great. Hours of Dawn and her girls without my father as a buffer. Not my favorite way to spend a Saturday.

"How are you?" I asked. Now that she was upright, her color had returned, and she seemed a little more like herself.

"I'm tired all the time, and I don't even *do* anything," she laughed. "You know me. I can't stand still. Keeping off my feet is a challenge."

I laughed too. "I don't think I've ever seen you lying on the couch in the middle of the day."

"Would you mind getting the shades?" she asked.

I opened all the shades, letting in the afternoon sunlight, bathing the room in a soft glow. Books and magazines lay in abandoned piles. The girls' toys sprawled across the floor. Barbie dolls were piled high in an armchair. Legos lay scattered across the coffee table. Empty glasses and half-empty bottles of juice and water littered the end tables.

"What a mess," Dawn said. "Oh well. I'll get the girls to pick up when they come inside."

"That ought to be easy," I said.

"You're right," she sighed. "They haven't embraced my imposed bed rest too well. So much change. Someone comes in every day for cooking and cleaning, but not on the weekends. Geneviève's a big help, and your father has taken over everything else. He just can't be here today."

"I can help," I said, picking up glasses.

"No, Aerin, you don't need to do that," she said, but I persisted, removing all of the glasses and setting them in the dishwasher. I picked up the half-empty bottles of juice and water and put them in the fridge. I grabbed a clean sponge, dampened it, and wiped down the glass tabletops.

"That's enough," Dawn said. "Sit down. I want to talk to you about something." She patted the sofa beside her. I took the chair across from her. She pretended not to notice the distance I'd set between us.

"Your father said you're going to a dance," she said.

I nodded. "Next weekend. It's at the church."

"That's exciting," she said, her eyes bright, cheeks flushed, a stark contrast to the woman I'd seen when I first entered the room. "Your first dance."

"Yeah, I guess so." I hadn't thought of it that way, but she was right. I'd never attended a dance, too busy swimming and studying.

"We need to buy you a dress."

"A dress?" I wasn't a dress kind of girl.

"Well, you're wearing a dress, aren't you? It's that kind of dance?"

"I guess so," I said, unsure, thinking hard about what Mel had said she was wearing. I was pretty sure I'd heard the word *dress.* I had a few in my closet back in Manhattan but hadn't brought any to Two Rivers, not suspecting I'd need one.

"If I wasn't glued to the couch I'd take you shopping for a whole new outfit, but I'm stuck here. So, here's what we're going to do. Once the girls come in from practice and Geneviève settles them down for reading time, you and she will go to the mall and pick out the prettiest dress you can find, and the shoes and accessories to match. I'll give you my credit card. Three hundred ought to be enough, right?"

"Three hundred?" I asked, stunned by the offer.

"Three hundred dollars," she said.

"Yeah, that sounds about right," I said, having no idea how much such an ensemble would cost. My mother did all my clothes shopping with me. I thought of her confined to her room at the correctional facility and longed for her to go on this shopping trip. Impossible.

"Thank you," I said. "I'd like that."

"I wish I could go with you. I love dress shopping." Her eyes gleamed. "Maybe next time."

The sound of a door opening and slamming against a wall, followed by footsteps and voices raised in argument shattered the peace in the room.

"I'm telling Mom," Avery said.

"Go ahead, you big baby," Emily said.

"Girls, girls, shhh, Maman is resting," said Geneviève, bringing up the rear.

They burst into the room. Avery and Emily surrounded their mother, bombarding her with their argument. Geneviève stayed out of it, meeting my eyes and rolling hers. "Happens all the time," she mouthed.

"I know," I mouthed back.

"Enough, girls," Dawn said in her tone that silenced them. "Wash up and get a drink of water. Then come back here and pick up your toys before reading time." They didn't argue but followed her orders with foot-dragging and exaggerated pouts. Silence again descended on the room, and I felt a moment of extreme gratefulness.

Dawn explained her plan to Geneviève, who perked up at the prospect of a trip to the mall. She ran up to her room to get her purse. Dawn reached into her purse and extracted a Visa card. She handed it to me with a smile. "Have fun," she said.

"I will. And thank you. Keep your phone handy. When I find something I like, I'll send you a picture, and you let me know what you think."

She seemed touched. “I will. And thanks for keeping me in the loop.”

“No problem.”

Chapter 35

My dad came home long after the girls and Dawn had gone to bed. Geneviève and I were in the family room engrossed in a movie. He plopped down on the couch beside me with a groan.

"Long day," I said. Years ago, when he, my mom, and I lived together, long days were the norm, but since he'd started his practice and ran things from his home office he wasn't usually out late. He looked beat.

"I'm sorry I wasn't here for you today, but we hammered out the details of the contract. I won't have to meet with them tomorrow, so we'll do something fun," he said. "How was your day?"

"Great. Geneviève and I went shopping for the dance and Dawn paid for everything. Want to see?"

I jumped up from the couch and took my dress and the accompanying bag of accessories from the hall closet. The salesgirl had packed the dress in a fancy white box. I peeled back the tissue paper and held the dress up for his approval. It was a short – but not too short – lavender – but not purple - creation, strapless with a sweetheart neckline, pleated bodice, and a twirly skirt. The back tied together like a corset. Geneviève and I found it after I tried on almost a gazillion dresses. It took hours, and we visited every store in the mall. Drained, but still optimistic, we ventured into the last store and found it, the most beautiful dress I'd ever seen. It fit like it was made for me, too.

I also found a strappy pair of silver sandals with the highest heels I'd ever worn. A visit to a jewelry boutique completed the outfit with a tiny amethyst pendant and matching earrings. I modeled everything for Dawn when we got back, and she was almost as excited as I was.

"Pretty," my father said.

"Wait," I said, "I'll try it on so you can get the whole effect." Geneviève and I went up to my room, and I put everything on. Dad was half-asleep when we came back downstairs but almost jumped out of his seat when he saw me.

I twirled in front of him, beaming. "So? What do you think?"

"You look beautiful," he said, "but where did my little girl go?"

"Oh please, don't get corny."

"You'll be the belle of the ball."

"Stop."

"Honey," he said, "you look great. Make sure you take lots of pictures."

"Of course. I have to send them to Mom. She's bummed out she's going to miss everything."

A somber moment passed, but I broke it with a smile, grabbing my hair up and piling it on top of my hand. "What do you think? Up?" I dropped it and let it swirl around my shoulders. "Or down?"

"Down," said Geneviève.

"Down," Dad agreed. "You have such pretty red hair, like someone else I know." We both shared the same thick auburn hair, but it looked better on me.

"Maybe I should get a trim," I said, holding the ends up to the light. Hours in the chlorinated pool made my hair dry and split the ends.

"I can do that," Geneviève said. "We'll do it now, before bed."

"Okay," I said, "and thanks for the dress and everything, Dad."

"Don't thank me, thank Dawn. It was her idea."

That stopped me in my tracks. "Well, it's very nice of her."

"She's known to be nice sometimes," he said with a smile.

I nodded, collected all the packaging for my party outfit, and started upstairs. "Good night, Dad. See you in the morning."

"How do you plan to get home with all that stuff?" he asked. "A bit awkward for the train. I'll drive you back to Maggie's, okay?"

"Good idea," I said. "I hadn't thought about getting all this stuff home."

"What time are you leaving?"

"I was planning to take the two o'clock train."

"Then two it is. That'll give us time for lunch."

I handed my purchases off to Geneviève and backed down the steps, meeting him at the foot of the stairs. I pulled him in for a hug and laid a kiss on his cheek. "Goodnight Daddy."

He hugged me back and ruffled my hair. "Goodnight Princess." He hadn't called me that in a long time, and the sound of his voice wrapped around the word warmed me all over as I went upstairs.

Chapter 36

Sunday mornings at Dad's house were laid back. He and Dawn didn't attend church. She was Episcopalian and he was Catholic and they hadn't yet figured out how to practice together. We all slept in, including Emily and Avery, who strolled into the kitchen long after Geneviève and I had finished breakfast. My father had gone out for bagels, and as soon as we'd cleaned up the kitchen after our breakfast he had to make a second meal for the girls.

"What are we doing today?" Avery asked as she smeared strawberry cream cheese on half a bagel. Her hair was a mess, sticking up every which way, and she had lines etched into her right cheek from snuggling up to her blankets.

"We're going to clean this place up," my dad said, shuffling the Sunday papers. He read the *Times*, the *Wall Street Journal*, and the local paper.

"Why do *we* have to clean up? Isn't that lady coming here tomorrow?" Emily asked as she poured herself a glass of orange juice. She was put together better than her sister, her hair brushed back into a tight ponytail, her pajamas swapped for jeans and a pink sweatshirt with a ballerina on it.

"Yes, she is, but we need to clean up today," Dad said.

"I don't want to stay in and clean the house. I want to go out and do something," Emily said.

"Me too," said Avery. She licked at a dot of cream cheese stuck to her wrist.

"After we clean up, we'll do something fun. What did you have in mind?" Dad organized the different newspapers into neat piles.

"I want to go to that funny new movie," Emily said. "Everyone at school will see it this weekend."

"I thought you didn't want to stay inside," I said.

"I don't want to stay inside this *house*," she clarified.

"No, you've watched too many movies," my dad said. Emily gave him a dark look and was about to open her mouth again when he said, "Hey, I've got a great idea. Why don't we go apple picking? We can go to the orchard and then drive Aerin home."

"I want to go to the movies," Emily said, sitting back in her chair and folding her arms, ready to fight. "I'll be the only girl in school who misses it."

"Come on, Ems," Dad said. "Look out that window. It's gorgeous out there, and we all need some fresh air and exercise. We'll go to the movie another day this week."

She looked out the window. The sun was shining, the sky an azure blue and cloudless. The leaves were already starting to turn their fall colors. "Well," she said, drawing it out, "I'll do the apple thing but only if we go to the movie one day after school, like *tomorrow*, and I'm not going on any long car rides today." No doubt she'd be a major player in some law firm someday.

"Then I'll bring you and your sister back here after the orchard, and you can stay with Geneviève and your mother while I drive Aerin home. Deal?"

"I want Mama to come," Avery said, teary-eyed, the second half of her bagel forgotten.

"Mama can't come," Emily told her, "she has to stay home because of the new baby."

"Mama can't do anything anymore," Avery said, her lower lip

trembling. Oh no, here come the waterworks.

"The baby will be here before we know it and Mama will be back on her feet," my dad said, steering them in a new direction. Meltdowns would spoil the rest of the morning. "Who's done with breakfast? Let's clean up and when we're finished we'll pick some apples. Later we'll make some applesauce, okay?"

It didn't take long to tidy the house, and the girls helped, making their beds, taking their laundry to the laundry room, and putting their toys away. Dawn reclined on the sofa in the family room reading a book.

"You girls are doing a great job," she said when they came to say goodbye. "You're my little helpers."

"I'll pick you a nice big apple, Mama," Avery said, wrapping her arms around her neck and giving her a wet kiss.

Emily hovered over her, fussing with her blanket.

"Thanks, Em," Dawn said, giving her a beautiful smile.

Emily shrugged. "We're making applesauce later," she said, "Gordon promised."

"Yes, I did," my father said. He kissed Dawn on the forehead. "I'll pick up a rotisserie chicken on the way home, and throw together some sides for supper."

"Yum," Dawn said. "That sounds good."

Emily and Avery argued over who would ride shotgun, but my father squashed that argument by putting me in the front seat and the girls in back with Geneviève. Their pouting didn't last long, though, as we headed into the countryside to an apple orchard about fifteen miles away, enjoying the crisp air with the windows down, and counting the number of trees that had already turned full color.

The orchard was chaos with people coming from miles away for apple and pumpkin picking, and jugs of fresh apple cider. We picked a half bushel of apples, all kinds, and sampled the homemade cider donuts. Emily and Avery wanted to choose pumpkins for carving and spent a half hour in the pumpkin patch making their selections.

Dad bought two gallons of cider, and we were on our way home.

After a quick lunch of PB and J sandwiches and milk, I packed up my stuff, and Dad and I headed to Maggie's.

Chapter 37

This was as good as it got: my father all to myself for ninety minutes, maybe two hours if traffic was heavy. No bickering from Emily and Avery in the back seat. No giving up the front seat to Dawn. I was again riding co-pilot.

I adjusted the AC on my side and tuned the radio station to today's top hits. My father turned down the volume from the controls on the steering wheel.

"Did you have fun at the orchard?" he asked.

"Yeah," I said. When I was younger, my parents took me apple picking every autumn, driving out to Long Island for the day, filling our baskets to overflowing and spending the rest of the weekend baking apple pies and making applesauce. A sweet memory from my childhood.

"I think the girls enjoyed it. Of course, they would have had a better time if Dawn had come along, but we're learning to spend time together on our own, and that's important."

"I suppose it is," I said.

"The pregnancy is tough on them. They're too young to understand."

"It won't last long, and when the baby's born I'm sure they'll be ecstatic."

"I hope so," he said. "What about you? Will you be ecstatic?"

I shrugged. Sometimes the thought of a little brother or sister excited me. Other times, I suspected he or she would just be someone else coming between my father and me. "I just hope there's enough of you to go around."

He didn't respond, the miles speeding behind us on the Thruway. "You feel left out," he said at last.

"Left out. Left behind."

"It doesn't help that we live so far apart."

"No, but I can't live with you and Dawn and the girls. It's too much."

"You know I'd do anything to have you with me."

"No, you wouldn't," I said. "If that was so, you'd have to leave them, and that's not happening." These words were difficult to speak aloud. I guess I'd been hoping he'd wake up one day and realize his marriage to Dawn was a mistake and come home to my mom and me, or, at least, move out of the McMansion. A baby erased all possibility of that happening.

"This is my new life, Aerin. Nothing is going to change. I have you, Dawn, Emily and Avery, and this new child. You have to accept it."

"I know," I said, my voice small.

"It's been four years."

I nodded, not trusting my voice.

"I'm sorry I've hurt you."

I waved my hand at him to stop. "We're so past that," I said willing my voice not to quiver.

"Are we?"

"Yeah."

He nodded and tapped out a rhythm on the steering wheel. The mood in the car seemed lighter. I sat back in my seat, more at peace than I'd felt in a long time. Coming to terms with him and his new life was a long time coming, but now that I'd accepted our new normal, I knew everything would be okay.

"We haven't had much time to talk about you. Everything all right?"

"Yeah."

"Have you heard from your mother?"

"I got a letter the other day." She'd written three pages, most of it about her progress with her therapy, her swimming, and her new job in the library, sorting and shelving cartons of books some church had donated. "She's doing okay, adjusting to life in that place. She said she might be getting some new privileges at the end of the month, and maybe she'll be able to send email."

"That sounds good. I've only heard from her once. I wish she'd write again."

"I'll tell her."

Traffic backed up on the Thruway, and we idled a while. In the late afternoon, the leaf peepers and apple pickers headed home. Poor Dad. He'd have to face the same traffic in reverse after he left me at Maggie's.

"It's unfortunate your mother had to go to such extremes to get help for her problems," he said, his eyes fixed on the car ahead as he inched us forward.

"She never does things the easy way," I said. "I think she's learning to slow down, to realize that it's not her job to save the world."

"That's what I loved about her," he mused. "She was never afraid to fight for her beliefs. She put everything she had into righting wrongs. Sometimes she put in too much."

Like us, I thought but didn't say it, understanding that the same words reverberated in his head, too.

"You were once the same way," I said.

He nodded. "The two of us made a formidable pair. From day one it was Gordon and Devon against the world."

"What happened?"

"We grew up. We wanted to change the world, but when we took on jobs, marriage, a child, a mortgage, we didn't have time to fix the world. We barely had time to build a decent world for ourselves.

"I realized it a lot sooner than your mother did, and chose a more stable work environment where the risks were small and the rewards were great. Devon kept going, trying to save the world one patient at a time at St. Vincent's, rattling the powers that be about healthcare for the homeless, volunteering at soup kitchens and shelters, always striving to do good no matter the cost. I'm not saying her work wasn't necessary or important, but it took a lot away from what we were trying to accomplish as a family."

The traffic started moving, and he shifted gears, accelerating and moving into the left lane to pass the minivan in front of us.

"I managed to get out of that trap, but your mother loved it," he continued as we once again sped down the Thruway. "She thrived on it, and couldn't stop. Then the worst catastrophe that ever hit our country occurred and she was right in the middle of it, and couldn't let it go. I can't blame her – I almost gave up my job at the firm to get involved with the post-September 11th effort - but by that time our marriage was in trouble and showed no signs of reconciliation, so I stayed my course to keep things afloat at home."

His version of the story sounded a lot like Maggie's, and I saw no reason to disagree with him.

"Her joining the Army Reserve ended things for us."

"She couldn't help it," I said in her defense. "She was compelled to join."

"I get that," he said, "but I couldn't accept it."

"And here we are now."

"And here we are now."

A mile or two rolled by in silence as we each absorbed these words. We couldn't go back to what we were before. Our lives had diverged in such different directions. I was the one caught in the middle, pulled two ways, and at the same time preparing to embark on my own undefined journey. Scary.

"Change of subject," he said, breaking the silence, which had gone on too long. "How's school?"

"Okay," I said. "I'm keeping up with all my classes. My GPA is right where we want it. I'm even doing well with physics." I left out the part that I had a tutor. Justin continued to help me complete lab reports and study for tests and quizzes.

"What's going on with college? Many schools are holding open houses. Any you want to visit?"

"Most of the schools I'm interested in are far away. Let's wait until I get in before we spend the time and money to visit."

"Are you thinking about the big swim schools again?"

I shrugged.

"Are your times good enough for these schools?"

"Are you kidding?" I asked, turning to look at him.

"I'm tracking your events online, and I've got to admit I'm not impressed."

"I'm keeping up," I said. "I made the cuts last season. I still have half a season left."

"They're evaluating you on what they see right now," he said. "I guess you're sticking to your plan to swim to keep your head straight, and not to win." He shook his head and laughed.

"What?" I asked, annoyed he was mocking me.

"How do you not win?" he asked. "I can't believe it's easy to slow down, especially after what you've achieved in the past."

"It's not easy," I said. "It's actually kind of hard."

"How do you do it?"

"I train like I always do, for the most part, but peter out towards the end of practice. In an event I make dumb mistakes, like slip off the block, take extra breaths, and make rookie turns, just enough to blow the race but still make an acceptable time."

"Only you could do that," he said.

"It is getting old," I admitted. "Sometimes the adrenaline gets going, and it's hard to pull back. I want to let it all out, but once I do, Coach will be all over me and expect me to win all the time, maybe even beat Tatiana and win that scholarship." As soon as I said it, I knew I'd made a terrible mistake.

"What scholarship?"

I had no choice but to tell him about the Allison Singer challenge and the fifty thousand dollar scholarship.

"Why am I just learning about this?" he asked. "You need to go for it, Aerin. You have a good chance at breaking that record and winning that prize."

"I knew you'd say that, which is why I didn't tell you. Do you know how much pressure Tatiana is under because of that scholarship? Everyone, and I mean *everyone,* is on her back about it: Coach, her parents, the other girls, her best friend, the principal, the teachers, even the sports writers at the newspaper. She's the best in the school and the division. She's two seconds off! She seems all calm and collected, but I bet she's a nervous wreck inside. Every day, I tell myself, 'Thank God I'm not Tati.' I couldn't handle the stress."

He chuckled and threw me a sidelong glance. "The funny thing is, your best time in the 500 is better than Tatiana's best time."

"Yeah, well, nobody knows that."

"You know it."

I fidgeted with the knobs on the dash. He knew just how to get to me.

"Don't tell me you haven't thought about shattering that record."

"It's not something I want to do."

"No, it's something you *have* to do. You're a champion, Aerin, everything about you screams winner. If you set your mind to breaking that record, you'll break it."

"But it's not my record to break. It's not my school. It's not my team."

"It is right now. I say you should take advantage of every

opportunity to position yourself for the future. Break the record and you'll get into the college of your choice. Win that scholarship and you'll have plenty of money to help pay for that college. We're looking at more than fifty grand per year at each one of those schools. Any scholarship money will be more than welcome."

"I should have kept my mouth shut," I said, as he exited off the highway. We were just minutes from Maggie's.

"Look, I just want you to think about it, okay? Promise me. Give it some real thought. It can make all the difference for you and your future."

"All right," I said, knowing he was right. "But I don't want you pressuring me. Don't bring it up again."

"Hands off," he said, lifting his hands off the steering wheel. The car swerved to the right and he deftly regained control.

Minutes later, we were at Maggie's. I didn't linger for a long goodbye, anxious to end the conversation. "I've got it," I said. "You don't have to get out of the car. They're waiting for you at home." I hoisted my backpack over my shoulder and picked up my dress box and the bag with the shoes and everything else in it.

"Tell Pat and Maggie I said hi," he said.

I nodded and closed the door. I walked up the driveway, listening for the sound of his car driving away. I peeked out the kitchen window and watched his tail lights disappear.

"What have I done?" I moaned. And did I do it on purpose? I knew he'd be all over the Allison Singer thing. Even if he kept his promise and didn't bring it up again, I'd see it in his eyes as the season wound down and I didn't step up. He'd be hurt and disappointed. He wanted me to do my best. To be my best. He was my number one fan, even more a fan than my mother, who had always coached me from the sidelines, working on technique and motivation. My father didn't understand the fine-tuning of swimming. He wasn't an athlete.

He was a dad, a dad who wanted to see his daughter excel.

Week Seven:

Spotlight

Chapter 38

We were officially mid-season and looking good, 8-0. Since most of the girls had made the cut for the Division Championships, Coach was happy most of the time, which made practice bearable as the yardage kept creeping up and we were now putting in close to 10,000 yards a day. My muscles ached in places I'd forgotten, and most nights I was sound asleep by 9:30.

I felt good about the season. At first, I figured I'd just get in the water every day, run through the practice set, get a great workout, clear my head, and leave. It's pretty much what I always did, except I'd left out the intensity and the drive to win, the mental game I played that kept me pumped up, maintaining my spot as number one, the swimmer to beat. I was determined not to allow Mel and Justin's' criticisms and Jordan's threats throw me off course. These things hurt - Jordan passing judgment on me the first day, Mel and Justin's insinuations that I was slacking off. Add in my disappointment when I finished a race and saw someone else in first place, even though I intended to lose all along.

These things burned me up, clouded my vision, and made me think twice about what I was doing here. My parents expected me to succeed, to win the way I always did. We'd invested a lot of time, energy, and money into the sport hoping for a scholarship and a shot at the Olympics.

When my family broke apart, swimming at champion level kept me sane, and gave me something else to focus on, something positive with achievable results. I didn't have to think about anything because I was consumed with practice every morning and afternoon, competition, and school work. I had little time for anything else, and the system worked well.

I went about my routine with blind eyes, focusing on the next practice, the next meet, improving my times and technique, earning praise from my coaches, meeting with recruiters from the big schools.

It was all about *me*, and when my mother's situation hit crisis mode, I had no idea she'd been sliding into big trouble for months.

She worked 12-hour shifts and our paths sometimes didn't cross for days.

She lost thirty pounds and her eyes had a sunken, haunted look.

She slept a lot and had pain from her war injuries.

Yet she managed to put a smile on her face when we did cross paths, and made it to most of my meets.

Then one afternoon my father pulled me out of practice and told me she'd been arrested. Something about stealing drugs from the hospital where she worked.

It wasn't the first time, he said.

She was addicted to painkillers, he said.

I cried, not because she was in trouble, but because I hadn't noticed she was hurting. I figured that once she came home from her tour of duty our normal life would resume. I didn't know about PTSD, or addiction to painkillers, or depression. I didn't know I was supposed to make sure she was all right. It was just the two of us at home; no one else to help out. And I was too busy with my own agenda to make sure she was okay.

She wasn't okay. While I was perfecting my technique and winning titles, she spiraled downward until she hit rock bottom. She stole drugs meant for her patients. She went to work under the influence and made mistakes that caught the attention of her superiors. She got fired, arrested, and the state board of nursing suspended her license.

What a load of trouble.

I thought about my mom, going through her rehab, serving her sentence, healing, transforming herself back to the woman she once was, guiding me through the next stage of my life.

I thought about my father, too, trying to make his new family work in spite of the obstacles Emily and I put before him, worrying about and taking care of Dawn during her risky pregnancy, trying to play the role of both parents for his stepdaughters and for me, while holding down his practice.

I also thought about Travis, who might never play football again. He needed an athletic scholarship if he wanted to get into a good school, and, in just seconds, that possibility was taken from him. And yet he rallied, not missing a day of school, sitting out practices on the bench and urging on his teammates, while he healed and waited for medical clearance to put him back into the game, an unlikely possibility.

I thought of the three of them and realized I wasn't the only one hurting, but I was the one who had given up.

At mid-season, my team was undefeated. My performance was respectable, my times acceptable, and I was staying under the radar the way I'd planned. All was good, except it didn't feel right because I could do better. I was cheating myself, my parents, my team, and my school of what I could achieve.

True, the Blazers didn't need me to be a superstar to win the division title. They were on their way while I played the role of average performer. But if I stepped up my game they were guaranteed to win their fourth consecutive title. And if I wanted to, I could take on the Singer challenge, break her record, win the scholarship, and win the Division and State Championships.

I had only one reason to continue in my role as a middle performer: my friends. What would be their reaction if I became a contender for the scholarship race? If I started winning events? If I beat Tatiana? Was I willing to sacrifice my new friendships? That was the question that wouldn't go away.

Chapter 39

At next practice, the pool deck was in a state of total confusion. A news crew from the local TV station had set up to interview and film Tati for a piece on the Singer scholarship. Coach told us to get in the pool and start our warm-up – the shoot was almost over – but few of us could concentrate. The girls popped their heads out of the water at every turn, stopping to see what was going on, distracted by the news crew with their bright lights and big cameras.

I jumped into my lane and started swimming, trying to ignore the commotion. I was good at blocking out external stimuli, so I was able to keep my focus and make my intervals on time. When I finished the first set, I stopped for a breather and found Mel and Erica resting at the pool's edge.

"She's a real celebrity," Mel said.

"She earned it," Erica said.

"It's all anyone talks about around here," Mel said.

"It could be worse," Erica said as she tugged at her swim cap. "It could be *you* under those spotlights."

"No way," Mel said, and laughed.

"I feel sorry for her," I said. Mel's eyebrows shot up. "She's under a lot of pressure. The least we can do is support her. She makes the whole team look good."

"When did you become a Tati fan?" Mel asked.

"Hey, she brings in the recruiters from the best colleges and that helps us all," Erica said.

"You're a member of the Tatiana Reese fan club too?"

"Just saying," Erica said.

"I suppose," Mel conceded. "But every year it's Tatiana this, and Tatiana that."

"Come on, Mel, her name dominates the leaderboard. She's broken every record in every event she swims, except for the 500, and that's because the record's crazy fast! If she breaks that, it will be a real achievement, plus she'll get the scholarship," Erica said.

"Like she needs it," Mel said.

"Well, if she breaks the record she deserves it," I said.

"You ought to take her on," Mel said. "You're her only competition."

"No thanks. I've got enough to worry about."

"Look Aerin, even if you don't break the record, you'll motivate her to train harder. That might be what pushes her over the edge."

Lightbulb! She was so right. Sometimes the best competition is a teammate. We spur each other on, challenging each other to work harder, swim faster. To win. Tatiana could use a little push.

The camera crew filmed her talking with the reporter, a guy I recognized from the nightly news. She seemed so at ease, dressed in her warm-up suit, her face lit with confidence and pride, such a pretty girl. Her poise was remarkable. She had to be a bundle of nerves inside. If it were me, I'd be a basket case.

The door to the pool deck opened and Calvin Reese strode in. He walked to where Coach supervised practice and kept an eye on the film crew, and they exchanged a few words. Mr. Reese caught Tati's attention and gave her a tiny wave. She acknowledged his presence with a little smile, but her facial muscles tensed, and she looked ill at ease. Her father had that effect on people. I didn't like to be around him, and I sensed a lot of others felt that way. He was another reason I empathized with Tati – he put incredible pressure on her, and I doubted he gave her the support she needed.

"Back to practice, girls," Erica said, donning her goggles, "before Coach starts barking at us." She pushed off and hit the water, Mel and I right behind her.

When everyone had finished their practice sets, Tatiana got into the pool and performed for the cameras. Her stroke was beautiful, technically flawless. She glided through the water without apparent effort, her turns right on, her breath in perfect rhythm. I rarely saw her swim because we always swam together. I appreciated her style.

"Let's get out of here," Mel said, urging Erica and me to the locker room. "We can catch the whole thing on TV later."

Chapter 40

The meet against the Spartans was a huge competition because Coach was a Spartan back in the day and a former teammate ran the team. The night before, the Boosters took over the school's kitchen to serve a carb-loading feast - spaghetti, meatballs, tomato sauce, salad, and garlic bread - catered by a local restaurant and paid for by Allison Singer. After practice, we gathered in the school cafeteria, crowded with swimmers and their families. As soon as I walked in, I found Aunt Mags and the twins.

"Hey Aerin," Mags called and I joined her at her table. The twins had coloring books and crayons spread out and practiced their artwork with deep concentration, not even glancing up when I said hello.

"How was practice?" Mags asked.

I shoved my swim bag under the table and took a seat.

"All right," I said. "I made all my intervals. Coach had us running some sprints and my time improved. I went 26.33."

"That's good?" she asked. She tried to keep up with the fine details of swimming but sometimes became a little confused and overwhelmed with talk about times, strokes, and technique. I sometimes forgot she was new to the sport.

"That's very good," I said.

"But you're a distance swimmer."

"Yeah, but Coach has me in the 200 free relay after the 500 as a cool down, and I want to be able to hold my own."

The line at the buffet table began to form, and I got up. "I'm starved. Let's eat."

I ate with Aunt Maggie and the twins, then made my rounds through the cafeteria, stopping to visit with some of the other families.

"Where's Justin?" I asked Mel. He wouldn't miss our eating fest for nothing.

Mel sat with her mother, both of them finished with the mounds of spaghetti that had filled their plates. "He had to work," she said. "He's picking up more hours at the Y."

"He wants to make some extra money before his swim season starts and he won't be able to work for a while," Dr. Ford said. "Excuse me, girls. I'd like to speak to Maggie Flynn for a few minutes." She made her way to Aunt Mags' table.

"Last minute dance details," Mel said. "I think she's going to recruit your aunt for set-up duty."

"She'll love that," I said.

"You all set for the dance?"

I'd already shown Mel my dress, shoes, everything, and she'd drooled with envy. She planned to wear a dress from last year, never before seen by our crowd as she'd worn it to a family wedding.

"Yeah. You?" I asked.

"Yes," she said. "We should all get together before the dance to get ready. I've got a ton of stuff, all kinds of makeup and hair products. I picked out some styles in a magazine I'd like to try. One of them will look great with your red hair."

I smiled, elated with the thought of having girlfriends to do hair and makeup with, to prepare for a dance, to have a dance to attend.

"Let's ask Erica to join us," Mel said.

"Kelsey too," I added.

We caught up with Charlie at the dessert table and helped ourselves to brownies, debating who had the most homework that night. Mel was the winner – she had something in every class – and she was itchy to go home and get started.

"Look, she's here," she suddenly said, pointing toward the cafeteria's entrance.

I turned to see who had caught her attention. My eyes rested on a well-dressed woman in a business suit talking to Coach and Calvin Reese.

"Who is she?" I asked.

"That's Allison Singer," Erica said, wide-eyed with awe.

Charlie and I stared at the woman who had set the legendary record and now offered the unheard of scholarship to the swimmer who broke it.

"Wow," said Charlie.

"She looks like a million bucks," Mel said.

She did look like a success story, in a tailored suit and shoes I doubted she picked up at the mall. Her sophisticated hairstyle flattered her lovely face. She wore a trio of gold bracelets on one arm and diamond studs in each ear.

"Figures Calvin Reese is right on top of her," Mel said. "What a dork."

A crowd of parents soon engulfed Ms. Singer, all of them laughing and chatting like old friends. The swimmers hung back, waiting for their opportunity to approach the superstar.

"Come on," said Mel. She rose first, and we followed her to the crowd at the front of the room, jockeying ourselves for the best position to be next to greet our special visitor.

At the center of the group was Calvin Reese and his wife, with Tatiana smack dab in front of Ms. Singer, everyone smiling. Tatiana's smile looked glued to her face. Ms. Singer asked her a question, she answered, and they all laughed.

"Don't they look all BFF," Mel said.

"Shush, Mel, you'll get your turn."

The Reese's moved aside, and other people took their places, trying to get a moment with our prestigious alumna. The four of us hung back, waiting to speak to her with some degree of exclusiveness. At last, we had our chance. Ms. Singer had a free moment, and Mel approached her with a bottle of water.

"Would you like a cold drink?" she asked.

"You're a lifesaver," Ms. Singer said, reaching for it. "I'm dying of thirst." She took a long swig and replaced the cap on the bottle. "I think I remember you. Melanie, right?"

Mel beamed at being recognized. "Yes," she said, holding out her hand. They shook. "It's nice to meet you again."

"You're a sprinter, aren't you? Not up for breaking my record?"

"That's right," Mel said.

"How's your season?"

"It's great. It's my last season and I already made it to the championships."

"That's wonderful. And who are your friends?"

Mel introduced her to Charlie and then it was my turn.

"Aerin is new to the team," she said. "She's from the city."

"I love the city," said Ms. Singer. "Manhattan?"

"Midtown," I said.

"Do you swim for Manhattan Swim Club?"

"Yes, ten years now."

"Great coach," she said.

"Aerin's a distance swimmer," Mel said.

Ms. Singer arched her eyebrow. "Are you setting out to break my record?"

I blushed, not knowing what to say, annoyed that Mel had put me on the spot.

"I keep telling her she needs to give Tatiana a run for the money," Mel said, "but she's not convinced."

"If you think you're good enough you should try," Ms. Singer said. "The opportunity to prove yourself the best doesn't come around too often, and the reward is great."

I tried to smile. "Yes, Ma'am." Did I have to be so tongue-tied? She wasn't a *real* celebrity. Still, the way she carried herself and commanded respect made me want her to like me.

"I'll be looking for you at the championship meet, Aerin," she said. "Something tells me this is the year someone knocks me off that leaderboard."

We said our goodbyes, and in seconds a group of parents crowded around her.

"Thanks a lot, Mel," I whispered.

"No need to thank me now," she said. "Thank me later. After you've won."

"Let it rest. You have no reason to believe I can break that record."

"I have eyes, don't I?"

~

We won the Spartans meet: 98-96.

What a night.

We switched positions each event.

We were on top; then they were on top.

The tension was thick, the energy electric. The stands were rocking with fans because the Spartans came from the next town, and it seemed every resident turned out to cheer for them, blending in with our own home crowd.

At the end of the meet, the Spartan's coach shook hands with Coach and then jumped in the pool, fully dressed, sneakers and all, fulfilling a tradition for the losing team. Swimmers from both teams went wild, and then everyone was in the water, including Coach after Jordan, Tati, and some of their friends pushed him in.

Chapter 41

Physics test on Friday. Justin and I met in the library during study hall and reviewed the latest chapter and my notes. We sat in the rear at a table for two. I tried to follow his instruction, but his silky blond hair distracted me, and I wondered what he would do if I reached out and ran my fingers through it.

"Earth to Aerin," he said, jolting me out of my fantasy.

I sat up straight. "I'm listening."

"Oh yeah? Well, explain it back to me."

I looked down at my notes, opened my mouth, tripped over my tongue, and gave him a sheepish look.

"Sorry. I guess I'm a little distracted."

"What's on your mind?"

I shrugged. No way I was telling him *he* was the only thing on my mind at the moment.

"Worried about the meet?"

"Tomorrow?" I asked. "No. Everyone says it will be an easy win."

"Never underestimate an opponent," he said, spinning a pencil between his fingers. "Although we haven't lost to the Eagles in the last five years that I can remember."

"I don't underestimate anyone," I said.

"Good. When we get complacent, bad things happen, like losing."

"Sounds like you have personal experience," I said, leaning forward, my arms resting on the table. "Tell me more."

He pulled his chair closer to the table and leaned into it, his face just inches from mine. His blue eyes were dark and intense, lit by an inner glow I recognized all too well – the glow from the desire to win.

"Last season we were up against the Eagles," he explained. "I'd heard they had a new hot shot, some kid who moved up from New Jersey and was setting some awesome times. I took one look at him and said, no way. He was a skinny little thing, looked weak. It was the 200 IM. I started out solid, like always, and kept the lead. Next thing I know, he comes off the wall like a rocket on the last turn and blows right past me. I hustled and caught up, but he still beat me by half a second. Coach reamed me out pretty bad for that one."

"That happened to me a couple of times," I said. "I try not to pay attention to who's in the lane next to me and swim against myself."

"The best strategy," he agreed. "How do you feel about the physics?"

"Better. Thanks for all your help." Without him, I'd be in danger of failing. I looked forward to our study hours more than he knew.

"Ready for the dance Saturday night?"

The dance! I got a rush of adrenaline every time I thought of it. I'd hung my dress on the outside of the closet door, so I saw it first thing in the morning and last at night, falling asleep to dreams of dancing with my friends, of dancing with Justin. "I've never been to a dance before," I confessed.

"No? Didn't they have dances at your other schools?"

"They did, but I was always too busy. Plus I didn't have anyone to go with."

"Who are you going with on Saturday night?"

"Aunt Maggie is driving me."

"That's a shame," he said.

"What is?"

"That your aunt is driving you to the dance. You deserve your own special chariot."

"Like Cinderella?"

"Yeah, like Cinderella, only your chariot won't turn into a pumpkin at midnight."

"How do you know?" I asked.

"Because I drive a Jeep, and everyone knows Jeeps don't turn into pumpkins."

"Are you saying you're Prince Charming?" I asked, a little breathless.

"I can be," he said, all serious now.

I didn't respond, afraid I'd misunderstood, and the correct answer wasn't yes, of course, I'll go to the dance with you.

"So? Will you go to the dance with me?"

The bell sounded, signaling the end of the period. Kids were packing up their books and bags and leaving the library. Justin and I lingered, time suspended. A wave of happiness rolled through me, and I paused, waiting for it to pass before answering. As the seconds ticked on, he began to look uneasy, and I realized I had to release him from his torture.

"Yes," I said.

He flashed me that megawatt smile. "Great, I'll pick you up at 7:00, okay?"

I nodded, picked up my books and tossed them into my bag.

"What color is your dress?" he asked.

"Lavender."

"Got it," he nodded, hoisting his backpack over his shoulder and matching my stride as we headed out of the library. Once outside, we prepared to go in opposite directions.

"I'll see you later," he said. "And remember: don't underestimate the competition."

"You're starting to worry me. Do you know something about tomorrow that I don't know?"

"That's for you to discover. Analyze the stats."

"I don't do stats."

"You might want to start." He walked backward down the hall, keeping his eyes on me. Last minute stragglers rushed by, trying to beat the bell to the next class. I walked backward too, not wanting to take my eyes off him. A second later, he disappeared around a corner, and I had seconds to get to class on time.

Chapter 42

Practice was tough that afternoon. Coach put us through the paces, working us hard.

"What is he doing to us?" Mel asked between sets. We'd stopped in the shallow end to regroup. "It's only the Eagles. They're 5-3. We've got this."

"They beat the Boxers yesterday," Tati said.

"No way!" Mel said. "Only two teams ever beat the Boxers – the Bears and us."

"They've got some new stars on their team: a flyer, a sprinter, and a distance swimmer. And their relays are crazy fast. Coach is worried."

"A sprinter? How fast?" Mel's eyes bugged out. She was starting to frighten me.

"25.75 yesterday, a win."

Mel sagged against the pool wall. "Sometimes I wish I didn't know these things."

"Sorry," Tati said. "Does it make a difference?"

"Well, yeah, because I'll be up all night worrying about the 50's when I'd rather sleep like a baby."

"Don't psych yourself out, Mel. Think positive. Envision

coming in first. If you see it, you'll believe it, and if you believe it you'll achieve it." Tati quoted Coach. She was turning out to be a great team captain, understanding everyone's strengths and weaknesses and acting as head cheerleader.

"A little competition is a good thing," Erica said. Her season was right on track. She'd qualified for the Division Championships in all of her events, beat her personal best in the fly twice, and had recruiters sending her emails and letters every day.

"It's good for all of us," Tati said, the reigning queen. So far, no one was positioned to steal her crown. Other than the event where she lost to the Chinese exchange student, she'd won all of her races – the 100, the 200, the 500, and all of her relays. Her times hovered close to her personal bests. She was on target to break her own record in the 100 and 200, and then smash Allison Singer's 500 record and win the scholarship. It was her year. Her father probably had his phone glued to his ear 24/7 fielding calls from recruiters. To date, Tati hadn't said a word about which college she planned to attend.

"What about their breaststroker?" asked a worried Charlie.

"No worries, Charlie," Tati said. "You've got it."

Charlie smiled.

"We need to move," Erica said. "We've got another set to do and here comes Coach."

One by one, we pushed off, chasing each other from end to end like a school of fish.

Never take anything for granted, my father always said. We thought the meet against the Eagles would be another easy victory, but Coach's ambitious routine the day before alerted us not to be complacent. He never said we had anything to worry about – it wasn't his style to scare or worry us – but his unspoken expectations at practice and on the way to the meet set the scene. We needed to be at our best or else we'd be in for a big surprise.

Tati's pep talk worked to our advantage. Everyone was diligent. No one slacked off or made errors that would cost an event. As the meet unfolded, we faced stiffer competition than expected, lost a few races to some exceptional swimmers, but managed to stay in the lead.

You don't need to win every event to win a meet. Coming in second, third, and fourth can earn you more points, and Coach positioned us in the lineup so that's what we did. Of course, Tati won all of her events with me right behind her in second. Charlie won the breaststroke. Erica finished second in the fly and first in the IM. Mel finished second in her sprints – the 50 free and the two relays – and the 100. The final score was close: 98-88. Blazers were now 9-0 for the season.

As we headed into the second half of the dual meet schedule, we were the strongest team in the division. If we maintained our momentum and motivation, and no one got hurt, we'd win our fourth consecutive championship title.

Chapter 43

Saturday afternoon, two hours before the dance, all four of us crammed into my little attic room. Mel had wheeled in a suitcase full of makeup, hair, and skin products, most of it brand new and still in its original packaging. She also had a few curling irons and hair straighteners, several cans of hair spray, and a box full of hairpins, headbands, and other stuff.

She unloaded the suitcase on my bed while everyone looked on, mesmerized by the collection of eye shadow, mascara, foundation, blush, and lipstick.

"I had no idea you were such a beauty queen," I said.

"You don't think all this cover girl beauty is natural, do you?" Mel asked, pointing at her carefully made up face. She went back to evaluating the assortment of hairbrushes in her hands and then put half of them back in the suitcase.

"Sure you don't want to be a hairdresser or a makeup artist after graduation?" I asked. She was so serious about arranging her supplies. I didn't own half the stuff she pulled out of that bag.

"My Aunt Julie owns a beauty shop in the city. She gets tons of samples from salespeople, stuff she doesn't want to use or stock, and gives it to me. She taught me everything I know."

"Aunt Julie is the best," said Kelsey, who came along with them and sat on the other side of the bed.

"Who's first?" Mel asked.

No one moved, so Mel said, "Get in the chair, Kels, you're up."

I relinquished the chair to Kelsey and took her place on my bed. Erica joined me and we paid attention as Mel went to work, explaining what she was doing and why. Kelsey sat with her eyes closed while Mel released her unruly blonde hair from its French braid and brushed it until it shone. No one said a word as Mel picked up the hair straightener and piece by piece turned Kelsey's stubborn locks into a golden blanket of silk that hung halfway down her back and covered her shoulders. Mel stepped back to observe her work.

"She looks beautiful," I said.

Kelsey opened her eyes and looked in the mirror on my dresser. She turned her head from side to side, admiring her reflection, her cheeks pinking, a smile lifting her lips. "Wow," she said.

"Good job, Mel," said Erica.

"What color is your dress?" Mel asked Kelsey as she rummaged through the makeup piled on my bed. She had dozens of eye shadow palettes in a rainbow of colors and picked through them, her brow furrowed in concentration.

"Navy blue," said Kelsey.

"Perfect," said Mel. She picked up some neutral shades and applied layers of color to Kelsey's pale eyelids, giving us a brief lesson in how to apply eye makeup as she went along. She added a little eyeliner and finished with two coats of brown mascara. Her final touch was a smudge of pale pink blush to Kelsey's apple cheeks and a dab of clear lip-gloss.

"She looks fantastic," Erica said.

"She doesn't even look like she's wearing makeup," I said. She'd transformed Kelsey from a plain girl to a cover girl hopeful.

"Get out of the chair, Kelsey. I'm next," Erica said.

They swapped places and as Mel worked on Erica, we no longer looked on in silence but started talking about everything and everyone.

"So tell us, Mel," Erica said, as Mel brushed out her shoulder-length hair. "How'd you get Matt Kendricks to ask you to the dance?"

Mel stopped mid-stroke and gave us a coy smile. "Who said he asked me?"

"I thought you said you're going to the dance with him," Erica said, gesturing at her to continue brushing.

"I did, and I am."

"Then how - ?" Erica asked, but I interrupted.

"Tell me you didn't!" I shouted.

"Oh yes, I did," Mel said, her face aglow.

"What did you do?" Kelsey asked, not getting it.

"I asked him," Mel said.

"No way," said Erica, almost rising out of the chair but staying put at the last second as Mel whipped the brush through her hair. "Ouch!"

"Stay still," Mel ordered. "And, yeah, I did ask him, the other night. And why shouldn't I? He was beating around the bush, not able to spit the words out, so I just put it out there and he said yes."

"What if he said no?" Kelsey asked.

"The thought never crossed my mind," she said.

"I could never do that," Erica said.

"And that's why you're going to the dance with Kelsey and not Brian," Mel said.

"He said he'd meet me there," Erica said.

"Not the same thing," Mel said.

"I'm good with it," Erica said and turned her attention to me. "How'd you get Justin to ask you?"

I shrugged. "I don't know. He just asked."

"He's been dying to ask you for weeks, but don't say you heard it from me," Mel said around a mouthful of bobby pins. She'd gathered Erica's chestnut hair in a sleek ponytail at the top of her head. Erica grimaced as Mel pulled and twisted it into a tight little bun, then fastened it with the pins.

"Justin's hot," Erica said.

"Oh yeah?" Mel asked, putting in the final bobby pin with a little too much force.

"Careful!" Erica cried. "That's my scalp."

"That's my brother you're talking about," Mel said.

"Everyone thinks he's hot, Mel. That's not news," Erica said, reaching up to massage the sore spot on her head.

Mel batted her hand away. "Stop. You'll mess it up."

"He's the hottest guy in school," Kelsey said.

"I wouldn't go that far," Mel said. She started poking through her pile of makeup, picking out what she wanted to use on Erica.

"Well, of course you think Matt's the hottest guy," Erica said.

"Of course," she said, applying a sheer foundation to her face. Erica's skin was dry and pimply from the pool – we all had our little skin issues - and Mel smoothed it out until it looked flawless. She unwrapped a brand new eyeshadow palette in varying shades of blue, and seconds later Erica's hazel eyes popped. Erica remained silent while Mel worked on her, applying a double layer of black mascara, a hint of pink blush and a smear of cherry lip-gloss. Mel had a knack for this. I couldn't wait to see what she did for me.

"You know," I said from the sidelines, "you really should rethink the whole college thing, Mel, and become a professional makeup artist. You're *that* good."

Mel beamed. "I haven't gotten around to you yet," she said. "Let's hope I can work a miracle."

"Hey!" I said and swatted her on the backside as Erica and I moved to switch places.

"Sit down, I'm only kidding," she said. "You need the least work of all."

"Hey!" Erica objected.

"That's not nice," Kelsey said.

"Just joking," Mel said, "take it easy." She pulled my hair out of its usual messy bun. I sat back as her fingers raked through it. It had been a long time since someone had done that. My mom and I often brushed each other's hair while we watched TV, and considered it one of life's simple pleasures. Another thing I missed about her.

"I can't wait to straighten these curls," Mel said, wielding her straightener.

"Go ahead," I said, "but I'm warning you. It's thick and takes forever."

Erica moved about my room, inspecting my belongings and space. "You've got a cool setup here," she said. "I have to share a room with my little sister."

I watched in the mirror as Erica and Kelsey examined my things, inspecting the books on my bookcase, the pile of CDs on my nightstand, the posters and pictures on the walls. It seemed surreal, having three girls in my room, and all at the same time. The most friends I'd ever entertained was one, and not very often. Once again I was reminded of all that I'd gained in Two Rivers. I had friends, girls I swam with, ate lunch with, went to dances with, and hung out with doing makeovers and manicures. A sudden surge of happiness rippled through me, and I let myself enjoy it, not push it away afraid it would burst.

"Is this your mom?" Erica asked. She held a framed 8x10 photo collage of Mom and me up to the mirror.

"Yeah," I said, wishing she'd put it down.

"Let me see," Mel said. She'd finished straightening my hair and was experimenting with different ways to put it up.

Erica brought the photo to her, and Kelsey also crowded around it. The collage was pictures of my mother and me at different times in my life: birthday parties, Christmas, vacations. There was a shot of her in her Army fatigues, dusty and dirty, but she looked happy. It was my most recent picture of her. We hadn't taken any lately, and I was grateful we hadn't documented her decline. I wanted to forget those images. I said nothing, waiting to hear what they had to say.

"Your mom's pretty," Mel said, "but you don't look like her at all."

"I hear that all the time."

"Your father must have the red hair."

"He's in that picture," I gestured toward a small table on the other side of the room. Erica handed the photo collage to Kelsey and went to get the photo of my father.

"Yup," she said, handing the picture of my father and me to Erica. "You're a chip off the old block. You look just like your dad."

Dawn had snapped the picture last summer when I spent two weeks with the four of them at a beach cottage in Wellfleet on Cape Cod. We took a vacation every summer, *family time*, which wasn't too bad because no one expected me to babysit the girls and we spent most of each day at the beach, playing in the waves, building sandcastles, and taking long walks along the shore. Everyone relaxed. Even Emily put aside her usual crankiness and had a good time. At night, we ate lobsters, steamers, and fried clams. We forgot about movies and TV and played board games until dark. Everyone was asleep by ten o'clock and up bright and early the next morning to get a start on the day.

After about a week of that routine, I was comfortable with everyone. At the end of two weeks, I felt like part of their family. But it wasn't long after our return to New York that I started to feel like an outsider again, shuttling back and forth to their house every other weekend, a visitor, and sometimes not sure if I were a welcome one. My dad said that was my perception and not what he, Dawn, and the girls intended. He said it was the result of my resentment and anger over my parent's divorce. I needed to make peace with that, and soon. Looking at the photo of us standing with our backs to the ocean reminded me of those good days, and I resolved not to dwell on the hard feelings and disappointments anymore.

Erica and Kelsey placed the pictures back where they belonged, and Mel returned to styling my hair.

"Maybe she should wear it down," Kelsey suggested.

"It's so smooth," Erica said.

"Her dress is strapless," Mel said. "An updo would be more sophisticated."

"What do you think, Aerin?" Erica asked.

I didn't have to answer because the door swung open and Aunt Mags and Paige came in bearing a platter of fresh-baked brownies, a pitcher of milk, and four glasses.

"How's it going, girls?" Aunt Mags asked. "Wow, you all look beautiful."

"Hi Mrs. Flynn," Erica said. "Are those for us?"

"Of course, and just out of the oven."

"They're still warm and gooey," Paige said, her eyes round with wonder as she caught sight of all of the makeup scattered across my bed.

"Look at that," Aunt Mags said, "it looks like a professional makeup artist dropped in." Aunt Mags was not a woman who wore much makeup. She started picking through the products, examining each one.

"Help yourself," Mel said. "Try that lipstick. It's perfect for you."

Mags examined the lipstick. Paige peeked over her shoulder.

"What do you think, Aunt Mags, up or down?" I held half of my hair up and left the other half down.

"With that dress," Mags gestured toward the lavender confection hanging on my closet door, "I'd say up. It's more sophisticated."

"I told you," Mel said, smirking. She started pulling my hair into a low ponytail.

"That's my head," I said when it felt like she'd tear it out by the roots.

"No pain, no gain," she said.

"I have to leave for the parish hall in a few minutes," Mags said. "Last minute decorations and setting out refreshments. But I'll be back to help you get dressed, Aerin." She was in the Women's Group and had been at the church all morning getting things ready.

"My mom will be there, too," Mel said. "She said you ladies went overboard and the parish hall looks incredible. I can't wait to see it."

"They always do a nice job," said Kelsey.

"Just you wait and see. We turned it into an autumn wonderland," said Mags. She'd chosen a lipstick in a neutral shade, something called buff. She slicked it over her lips and in seconds looked like a different woman.

"Wow," said Paige, "you look pretty, Mommy."

"Come on, honey," Mags said. "Let's leave the girls so they can finish getting ready."

"Can I stay? I want to watch," said Paige. She was twelve and fascinated with the whole makeover thing.

"She can stay," I said.

"All right," said Mags. "Thanks for the lipstick, Mel."

"Thanks for the milk and brownies, Mrs. F," Mel said. Erica and Kelsey had already helped themselves, and scattered brownie crumbs everywhere.

"They're delicious," Erica said around a mouthful. Kelsey nodded, too busy eating.

Chapter 44

Mel put the final touches to my updo, a low ponytail twisted upwards and fastened against my head. She called it a French twist. The front was parted on the left and swooped down across my forehead, giving me an exotic look. She secured it with a few pins and half a can of hairspray. The whole thing was sleek and shiny. I turned from side to side inspecting my reflection in the mirror.

"This is something else, Mel," I said.

"Hey," she said, "I can't let my brother go to the dance with a frump."

She got to work on my face. My eyes were closed and I couldn't see what she was doing. She stroked my cheeks with a soft brush, smoothed something creamy on my eyelids, and tickled my eyelashes with mascara. When she stepped back, I opened my eyes and gasped. A peachy blush enhanced the fairness of my complexion. My hazel eyes were luminous, the lashes long and flirty. I parted my lips and she coated them with a glossy russet lipstick.

"Well?" she asked.

"You're a magician."

She smirked.

"Who's going to do you?" I asked.

She looked at me like I was nuts. "Who do you think?" she asked. "Me. I'm not going to let any of you amateurs touch my head or my face."

"What about me?" Paige asked.

"Hop up here small fry and I'll see what I can do," Mel said.

Paige wasted no time jumping into the hot seat, and Mel turned her shoulder-length dark hair into a mass of curls. She brushed a light layer of pink blush on her cheeks, outlined her almond shaped brown eyes in neutral tan shades, and coated her lashes with clear mascara. She smoothed a smear of pink lip-gloss across her lips.

"What do you think?" Mel asked.

Paige admired herself in the mirror, eyes shining. "I wish I could go to the dance too."

"Maybe next time," Mel said. "Now scoot." She picked up her brush and pulled it through her own hair, wincing when she caught a tangle. "You guys might want to get working on your nails before it gets too late," she told us.

We finished the brownies and downed the milk, washed our hands, and then picked through the bottles of nail polish Mel had brought. We each selected our color and started painting.

Mel's hair was stick straight, and she took the curling iron to it, forming long, spiraling curls. "What do you think, Kels?" she asked as she twirled and released her hair. "How are we looking for the invitational?"

The following weekend was the Long Island meet. We'd leave Friday right after practice and take the bus to a hotel, where we'd spend the night before heading to the meet the next morning. Some of the top teams in metropolitan New York, Long Island, and the Lower Hudson Valley would be there, nineteen of them, hundreds of swimmers. We would not be the best, but each year finished in the top four. Coach expected us to finish in the top three this time. Mel said the best part of the whole thing was spending the night away from home, sharing a hotel room with our teammates – four to a room – going out to dinner at a nice restaurant, followed by board games before bed. It would be my first sleep away meet, and I was as excited as the other girls.

"Coach is right," Kelsey said, pulling her phone out of her pocket. She tapped on the screen and opened an app. "By my calculations, you guys will come in third, but you might be able to pull off second if we have a couple of surprises."

"Who needs to pull off a surprise?" asked Mel.

"Everyone has to swim close to her personal best, no slacking. Several of you are close to breaking your best, and now would be a good time to do that. You, Mel, are on that list, so is Charlie, so is Tatiana, and so is Aerin."

I gulped. *Close* to beating my personal best? I hadn't come close to that this season and didn't intend to, but then I realized that she referred to my best on this team, and I understood. I could break that best, and maybe now was the time to do it, to give the team a better finish at this all-important meet.

"You hear that Aerin?" Mel said.

"You too, Mel," I retorted. "Think you can step it up?"

"Oh, I intend to. I'm not even close to peaking yet."

"Me neither," said Erica.

"I want to see you beat Tati," Mel said, catching my eye in our reflection in the mirror.

"Dream on. I'm not beating Tati."

"What makes you think she can beat Tati?" Erica asked, blowing on her freshly polished nails.

"My gut," said Mel, still working the curling iron.

"You keep saying that but I don't see it," Erica said.

Thanks, Erica, I thought, but at the same time, it annoyed me she doubted my abilities.

"Why would she want to try to beat Tatiana? You know how Tati responds to competition. It makes her faster," Erica said.

"Tati blew it last year," Mel said.

"She wrecked her shoulder," Erica said. "She didn't blow anything."

"That's not what I saw. I think she could have broken Allison Singer's record, but for some reason, she chose not to," said Mel.

"Is there a choice between winning and not winning for someone like Tatiana? Come on, Mel. We've discussed this a million times. Tati wrecked her shoulder late last season and didn't get back to her game in time to break the record. She missed it by four and a half seconds. She didn't fake anything."

"Tati works through the pain," Mel said. "She's never let that stop her from winning. Remember when she hurt her shoulder at the Bears meet two seasons ago and we had to drag her out of the pool? She couldn't climb out by herself. But she won. That's the difference between her and everyone else. She doesn't let anything get in her way."

"Mighty Mouse," said Kelsey.

"Exactly," Mel said. "And at championships last year she let that bum shoulder get the best of her, or that's what everyone thinks."

"Why would she want to lose, Mel, after working so hard all season? That's crazy," Erica said.

"Check her out when her father's around," Mel said. "If you ask me, I think the two of them are having some kind of battle. He wants her to break the record, and she doesn't want to give it to him."

"You better not say those things about Tati outside this room," Erica said.

"I'm not stupid," Mel said. "This is between the four of us, okay?" She met all of our eyes in the mirror, and we each nodded, sealing ourselves to silence.

"Tati's been swimming and winning a long time. Her father puts a lot of pressure on her," Mel said.

"Her father gives me the creeps," Kelsey said.

"Me too," I said.

"He is a creep," Mel said.

"Creep or not," Erica said, "Tati's going to break the record, get the scholarship, and go off to some big swim school far away from here. I would if I were her."

"So would I," Mel said.

"What about you, Aerin?" Kelsey asked. "What would you do with the scholarship?"

"I don't know," I said. "I don't think about it."

"Liar," Mel snorted. "It's your event. I can't believe you're not trying to break that record. What's wrong with you?"

I shrugged. The conversation was getting old. I glanced at the clock on my nightstand. It was getting late, and the other girls needed to go home and dress for the dance. "Is everyone done with their nails?"

Erica and Kelsey flashed their sparkling fingers at me. I put the bottles of nail polish back in Mel's bag. She leaned on my dresser, peering into the mirror as she finished putting on eye makeup with a double coat of mascara. She stood back to look at herself. Her hair was a cascade of curls, swept up on one side and held behind her ear with a bejeweled comb. Her makeup was flawless, her blue eyes sparkled, and her lips shimmered.

"How do I look?" she asked.

No one said a word, mesmerized by her beauty.

"Well?"

"Matt's going to flip when he sees you," Erica said.

"He's going to freak out," Kelsey said.

"You look awesome, Mel," I said.

"Good." She started packing up her stuff. "Look at the time! We need to get out of here and get dressed. Don't want to be late. Matt's picking me up in forty minutes."

We helped her reload her bag, then filed out of my room and downstairs, our voices rising in a frenzy of excitement as we said goodbye. In an hour we'd reunite at the dance. When they had all left, I went back to my room to finish dressing.

Chapter 45

Aunt Maggie helped me step into my dress and zipped me in. I stood in front of the full-length mirror and stared at the reflection in wonder. Who was that tall, curvy girl in the lavender confection, her abundant coppery hair swept up, her skin flawless and glowing?

"What do you think?" I asked.

"Honey, you're gorgeous," she said, standing behind me in the mirror. "Just perfect. Let me get my camera. I need to send a picture to your mother."

She hustled out of the room and left me slightly deflated, as thoughts of Mom missing this moment crashed down on me. My eyes welled with tears, but I shook them off, not wanting to spoil my makeup. Mel had done a superb job. I could never repair the damage, so no tears. She'd scream if I ruined her look. I set aside sad thoughts and twirled in front of the mirror, admiring my image from all angles. A shiver of delight ran through me.

Maggie came back with the camera and I posed while she clicked away, capturing me from every possible position.

"Please send some pictures to my father and Dawn," I said. She nodded.

A knock on the door interrupted, and Paige stuck her head in the room. "He's here!" she said, her face bright with anticipation, Mel's artfully applied makeup smeared, her bouncy curls limp.

I felt lightheaded, unsure of presenting myself to Justin. Would he like the way I looked? My dress? My hair?

"Are you ready?" Mags asked.

I took one last look in the mirror and nodded. "Yes," I said, and gathered my purse, a small silver clutch borrowed from Mags, and a knitted white shawl also provided by Mags. Taking a deep breath, I followed her and Paige out of the room and downstairs.

Uncle Pat and the other kids clustered around Justin. He had his back to me as I descended the stairs into the living room, where Maggie and Paige had joined his field of admirers.

"Very nice," Maggie said. "You clean up well, Justin."

From the back, he looked like a model, dressed in a black suit that fit like it was made for him. He wore shiny black dress shoes on his flipper feet. His blond hair brushed his shoulders, one lone piece refusing to stay in place.

"Here she is," said Uncle Pat, looking up at me, refocusing everyone's attention. "You look lovely, Aerin."

Everyone turned toward me, and I blushed, uncomfortable being in the spotlight. I put one foot in front of the other and made it down the stairs without tripping or turning my ankle. I looked up at Justin, who stared at me, his mouth hanging open, his blue-green eyes round with wonder.

"Wow," he said. "You look beautiful."

I blushed again under the heat of his gaze. He, too, looked beautiful, his face scrubbed pink and freshly shaved, his eyes sparkling. He wore a dark purple shirt and a tie in a geometric pattern with several shades of purple, including one that matched my dress.

"Thank you," I said, not taking my eyes off him.

He held out a box. "This is for you."

Inside was a wrist corsage made with three tiny white roses and lavender ribbon.

"Would you like me to help you?" Maggie asked.

I nodded, and she took the box from Justin, opened it, and extracted the delicate corsage. "You may do the honors," she said, handing him the flowers.

I extended my arm, and he slipped the corsage over my hand and around my wrist. The roses' perfume drifted toward my face, and I inhaled. "Thank you," I said.

Behind us, the Flynn family cheered, and it was his turn to blush.

"You two need to get going," Maggie said.

"Ready?" I asked.

Justin nodded and took my arm as we walked toward the door.

"Have a good time!" Uncle Pat called as he and the rest of them followed us out.

We left through the front door and walked down the path leading to the street. Justin's Jeep was parked in front under a streetlight, clean and shiny, looking like he'd spent the better part of the day making it perfect for this night.

"The Jeep looks great," I said as he opened the door for me.

"A chariot for a princess," he said.

"Ha ha." I climbed into the passenger seat, losing all pretense at gracefulness. "I don't feel like Cinderella."

He smiled and said, "You look like her," as he closed the door.

Chapter 46

The St. Joseph's Church Women's Group had turned the parish hall into an autumn wonderland, just as Aunt Mags had said. Justin and I paused at the entrance, in awe as we looked at all the decorations.

"Wow, they went all out," he said. "Check out the lights."

Hundreds of strands of string lights draped across the ceiling, wall to wall, giving a festive glow to the otherwise drab and utilitarian room.

"I wonder who climbed all the way up there to hang them," Justin said.

"That would be the perfect job for you, Mr. Rock Climber."

"Maybe next time."

Mel glided over to us, Matt Kendricks in tow. "What are you guys gawking at? Are you coming in or what? You're blocking the door."

We stepped aside to let some others enter. Justin and Matt shook hands and moved off to the left, talking about last night's football game, leaving Mel and me on our own.

"This place looks incredible," I said. "I've never seen anything like it." Clusters of red, orange, and gold balloons floated overhead.

Gold, orange, and white tablecloths covered the tables, and mini pumpkins and gourds sat on each one amid fall leaves, real ones. Now I understood why Aunt Maggie and the twins had spent the morning collecting leaves from the backyard. Tall glass vases full of fresh flowers in shades of red, rust, and gold also decorated each table and lit votive candles at the base of each vase lent a dreamy glow.

"Follow me. I grabbed us a table." Mel took me by the hand, and I trailed after her, still spellbound by the transformation of the parish hall, like Cinderella at the ball.

Mel had secured a table in the back corner, away from the DJ and his booming speakers and just a few feet from the snack table. Justin and Matt followed us but detoured to the table covered with drinks and treats.

"Animals," Mel said, but she was smiling. "They think they'll starve if they don't eat hourly." A crowd of guys surrounded the snack table, stuffing their faces with chips, dips, salsa, and tiny sandwiches. "Justin had a burger and double fries an hour ago."

"Hey Aerin," Erica said. She sat at the table next to Kelsey, both of them still looking fresh in the hair and make-up Mel had done.

"I saved you a seat next to me," Mel said, pulling out a chair. I draped my purse and shawl around the back of it. A pitcher of ice water with floating lemon slices sat on the table with a stack of plastic cups. I poured a cup for each of us, handed them out, and took my seat.

Moments later Justin was beside me, a plate of chips, dips, and miniature egg salad sandwiches in his hand.

"Hungry?" he asked as he placed the plate on the table in front of us. I shook my head.

"I had dinner."

"So did I, but that never stops me." He picked up a sandwich and ate half in one bite.

"Wait for the desserts," Mel said. "They're all homemade and lots of chocolate."

The music was too loud for serious talk, so we sat for a while as everyone else came in, met up with friends, and found seats. All the girls wore pretty party dresses and most of the guys sported suits or dress pants and a shirt and tie. As the crowd grew, the party atmosphere rose to a feverish pitch. The DJ played his music loud, the bass booming through the speakers, the playlist made up of the most current hits with a few classics thrown in. Not long after I'd sat down, a few brave souls ventured out onto the dance floor. Mel, Erica, Kelsey and I sat in our seats bobbing and weaving to the beat of the music, watching the dancers. Justin, Matt, and Brian, who had met up with Erica as planned, ignored the dancers and seemed oblivious to our desire to join them.

"What are we waiting for?" Mel asked. "I didn't come here to sit on my butt all night."

"I love this song!" Erica shouted.

We all pushed back from the table at once and left the guys behind as we made our way to the dance floor. Three songs later, I did a turn and bumped right into Justin.

"May I have this dance?" he asked.

I was already breathless, but his sudden appearance took my remaining breath away. The DJ switched from fast songs and started a slow one. I faltered just a moment but then allowed Justin to take me by the right hand, the other resting on my left hip, and lead me into some version of a slow dance.

"Are you having a good time?" he murmured in my left ear. A tingle coursed through me. I didn't trust my voice, so I nodded. He danced like he knew what he was doing, which was good because I didn't have a clue. I'd never danced with anyone other than my mom and dad, and even that was just in fun. Justin was smooth on his feet, confident and comfortable.

"You're a great dancer," I managed to spit out.

"Thank my mom," he said. "She made me take lessons even

though I threatened to run away from home if she wouldn't let me quit. I guess it all paid off in the end." He twirled me away from him, and I felt light as a feather, the skirt of my dress billowing around me. As the song ended, he pulled me closer and then reluctantly let go when the next song changed the tempo. At that song's end, I was overheated and breathless, and looked for an escape route as the crowd started dancing to another fast-paced song. Justin led me through a maze of dancers until we emerged from the crowd close to our table. I plopped down in my chair and fanned myself.

"Whew, that was fun!"

"Want a drink?" he asked. He refilled our cups, and we downed them. We sat down to catch our breath and watch the crowd.

The evening continued in much the same way. We rejoined the dancers and took turns dancing with Mel, Erica, Kelsey, Matt, Brian, and any others who joined our little band. In between we visited the snack table and pigged out on little hot dogs, sliders, nachos, and a dessert table loaded with brownies, chocolate chip cookies, and red velvet cupcakes.

"My stomach's going to bust," Mel moaned, clutching her abdomen.

"Good thing Coach isn't here," Erica said. "He'd kill us if he saw us eating all this junk so late at night."

"Maybe we should work out tomorrow to burn it off," Mel said. Erica and I looked at her in horror. "Just kidding! You two need to relax. It's a party for heaven's sake."

"We can dance some more," Justin said, meeting my eyes. "That'll help burn off some of these calories."

"In a minute," I said. "I'm still pooped. Let's sit."

He sat beside me, and we judged the crowd on the dance floor, picking out the good dancers and critiquing the not so good.

"Hey everybody, having a good time?" A familiar voice right behind us interrupted. I turned to see Tatiana and Sean. Justin rose to greet Sean and gave Tati a friendly hug.

"Hi Aerin," she said. "I love your dress."

That was the most she'd said to me in weeks. "Thank you. Yours is beautiful, too." Her dress was white and fluffy, strapless, with a gold band around her waist. A gold headband that matched the band on her dress held back her short dark hair, a pile of curls that looked both wild and controlled. Glittering gold pumps added three inches to her height, but because of my own high heels, she still looked petite to me, soft and sweet, no hint of Mighty Mouse tonight.

"How do you like the music?" she asked.

"The DJ's good," I said, "and he has a great selection."

She nodded. "He offered to play for free tonight. He says it helps him get gigs for other parties, weddings, stuff like that."

"How do you know?" I asked, curious.

"I'm on the dance committee. With Mel."

Mel hadn't mentioned that, but I shouldn't have been surprised. Tati was into everything. I doubt she ever slept.

"Well, you've done a great job. Everything looks beautiful. The music is good, and the food is delicious."

She smiled. "I'm glad you're having a good time."

"Where's Jordan?" I asked. "I thought she and Travis were coming tonight."

"Something came up at the last minute," she said. "She was disappointed to miss this." She stepped away and joined Justin and Sean, smiling up at her date and gesturing that they needed to move on. They said their goodbyes and glided away like the dance was all theirs.

"The Golden Couple," Justin said as he returned to his seat.

"I thought Sean was your friend."

"He is, but Tatiana has him acting like they're king and queen of the ball."

"They're like that all the time," I said, dismissing them. Tatiana and Sean ran the school as if it was their own reality show, both of them star athletes and honor students from wealthy families. "Some people peak in high school, you know."

He pulled back and raised his eyebrows. "Don't tell me you're jealous."

"Jealous?" I sputtered. "Me? Of them?"

"Yes," he said, teasing. "Jealous of Tati and Sean."

Was I? I wondered. After all, Tati had deep roots in Two Rivers. Her father owned half the town. A winner since birth, she was destined for great things. She was sure to win every event she competed in in the Division Championships, break the Allison Singer record, win the scholarship, and make the All-American team. Recruiters from across the country called her daily. Her boyfriend, one of the hottest guys in school, adored her. She was the queen of Two Rivers High School. But I wasn't the jealous type. Whatever she had going for her didn't detract from what I had going for me.

Before I could give Justin his answer, Mel joined us, flushed and out of breath after dancing the last two songs with Matt.

"What did Tati want?" she asked as she poured two cups of water.

"Just checking on us," Justin said, "making sure everyone's having a good time."

Mel rolled her eyes. "Queen Tati. Now she thinks she owns the church."

We all laughed.

"Somebody better set that girl straight," Matt said.

"Oh," Mel said, looking right at me, "trust me. Somebody will."

"I'd like that dance now," I told Justin, rising from the table and not waiting for an answer. The last thing I wanted was to listen to Mel fantasize about my beating Tati. She couldn't let that rest, not even at the dance, with our dates, having a good time. She was the one who needed to be set straight.

Chapter 47

We were among the last to leave the dance, reluctant to end the evening. Someone had turned off the pretty party lights and switched on the full fluorescents, which beamed down on us, killing the room's party glow, turning it back into the no-frills parish hall. Erica and Kelsey had gone home long ago, most of the crowd had thinned, and the DJ packed up his gear. Members of the Women's Group cleared the tables.

Mel and I sat at our table, massaging our aching feet.

"We'll be lucky if we can walk tomorrow," I said.

She groaned. "Why do women wear such ridiculous shoes, anyway?"

"They look great," I said, glancing at our strappy, spiky sandals lying in a pile under the table.

"Well, they don't feel too good." She pointed and flexed her foot. "I think I've got a cramp."

"You girls ready to go?" Justin asked as he and Matt returned from helping the DJ wheel his equipment out to his car.

I dreaded the evening's end, but the hour was late, and we had church in the morning. I put on my shoes and grabbed my purse and shawl.

"See you in the morning, Mel."

I'd never danced so much in my life and was as tired as after any monster practice. Justin and I walked out of the hall, saying goodbye to those staying behind for cleanup. Outside, the chilly night air woke me up, and I wrapped my shawl around my shoulders, wishing I'd worn something warmer. The Jeep was parked and running at the door.

"Your chariot awaits," Justin said as he opened the door.

"When did you do this?" I asked as I climbed in, grateful the heater was running.

"When I came out to help the DJ load his truck I figured I'd start the Jeep and warm it up for you." He shut the door.

His foresight and thoughtfulness touched me. "Thank you," I said as he settled into the driver's seat. He shrugged and headed the Jeep toward home.

Minutes later, we parked outside Maggie and Pat's.

"All tucked in for the night at the Flynn's house," Justin said. He left the Jeep running while we observed the house.

"Well, it is almost midnight," I said.

"Looks like someone waited up for you." The living room lights lit the windows, and the glow of the TV was visible through the drapes.

"Probably Aunt Maggie."

"I'd better get you inside."

He opened the door and helped me climb down from the Jeep. Taking my arm, he walked me up the short pathway to the front door. The porch light was on, and I heard the murmur of the TV.

"I had a great time tonight," he said. "Thank you for coming to the dance with me." He edged closer toward me.

I blushed as the space between us grew smaller. "I'm glad you asked me," I managed to get out, remembering my manners. "I had the best dancer on the dance floor."

He smiled. "You're a great dancer, too. Maybe we can do this again sometime."

The idea of future dances with him sent a burst of energy through me which I hoped he couldn't detect. "Okay," I said, trying to sound noncommittal.

"You know I want to kiss you good night," he whispered, edging even closer so that now his warm breath brushed my cheek.

"Okay," I mumbled, not knowing how to respond to *that.* I'd never been kissed before and hadn't expected to be kissed tonight, although the thought had crossed my mind.

Justin leaned in closer, and a second later I felt his lips against mine, soft and smooth. He lingered a moment and then put his arms around me in an embrace, our lips locked. He broke the kiss with a sigh and buried his head in my hair.

"You smell so good," he said.

I was still reeling from the kiss, my eyes closed, as I returned his embrace and held him close. I needed to catch my breath and slow my racing heart, almost impossible with him so close. "You mean I don't smell like chlorine?" I asked, defusing the moment before the excitement carried me away.

He laughed and pulled his head back, relaxing his grip on me. "Not at all."

I let go of him and smiled up into his beautiful blue eyes.

"You need to go inside, and I need to go home. I've got an early shift at the pool tomorrow, and I'm doing a set right before."

"You swim on Sundays?"

"I swim every day I can, Aerin, whether it's morning practice at the high school or lap swim at the Y."

"Morning swim?"

"Most mornings. If I'm scheduled to work, I skip the a.m. practice and do my laps either before or after my shift."

"You're driven," I said. "I used to be like that."

"What happened?"

I shrugged. "Too much to talk about right now."

"Maybe you can tell me about it tomorrow."

"Maybe."

Justin looked at his watch. "Look, two minutes before midnight. I guess the Jeep's not turning into a pumpkin tonight." He reached for the doorknob and opened the front door.

I entered the house without a sound, not wanting to disturb anyone and not wanting to see him go. "Good night," I said, "and thanks again."

"Good night Aerin. Sweet dreams." He gave me one last smile before I pushed the door closed. I rushed to the nearest window and watched him saunter off the porch, down the front path, and climb into his Jeep. As he pulled away from the house, he gave a tiny beep. I stared out the window until he disappeared around the curve at the end of the street.

Aunt Maggie was awake, reading a book. Uncle Pat sat in his recliner, asleep, old Salty at his feet.

Maggie roused when I came in. "Did you have a good time?" she asked.

I nodded, not sure where to begin. "Everything was wonderful."

"Tell me all about it in the morning. It's late, and we both need to get to bed." She switched off the TV.

"I don't think I can sleep tonight," I said. "I'm pretty wired."

"That good, huh?" she asked as we headed for the stairs.

"Yeah," I said, hoping she couldn't see me blush.

"Oh, to be young again," she said. "Do you want me to help you get undressed? Take down your hair?"

"That would be great."

She followed me to my room and closed the door. The house was in night mode, all the kids asleep, the drone of the furnace the only noticeable sound. She helped me undress and get ready for bed, while I shared with her every detail of my evening, until I was so tired I couldn't talk anymore.

She tucked me into bed, and said, "I'm glad you had a good

time."

I nodded and drifted off to sleep, a silly smile on my face.

WEEK EIGHT:

Breakout

Chapter 48

Over the next few days, I floated on a cloud of happiness. Justin and I were officially boyfriend and girlfriend. He found excuses to be on deck during practice, walked me to some of my classes, and came to Maggie's house every night to help me study. We hadn't shared any more kisses since the night of the dance, but I relived that sweet first kiss every night before I went to sleep.

Swimming was going great too. With the big invitational coming up on Saturday we only had one meet during the week. We thumped the Mavericks, a small team not in our division that Coach put on the schedule to help us keep our momentum. We trained hard in practice, though, increasing our yardage and time in the weight room. At the end of the week he let up a little bit, allowing us to rest for the weekend's tough races.

Saturday came quick.

Coach said it was important to arrive early for the big meets, to stake our claim on our space for the day, start warming up, and watch everyone else walk in behind us. He preferred that to trying to get our bearings in a noisy, crowded natatorium. He said it gave us room to breathe, to relax before the excitement mounted and the energy became palpable. I agreed. I never liked walking onto a pool deck packed with swimmers.

We arrived at the natatorium two hours before the start of the meet, first on deck, beating the home team to their own event. We unloaded our gear, and got in the water before the next group showed up, filling the pool with hundreds of swimmers all looking for space, like salmon in a run.

After the warm-up, I joined Mel, Erica, and Charlie on our yoga mats on the pool deck. The air was cool, and we wore our team sweat suits. We sat in a circle, kneading the neck and shoulders of the girl in front of us. At this point in the season, we accepted our sore muscles as badges of honor. Complaining was futile, so we worked through the pain.

While I stretched and kneaded Erica's shoulders, I kept one eye on the action in the pool. I'd gotten a glimpse of the psych sheet, and spotted a few familiar names from previous teams and seasons, swimmers I'd bested in races, coaches I'd met. I wondered if any would recognize me.

The crowd in the stands started filling in. My father was due to arrive any moment, and I scanned the crowd for him, Geneviève, and the girls. Dawn, still on strict bed rest, would not be joining them. The first event was just minutes away, and I hoped they would arrive before they lost out on the best seats.

We pulled together one more time before the meet started for last minute instructions. Coach pulled us in close, a tight huddle, our arms draped over each other's shoulders, as he reviewed the lineup. When he finished, he said, "There are some tough teams here, and some tough swimmers, many we've faced in the past, a few we've beaten, and a couple who beat us. You girls have everything you need to make a strong statement today. I trust everyone to do her best. Now go get 'em!"

Mel and Tati led us in a cheer and we shouted to the rafters, "Blazers Pride!"

Up first was the 200 medley relay. All nineteen teams competed, each with two relay teams, so 152 girls swam the race. Coach ordered all of those not swimming to cheer from the sidelines, so I joined my teammates at the pool's edge to root for our teams. Our "A" team with Taylor in backstroke, Charlie swimming the breaststroke, Erica in fly position, and Kim anchoring the freestyle finish, came in fifth. Our "B" team with Jordan doing the breast finished in 22nd place. The "A" team, breathless and exhilarated, crowded around Coach for high fives. Jordan slunk back, head down, not looking at anyone, and slumped on the bleachers.

My first event, the 200 free, was next, and the first heat was already in progress. I was in the final heat, so I had some time to prepare. I joined the swimmers in lane five, and stretched out, all the while searching the crowd in the packed-to-capacity bleachers for my father, Geneviève, and the girls. Where were they? He said they'd be here before the meet started and we were twenty minutes in. I watched the swimmers ahead of me, the lines moving quickly as each heat lasted less than three minutes.

My time came, and I hopped up onto the block, adjusting my cap and goggles, swinging and stretching my arms before the buzzer signaled the start of the race. I had a second to search for my father in the stands one last time. No sign of him. The starter announced the event, and I entered race mode, banishing thoughts of my absent father. It wouldn't be the first event he'd missed.

"Swimmers, take your mark," the announcer said. I assumed start position, my muscles poised to leap off the block the instant the buzzer buzzed. It did, and we launched, the meet's top swimmers in this event, hitting the water in the same second.

I plowed through the water, in my zone, counting my strokes until the turn, and ricocheting off the wall, seven times, oblivious to anyone around me, focusing on my breath, my arms, my legs. At the finish, I touched the wall full force and popped out of the water, panting. I checked the clock: 2:01.22, fifth place. My best time this season, but a few seconds shy of my real personal best. Coach expected me to finish fifth, and I didn't disappoint. I climbed out of the pool, pulled off my cap and goggles, congratulated Tati on her second place finish (her personal best) and found Coach.

He gave me a high five and a pat on the back. "Great job, Aerin," he said. "I knew I could count on you. Now get something to eat and drink and rest up for the 500. I need another fifth place finish from you."

I nodded, still out of breath, but pleased with my performance, and took a seat on the bleachers. I scanned the crowd of spectators again, searching for my father. His absence was getting to me. He'd *promised* he'd come. He'd missed all of my meets this season because he lived so far away, but this one was close to his home. How could he blow it off?

I fished around in my bag, found my phone, and sneaked a peek to see if he'd left any text messages. Nope. Nothing. Not a word. No email. No missed calls. I sent him a quick text - *Where are you???* - and dropped the phone back into my bag. I grabbed a bottle of water from our cooler, sucked half down in a single gulp, and resumed my seat on the bleachers.

The 200 IM was midway and we had several girls in the event, including Erica. Mel gestured to me to get up and cheer for our teammates, but I stayed put, not in the mood to play cheerleader. I sipped my water and viewed the pool from the bleachers, seeing the swimmers but not following the races.

"What's the matter with you?" Mel asked when the event ended. Erica had come in fourth, and two of our other teammates had finished in the top sixteen. Nice wins.

"I'm tired," I said.

"You have no time to be tired. Get up and start cheering. I'm up next." The 50 free was about to start. "I better finish in the top five," she said. She took off to join the competition.

I took my usual place at the end of the pool to urge Mel on when she made the turn. While I waited for her heat to begin, I searched the crowd of spectators for familiar faces. Not even one. The meet was too far from home for most of our parents to attend. We didn't expect many supporters. But my father lived *so close,* and it was Saturday. He could still make the 500 and the relays. He'd only missed my first event. Perhaps he was stuck in traffic. He'd probably walk in any minute.

At last, Mel was in the water, ripping through it like a storm. As she approached the turn, I leaned forward and shouted "Go!" She flipped and pushed off the wall in tandem with everyone else. It was a close race, the top eight swimmers in the meet. I followed them back to the finish, cheering Mel on all the way, checking the clock to see how it ended. Mel came in fourth at 26:03, her personal best. She looked up at the clock in disbelief, trying to catch her breath, triumph plastered across her face. She caught my eye.

"I did it!" she cried, waving. "Fourth place!"

I waved back, proud of her. She worked so hard, and it was beginning to pay off. She was just .04 seconds away from meeting her goal of finishing in less than twenty-six seconds.

Diving was up next, giving us a chance to regroup. Those of us not swimming for a while ate our lunch of turkey sandwiches, carrot sticks, and an apple or banana. We had four divers on our team and cheered them on, knowing they'd each place in the top 16. I kept one eye on them and one eye on the stands, hunting for my father. He still hadn't arrived. I snuck a look at my phone. No text messages. No missed calls. No emails. Nothing from Geneviève, either. I tossed my half-eaten banana in the trash, no longer hungry. He'd let me down, and he knew how important this meet was to me.

"Earth to Aerin," Mel said, startling me. "You're a million miles away, and it doesn't look like a happy place. What's going on with you?"

"They're not here," I mumbled.

"Who's not here? Your father?" I'd told her they were all coming, and she'd get to meet my dad, the stepbrats, and Geneviève.

I nodded, averting my face, not wanting her to see the tears in my eyes.

"They're probably stuck in traffic."

"On Saturday?" I countered.

"Maybe something came up."

"He would have left me a message if he couldn't make it. He just doesn't care. He blew me off." My disappointment was giving way to anger, a familiar emotion when it came to my dad. I'd been trying so hard to replace it with understanding, tolerance, and patience. Yet I couldn't help being angry. He'd *promised*, and this was the only meet he'd get to this season. I felt so alone, even though I was with Mel and all the other girls. I wanted someone in the stands for *me*. Hundreds of other parents had made it, but none of them cared about *me*.

"I bet he's doing something for the girls," I said. "They have soccer on Saturday mornings. He said they'd skip out early today to make the meet, but maybe they were playing well, and he decided to let them finish their games. He wouldn't want to mess up *their* day." Of course not. He was their chauffeur, coach, and head cheerleader. Heaven forbid they suffered any disappointment when it came to Saturday soccer.

Anger simmered, and I tried to brush it off, but as each minute ticked by without them in the stands, I grew angrier. I checked my phone every five minutes, risking Coach catching me and confiscating it. No word from any of them. Again, I sent a text. *Where are you?*

Diving ended, and our girls finished as expected.

With the first half completed, Coach was smiling, pleased with our performance.

Funny thing about big meets: there's tons of down time, waiting around for your next event, cheering on your teammates, drinking lots of water to stay hydrated, listening to music on your iPod, or catching up on homework. I tried to distract myself by lying on the bleachers, my ear buds plugged in, listening to music, and pretending I wasn't enraged that my father had ditched me.

The meet went on, our girls ratcheting up points in the fly and 100 free, Erica, Mel, and a few others making their season's bests and qualifying times for the Division Championships. Coach was everywhere, urging on every swimmer, writing nonstop on his clipboard, keeping score. As we continued to show our strength, we grew more excited, that is, everyone but me, because I was still fuming that I hadn't heard a word from my father and he was nowhere to be seen.

It was time for the 500, my big event. I took one last look at my phone, and this time I had a message.

Sorry, honey. I can't make it. Something came up.

I stared at the text message, incredulous. Something came up? What something? And why wait until now to tell me? The meet was half over. If he couldn't make it he should've told me long before now.

I tossed the phone back into my bag, grabbed my cap and goggles, and stomped off, seeing red, my heart pumping and the race hadn't even started. I got into my lane. I was seeded sixth. I pulled on my cap, adjusted it, and tugged on my goggles. I did some stretches and relaxed breathing to calm down. I studied the other swimmers in my event. Tati was seeded second, and stood behind the starting block two lanes to my left. Two of the Chinese exchange students we'd met up with before were also in the race. They too looked calm, serious about the race, not thinking of anything else.

I looked up into the stands one last time, hoping I'd see my dad, but knowing he was miles away busy with something else, and remembering me at the last minute, like an afterthought. That was me, second place, the left behind daughter who came out only on weekends and holidays per the divorce decree.

Angry tears filled my eyes, and I couldn't wipe them away because I was wearing my goggles. My nose starting running and I swiped at it. It was my turn to get up on the block. I jumped up and got in position. Right before the starter announced the race I glanced up into the bleachers. Calvin Reese stood in the top row wearing a Blazers T-shirt. He shouted, "You got this one, Tatiana. Go get it!"

Before I could react, the buzzer buzzed, and I flew off the block, hitting the water hard, and started to tear through it. I banished all thoughts and concentrated on breathing and moving. I focused on the black line and hit the walls with all I had, my flip turns flawless, my stroke perfect. All the while, my heart was breaking. I cried soundless tears, thankful that I was in the water where no one could see me cry.

As the tears fell, I beat at the water with my anger, taking it out on its choppy surface, oblivious to the swimmers competing against me. I didn't care if I won or lost. I just wanted these horrible feelings to go away, and the best way to get rid of them was to leave them in the pool.

Mel was my lap counter, and I counted off each lap as she turned the numbers, 13-15-17 lengths. As I approached the turn for the last lap, I heard the shot of the starting pistol that signaled the first swimmer had reached the final lap. I flipped and rebounded off the wall with no idea as to who that first swimmer was, and not caring. I didn't let up on my stroke, even though my chest was heaving and my muscles burned. I used everything I knew about this race to swim it on autopilot, flushing out my emotions and replacing them with physical pain.

As I approached the final turn, Mel waved the number 19 at me, and I flipped again, pushing off the wall with all I had, racing toward the finish, hearing the dull roar of the crowd over the splashing of the water, lost in my zone, unaware of the other swimmers. I approached the finish and sped up, arms streaking through the water, my feet kicking liked I'd just started the race. I hit the wall with all I had left. Depleted and spent, I waited as the other swimmers came in behind me. I tugged off my goggles and looked at the scoreboard. I'd won the race, 4:54.16, and finished three seconds ahead of Tatiana, who came in second.

Chapter 49

I gasped, struggling to catch my breath and make sense of what had just happened. I looked at Tati, who stared back at me, astounded.

The swimmer to my right leaned over to high five me. "Great race," she said as we shook hands.

I was the last swimmer to climb out of the pool, still in shock, not comprehending what I'd done and afraid of the reaction from Coach and my teammates. I walked back to our spot on the pool deck, head down, ignoring the congratulations from the other coaches.

The first person to approach me was Coach. "What was that all about?" I couldn't tell if he was angry or stunned. "You just broke a meet record."

It was worse than I thought. I shook my head, not meeting his eyes.

"I've never seen anyone swim like that," he said. "You and I need to have a little talk. In my office tomorrow, right after school."

I met his eyes and nodded.

"Get a drink and then head back down to the blocks," he said. "You're up again in the 200 free relay. And congratulations.

Excellent swim."

I rejoined my team and plucked a bottle of water from the cooler.

"I knew it!" Mel was in my face. "I knew there was something special about you. Why did you lie to us? Why did you lie to *me*?" She looked angry and hurt, her face red, brows knit together, blue eyes smoldering.

The last thing I wanted to do was talk to Mel. The other girls stared at us, speechless. Tatiana huddled with Jordan and her fan club, still wearing that expression of astonishment. Jordan's lips moved a mile a minute as she hissed into Tati's ear, her icy blue eyes riveted on me.

"You do know you broke a meet record?" Mel would not let up.

I nodded and took a long swig of my water. "We don't have time to talk about this, Mel. The relay's about to start." Already the lines had formed.

Coach D came over and said, "You guys better get moving. You're up next."

Tatiana led the way, Mel and Erica following. I walked a few feet behind, not wanting to have to talk to anyone. As we lined up, Erica said, "Way to go, Aerin, breaking the meet record. You surprised me."

"She surprised *everyone*," Mel said.

Little did they know, I surprised myself.

"I didn't know you could swim like that," Tati said, her brown eyes dark, lips tight.

"I'm just having a good day," I said, struggling to defuse the tension between the four of us.

"Good day?" Mel asked. "No one has a good day like that. They seeded you *sixth*. You shaved more than ten seconds off your best time! You won the event, *and* broke a meet record."

It was our turn to race. Tati was lead, then Erica, me, and Mel finishing up. We took our places, tugging our caps and goggles into place.

“We’re not done talking,” Mel said. “You need to tell me everything.”

I had no time to respond. The starter announced the event. Our race was on.

Chapter 50

Our relay team was seeded fifth. All the turmoil that came before it had its advantages. We finished third. Two more events stood between my final event, the 400 free relay. I needed fresh air.

I zipped up my team jacket, stepped into my flip-flops and walked off the pool deck to the lobby. I pushed against a milling crowd buying food at the snack bar, and browsing through the T-shirts, caps, goggles, and other gear the swim vendors had brought in. Minutes later, I was out the door in the afternoon sunshine, where the air was free of the smell of chlorine. I leaned against the brick building, closed my eyes, and inhaled.

"I figured you'd be out here," Mel said, startling me.

I groaned. "I want to be alone, Mel. Please give me a couple of minutes."

She leaned against the building beside me. "Everyone is talking about you, and it's not nice," she said.

My stomach flipped. Just what I'd been dreading. "What are they saying?"

"Jordan's calling you a liar. She said you joined the team under false pretenses, acting like you're just an average varsity swimmer, and then beating Tatiana in her best event."

I had no response. I had been lying, to everyone, including myself, trying to be just one of the girls, not making swimming the biggest thing in my life.

"Jordan says you broke some code of honor or something. She's trying to turn the other girls against you. She's starting a petition to demand Coach kicks you off the team."

"She's nuts. She cares that much?" I asked, knowing that of course she'd try to get me kicked off the team. I was a threat to Tatiana and Jordan was riding on her success.

"Of course she's upset you beat Tati. She's president of her fan club. She can't wait for Tati to break the 500 record. She's got a huge publicity campaign all planned out, and she'll be right beside her when the cameras start rolling and the flashes go off."

"What are the others saying?"

"Most of them don't understand what's going on, but Jordan's rallying them for Team Tati. You better watch it."

What could they do to me? Coach would never throw me off the team, knowing he had a star performer. I wasn't worried about the other girls. I wasn't close to them. The only ones I cared about were Mel, Erica, Kelsey, and Charlie. I couldn't bear to lose their friendships.

"What do you think?" I asked.

"Me? I don't know how you do it. Or why. If I could swim like that, I'd want to win all the time."

"Well," I said, "winning isn't everything."

"Easy for you to say. I bust my butt to win. I think about it all the time! Everything I do is geared toward winning. I can't imagine trying *not to* win. Can you explain that?"

I sighed. She'd never understand. "It's not easy. I actually have to work at it." I laughed. She didn't. "Look, Mel, I never intended to hurt anyone. So, I won a race. Big deal. I doubt I'll win another one."

She regarded me through knowing eyes. "I had you pegged," she said, "but you surprised me, too. I suspected you were a better swimmer than you let on. I can tell you've had excellent training. You've got the best technique I've ever seen. When I asked about your best times or if you'd won any titles you evaded the question, and I let it slide. So, what's the truth, Aerin? What *is* your best time in the 500? Have you won any titles?"

My staying under the radar was over, and after today, everyone would expect great things from me. I hesitated just a second, thinking it would be better to tell another little white lie, but realized it would make things worse.

"Okay," I said. "You deserve the truth. I won my varsity and club championships in both the 200 and the 500 the last two years. Up until last winter, I was preparing to swim for a Division I school and prepare for the Olympic trials. My best time in the 500 is six seconds faster than Tati's. My 200 is even better." Admitting all of that was like dumping a big weight.

"Numbers?"

I sighed. She was getting technical. "4:53.02. 1:50.12."

Mel stared at me, blue eyes round, mouth gaping. For once, she had nothing to say.

"That's it, Mel, okay? So can we go back inside? It's probably time for the relay and Coach will kill us if we miss the start."

"This is crazy," she said, shaking her head. "Those are New York State qualifying times, All-American Conference. Do you know what this means?"

I stared back at her, not following, and shrugged. "I made States?"

"Made States? You can *win* States! You can win the division title and the fifty thousand dollar scholarship. This is *terrible*."

"Don't worry, Mel. I don't plan to win big. I've given up on winning. I just want to swim for fun and keep my head clear."

She shook her head. "I don't believe you," she said. "No one who can swim like that would try to lose, try to pretend she was something less. You're crazy. And you know something else? Not only did you lie about your performance in the pool, but you also lied about your mother. You told us she's a nurse serving in Afghanistan, but she's really a thief and a druggie locked up in some rehab jail. Jordan's right, Aerin, you *are* a liar."

Her harsh words stunned me. How could she talk about my mother like that after I'd confided in her? I thought she was on my side. That little ball of anger I struggled to contain sparked and my heart started pounding as my face grew hot. I clenched my fists. "What did you say about my mother?"

"You heard me. Or maybe all of that was a lie too? You've only been here a few weeks. No one knows much about you. I bet you had a good time tricking everyone into thinking you were one of us." Her voice was thick with emotion, her eyes dark and angry. I'd never seen her like that.

"Of course I didn't make up the story about my mother. Why would I? It's a horrible story." I could barely speak, consumed with anger and hurt. One thing I knew for sure: I did not want to lose Mel's friendship. "Mel, I'm sorry. I didn't mean to hurt anyone – "

"You know, the whole team is going to turn upside down. Jordan's already splitting sides, and you don't have too many on yours. I welcomed you onto this team, befriended you when you knew no one, welcomed you into my home, helped you make friends. Now I feel like an idiot because you were playing us the whole time." She started to walk away.

"Mel, wait," I cried, following.

She pulled open the door to the natatorium and stalked off. I was sick to my stomach, my cheeks wet with tears. I had to fix this. I followed, chasing her back to the pool deck. Halfway there, I bumped into someone who felt like a wall.

"Excuse me," I said and looked up into the furious face of Calvin Reese.

"Aerin Keane." He sneered at me, looking like the big bad wolf. "You should watch where you're going."

I stopped in my tracks. Was he threatening me?

"Get moving. Don't you have another event?" he snarled.

Without saying another word, I rushed past him. I did have one more race today.

Chapter 51

We finished the meet in fourth place, as expected. Several of the girls made their personal bests. A few more made division cut times. I, of course, broke a meet record. Our mood, however, was subdued.

The tension on the pool deck was thick as we packed up our gear, put on our sweats, and headed for the bus. No one spoke to me, not even Charlie, who wouldn't meet my eyes. I swallowed a lump in my throat, determined not to cry until I was alone. I held my head high and followed everyone out to the bus.

I was the last one on, and as I headed down the aisle in search of a seat, no one looked at me or offered to let me sit with them. Every other day I sat with Mel, but when I passed her she made a point of setting her bag on the seat next to her to show me I was not welcome to sit there. I strode to the rear of the bus, took the last seat and spread out, leaning against the window. I pulled my phone out of my bag, checked my messages – none – and plugged in my ear buds, listening to my swim playlist all the way back to Two Rivers.

Back at the high school, I waited until everyone got off the bus and didn't get up from my seat until the driver asked me what I was doing. I left the bus and started heading toward Maggie's. I didn't get too far before Justin's dusty Jeep pulled up alongside me, Mel in the front passenger seat. "Hey Apple," he said. "Can I give you a lift?"

"Come on, Justin, let's go," Mel said, her eyes flicking over me. "I'm in a hurry."

"No," I said, my heart sinking. "I'm okay. I need to clear my head. Walking will do me good. It's been a long day."

"If you're sure," he said, smiling. "I'll see you Monday? Physics in the library during study period?"

I nodded, and he drove off. I hoisted my bag onto my shoulder and started walking. It was early evening and an autumn chill rushed through me. I pulled the hood of my jacket over my head and quickened my pace, anxious to get home so I could take a hot shower and have something loaded with carbs for dinner. Aunt Maggie and her family had gone to visit her sister in Brooklyn, an all day trip, and I did not expect them back until late. I had the whole house to myself. No one would witness my meltdown.

Salty met me as I entered, crying to go out. I closed the door behind him and dropped my bags, leaving them in the foyer. Plenty of time to unpack after I filled my stomach. In the kitchen, I set out Salty's dinner so I wouldn't have to hear him whine when he came in, and checked what Maggie had left for me in the refrigerator. A stack of plastic food containers had my name on them. I heated their contents in the microwave and feasted on chicken, baked beans, and mashed potatoes. I finished with a thick slice of apple pie, washed down with two glasses of milk.

It was after eight o'clock and still no sign of Maggie, Pat, and the kids for which I was very grateful. I was in no mood to talk about my day with my game face on. I cleaned up from dinner, emptied my swim bag, started a load of laundry, and headed for the shower.

I climbed into bed, still damp, lights out, and pulled the covers up to my shoulders. I lay quiet for a while, numb, trying to clear my head, ignoring the rush of memories that threatened to overcome me.

Waiting for my father to show up at the meet.

The sick sensation in my stomach that got worse every time I searched the stands and didn't see him.

The numbers on the clock after my heat in the 500.

The roar from the crowd when I won the race and broke the record.

Jordan's reaction to my win.

Mel's harsh words about my mother.

My teammates ignoring me on the pool deck and the long ride home.

I was used to being the lonely girl, singled out, unapproachable, no time for friends or fun. This was not a new feeling. Still, it hurt, because in Two Rivers I'd found friends who liked me for *me*, and not for what I did in the pool.

I glanced at my phone. No more messages from my dad. What was going on? I was sure I'd have heard from him by now. It was getting late, and the girls' soccer game was long done. In spite of my curiosity, I was determined not to call him, turned off my phone, and rolled over to go to sleep. That's when the tears came.

Chapter 52

Sunday morning, I lounged in bed, ignoring the noisy kids tearing through the house and the sounds and smells of Uncle Pat making breakfast. At ten o'clock, I decided to rejoin the world. I checked my phone – nothing, no missed calls, no emails, no text messages. Nothing screamed outcast louder than a silent phone. Its battery was running on empty. I got up and plugged it into its charger on my desk.

An envelope caught my attention. A letter from Mom. I must have been so engrossed in my pity party last night I hadn't noticed it.

Her perfect cursive filled the pages.

'My dear Aerin, I can send email now, and it's so much quicker, but I got used to writing these little letters and don't want to stop. They seem much more personal and I want to feel close to you although we're apart. Things are going very well here. I'm teaching classes! Health classes. We talk about women's issues, fertility, pregnancy, breast and heart health, nutrition and fitness. I'm even teaching a few of the women how to swim. I'm doing 1,000 yards a day now, what do you think of that? I haven't put in so much yardage in years! But it feels good, and I've gotten so much stronger. I've even got a little muscle on my biceps.

My therapy is also going well. I'm in three groups and meet with my counselor twice a week. I'm getting a much better handle on what happened in

Afghanistan. When I get out of here, I'm going to join some veterans' groups and try to get connected with some others who may have experienced what I've had. I realize I can't go through this alone. I need to be able to share my fears and worries with people who understand where I'm coming from. No more hiding.

Anyway, I'm halfway through my sentence, can you believe it? Before you know it I'll be home. We need to talk about that. I don't want to uproot your life in the middle of your senior year, but I also don't want to go home without you. I'm working on it with my counselor. On my next visitation day – in two weeks! – you and I will have to figure it all out.

I'm so happy you sent the pictures from the dance! You looked breathtaking. This young man, Justin, is very handsome. Maggie said he was from a nice family. I printed out all of the pictures and posted them around my bed. Everyone who enters my room tells me how beautiful you are.

I trust school is going well? And swimming? Maggie said you're doing okay, but not winning. (Sorry, I had to ask her.) Remember what I said. Don't give up on swimming. Stick to our plan. Trust me. I know. But enough pressure. I'm sure your father is riding you pretty hard. Speaking of Gordon, is he okay? I never hear from him. How are Dawn and the baby?

It's getting late, and I need to wrap it up before they shut the lights off. I miss you. I love you. I'm getting better. I'll be home soon, and we'll get on with our lives. I promise. See you in two weeks. Write back in between. Love, Mom

I read the letter three times, folded it with care, and placed it back in its envelope to join the others in my desk drawer. The little stack was growing thick with her writings.

There was a knock on the door. "I thought I heard signs of life in here," Maggie said as she opened it. "May I come in?"

I nodded, and she entered.

"Pat made bacon and eggs. I saved you some. We're getting ready for church. Are you coming?"

I'd forgotten about church. I was in no mood to see Mel and shook my head. "I'm exhausted," I said, which was true. "Is it all right if I skip?"

"That's up to you. I can't force you. Tough meet yesterday?"

"Yeah," I said. "In more ways than one."

"The paper has a big write up about it," she said. "Something about you breaking a meet record."

I groaned. The paper! I hadn't thought of that.

"Oh boy," she said, looking sympathetic. "What happened?"

I told her the whole story, beginning with my father not showing up and ending with the miserable bus ride home. She let me spill everything without interruption, and handing me the box of tissues when the waterworks started.

"I'm not surprised this happened," she said when I'd run out of words.

"You're not?" I mumbled, my voice thick with tears.

"I knew you couldn't put on the 'I'm just an average swimmer' act for too long. You were bound to flub up."

"What do I do now?" I asked.

"You're going to go downstairs and eat breakfast. Then you're going to get dressed and go to church with us. Take it easy today, do your homework, go to bed early, and get up at five a.m. tomorrow morning to go to practice. I'll drive you."

"Morning practice?" I gawked. "No way. I may never go back to the pool, let alone hit morning practice."

"Isn't that what you do? The real Aerin Keane? You go to morning practice. You go to afternoon practice. You swim. You win. Swim, school, swim, study, sleep. That's the routine, isn't it?"

"It was," I said, hating the idea.

She ruffled my hair. "Get back on the block."

"I can't go back. Everybody hates me."

"They'll get over it. They know you're a great person. When they see how great of a swimmer you really are they'll be thrilled you're on *their* team."

"I hope you're right," I sighed, not convinced.

"Let's get you something to eat," she said. "You'll feel better."

Chapter 53

I followed her downstairs and tackled my breakfast. After I devoured a plate of eggs, bacon, home fries, and toast, I peeled an apple. The doorbell rang as I cut it into bite-sized slices.

"Aerin, you have a visitor," Maggie called from the foyer. She entered the kitchen with a knowing smile. Justin trailed behind her, not smiling.

I stopped slicing the apple, wiped my mouth with a napkin, and fluffed my hair, wondering if I looked like I'd just rolled out of bed.

"What are you doing here?" I asked.

"What kind of a greeting is that?" Maggie asked. She poured herself a cup of coffee. "I'll be in the living room if you need me."

"Hey," he said, taking a seat across from me. He wore his Sunday best: dress pants, shirt, tie, and shiny black shoes. His hair was damp, track lines from his comb still showing. His face was scrubbed clean and pink. Seeing him sitting across the table was the best part of my morning.

"You heard?" I asked, unsure as to whether or not he was as angry with me as everyone else was.

"I heard," he said, "but I'm not surprised. You're not as good an actress as you think."

I blushed. "What gave me away?"

"Aerin, you and I are alike. We're serious athletes. We work hard, train hard, and play harder. Most of the swimmers we compete against have no clue. They're not driven the way we are. I saw that in your eyes the day we met, and every time you raced. I sensed you holding back, and not liking it. Tell me, was it as hard as it looked?"

"Was what as hard as it looked?"

"Losing."

I didn't have to think about it for a second. "Well, yeah, especially when the competition's so thin."

He burst out laughing and slapped his leg. "That statement won't go any farther than this room, okay?"

I rolled my eyes. "That sounded terrible."

"Yeah, but it's true. Tatiana's your biggest competition and maybe a couple of those Chinese exchange students, but other than them you own the pool. You can beat Tati in the 500 and win that scholarship. Is that your plan?"

"I wasn't planning to. I mean, I am the new girl, and Tati's been working on it for years. It seems unfair to take it away from her."

"Hey, may the best swimmer win."

I shrugged. "So, you're not mad?"

He shook his head. "No, I'm not mad, but Mel's pretty hot, and the phones have been lighting up all night and this morning with the buzz. That's why I'm here. I wanted to make sure you knew."

A sense of foreboding came over me. "Knew what?"

"Jordan's been trashing you on her blog."

The blood drained from my face, and my breakfast started working its way back up.

"You haven't checked her blog?"

"I don't have time for Jordan's two-bit blog."

"Jordan has nothing but time and she's been pretty busy since yesterday afternoon. She Googled you and found out all kinds of stuff: your real name, your former swim teams, your stats, pictures, everything."

"No," I said. This couldn't be happening.

"And she plastered it all over her blog."

I dropped my head in my arms and collapsed on the table. It was worse than I thought. "And?" I lifted my head and looked at him. "What's she saying?"

He pulled his cell phone out of his pocket, pulled up Jordan's blog, and handed it to me. I took it as though it would burn my hand and scrolled through her long-winded post.

Aerin Keane is a liar, she wrote. *She pretends to be an ordinary swimmer when she's really* Margaret *Keane, an Olympic hopeful. What other lies has she told?*

Jordan had done some deep research and discovered my swimming records in the data base where every race I'd ever swam was documented. I was listed under my given name, Margaret Keane.

"Margaret?" Justin asked.

"Yeah," I said. "I'm named Margaret Aerin after my maternal grandmother, who passed away before I was born. But my parents called me Aerin from day one. When my mother signed me up for club swimming she did it under my full legal name."

I scrolled through the post, shaking my head at the photos Jordan had downloaded from the internet and used to help make her point, pictures of me wearing first place medals for the 500 free at last year's varsity and club championships. Jordan had also added links to an article in a swimming magazine that talked about my prospects for the Olympic team.

Leave it to her to blow my cover.

Dozens of comments from teammates and others followed, none of them kind.

Tears stung my eyes. People I'd thought of as friends had written awful things about me. The consensus was I was a fake and a phony and didn't deserve to live. I scrolled through the comments from the last twelve hours growing sicker and sadder. I handed the phone back to Justin.

"Well," I said, my voice wavering. I wiped the tears away. "Guess I can't do much about that."

"Don't worry. The school has an anti-bullying policy. Zero tolerance. Jordan will be in Principal Sorenson's office first thing tomorrow morning."

"That won't change anything," I sniffled.

"That will put a stop to her bullying. In a day or two, something else will happen, and this will be old news."

"Whatever. I'm not going back."

"What do you mean?"

"I'm calling my father and telling him to come and get me. I'll stay with him, go to school in his town."

"You can't leave Two Rivers!"

"Why not? Nothing here for me now."

He looked stunned, then hurt. "I thought I was here for you."

I didn't think I could feel any worse but I was wrong. "That didn't come out right. I know you're here for me, and I appreciate it."

"That's it?"

I gave him a blank look.

"Because I thought we had something special and I wanted to see where it was going."

That one sentence almost made up for all the hurt Jordan had caused me. "You mean that?" I whispered.

He nodded. "Please don't call your father. We'll work this out."

"You've got a plan?"

"As a matter of fact, I do. An excellent plan." He moved closer to me and reached for my hand. "This is what we're going to do."

Week Nine:

Back in Action

Chapter 54

At 5:15 the next morning, I stood in front of my mirror dressed for practice and recited one of my old mantras: *You are a winner. This is your race. Do not be afraid.*

Throughout my years of training, coaches had instilled in me the power of positive thinking and positive self-talk. I'd practiced their advice and had several affirmations to recite over the course of each day, especially before a big meet or event. I'd cast them aside this season, buried them deep inside me. This morning, with my new attitude, as Justin called it, I pulled them out and spoke them aloud, with more conviction each time.

It took a few seconds, but after several repetitions, I felt stronger. I needed to fortify myself before hitting the deck. Justin said most of the girls attended morning practice before tapering for the championship meet, now a couple of weeks away. Everyone who mattered would be at the pool.

I'd grown accustomed to "sleeping in" until after six each weekday, although early a.m. practice was part of my DNA from years of training. I'd wake up once I hit the water and the extra yardage would improve my performance, even if it meant I'd be exhausted come dinner time.

I made it to the door just as the lights from Justin's Jeep lit up the front lawn, slipped out of the house without a sound, and climbed into the passenger seat.

"How are you?" Justin asked as he inched away from the house trying not to disturb the neighbors.

I settled my gear on the floor in front of me. "I'm good."

"Did you stay off the internet?" he asked.

I nodded. "I was off the grid all day, no computer, no phone, except to talk to my dad. I finally decided to answer his calls and texts yesterday afternoon."

"And? What did he have to say? Did he have a good reason to skip your meet?"

Thoughts of my father made me sick. It turned out he had an excellent reason to miss my meet. "My stepmother's not doing well. She's in the hospital. She's in danger of losing the baby, and they have her hooked up to all kinds of monitors and things to try to control the situation. My dad said it's touch and go. He hasn't left her side. In all the excitement, he forgot about the meet."

"I'm sorry to hear that," he said.

I nodded. "We just have to wait and see. I hope everything works out, because Dad said if this pregnancy fails, Dawn might have to have an operation and won't be able to have more kids."

We arrived at the school seconds later. The place was dark and deserted, although dawn was beginning to show itself. We parted outside the natatorium, and I braced myself to enter the girls' locker room. It was empty, giving me a moment to prepare for what lay waiting for me on the pool deck. I peeled off my sweats and stuffed them into my locker with everything else I carried: swim bag, book bag, and a lunch bag holding my breakfast. I tugged on my cap and goggles, met my eyes in the mirror, and said, "Go get 'em, girl. You've got this."

~

A blast of cold air enveloped me as I pulled open the heavy door and stepped onto the pool deck. I stood tall, erect, stretching out all of my sixty-eight inches, then walked with confidence toward the blocks, not looking at anyone. A small group had assembled by the bleachers. Mel, Erica, Tati, and Jordan formed a tight circle, talking and laughing while they ran through warm-up stretches. I strode toward the blocks as if I didn't see them. They went silent as I passed.

"Well, look who decided to crawl out of bed," Jordan called after me. "What happened, *Margaret*? Couldn't sleep?"

I kept moving, readjusted my cap, pulled on my goggles. "Don't listen to her," I told myself. "You don't need them." I climbed onto the block in lane four, the girls' fast lane, and stared down at the water, its glassy surface unmarred. I dropped into starting position, counted to three, and dove in. The water broke for me and I streamlined close to the bottom, swimming halfway across before surfacing and starting my set.

I kept up a steady pace, focused on the black line, the wall, and the flags, getting into rhythm, stretching out my arms and legs, taking relaxed breaths, timing it just right, smooth and easy. In minutes, my mind was clear, and I no longer saw or heard Jordan and the others.

The water around me grew choppy, and I realized they'd started their sets and swam alongside me. As the clock ticked, I went about my routine as though I'd never stopped training at this level, executing perfect flip turns, my feet kicking nonstop, my arms arcing overhead in synchronicity, my hands cupped and pulling the water away from me, clearing my path. After 1,000 yards of freestyle, my fastest this season, I stopped to catch my breath. Coach was on deck now, sitting in his usual chair with his ever-ready clipboard in one hand and an enormous cup of coffee in the other. We made eye contact, and he mouthed, "Good move." I gave him a grim smile and pushed off to start my next set of 400 fly.

I killed the set, the first one out of the pool. I stood on the deck alone, drying off, and watched the action in the water. Justin was finishing up, ahead of the rest of the guys. I smiled; we really were an excellent match.

Tati and Mel led the girls, pushing on. Mel looked like she was struggling to keep up with Tati. I had to hand it to her – she gave it her all every time she hit the water. A wave of sadness washed over me. I missed her friendship already.

"No way you're done first." Jordan stood in the door of the locker room, exiting, on her way back to the pool. She had a habit of disappearing during sets. She claimed she had a "weak bladder." I figured she was just lazy. She focused her icy blue eyes on me and stalked toward me.

"So what if I am?" I asked, squeezing the excess water out of my hair.

"You're not that fast." She tried to sound snarky, but her lower lip trembled.

"You should know how fast I am, Jordan," I said, wrapping my towel around me. "You spent most of your weekend investigating me."

Her eyes narrowed. "Well, someone had to find out who you are, *Margaret*."

"And now everyone knows, including me," I said, brushing past her.

Before I could reach the locker room, Coach stopped me. "Don't forget our meeting this afternoon, right after school."

How could I forget?

Chapter 55

I rushed through my shower, plaited my wet hair, and pulled on my jeans and sweater in time to get out of the locker room before the other girls came in. I was not up to any more conversations like the one I had with Jordan.

The school was almost deserted that early in the morning. I found a booth in the back of the cafeteria and ate my breakfast – ham and egg sandwich, orange juice, and a banana - then reviewed my physics homework and double-checked the math problems I'd completed last night.

Justin slid into the seat across from me, his hair still wet, cheeks pink from his morning set. He stretched out and placed a long, lean leg on the bench beside me.

"You looked good this morning."

"Thanks," I said.

"Coach was impressed."

"He said something?" The last thing I wanted was Coach talking about me with the other swimmers.

"He said something like, 'Good to see Aerin Keane decided to meet her potential."

I dropped my head into my hands. "He didn't," I moaned. "I've got more than enough pressure on me. I don't need this."

"I think he meant it in a positive way."

"That is precisely what I wanted to avoid."

"Yeah, can you explain that to me? I still don't get it."

"What don't you get?"

"Why you don't want to win."

"It's not the winning," I said. "It's the time it demands, the concentration, the drowning out of everything else. My *whole life* was focused on swimming. And it fell apart while I was in the water. My parents split. My mother ended up in jail. In the end, winning wasn't worth the sacrifices I made."

"You do realize you have no control over what your parents do," he said.

I picked at a hangnail, avoiding his eyes. I'd heard that *way* too many times. "No, I can't control them or their actions, but if I had been *paying attention* I might have been able to keep things under control."

"You believe that?" He leaned back, consuming the entire bench, a skeptical look on his face.

I met his gaze. "Yeah."

"Okay," he leaned forward, all serious. "Let's say you slacked off on swimming, for what reason I do not know, but let's say you did, and you didn't win, and you weren't in the pool five, six hours a day. What would you have done about your parents?"

I leaned back in my seat and exhaled. I hadn't thought of it like that, in practical terms. "Well, I guess I would have seen the tension between them. My father wasn't happy when my mom joined the Reserve. My grandmother was living with us then and took me to school, swim practice, and meets. I didn't see too much of my dad. I always thought he was working, but I found out later he was seeing Dawn."

"You could've stopped that?"

I squirmed. "I suppose not. But when my mother came back

from her second tour and she was all messed up, maybe I could have saved her from falling into that rabbit hole she got stuck in if I had been paying attention."

"What would you have done to stop that?"

"I don't know! Maybe I would've told someone. Maybe I would've made her face up to what was going on. I wouldn't have sat by while she turned into a drug addict."

"People hooked on drugs don't want interference, and they don't want help until they're ready. Even if you had quit swimming and stayed with her 24/7, it wouldn't have changed what happened."

"Well, that's something we'll never know. I'll never forgive myself for being self-absorbed and letting her get so bad."

While we talked, the cafeteria filled with students coming in for breakfast. On the other side of the cafeteria Mel, Erica, Tatiana, and Jordan sat together, sharing their meal, laughing and joking. Although I was sitting with Justin, I felt left out. He caught me looking their way and said, "Don't worry. They'll come around."

"I don't care about Tati and Jordan," I said. "I just want things to be okay with Mel and Erica."

"They will be. Trust me. Once all of this blows over everything will be back to normal."

Chapter 56

The day wore on, and I found myself the subject of much curiosity. A girl in my English class who had never spoken to me stopped by my desk and asked, "Are you really going to the Olympics?"

Everyone grew silent, waiting for my response.

I gave her a puzzled look, and said, "How would I know? The Olympics are a long way off."

"I thought I heard something about it," she said, moving on and taking her seat at the back of the room.

For the rest of the class I sensed everyone's eyes on me, and even Mr. Evans, our teacher, stared at me when he thought I couldn't see him.

After my last class, I raced to the natatorium, first one on deck. Coach was in his office, studying some swim stats on his computer, clipboard in hand. He looked up when I announced myself from the doorway, turned off the monitor, spun around in his chair, and studied me over the reading glasses perched on his nose. "Come on in, Aerin."

I took the seat opposite him. For a few moments, we just sat there, him staring at me, and me not meeting his eyes. At last, he broke the silence.

"When a swimmer unknown to me joins my team, I check her out and review her stats. We have an interview. I may call her former coach. But with you, Aerin, I didn't do any of these things. You showed up here at the last minute and no other candidate came close to qualifying, except for Charlie, and I gave you a spot on the team." He picked up the cup of coffee on his desk and took a sip.

"From the first day, I saw that you are an incredible athlete, with huge talent nurtured with excellent training. I also saw that something troubles you, and I decided to wait and see if you might resolve your issues and break out. At every meet, I hoped you might reveal your strengths. It took a while, but last weekend you showed everyone what you can really do." The phone rang and he ignored it, letting it go to voice mail.

"Now, I'll admit I'm preoccupied with Tatiana Reese and the Singer challenge," he said. "This school has been waiting for someone to break that record for years, and I expect Tatiana will break it. But after what I've seen and read about you, I think you could break it too."

"I don't plan to challenge that record," I said. "Tatiana has every right to win that challenge."

He leaned back in his chair and folded his arms across his chest. "The best swimmer has the right to win that challenge. It's no secret I hope it will be Tatiana. I've been her coach for six years. I've seen her develop into a champion. But if a swimmer stronger and faster challenges and breaks the record, she deserves the rewards."

His neutral stance surprised me. Until now, he'd been rooting for Tati, positioning her to win all of her events, training her to break the record. It was almost a given. The team expected it. The whole *school* expected it. And so did the town. I guess I'd reached that impasse Maggie and I had talked about on the way home from the visit with my mother. I had it within me to break the record. The question was, did I want to? And did I want it enough to damage my relationships with everyone on the team, and perhaps everyone in the school?

"I've seen you blossom here, Aerin, making friends and enjoying your senior year. You struggle to keep up the appearance of being an average swimmer. It must be so hard to lose when you're used to being a winner. I've never seen anyone do that. I read a little bit of your story online and talked to Mike Starling at Manhattan Swim Club. I've read the write-ups, I see your potential, and I believe you can reach your goals. My advice is for you to let go of whatever it is that's holding you back. Opportunities like this come once in a lifetime, if at all. You don't want to look back ten or twenty years from now and wish you'd made a different choice. If I can do anything to help you succeed, just ask."

His generosity astounded me. I'd expected him to ream me out for causing all this controversy. But I was gold, and he knew it. Even if I wanted to quit, I doubt he'd let me. Still, I had not expected him to be so kind, thoughtful, and helpful.

"Thank you," I said. "I appreciate your letting me swim here. I'm sorry if I pretended to be something I'm not. I apologize if I've let the team down. It was never my intention to draw attention to myself or to hurt the other girls. From now on, I promise I'll do my best."

"I'm counting on it," he said, rising from his chair.

The noise outside the office suggested practice had started. Coach D blew her whistle from the other side of the pool. I needed to get wet.

"And I mean it, Aerin," he continued as we exited the office. "May the best swimmer win." He extended his right hand.

"Thanks, Coach." We shook on it.

"Do me a favor," he said. "Tell Jordan to come to my office right now."

Chapter 57

I walked to the bleachers and stepped out of my warm-up suit. A moment later Charlie approached me.

"Hey Aerin," she said, all smiles. "Guess what? I got an 'A' on my algebra test."

I smiled back at her. "High five!" I said, and we slapped hands. "Excellent! I told you all of that hard work would pay off."

"Charlie," Jordan called from the other side of the bleachers where she sat with Mel, Erica, Tatiana, and a few of the other girls, all with their heads bowed, deep in discussion, no doubt talking about me. "Come here."

"In a minute," Charlie responded. "I'm talking to Aerin."

"I said come here *now*," Jordan said, lasering her icy blue eyes on Charlie.

Charlie looked at me, a question in her eyes.

"You better go," I said. "You don't want to get on Jordan's bad side."

"I don't get it. Are you on Jordan's bad side?"

"I guess you didn't see her blog posts."

"What blog?"

"Never mind. You're not missing anything. Just get in the water before Coach gives you a double set. I'm right behind you."

She grinned, her mouth full of braces, and sauntered off to start her routine. I tugged on my cap but before I could pull on my goggles Jordan and the rest of the girls marched up to me.

"We want to talk to you," Jordan said, assuming the role of their leader.

"What's up?"

"Are you planning to challenge the 500 record?"

"To be honest, Jordan," I said, "I haven't put much thought into it."

"Don't," she said, "because that belongs to Tatiana. We don't want some outsider to come along and take it away from her."

That word, *outsider*, stung, yet I couldn't blame her, or them. They were protecting their own. I looked at Mel and Erica, who would not meet my eyes. Just a few days ago, we were best friends, the best friends I'd ever had. I bit back my tears, unwilling to let them see they'd gotten to me.

"Fair enough," I said. "I haven't made up my mind one way or the other, but I will say that if I do decide to take this challenge may the best swimmer win." I directed these last words at Tatiana, who stared back at me, her face neutral. We locked eyes for a moment, one opponent to another, each of us knowing what was at stake and that it could go either way.

Tatiana thought she had it all figured out, knowing the competition in the division, which wasn't much other than the Chinese exchange students whom no one had anticipated. Now she had to contend with me, competition from a direction she hadn't expected. In the middle of the season, she now had work to do. I almost felt sorry for her. We each took measure of the other, and as I stared her down that stirring started deep inside, the one I'd been suppressing all season, that hunger, the urge to overcome my opponent, to win, to be the best. I wondered if she felt it too.

She turned her eyes away from mine, and said, "Come on, let's go," leading the way to the blocks. The others followed, not meeting my eyes as they filed past.

"Oh, Jordan," I called out, "Coach said he wants you in his office again right now." She'd spent more than her fair share there, and was on probation off and on for all of her tardiness, slacking, and harassing of the younger girls.

She faltered, dropping out of step and turned back. "When?"

"Now. He's waiting, and he looks hot."

Her mean girl façade cracked a bit, and a glimmer of fear crossed her face, but she shook it off, maintaining her composure. "Did he say why?"

"No," I said, "but I wouldn't be surprised if it has something to do with all your recent hard work."

"What?" She looked confused.

"He's waiting, Jordan. Clock's ticking." I walked past her and joined the girls at the blocks, waited my turn, and then dove into the impartial water.

Chapter 58

I went through the set with purpose, all pretensions cast aside. Now that everyone knew what I was capable of I couldn't hide it any longer, nor did I want to. Their reaction to Jordan's outing me hurt, but once I got past it I was reconciled to the fact that these girls weren't my friends. They were teammates, fellow swimmers, and classmates. Once the season ended, we'd drift apart. I'd join the Marlins and swim with the die-hards – Mel, Erica, Tati, Charlie, and a few others – but we wouldn't hang out anymore. We wouldn't have time. I'd get used to it. It's how I'd always lived, and it suited me just fine.

I went through the routine, not trying to make any statements, but finished first. I climbed out, dried off, and walked over to Justin who was fiddling with the sound system.

"Hey," I said, "Think you can fix it?"

The sound system had cut in and out at the last meet, and Coach asked Mr. Gearhead to see what he could do with it.

"Almost done," he said. "See? This wire's frayed. I'm replacing the entire cord. She'll be as good as new for tomorrow's meet."

The meet was against the Falcons, a team that inspired no fear. Coach would put together an easy lineup, mix us up a little bit to keep us in shape, let us make division times in other events, and we'd win by a pretty good margin. Most likely, I wouldn't have to face Tatiana in the 200 or the 500.

"You look serious out there," he said. "You make the other girls look like amateurs."

I rolled my eyes. "Don't say that too loud. They might conspire to get me kicked off the team."

He laughed, "No way. You're Coach's Golden Girl now."

"Great," I sighed. "This wasn't what I wanted. In fact, it's what I *didn't* want."

"Whatever," he said. "Make the most of it. And don't let Jordan and the other girls get to you. They're scared."

"They've got nothing to be scared of. Tatiana can have her record. Why should I care?"

"For Tati it's all about the record, but for anyone else it would be about the money."

"Yeah, there is that," I conceded.

"You don't have any loyalty to her or to this team. You should go for it. If I were in your place, I would."

"Everyone will hate me."

"Not everyone," he said, grinning up at me, giving me those butterflies again.

Mel had finished her set and stood by the bleachers drying off. She called to Justin, "Where's Jordan?"

I had forgotten all about Jordan. I looked for her in the pool and on the deck. Missing. *Again.*

"Coach benched her. She's out of here," Justin said, a wicked grin on his face.

"For how long?" she asked.

"Today and tomorrow. She'll miss the Falcons meet."

"He pulled her out of the meet?"

By now, Tatiana and Erica had joined us and jumped into the conversation.

"Jordan's benched?" Tati asked.

"Yep. And suspended three days. Guess Coach and Principal Sorenson didn't appreciate her investigative reporting," Justin said.

"Well, that stinks," Erica said. "Jordan still hasn't made a qualifying time for the championship meet. She was hoping she'd do it tomorrow."

"We've only got a few meets left, and she's running out of time," Tati said. "This is so not fair."

"I'd say it's fair," Justin said.

"You would," Mel said, her eyes narrowing at her twin. She turned her focus to me. "This mess is all your fault," she said.

Up until now, I'd been a quiet observer, but I wasn't going to take the blame for Jordan's punishment. "She got what she deserved. She knows what the rules are about bullying other students."

"I'd say she did us all a service," Mel said, staring me down, hands on hips.

"Calm down girls," Justin said. "Remember, you're all friends."

"Not anymore," Mel muttered.

"Come on, Mel, you know you don't mean it," Justin said. "So Aerin pretended to be less of a swimmer than she is. So what? She didn't mean to hurt anyone, and now that everyone knows what she can do, she's a real asset. When she starts swimming her best, you guys are sure to win the division title. Remember, it's all about the team. Isn't that right?"

"Oh, for crying out loud," Mel said, frustrated with her brother. "You sound just like Coach."

"You know I'm right."

Mel wrapped her hair in a towel, grabbed her swim bag, and stomped off, Erica and Tatiana close behind.

I'd be forever grateful to Justin for defusing the situation.

"See?" he said. "They're already starting to come around. In the end, they'll realize that what's best for the team is most important. And you're best for the team."

"As long as I don't take on Tati in the 500 challenge."

"Don't fool yourself. You may be the best thing that happens to Tatiana. Some real competition is what she needs to break that record."

He was right again. I could be the catalyst to force Tati to push herself beyond her limits, to break the record, although it would also put me at risk of being the record breaker.

"I finished fixing the cord, and it's getting late. I need to get home for dinner."

My stomach rumbled. I'd had nothing more than a protein bar on my way to practice. "Thanks," I said, folding my wet towel into a tidy square.

"For what?" he asked as he picked up his tools.

"For sticking up for me. No one has ever done that before."

"I stick up for what I believe in, and I believe in you."

"I'm sorry if I messed things up for you and your sister."

"Don't worry about that. Like I said before, she'll get over it. I know Mel."

I tugged on my sweats and stepped into my sneakers.

"Need a ride home?"

"Yeah, that would be great." It was starting to get dark early, and I didn't like to walk home alone.

"Then let's go," he said grabbing my book bag.

The meet against the Falcons went as expected. Coach placed all of us in races we didn't usually swim so we could make division times in other events. His goal was for each girl to qualify in a minimum of two events and two relays, the most we could swim in the competition. I had already made the cut in the 50, 200, and 500 freestyle, and the 200 and 400 free relays. Coach wanted to see what I could do in the fly and the IM. In past seasons, I had qualified in those events too, but given the state of my team, I decided to take it easy and not do anything outstanding. No need to rub salt in any wounds.

Tatiana made the cut in the backstroke and the 50 free, as well as her other events. Erica, who had already qualified in the fly and the IM, almost made it in the 500 free but didn't come close in the breaststroke. Mel, who would swim the 50 and the 100 free in the championship meet, now qualified in the 200 free and the back. Charlie, our little dynamo, more than qualified to swim in the breaststroke, and qualified in the 50 free too.

Although on suspension, Jordan still had to attend meets and sat on the sidelines in her team sweats, cheering on Tati, Mel, Erica, anyone but me. Word on the deck was Coach told her to clean up her act or he'd cut her from the team. Although some of the girls still acted distant toward me, I sensed a thaw coming, as some of them chose to sit beside me on the bench, and a few cheered for me during my events. Charlie, innocent and unaffected by the drama, defied Jordan, and ignored her icy glares and veiled threats, sitting beside me between races and rooting for me at the turns. Her loyalty moved me. My Little Sister was the bravest girl on the team. She looked up to me, and I was determined to show her she had not misplaced her trust.

Chapter 59

Nine weeks into the season, and the daily drill of morning practice, classes, after school practice or a meet, and then homework had all of us exhausted and cranky. Everything hurt: our shoulders, our legs, our backs, and, in some cases, our pride.

Too many girls visited the trainer to ice injuries and stretch stiff limbs. Some wore therapy tape on their arms and backs to relieve their aching muscles.

The younger girls started to slack off, missing intervals, wimping out in the weight room, whining, complaining, and crying.

The more experienced swimmers pressed on, knowing from previous years that hard work and pain were necessary to perform well and make the best of our season.

It was a grueling time for all of us.

To add to the misery, the end of the first marking period was in sight and we had projects, reports, and exams to contend with too. The seniors also had to check out colleges, take the placement tests, meet with visiting admissions counselors, work on a winning application essay, and figure out what we wanted to do with the rest of our lives.

The swim recruiters were also swooping in, sending head-spinning letters and emails, begging us to check out their programs, visit their campuses, attend a meet, spend a weekend with their team, and apply to their schools.

Navigating all of this without falling apart is what separated the winners from the others. Those who kept their mental game on and proceeded with blinders would do well in the Division Championships, and maybe earn a spot on a college team. Not all of the girls planned to swim beyond high school, but the ones who did – me, Tati, Mel, Erica, and a few of the juniors - talked nonstop about which coach sent the latest letter and which school they'd visit next.

My plans were still undecided, but the pile of mail on my desk grew taller each day as recruiters and coaches tempted me to consider their programs. I'd received dozens of letters in the past, but tossed them in the trash unopened because I was interested in only a handful of schools and had no interest in the others.

Now I stacked them, many unopened, in a corner of my desk, and picked through them at least once a day, weighing the possibilities. Swimming remained in my future. I just needed to figure out where it fit and how much of my time and energy I wanted to devote to it.

Physical exhaustion, injuries, tests, projects, reports, and worries about college and life beyond high school had everyone's nerves on edge. The last thing the team needed was unnecessary drama. My win at the Long Island meet and Jordan's campaign to discredit me added a new dimension of stress and tension. A few of the girls ignored Jordan and supported me. Jordan's minions supported Tati and gave me the cold shoulder. Mel and Erica remained neutral, not taking sides, like Switzerland. Our team was split in two. All of Mel and Tati's hard work to build a cohesive unit was crumbling, and it was my fault.

Sometimes I wondered what I was doing here.

Chapter 60

Part two of Justin's excellent plan included night swimming, something forbidden, because Coach demanded we stick to his training program alone, and not go off on our own to work out or train in case we hurt ourselves and missed practice, or worse, meets, due to injury. I'd trained with many coaches and knew lots of techniques and training methods. Coach Dudash's methods worked just fine, but Justin said he saw room for improvement. I'd gotten sloppy in some areas because I wasn't utilizing all of my skills, and he wanted to train with me one-on-one to bring me back to my winning form.

He picked me up after dinner and we drove to the Y where he worked as a lifeguard and swim instructor.

"Are you sure bringing me here is okay?" I asked as we entered the natatorium.

"Trust me; it's fine."

"I'm not a member," I said. The pool area was much smaller than the one at the high school, but had 25-yard lanes and diving blocks, which was all we needed.

"Well, I am, and you're my guest, so don't worry." He dropped our swim bags to the floor and pulled off his sweats, stripping to his swimsuit, black jammers with blue racing stripes. "Get ready. We don't have all night." He pulled his goggles out of his bag and stretched them over his head, snapping them in place.

I undressed down to my suit, stuffed my hair under a cap, and tugged on my goggles. I followed him to the blocks.

"Hey, Reggie," he said, greeting the lifeguard on duty.

Reggie stretched out in his guard chair, looking down at us. "How ya doing, Justin? Private lesson?"

"Yeah, private lesson," Justin said, "as in don't tell anyone you saw us here."

Just two swimmers used the pool, a couple of old guys doing laps at a steady pace.

"What about them?" I asked Justin.

"They're cool," he said. "I taught both of them how to do flip turns. They love me. Besides, no one cares if you're here. I just don't want Coach to find out. Reggie goes to the high school and we've been friends forever. He won't say anything."

"What if Coach finds out? What will he do?"

"Scream at me. He doesn't like me messing with his swimmers during swim season. He won't bench you if that's what you're worried about."

"There's so much tension on the team. I don't want to cause anymore," I said, dipping my toe into the water. It was cold, and I shivered.

"It's okay. The ends justify the means." He gave me a little shove and I fell back into the pool. He jumped in beside me.

I surfaced and sputtered, "Jerk!"

"No more talking," he said, laughing. "We're here to work, remember?"

And work we did. I had no idea Justin was such a tireless taskmaster. We warmed up with an easy 500, side by side in separate lanes. Then Justin climbed out of the pool and into the guard chair across from Reggie to watch me do another 200.

"I've never seen anyone like you," he said, shaking his head. "What do you think, Reg? Close to perfect?"

"Looks perfect to me," Reggie said.

"You have a natural talent fine-tuned with top-notch training."

"Why do you sound surprised?" I asked, shaking the water out of my ears. "I swam with the Manhattan Swim Club for nine years, and trained with Mike Starling."

"Mike Starling?" Justin's eyes widened in wonder. "He's, like, *a legend*. Did you hear that Reggie? She trained under *Starling*."

Reggie shrugged. Although a lifeguard, he didn't have the look of a swimmer and I doubted he'd ever heard of Mike Starling.

"He's trained a ton of NCAA champions, some who went on to the Olympic trials," Justin explained to Reggie, who looked back at him unimpressed. "He was at Berkeley before he moved to New York to start his own club." He turned to me. "What's he like?"

I shrugged. "Tough. Demanding. No fooling around." I was so used to Coach Mike he'd stopped fazing me years ago. He was well-respected, and turned out top swimmers as though he molded them from clay. Everyone wanted to work with him, but he was selective. I was lucky to catch his eye when I first started at the club, and he put me in his group of top performers.

After the way things had gone down at the end of my last season with the Manhattan Swim Club, Coach Mike was the only person I wanted to keep in touch with. The situation with my mother deteriorated rapidly, but I hung on through championships because swimming helped ground me. When the season ended, I told Coach Mike I wasn't coming back. He stayed in touch, though, and we communicated weekly through text messages and email. He wanted me back on the team, but I wouldn't make any promises until after Mom came home.

"What I wouldn't give to spend a few weeks with him," Justin said, still starstruck.

"What makes you think you can help Aerin improve after she

trained under that guy?" Reggie asked.

Justin returned to earth with a crash. "Not much, I guess," he said, deflated, and then brightened. "Still, it's been a while since she's worked with him, and I can see where she's fallen a little off the wagon. I can help her get back on track."

"Yeah, right," Reggie said, smirking. "I keep forgetting you're a mini Michael Phelps."

"Hey," Justin said, his face reddening. "I've had some excellent training myself. Don't forget I went to that Olympic swim camp last summer."

"Like Tati?" I asked, remembering that she'd gone to some hotshot swim camp in California.

"Similar. I spent a week training with a bunch of elite swimmers in a program supervised by some former Olympians. They helped me work on a few technical issues I've noticed in your technique."

"Did it help?" I asked.

"Sure did. I improved my time in the IM, back, and fly. I might break a few records myself."

"Ok. If you're so sure of yourself, let's get going."

Justin proceeded to work with me on my turns, analyzing me while I did flip turn after flip turn, focusing on how I turned my body, tucked my head, and planted my feet when I pushed off the wall. I'd worked that drill thousands of times, but I'd grown sloppy, making silly mistakes I'd left behind years ago. These mistakes cost me precious microseconds. Now that I wanted to get back to my real game, I had to break these new bad habits.

When I was flip turned out, Justin walked me to the blocks to work on my starts. I'd always had a great start and resisted his efforts, but after a few attempts I had to admit he was on to something. I realized I wasn't hitting the water the way Coach Mike had taught me, reverting to old bad habits and poor technique in my attempt to fool everyone. I had to laugh. Turned out I only fooled myself.

I stood on the block, arranging my arms and legs while Justin stood behind me and perfected my posture, adjusting my feet, straightening my knees, grasping my hips and pulling them back. The feel of his hands on my body was strange and exhilarating. He touched me like a coach, but I was thinking of something else and grew flustered, my face flushed, my heart pounding.

"Earth to Aerin," he said. "You with me?"

I reconnected with the situation and stammered, "I'm here."

"I thought I was losing you," he said.

"Oh no," I answered. "I'm right here."

"Well, then try it like this," he ordered and I did, grateful for the release and the plunge into the cool water which set things right. I swam to the surface, gazing up at him for his assessment.

"I think you've got it," he said.

I splashed at him, soaking his feet, and he jumped back with a yelp. "I've got it *back*," I corrected as I climbed out of the pool. "Don't give yourself too much credit." We locked eyes for a moment and he shot me that irresistible grin.

"Coach Mike would be proud," he said.

"Keep it up and maybe I'll introduce you to him one of these days."

"You'd do that?" he gasped.

"Yup, but only for my best friends."

"Okay, lovebirds," Reggie called from the other side of the pool. "Time to lock up."

We toweled off and pulled on our sweats. I wrapped my hair in a towel for the ride home. We grabbed our bags and met Reggie at the door, waiting for him to close the pool.

"You look good in the water, Aerin," he said as he double-checked the door was locked.

"Remember," Justin said. "We weren't here."

"'Coach Dudash, I never saw them'," Reggie said with a grin.

"Thanks, bro. Are we all set to come to your place tomorrow

night?" Reggie had a weight room in his basement where the guys on the team worked out in the off-season. Justin and I planned to train together a couple of nights a week. That would be in addition to the hours I spent training with my team, and another no-no. We were breaking several rules, and I still hadn't decided whether or not I'd challenge Tatiana for the 500 record. Justin was taking a lot of risks for me.

"All set. I told the guys my parents said no weight room for a while. It's cool."

We walked out into the dark parking lot, our cars the only ones left.

"See you tomorrow," Justin said, clapping Reggie on the back. Reggie nodded and walked off toward his own car.

Justin and I got into his Jeep. I turned the heater on, feeling chilled from the October night air, my hair still wrapped in a wet towel.

"Thanks for doing this for me," I said.

He shrugged. "I want you to do your best."

"Well, it's sweet of you to go out of your way for me. We haven't known each other very long."

He glanced at me and grinned. "I know you well enough. You're gonna kick butt the rest of this season, shake things up a little bit. And Two Rivers needs shaking up."

"Are you talking about Tati?" It sounded like he shared his sister's dislike for the team's star swimmer.

"Yeah, Tati, Jordan, all of them, but Calvin Reese, too, because he thinks he's better than everyone and holds the town in his hands. And Coach, too, because he has his favorites, and doesn't always give the other girls the attention they deserve."

"What do you mean?"

"He spends a lot of time working with Tati and the new girls on the team, and forgets he has about twenty other girls in need of coaching."

I hadn't noticed, but then I'd been focused on staying invisible, not looking for any special training or attention. "Mel?" I asked.

He nodded. "Mel has worked harder than any other girl on that team for the last six years and still hasn't met her goals. Her starts are erratic, her turns can be sloppy, and he just pats her on the back and tells her 'good job' when she comes in second or third, her best time not much better than three years ago."

"Don't you work with her?"

"Coach won't let me and my parents told me to back off."

"She didn't go to the swim camp?"

He laughed. "Mel chooses to spend her money on other things." The Jeep pulled up in front of Aunt Mags' house. "My parents made me pay my own way to the camp. I saved all year. Mel spent her money at the mall."

"I didn't know she was a shopper," I said, but then I recently learned I didn't know Mel well at all.

"Shopaholic," he said. "Never met a boutique she didn't like. Her closet is stuffed with clothes and shoes, some still with price tags. I'm afraid one day she's going to be one of those old lady hoarders."

I laughed. "You exaggerate."

"No, I don't. During swim season, she wears nothing but sweats and T's, but once the season's over you'll see a new Mel, looking like she just stepped out of some fashion magazine." He shook his head.

"Okay," I said, doubtful. His picture of his sister didn't jibe with mine. "I can't wait to see that."

He switched off the ignition. "Ready to go in?"

I looked at the clock on the dash; almost ten thirty. All the lights upstairs at Maggie's house were out, and a single lamp burned in the living room. The flicker of the TV screen in the window told me she was waiting up for me. I picked up my bags and opened the door. "You don't have to walk me inside," I said. "It's late. You should go home."

He climbed out his side of the car. "No one will ever say I failed to walk my girlfriend to the door late at night."

He took my bag as we walked up the path to the house in silence, tiptoeing on the porch steps, mindful of the sleeping family inside.

"Don't forget, morning practice in seven hours," he said.

I stifled a yawn. How could I forget?

"Should I pick you up?"

"That would be great because I won't have to bother Aunt Mags. She's too busy in the morning getting everyone off to school to have to worry about me."

"Make sure you're ready," he said. "I don't like to be late. Should I send you a wake-up text?"

"Yeah, that would be helpful."

"Will do." He handed me my bag, signaling the end of our evening. We looked at each other, unsure of what to do next. Before the moment became awkward, he leaned in close and gave me a light peck on the cheek. I hid my disappointment as he backed away and started down the steps. He waited while I pulled open the front door, making a squeak. I cringed, hoping I hadn't woken anyone. The house remained quiet. Not even Salty made a sound. I let myself in and turned back to see Justin heading for his car. I closed the door but peered through the window as he drove off.

I stuck my head into the living room. Maggie was spread out on the couch, half-asleep, Salty at her feet. They both startled when I said good night.

"Oh, good, you're back. How was practice?" She sat up, yawned, and rubbed her sleepy eyes. Salty rose and walked over to me, sniffing. I reached down to scratch his tawny head.

"Justin is a killer coach."

"I've heard he was a great team leader."

"Like Mel," I said.

"Are the girls still giving you the cold shoulder?"

I nodded.

"This too shall pass," she said, patting me on the back. "Trust me."

"I wish it would hurry up."

She turned off the TV with the remote and stood, pausing to stretch. She twisted at the waist and her spine cracked. She moaned in pleasure and stretched all the way up to the ceiling, her arms arcing overhead.

"That's better," she said. "Not a good idea to crash on the couch."

"You don't have to wait up for me, you know."

"I don't mind. It's good practice. Before too long, Paige will be going out at night."

"And you've got four others right behind her. I guess I am good practice."

Maggie turned off the light. We headed upstairs to our bedrooms and in minutes, the house was dark and silent.

Chapter 61

I was on autopilot, a skill I'd used in the past to get through each over-packed day. The days blended into one another, each a repeat of the one before. Up at the crack of dawn for morning practice, then school, afternoon practice or a meet, followed by dinner, homework, and a workout with Justin either in the pool or at Reggie's. My muscles started to ache, but when I looked in the mirror I saw definition in my arms and abs I hadn't seen for a long time, and it thrilled me. Although I was exhausted, I performed better in the pool and had improved on my intervals. We had three meets left before our showdown with the Bears, who were also undefeated. It was all we talked about on the pool deck.

Kelsey kept us up to date on how each team in the division was doing. She'd created an Excel spreadsheet with a page for every team, for every star swimmer. From her calculations, we were in line to win the division title again, undefeated, even though the Bears would challenge us in almost every event down to the last hundredth of a second.

"Are you sure you don't want to be a sports analyst?" Mel asked her more than once.

"No way," Kelsey said. "I'd rather analyze literature and teach it to kids."

She'd excel at that, too.

Speculation about whether or not Tatiana was on track to beat the Singer record was intense. Her time wasn't much better than at the close of last season, and I could tell she was getting tired and starting to buckle under the pressure. Not a day went by that someone outside the team didn't bring up the challenge. The local media also didn't let up, covering the team with a microscope, reporting on all our meets and including pictures of all of us, but mainly of Tati.

"Channel Six is here again," Erica said when we came on deck for the meet against the Raiders.

A camera crew was setting up to shoot video.

"This is getting old," Mel said.

"You're just jealous because no one's writing about you," Jordan said, her blue eyes flashing. As the season ground on and Tati made little to no progress toward breaking the record, Jordan grew tense and testy, snapping at anyone who had anything negative or critical to say about "her" girl.

"Now, why would I want that?" Mel asked, hands on hips. "All the added attention would only make me more nervous, and I don't perform well under pressure. What about you, Tati? Do you perform well under pressure?"

Tati ignored her, focusing on her pre-meet stretches, a blank expression on her face.

"Knock it off, Mel," Jordan said. "Stop trying to psych her out."

"Who? Me? Would I do that?" Mel asked the small crowd standing around her, Jordan, and Tati. A few of the girls snickered, but most looked like they debated the answer.

"You've been undermining her all season," Jordan said. "We're a team here, remember? Everyone cares. Give her some support instead of sniping behind her back."

Mel bristled. "Hey, Jordan, news flash: Tati knows she has my support. In fact, I can't wait to see her crash through that record. It will be the best day of my life. Well, almost the best day."

Jordan looked at her as though wondering if she was setting her up to look like a fool, but before she could make up her mind, Mel said "No, the best day of my life will be the day I break *my* personal record and meet *my* goals. Wouldn't that be the best day of *your* life, Jordan? Meeting your own goals? Oh, that's right, you don't have any. That's why you're so set on Tati breaking the record. Because *you're* not doing anything spectacular."

Jordan's frosty eyes darkened, narrowing to slits. An uncomfortable silence fell across the pool deck as everyone tuned into this confrontation. Even Tatiana stopped stretching, her gaze locked on Mel and Jordan.

"Well," Jordan said at last in icy tones. "I don't see *you* doing anything spectacular either, Mel. You haven't even won an event."

"I try," Mel said, hands on hips.

"Are you saying I'm not trying?"

"If the shoe fits...."

"What's going on here?" Coach said as he crossed the pool deck. "Aren't you supposed to be warming up? The clock is ticking. Now get in."

The girls looked relieved that the tension was broken and followed orders, diving in and starting their laps. Mel and Jordan squared off for a few more seconds and then Mel tugged on her cap and goggles and walked past Jordan to get on the blocks.

"This isn't finished," Jordan hissed behind her.

Mel acted like she didn't hear her and got behind the blocks.

Jordan and I were the last ones left, and she caught me staring at her. "What are you looking at?"

"Not much," I said, unzipping my jacket.

"Watch yourself Aerin, or should I say *Margaret*, Keane. I'm not finished with you."

The challenge in her eyes kindled something deep inside me,

something I thought I'd laid to rest a while ago. *Don't let her get to you*, I told myself. *She's not worth it.* "Shouldn't you be in the water? You did miss two days of practice *and* a meet."

It seemed impossible, but her eyes narrowed even more than they had before. She looked downright ugly. Still, she didn't scare me.

"I wish you'd never come to Two Rivers. You've been nothing but trouble," she said.

She was clearly insane. She was the troublemaker and had been long before I came around. "Just drop it, Jordan, okay? I need to focus on my performance, and you might think about doing that yourself." I took a step toward the blocks but she stopped me.

"So now you're telling me what to do, Miss Superstar?"

"Knock it off." I pushed her out of my way.

"I'm not done with you, Aerin."

I put her behind me and joined the rest of the girls in the pool.

The Raiders were no match for us and we took the lead right away in the 200 medley relay. Tati and I then faced off in the 200 free. We took our places, Tati in the lead lane and me two over on the right. The season was more than half completed, and I was still not used to swimming in the outer lanes. I had always swam in the lead lanes and it rankled me to swim by the wall, although I knew to never underestimate the swimmers on the edges. For years, I'd worked to be the lead swimmer, and the role of second best didn't suit me, even though I'd set myself up for it from day one.

As the officials readied the event, I looked at Tatiana, watching her adjust her cap and goggles, shake out her limbs, and take some deep breaths. I copied her movements, going through the same motions. I had four chances to beat her before the championship meet. Today was as good as any to stake my claim.

On our benches, Jordan and her minions called out

encouragement to Tati. The Viper's words just moments before burned through my brain, igniting a fire in me I hadn't allowed to flame in months. I looked at my teammates standing at the pool's edge, waiting for the race to begin. Half of them looked back at me, encouraging me with fist pumps and big smiles. Charlie huddled with a few of the younger girls, and called out, "You can do it Aerin!" as though she could read my mind. I drew in a deep breath to steady my nerves.

The announcer ordered us on the blocks. *This is it*, I thought. *Do it now*. I gave my cap and goggles one last tug.

"Swimmers, take your mark," the announcer said.

I caught a glimpse of Justin on the pool deck, his eyes trained on me. I met his gaze and gave him a slight nod. His smile lit up the room. I brought my gaze back to the lane of water in front of me and steeled my resolve. This would be my race.

The buzzer buzzed, and we shot off the blocks, hitting the water with a tremendous rush, breaking through its glass-like surface. My start was higher and tighter than I'd had all season, a comfortable position, and I streamlined halfway across the pool, surfacing at ten yards, taking a deep breath and then kicking, kicking, kicking as my arms churned through the water, pulling me across the length of the pool. I put my thoughts on hold and focused on nothing but moving forward, executing perfect flip turns, pushing off the wall with my feet in perfect position, and using my energy wisely to take the lead from the swimmer on my immediate left. Tati was just a stroke ahead of her. By the third lap I was gaining on both of them, and in the final turn, I let loose with my last blast of energy and shot off the wall, using the momentum to streak past the Raiders' swimmer and then shoot beyond Tatiana, who struggled to maintain her lead. I stopped breathing on the last five yards and pushed into the wall, Tati a full second behind me.

Tati hung on the wall two lanes over, catching her breath, staring at the clock, disbelief on her face. The other swimmers finished, and the Raider next to me in lane five reached out to shake hands. "Great race," she said, panting.

Pandemonium hit the pool deck as my teammates cheered and jeered for me, the younger girls, Charlie in the lead, shouting congratulations and Tati's crew booing. Coach stood off to the sidelines scribbling on his clipboard. Mel, Erica, and their tribe stayed out of it, casting wary looks at each other, pointing up at the scoreboard.

The game was on.

I climbed out of the pool, tugged the bottom of my suit into place and pulled off my goggles and cap. I slipped into my flip-flops and walked back to the bench, passing a still breathless Tati on the way. She looked at me with round eyes, her chest heaving.

Before I met up with Coach, Jordan intercepted me. "What are you doing?" she hissed. "Didn't you hear what I said?"

I pushed past her. "Knock it off, Jordan. I'm a swimmer. This is what I do."

"You're not going to do it here," she said, her eyes cold, her mouth a thin, grim line. She might scare the other girls, but she didn't scare me. I'd suffered crueler and meaner girls throughout my nine-year swim career. I kept moving, leaving her sputtering in my wake.

Coach looked up from his scribblings when I approached, trying not to smile. "You've made a decision," he said.

I shrugged.

"It's going to be interesting around here the next few weeks." He smiled. "Great race."

I grabbed a cup of water on my way to the bench, wrapped a towel around me, and sat on the end, watching the next event. Erica was in lane four, in the lead for the 200 IM. Mel stood at the pool's edge cheering her on.

Charlie plopped down next to me. "Good job, Aerin. You beat Tati."

I nodded, both exhilarated and exhausted. Now that I'd beaten Tati I'd be expected to do it again, and again. I'd joined the team for the pleasure I got from swimming, nothing more, and certainly not to make any waves. All season I'd been repressing my desire to win, my killer instinct, my competitive spirit. Once I unleashed it there'd be no going back. I'd carved out a sweet spot on the team, in the school. I'd gained a lot, my friendships with Mel, Erica, Justin, Kelsey, and Charlie at the top of the list. How much of that would challenging the record cost me? Mel and Erica were still not speaking to me, although the ice had started to thaw over the last couple of days. I looked at them now that the IM had finished, and Erica had won with a time close to her personal best. They huddled together at the blocks, Erica recovering from her event while Mel prepared for hers, giving each other high fives and cheers, byproducts of friendship and team bonding I hadn't experienced in days. I felt empty inside.

Mel took second in her event, and the Blazers led the meet. When we lined up for the blocks for the 500, I took my position in lane six again. I played it just like the 200, aching to win this event too. But losing the 200 had lit a fire in Tati, and she wouldn't let me get past her. She finished first, ahead of me by 2:03 seconds. When I surfaced from my finish, the natatorium was rocking with excitement. The competition between Tati and I ignited more than just the two us. The stands full of friends, parents, and other swim fans had caught the excitement and let loose with it. Aunt Maggie and the twins cheered from the top row, the twins holding a banner that read "Go Aerin!" I smiled up at them, and they waved back, jumping up and down.

When all the swimmers had finished the race, I climbed out of the pool and headed for Coach. Tati already had his ear and he high fived her, all smiles. At my approach, his smile turned into a more serious expression. Tati had moved back to the blocks for the 200 free relay, up next, and was out of earshot. He leaned in close to me.

"You almost had her," he said. "You slipped a little on the seventeenth turn and gave her an edge."

I nodded, knowing he was right. Even with all of the extra practice and tweaking of the small elements in technique that made a swimmer a winner, I was still not at my best. "I'm working on it," I said.

"You've made a lot of improvement the last few days," he acknowledged. "Be careful you don't hurt yourself. I want you in fighting form for the meets against the Bears and the Boxers, and of course Championships."

"I'm good. I know how much I can handle."

"I'll trust you on that," he said. "Now get back to the blocks. They're lining up for the relay."

The Blazers dominated the rest of the meet, beating the Raiders by almost 30 points. Everyone was happy and exhausted as we went into the pool for a 500-yard cool down when the meet ended. I followed Charlie and the rest of the newbies in lane five, relaxed, taking it easy, working out the kinks in my muscles. Cool down was always my favorite part of a meet.

I showered and changed into my sweats, pulling my wet hair into a ponytail, and set off to find Aunt Maggie and the twins to catch a ride home. I walked several yards behind Jordan, Tati, their minions and their mindless chatter, not paying attention to their words. One of them, a sophomore named Jazmin, glanced back over her shoulder and caught my eye. She leaned close to Jordan, said something, and Jordan stopped walking, the others jerking to a stop beside her. She turned as I caught up with them. No one said a word as I passed, but they stared at me, unblinking, eyes narrowed. I was a good ten feet away before they restarted their chatter. Let them talk all they want. Nothing Jordan or any of them could do would stop me now.

Chapter 62

After practice on Saturday morning, Maggie drove me to the train station and I headed to Westchester to visit my father. It would be our first visit since he stood me up at the Long Island meet and I reacted by breaking a meet record and becoming enemy number one. He knew nothing about that because we hadn't talked, just passed text messages letting me know that Dawn was stable and what time he needed to meet me at the station.

He was waiting when I arrived. He popped open the trunk and I stuffed my bag inside. I opened the back door to take my usual seat and found he was alone.

"Where is everyone? I thought you were picking me up right after soccer practice." I jumped into the front passenger seat and fastened my seatbelt. I turned on the radio and fiddled with the buttons, tuning in to my favorite station. How nice not to hear Emily's whine when I switched from top pop hits to alternative rock.

"The girls are spending the weekend with their father," he said as he pulled out of the arrivals lane and merged into the traffic leaving the station. "He picked them up after practice."

"Awesome." It had been months since I'd had a weekend with my father minus the girls. We had a lot to discuss, and it would be great to talk without their constant butting in and incessant demands.

"I figured you'd like that," he said, glancing at me with a smile. He looked tired, dark circles under his eyes and new wrinkles around his mouth.

"How are things going?" I asked. Dawn was still on bed rest. My father was managing the girls and the day-to-day household routines with the help of Geneviève, their housekeeper, and Dawn's supervision from the couch, in addition to keeping up with his legal practice. No wonder he looked exhausted.

"It's going okay. Dawn and the baby are stable, and the girls are doing well in school. Somehow we're managing to keep it together."

"How are *you* doing?"

"I'm hanging in there."

"Just four more months to go. Did you find out if it's a boy or a girl?"

"As a matter of fact, we did, but we haven't told anyone. We want it to be a surprise for the girls. How about you? Do you want to know?"

I thought for a moment. "No," I said. "I can wait."

We cruised along a few minutes in silence, both of us enjoying the peace.

"So, with the girls away what are the plans for the weekend?" I had nothing in mind. I was exhausted from swimming and working out with Justin and wanted to catch up on my sleep. I also had a lot of homework.

"Whatever you want to do," he said. "Dawn's not up for much except reading and TV. She suggested that you and I go out to dinner tonight, maybe catch a movie. What do you think?"

"Sounds good, but I have some school work I need to take care of before we go out."

Back at the house, we found Dawn stretched out on the sofa, remote in hand, an open book on her lap, and a chick flick on the TV screen. She looked up as we walked in and tried to sit up.

"Don't get up," I said as I walked toward her.

"I need to stretch a little bit." She came to a seated position and raised her arms overhead, stretching cat-like. The crocheted afghan covering her dropped to her lap, exposing the swell of her pregnant belly.

"Look at you," I said, "you're starting to show."

She rubbed her belly. "This little bugger's an active one. Want to meet your baby brother or sister? Put your hand here."

She grabbed my hand and placed it on the side of her belly. A moment later, something pushed through her abdominal wall and into my hand. I'd never felt anything like it before. My eyes widened with wonder. "Oh my gosh, is it kicking me?"

She laughed. "Got some kick, doesn't it?"

I sat next to her on the couch, keeping my hand pressed against her belly, waiting for another kick. When it came, I grinned up at both of them. Until now, I'd known the baby was coming, but it had seemed dreamlike, more of an idea than reality. But this was physical proof, and suddenly I felt a deep connection to whoever reached out to meet me.

"Aerin opted out of knowing whether it's a boy or a girl," my father said.

"Good idea," Dawn said. "We found out by accident because someone let it slip during all the testing. When I carried my girls, I didn't know their sex, and wish I didn't know now."

"Not that it does us any good," my father said. "We can't buy anything or decorate the room without letting it out, and we want the girls to be surprised."

"It can wait," said Dawn. "We've got plenty of time."

Her attitude surprised me. She was always so on top of things. *Normal* Dawn would have been in a major rush to decorate the nursery, buy all the furnishings, and order a complete wardrobe. I guessed the risky nature of the pregnancy and the limits it imposed had given her a new perspective, and she was taking it easy.

"So, what are you guys planning to do today?" she asked.

"We're taking you up on your suggestion of a father-daughter date night, but first Aerin has some homework she needs to take care of before we can go out."

"What about you? What will you do?" I asked her.

"Don't worry about me. I'll be right here. Maybe I'll finish this book." She picked up the book that had fallen beside her, losing her page. "I'll grab some leftover pizza from last night. Geneviève will be back in a while, and she can keep me company."

She seemed to be taking all of it in stride, although she must be bored out of her mind. Dawn was not a couch potato. I'd never seen her lie down in the middle of the day. Now she had hours upon hours of nothing to do and nowhere to go. "Will it be like this until the baby comes?"

"I hope not!" she said. "But if it has to be, I'll deal with it. Right now there's nothing more important than this baby."

I grabbed my book bag and suitcase and headed up to my room. The silence upstairs seemed strange. I peeked into Emily's and Avery's bedrooms. The housekeeper must have been in because everything was in order and the place reeked of disinfectant. I went on to my room and plopped down on the bed, listening to the rustle of the trees just outside my window. I peeked out at them, captivated with the rich red, vivid gold, and russet leaves. Autumn had arrived without my notice. I was so busy with swimming and school I hadn't seen it coming. I remembered my earlier resolve to pay attention to what was happening around me and took note of my surroundings. The heat was on, and I listened to the hot air blast through the vents. The room had a cozy, comfy feel and I dozed for a while.

When I awoke, the clock said almost five. It was starting to get dark outside, and the house was quiet. Dawn slept on the sofa, snoring. I'd never heard *that* before. My dad was in his office, squinting at the multiple screens attached to his computer and drinking a cup of coffee.

"Big case?" I asked as I sat on the couch beside his large oak desk, covered with file folders and papers in some organized mess only he understood. He glanced up at me over his black-framed reading glasses.

"Remember the chemical spill in the Hudson last year? I've been retained to help broker a deal on the clean-up. We have a big meeting next week."

"Whose side are you on?" Four years ago, I wouldn't have had to ask, but he'd changed so much since starting his new life I couldn't assume anything. I was almost afraid of the answer.

"The river's, of course," he said, smiling and sitting back. "I haven't changed that much."

I laughed, relieved. "Still an environmentalist then."

"Always," he said. He shut down the PC and monitors and swiveled around to face me. "Hungry?"

"Starved."

"I know a great Chinese place in town that serves the best shrimp with lobster sauce. You interested?"

I'd eat anything, but Chinese was my favorite. "Give me a few minutes to wash up and change."

Dawn awakened before we left, and my father helped her upstairs to take a quick shower. When we said goodbye, she was back on the couch eating a bowl of soup and reading the newspaper. She pushed us out the door, insisting she'd be all right. Geneviève had texted she was on her way home with a movie. Girls' night in for the two of them.

Thirty minutes later, we sat in a booth at Ming's Garden trying not to devour the bowl of fried wontons the waiter had placed in front of us.

"It's nice it's just the two of us tonight," Dad said. "It's been awhile since we've been able to talk without distractions."

"You said it," I said, relieved he was relaxed and focused only on me.

"So, tell me what's new with you," he said as he prepared his tea. He added two packets of sugar and stirred.

"Same old routine: swim, school, swim, study, sleep." I took a tiny sip of my tea, unsweetened and steaming, and placed the cup back on the table to cool.

"Wait a minute," he asked, looking up. "Did I hear *two* swims in that routine? I thought you gave up morning practice."

I had to fill him in. Our daily text messaging was brief and to the point, and I hadn't told him what happened since the Long Island meet. While we waited for our combination plates, I rehashed the meet, my record-breaking 500, the girls rally against me, and Jordan's cyber-attack. He listened, not butting in, waiting to get all the facts before reaching conclusions. When I stopped to catch my breath and ingest some General Tso's Chicken, he spoke up.

"I thought things were going well at that school."

"Well, they were, until everyone found out I'm a much better swimmer than I let on and now they hate me. At least, some of them do," I said.

"I'd expect they'd be happy to have you on their team," he said, spearing a shrimp with his fork. "You can lead them to a fourth division title."

"They don't need me to win the division title, Dad. They've won it umpteen times without me. It's my going against Tatiana Reese for the Singer challenge that's got them all fired up."

"What's her best time again?"

I took a sip of my now tepid tea, and murmured, "457.20."

"It's yours, Aerin. Just do it."

I sighed and looked down at my plate, no longer hungry. "It's not that simple." I pushed the plate away. "When I started this season I just wanted to swim. I never intended to break any records or win any titles. I just wanted to be one of the girls on the team."

"You have never been 'just one of the girls on the team.'"

"I know! And I hate it! I'm sick of everyone treating me like a freak because I'm faster than everyone else. I have friends, Dad, friends who like me because I'm me, and not some Olympic hopeful who makes everyone else look like they're not trying."

"I never thought of it like that," he said. "I guess your mother and I focused so much on your future we stopped paying attention to your present."

"Right," I said, relieved I'd finally gotten through to him, and in my last high school season. "We focused on what I did *in* the pool so much we didn't leave time for me to enjoy what happened *outside* the pool. And a lot's happening, Dad. Parties, dances, study dates, football games - "

He laughed and shook his head.

"What?"

"I've never seen you so excited about something other than swimming."

"I have friends, Dad. I have a *life*, in and out of the water, and I was enjoying it until I won that race. Now everyone expects me to win the challenge and break the 500 record. And if I do, everyone will hate me."

"Everyone?"

I thought of Justin. "Well," I conceded, "maybe not everyone."

He poured himself another cup of tea and stirred in some sugar. I pulled my plate back and picked through the remains, finding a nice chunk of chicken, cold, but I ate it anyway.

"Aerin, it's like this," he said, setting the spoon down. "You've come across an opportunity that most of us never get. You can do this, and it will better your life. I understand you don't want to lose your friends, but what kind of friends are they if they don't want you to do your best? You're a competitive athlete. It's not in your nature to back away from a challenge. If you don't rise to this one, you'll spend the rest of your life wondering what could have happened if you had."

I pushed back in my seat and absorbed his words. All of the

adults in my life said the same thing: Do it or you'll regret it. No one remembered how it felt to be seventeen and just wanting to fit in.

Yet I understood his point. We had prepared almost my whole life for me to excel, to make something out of this sport. Dreams of glory. Dreams of Olympic gold. Yes, my parents had planted that seed in my head, but I had let it take root, nurtured it, and allowed it to grow.

And we weren't a bunch of nutcases with delusions of grandeur. I had the stuff. Competing in the Olympics was a *real* possibility. I had demonstrated my talent and ability to people who knew the sport inside and out. They believed in me. *I* believed in me. That had not changed.

The circumstances involving my mother had caused me to stray from my path, a decision made in emotional turmoil, at my lowest point, when pain and confusion consumed me, and I did not know what to do next. I needed time off. Time to get my head together, to forgive myself for not seeing what was happening to my mother, for not holding her together. All that time underwater had waterlogged my brain, giving me tunnel vision as I focused on my goal. On winning. I wore blinders while everything important in my life slipped away.

Only my lingering guilt held me back. Could I release it and get back to my dreams, my goals, my plans? Winning the Singer challenge would change my life. It might cost me some friends, but if I won, I'd gain college money and a spot on a Division I team. Dad was right – I'd be a fool not to rise to the Singer challenge.

"452.50. That's easy." I plucked the last piece of chicken from my plate and popped it into my mouth.

Week Ten:

Sabotage

Chapter 63

Five a.m. Monday morning came too soon. I fumbled for my screeching alarm clock and switched it off, tossing it to the foot of the bed. I'd come home late Sunday night. My father and I took full advantage of the time without Emily and Avery and started the day with a long brunch with Dawn. His schedule was free of clients, calls, and computer work so after I finished my homework he saved me from taking the train back to Two Rivers and drove me there himself.

We stopped off at a huge mall halfway between his place and Maggie's and poked around in all the hip stores for cold weather gear for me - a new jacket, sweaters, and snow boots - and new sneakers and jeans for him. We then waited almost an hour for a table at a trendy burger joint. He dropped me off at Maggie's after nine. I climbed upstairs with barely a hello to her and Uncle Pat before I crashed onto my bed.

At the crack of dawn, all I wanted to do was burrow under the blankets and go back to sleep, but Justin would pull up in front of the house in a few minutes and I had to get moving. I packed my practice bag, threw on my sweats, grabbed my book bag, and stopped off in the kitchen for a glass of orange juice and a banana. I slipped out of the house when his Jeep rumbled outside. It was cold, and I jumped into the passenger's seat, grateful he was running the heater at full blast.

"Cold enough for you?" he asked as he started the drive to the high school.

"I hate the cold," I said, buckling my seat belt.

"Oh yeah? No skiing, skating, snowmobiling?"

I rolled my eyes. "I'm a city girl, remember?"

"Some city people like winter sports."

"Not this city person. How was your weekend? Did I miss anything?"

"No," he said. He reached for the bottle of water stuck between his legs and took a long sip. "I worked eight-hour shifts both days, and spent Saturday night at Travis' house, watching the Yankees win game three in the playoffs. What about you? How were things at your dad's?"

"The best time we've had in months," I said, and told him all about the weekend, showing him my new jacket.

"I'm glad things are working out with you and your dad," he said.

I thought about that for a moment, conjuring up a vision of my father as he sat across from me at dinner last night, relaxed and focused on me. "I loved not having to share him with Dawn and the girls," I said, "but I also understand they're important to him, and I have to respect that and do my part to make this whole thing work so we can all be happy."

"Do I detect some growth here?" he asked.

"Leaps and bounds," I said, smiling. We *had* come a long way these last two months.

"And you're visiting your mom this weekend?" He pulled into the school's parking lot.

I nodded. "Saturday, after practice. I can't wait. Her letters have been so positive. Talk about growth. She's been teaching some of the other women how to swim and helping them study for the GED exam. She says she's back to her normal weight and feels great."

"That's awesome, Aerin, I'm happy for her. And for you." He parked and turned off the Jeep. The school was in darkness except for the light over the door to the athletics wing. Three other cars sat in the lot: Coach's, Tati's, and Erica's. We grabbed our gear and headed for the natatorium.

The locker room was empty, and I realized we were a few minutes late. I hoped Coach hadn't chugged his second coffee yet and was still in his early morning fog, oblivious to our lateness. I wasn't in the mood for his disapproval nor did I want him to tack on an extra set as punishment. I switched my sneakers for flip-flops, grabbed my cap, goggles, and towel out of my practice bag, and stuffed everything else into a locker.

I walked on to the pool deck expecting everyone to be in the water, but was surprised to see them clustered on the bleachers, chattering as they stared at and scrolled on their phones. The door to the locker room swung shut with a whoosh, and a few of them looked up, spotting me on deck. They nudged each other, announcing my presence, and the group grew hushed. Some of the girls turned their backs.

"What's up?" I asked, my stomach now in knots as I realized whatever captured their attention had something to do with me.

Before anyone could answer, Justin exited the boy's locker room. He summed up the situation in a second and asked, "What's going on?"

They just looked at each other and then down at their phones as though hypnotized. Justin approached Mel and grabbed her phone out of her hand. He stared at the screen, scrolled down, and looked at me.

"What is it?" I asked, trembling.

He handed Mel's phone to me. "Where's Jordan?" he asked as I took it from him.

I forced my eyes to look at the screen, afraid of what I'd see. It was a picture of my mom, wearing an orange jumpsuit and handcuffs, standing in what looked like a courtroom. My father stood beside her. How had *this* gotten on Jordan's blog?

My knees went weak, and I almost crumbled. Justin threw an arm around my shoulders and held me up. No one said anything. I looked at them, still huddled together, and not one of them met my eyes.

"Where's Jordan?" Justin asked again, his voice booming.

I looked back at the phone and read the text that accompanied the photo. "Aerin Keane's mom is a druggie and a thief. She's in jail, not helping soldiers in Afghanistan. Aerin is a liar. She lied to all of us." She'd included a link to the newspaper article with all the details of my mother's arrest. The post was time-stamped 11:18 pm last night. A rush of heat rolled through me, head to toe, and I heard a roaring in my head. Then my body went numb, and my hands grew weak. I almost dropped Mel's phone. She took it from me and our eyes locked.

"How could you?" I asked, my voice like steel as I struggled to hold back my tears. I turned away from all of them and ran to the locker room. No one would see me shed a single tear.

Once in the locker room, I rushed into a changing stall and locked the door behind me before crumpling into a heap on the cold tile floor. I wrapped my arms around my legs and let out deep, wracking sobs, my face wet with tears. This vicious attack was too much. I could handle attacks on me, the name-calling, the stares, the whispers. I could *not* handle an attack on my mom, whom they didn't know, and who had never hurt anyone. It was unforgivable; a low blow, never taken back no matter what anyone did or said. My heart hardened against all of them.

Minutes later, the door opened, followed by the sound of flip-flops slapping against the floor.

"Aerin?"

Mel.

"Go away," I said. "You're the last person I want to talk to."

"Come on, Aerin, let me explain."

"There's no explaining, Mel. I can't believe you did that to me. I thought we were friends."

She'd followed my voice, and her feet appeared on the other side of the stall door. She plopped down on the floor, knees to chest, the thick layer of downy hair on her legs visible.

"I didn't do it, Aerin," she started to explain, but I cut her off.

"Only two people know about my mom - you and Justin - and he'd never hurt me like that." My nose was stuffed up, and my voice sounded muffled. I wiped the tears from my eyes with the towel still draped around my neck.

"No, of course not, and neither would I. You know me better than that. It's Jordan's work. She spent all weekend looking for ways to hurt you."

I lifted my head and stared at the back of the stall door. Of course it was Jordan. She'd already proven herself to be quite the investigator.

"Where is she?" I asked. I didn't recall seeing her on the bleachers with the others.

"She's not here. She skipped practice. I guess she didn't have the guts to see the damage she caused."

"Well, she can't stay away for long. I'll catch up with her." And she'd be toast when I did, burnt toast, black on both sides and stinking.

"Coach knows all about it. It's her second infraction. I think he might throw her off the team."

"Good," I said.

"She'll be suspended, too, for cyberbullying."

"Even better." I wiped my nose.

"Are you going to stay in there all morning?" she asked.

"I wish. What did everyone else say?"

"I don't think they know what to say. She made the post late last night, and no one saw it until we got here this morning. She wrote some other stuff too, about your mom's conviction and sentencing. The whole story's out."

"Great, "I said, "by the time I get out of here the entire school will know, and by the time I get to lunch the whole town will know. I'm going home."

"You can't go home. We have physics lab. Remember?"

"Ugh," I groaned. "Do we have to?"

"We have to. Neither of us can afford to miss lab."

Could this day get any worse?

"Come out," she said. "I don't want to talk to a stall door. And the floor is freezing my butt." She was in her swimsuit while I still wore my sweats.

I wiped my face on the towel and rose to my feet. The locker room's stench of sweat and chlorine was making me nauseous. I opened the door, and Mel moved aside so I could walk out. At the sink, I turned on the cold water, and splashed my face. I cringed at my reflection in the mirror, at my miserable face, red-rimmed and swollen eyes, my nose a blubbery mess. "I look terrible."

"You look okay," she said. "Once you put your goggles on no one can see anything. Besides, everyone's in the pool and too busy to notice you."

I dried my face on the towel.

"You know, Aerin, it's not as bad as it seems," Mel said.

"Oh? And how's that?" I asked as I wrapped my towel around my neck.

"At first, the posts and pictures shocked us, but when we read the stories we understood what was going on with your mom, and we felt sorry for her."

"My mother is not a druggie and a thief, Mel. She's sick and got into trouble."

"I know that," Mel said, "and I told that to the other girls, including Tati and her minions. They get it. Your mom's a hero."

"She is," I said, feeling a smidge better now that the other girls understood what she'd gone through. "She's the bravest person I know. That's why I can't tolerate anyone doing her harm, even if they're just calling her names. Jordan can say anything she wants about me, but my mother is off limits. She's not getting away with this, Mel."

"What are you going to do?"

It didn't take long to figure that out. "Why did Jordan do this? What does she hope to gain?"

"Dumb question. Jordan's motives are as plain as day. She wants you to back off the 500 so Tati can win the challenge."

"That little stunt of hers backfired," I said, a sly smile working its way across my face. "No way I'm backing off now."

Mel's face lit up. "You're going for it?"

"I'm not going for it. I'm getting it."

She put her hand up in the air for a high five and we slapped palms.

"You go, girl!"

"Jordan will be sorry she ever crossed paths with me."

Mel's smile faltered.

"What?" I asked.

"I'm just thinking about Tati. She's collateral damage."

That was what I'd been trying to avoid all season. I never wanted to cheat Tatiana out of a victory, a scholarship, another spot on the leaderboard. But she was best friends with Jordan, and while Jordan had started the battle, Tati had done nothing to stop her.

"May the best swimmer win," I said.

"Okay," Mel said, brightening. "There's still forty minutes left for practice. We better get in the pool or Coach will have a conniption."

I tugged on my cap and goggles, and she did the same. Before we reached the locker room door, Mel stopped.

"I want to apologize, Aerin. I wasn't a good friend to you when all of this exploded. I shouldn't have taken sides, and I shouldn't have let you down. Forgive me?"

I wanted to start crying again but held back. I nodded.

"We're okay?" she asked.

"We're okay."

Chapter 64

The day dragged on as I went from class to class, keeping my head down to avoid the stares and snickers. Everyone was talking about me, even the teachers. I wouldn't give them the satisfaction of seeing how upset I was, thinking about my mom and how Jordan had attacked her. The Little Mermaid was absent today, which wasn't unnoticed by the kids in my classes, who whispered her name as much as they whispered mine. Coward. She'd done her hit-and-run and fled the scene, but she couldn't hide forever.

In the lunchroom, I grabbed a deserted table in the back and pulled a peanut butter and jelly sandwich out of my backpack. I was halfway through it when Mel and Erica stopped at my table with their lunch trays and asked if they could sit down. Once they had settled into their seats, Mel said, "Erica, tell her what you just told me."

Erica stopped unwrapping her tuna fish sandwich and looked at me. "I was in Principal Sorenson's office just a few minutes ago. Mrs. Mendoza asked me to drop something off on my way to the cafeteria. Jordan and her parents sat in the office with Mr. Sorenson and Coach. No one looked happy. Jordan was bawling like a baby."

That news buoyed my spirits. Jordan was already in hot water because of her bullying and harassment. No telling what would happen now. I took a sip of my water. "What do you think they'll do to her?"

"Well, after the first incident, when she outed you as a star swimmer, Mr. Sorenson suspended her three days for cyberbullying, and Coach suspended her two practices and a meet." Erica pulled the last of the wrapper off her sandwich. She took a bite, chewed, and went on. "This time, I heard she's getting kicked off the team and a one-week suspension. Her parents are so not happy at the moment."

"There goes NYU," Mel said with her signature smirk. "Hey, she earned it. She's been pulling stuff like this for years, but what she did to Aerin is the worst. The other girls are mad at her too. She's not too popular right now."

"What about Tati?" I asked.

"Tati wants nothing to do with her, and she's upset Jordan dragged her into this ugly mess. It's not her style. I told you: Tatiana is okay. Jordan's the one to watch out for."

"Viper," Erica said.

Tatiana sat across the room with Sean and Travis, the three of them huddled together, whispering, no smiles. She looked up and caught me staring at them, frowned, and looked away. We had nothing to say to each other, both of us captured in Jordan's web of torment and intimidation. But the final showdown would be between the two of us. Jordan had made things tougher for Tatiana. Some best friend.

It was good to sit with Mel and Erica at lunch again. I'd missed their company, the jokes, and the laughter, their support. "Thanks for sitting with me, guys."

"We're a couple of dopes," Erica said. "We never should have followed Jordan and unfriended you after the Long Island meet. We were confused, and hurt, but what she did was terrible. And you've been a good friend ever since you came here."

I raised my eyebrows. "Even though I lied about my swimming

and my mom?"

"I don't understand why you lied about your swimming," Erica answered, "but I understand why you lied about your mom. If it were my mom, I'd lie too. People don't understand these things and are quick to judge. I'm sure it's painful, and you deal with it the best way you can."

"Thanks, Erica," I said, touched by her sincerity.

"The newspaper article said your mom is serving six months. When does she get out?" Erica asked.

"February."

"Will you be leaving Two Rivers?"

"I don't know. I was thinking of going back to the city to be with my mom, to help her get settled when she gets back. Things will be different for her, and I don't want her to be alone. She'll need me."

"Well, I hope you don't leave," Mel said. "We need you here, too."

"You won't need me much after swim season ends," I pointed out.

"Are you kidding? Who else will help us keep Jordan in line? We'll still have five or six months left to deal with her garbage."

"I'll be glad when we graduate and go off to college," Erica sighed.

The bell rang. Time to go. We packed up our wrappers and empty cartons and I followed them out of the cafeteria.

"What's up for tonight?" Mel asked.

I had plans to train with Justin but couldn't tell her that. "Homework and then bed. I'm exhausted after the weekend at my dad's and all this turmoil."

"Erica and I are catching a movie."

"Maybe next time."

"I'll remember you said that."

"Oh, I almost forgot," Erica said as we merged into the throng of students flooding the corridors on the way to seventh period. "The harvest is just about finished, and my parents said I could take a Saturday off to go to the city with you guys."

I had forgotten all about our plan to spend a day in the city as soon as Erica was free from farm chores. Right now, it sounded like fun, and I could use a day away from all the team drama. "Not this weekend. I'm seeing my mom on Saturday afternoon. But the following weekend I'm free."

"I'll check with my parents," Erica said before she went left while we went right.

"Me too," said Mel. "I'm sure they'll have no problem with it. After all, you are a city girl and know your way around."

"Piece of cake," I said. We high fived each other and walked into physics lab.

The rest of the day continued without incident. Aside from a few sidelong looks, whispered conversations that ceased when I came within hearing distance, and a lot of surreptitious texting accompanied by furtive glances my way, it was just like any other school day.

Mel and I got through physics lab and went on to practice with relief. On the pool deck, the mood was somewhat subdued. Coach sat in wait for us as we filed in and took our places in the bleachers, a grave expression on his face. No one said anything, waiting for him to explode. Once we assembled, he sipped his coffee, then took his time looking at each one of us. An awkward moment passed before he started speaking.

"I'm going to say this once. What's been going on for the last couple of weeks has to stop. Everyone knows the school's code of conduct: zero tolerance for harassment of any student or athlete. I understand you're all caught up in the excitement of the Allison Singer challenge. We have two athletes here today who can meet that challenge, and I'm confident one, if not both of them, will."

I focused on the pool deck, sensing twenty-six sets of eyes boring into the back of my head.

"This is going to be a fair contest," Coach continued. "Any harassment or bullying of either of these athletes will result in an immediate suspension from school and the team. Jordan Hastings is not here today for that reason. We are a team, meant to support one another, to help each other be the best we can be. Backbiting, sniping, and defamation affects all of us. Jordan's actions over the last twenty-four hours have harmed the team's reputation. She's hurt all of us, including herself.

"Anyone who continues to spread rumors via social media or any other method will share Jordan's fate. We have four meets until the Division Championships. Two of them are against our toughest competitors. You girls are having an excellent season. I don't want all of your hard work to be wasted because of one person's actions. Am I clear?"

Heads nodded all around.

"We need to focus on nothing but swimming and bringing home that division title. Now get in the water and start the Monster set."

A few groans erupted from the swimmers. The Monster set was the worst Coach could dish out. We'd only done it once this season and it ended in tears for many of us. A stern glance from Coach quieted the complainers. We rose, tugged on our goggles and caps, walked to the blocks, and dove into our lanes. I swam behind Mel, Erica, and Charlie, all of us concentrating on meeting the intervals. As the set progressed, I was soon in the lead and kept my pace, straining after each lap to go faster next time, getting into the rhythm of the swim, controlling my breathing as I emptied my mind of all of the stress of the last hours.

Near the end of the set, most of the girls had dropped off, maxed out and unable to continue. Soon me, Mel, Erica, and Tatiana were the only swimmers in the water, all of us exhausted and out of breath, meeting the intervals by just hundredths of a second. The other girls cheered from the sidelines. A few shouted encouragement to me, and as I launched into another lap, I smiled, touched by their support.

Minutes later, Mel dropped out and Erica dropped out right behind her. Tati and I were now the only swimmers making the intervals. After the pain and humiliation Jordan had caused, there was no way I'd let Tati beat me. I was determined to complete the set in record time.

I pushed on, ignoring my burning muscles and overtaxed lungs as I pulled and kicked my way across the pool, while Tati matched my pace in the lane beside me. When I surfaced for air, I heard the shouts and cries of our teammates as they urged us on.

We had one interval left. I pushed off a half second before Tati, and we raced each other, neck and neck, stroke to stroke, the water churning as we kicked our feet and plunged our arms into it. The girls on deck erupted into a frenzy of cheers. Most of them allied with Tati's team, but a few voices shouted my name. They spurred me on, and at the last turn I was ahead.

I took advantage of Tati's faltering and pushed off the wall as though my life depended on it, streamlining across the first ten yards before popping the surface and clobbering the water with my arms and feet, Tati right behind me, her hands at the level of my hips as she tried to draw even with me. She didn't have my determination or my drive and I streaked ahead of her, flipping off the wall in my final turn, leaving her in my wake as I plowed ahead, reaching the finish a full second before she did.

The noise on deck was deafening as the girls cheered for both of us. I clung to the wall and panted, straining to catch my breath. Tati came up beside me, also overwhelmed. We looked at each other, and she smiled. I smiled back, puzzled by her unusual response to losing. She climbed out of the pool and joined her minions on deck.

Mel leaned down and offered a hand as I climbed out of the pool.

"Good job," she said. "That'll show them."

"Don't be too confident," I said, still breathless. "This will motivate her to train harder. I just give her another reason to break that record."

"She's not a shoo-in," Mel said. "If she were, she would have already broken it."

No one on the team knew Tatiana better than I did. We weren't friends - we rarely spoke - but we were both winners, and I knew all about winning.

A winner wants to win. A winner has a burning desire to come out on top. She needs a challenge, an inner drive, something chasing her toward a goal. Perhaps Tati was biding her time, working slowly toward breaking the record, waiting for the last event to make her mark. That's how I'd play it. Creep forward, fall back a little to enthrall and entertain the others, then leave them all shocked and screaming when I break that record at the last possible moment, winning the challenge and all its glory and prizes.

That's how I'd do it.

Chapter 65

Justin picked me up at eight to do some weight work at Reggie's house.

"Everyone's talking about how you beat Tati in the Monster set," he said as soon as I got into his Jeep. "I'm sorry I missed it."

"It's just a practice set. It doesn't mean anything." I figured that news would make the circuit in no time. The gossip around here moved faster than the speed of light.

"Of course it means something," he said as he took the right turn out of Aunt Mag's neighborhood. "You've shaken things up around here. A lot of people would love to see you beat Tati for that title."

"Swimmers make and break records every day, Justin, you know that."

"Yeah, but not too many with a fifty thousand dollar prize attached."

I closed my eyes and leaned back. "Stop," I said. "You're giving me a migraine."

He stopped for a stop sign. "Seriously? If you don't feel well, I'll take you home." He looked so disappointed I had to laugh.

"I'm all right," I said. "Although I am pretty tired after that set today. I think Coach was punishing all of us for what Jordan did."

"She made the team look bad, and Coach doesn't like that. After school today, Principal Sorenson had a big powwow in his office with him, Jordan, her parents, and Calvin Reese."

"What was Tati's father doing there?"

He shrugged. "He's into everything."

"Are you thinking what I'm thinking?" I asked. "Is Tati's father strong-arming Coach and Mr. Sorenson to let Jordan back on the team?"

"I wouldn't put it past him," he said, parking the car and turning off the engine. "It wouldn't be the first time he went to bat for Jordan. He's tight with her father, too. Maybe he owes him a favor."

"What does Jordan's father do?"

"Real estate broker."

"Thick as thieves."

"You know it."

"It's not fair," I said, grabbing my gear and jumping down from the Jeep.

"When is life ever fair, Apple?"

"After all the trouble she's caused you'd think she'd get some punishment."

"I'm sure her parents are punishing her."

"I want her publicly reprimanded and off the team."

"So do I. Too bad we don't run the world."

We stood outside Reggie's door, waiting for him to let us in.

"Don't be too hard on me tonight. I'm tired and sore, and I have a meet tomorrow."

"The Knights are no problem. You'll beat them no sweat."

"I have to beat Tati," I reminded him.

"Like I said, no sweat."

Chapter 66

Justin was almost as good as Kelsey in predicting meets. The Knights were a small team with a few star performers, none of whom competed in my events. Tati and I went head to toe in the 200, a quick warmup to the main event – the 500. When we hit the water, everyone else on our team went wild, picking sides, some rooting for me, the others cheering on Tati. Mel, Erica, and Charlie urged me on at the turn. When I won by just a few hundredths of a second the three of them gave me a high five.

"Good race!" Mel shouted, slapping me on the back.

Tati and her minions walked back to the bleachers, skirting us as they chattered and consoled her. She shook them off and sat at the far end of the bench, alone.

"That's not the big race," I said. "She's all fired up for the 500 now. I'll have to push harder."

I grabbed my towel and dried off, then joined Mel poolside to cheer on Erica in the 200 IM. She won, and then Mel finished second in the 50 free. Our divers competed next and took first, third, and fourth. We were winning the meet by a landslide.

I took the blocks for the 500 and appraised the competition. Tati was on my left, tugging at her goggles, readjusting her cap. The swimmer between us looked like a little dynamo, poised on the edge of the block, locked between two powerhouses. I wondered if she knew it.

When the buzzer buzzed, I was ready, plunging into the pool with as much velocity as I could muster, using my legs the way Justin had shown me, depending on muscle memory to tell my arms what to do. It all came back to me - the physical moves, the mental game - as though I'd never stopped swimming at my best. My intentional slacking had done no damage. My skill, confidence, and technique were spot on.

In just a few minutes, I had the lead. Tatiana was right beside me, almost matching me stroke for stroke. At each turn, I gained a small advantage until I was half a body length ahead of her. The roar of the crowd and the rush of the water spurred me on although my lungs burned and my arms and legs were on fire. I hadn't swum that hard in months and was exhilarated and exhausted. I finished first, 4:54.28, less than two seconds from beating the Singer record. I clung to the wall, chest heaving, straining to catch my breath.

Tati popped up in her lane two and a half seconds behind me. She also clung to the wall, her breath heavy. She glanced up at the clock and stared at the numbers, her lips moving. She pulled herself out of the pool and joined her crew, who also stared up at the clock, all of them stunned.

When the meet was over, Coach told us to shower, change, and come back on deck before we left. Something was up. He never kept us after we'd dressed to go home.

Although we'd won the meet 101-86, the mood in the locker room was subdued. The tension between Tatiana and me, and the outcome of our events, diminished our usual energy and excitement following a win. Before the race, everyone knew there was a chance for a big upset. Now they understood that the possibility of the school's Golden Girl failing to meet a challenge she was just seconds shy of overcoming was real. The season might not end the way they expected, with Tati breaking another record and winning a huge scholarship.

She and I each had our supporters, although her group numbered twice as many as mine did. While they clustered together, getting ready, I huddled in the rear of the locker room with Mel, Erica, Charlie and a few of the others who rooted for me, taking quick showers and pulling on our sweats. We wrapped our dripping hair in big towels, packed our bags, and were first to take our spots on the bleachers, waiting impatiently for the coaches and the other girls to come out so we could find out what was going on and get home. It was almost seven, and I was hungry, tired, and had a mountain of homework waiting for me.

The other girls filed out of the locker room in twos and threes, and a few minutes later the entire team was in the bleachers, whispering to each other, wondering why we were sitting there.

Coach came out of his office and pulled his chair around to face us, straddling it in his usual position, leaning against its back. He took a quick headcount, and when satisfied no one was missing, cleared his throat. I sensed a lecture coming on.

"Listen up, girls." He had our undivided attention. "Jordan Hastings will be back on the team beginning Monday morning."

Before anyone could say anything, he continued. "Everyone knows the penalty for bullying a teammate on any sports team at Two Rivers High School is suspension and possible expulsion. Jordan violated the code of conduct not once, but twice," he held up two fingers, "and I stand behind my decision to expel her from the team. But there are forces at this school stronger than me, and Jordan appealed to these forces. She apologized for her actions, and asked for leniency so she can finish out the season. Principal Sorenson and Mr. Maxwell agreed to give her another chance. From this moment on, I want no more discussion of her actions and no retaliations. Do you understand?"

I looked at the rest of the girls, assessing their reactions. No one was happy. Even Jordan's staunchest of minions seemed troubled. Tatiana sat at the end of the row chewing her nails, not making eye contact with anyone, a deep frown on her face. I could almost feel her seething. Word around the school was that she and Jordan had a big blowout and still weren't talking. Jordan had dragged Tati into an awkward situation and damaged her name as well as her own. Mel said Tati wanted nothing to do with Jordan anymore. That would make Jordan's reappearance next week even more tempestuous for the team.

Coach looked tired, and not happy to have had his authority questioned. Jordan's actions had tarnished the team's reputation and embarrassed him. The whole thing was as hard for him as it was for us.

"So, come to practice Monday morning prepared to work. We have our last three meets in the next ten days, and I don't want any drama to interfere with our progress to date." He took a moment to make eye contact with each of us. "We're poised to have an undefeated season and win the division championship again, but we have to hold it together and compete as one cohesive unit. No more of this Team Tati – Team Aerin split. We saw today that either of these swimmers can break the Singer record and win her challenge. I have no doubt one of them will. We'll cheer for each of them impartially and equally and show the rest of the division we are a unified team. Do you understand?"

No one said anything, but we all nodded. The air around us bristled with unspoken tension. I couldn't wait to get out of there.

"Jordan's five day school suspension is postponed until after her season ends," Coach continued. "But before she comes to practice on Monday, she has to take down her blog and write a one thousand-word essay for the school's website on the effects of cyberbullying that includes a formal apology to Aerin."

Silence from the team, although I could sense everyone's head was spinning with unasked questions and unspoken objections.

"Now, go home, eat dinner, do your homework, and get into bed early. Tomorrow is another day." Coach dismissed us.

We couldn't leave fast enough, and pushed and shoved each other to get out of the natatorium. Once outside, we drifted into our various factions, our heads bent low as we discussed what had just happened.

"I don't believe it," Mel hissed.

"Teflon Jordan," Erica said, shaking her head. "Nothing ever sticks."

"I don't get it," Charlie said, her lips trembling. "I thought Coach cut Jordan from the team because of what she did to Aerin. Now he's letting her back?"

"It wasn't Coach's decision," I said. "He's upset about it too."

"Someone got to Principal Sorenson and Mr. Maxwell and got Coach's decision reversed," Mel said.

"How did that happen?" Erica wondered. "Not only did she break the team's code of conduct but the school's as well. How does she get off?"

"The whole thing is a farce," Mel said, increasing her pace.

Justin and his Jeep waited for Mel and me in the parking lot. "Did you hear about Jordan?" he asked.

"We know all about it," I said, "and no one is happy."

"Back on Monday like nothing ever happened." Mel dropped her bags. "How do you know?"

"Travis told me. He said Jordan, her parents, Coach, and Calvin Reese went to see Principal Sorenson together, and Mr. Maxwell and Mr. Howard, the *superintendent,* joined them. He waited for Jordan outside the office and when she came out she looked like a wreck. Her face was red and swollen like she'd been crying her eyes out. She was with her parents and Mr. Reese, and they were all smiles. Coach came out after them looking like he wanted to hit someone and stalked off."

"Politics," Mel scoffed. "I should have known."

"She's outlived her life on this team," Erica said. "I can't imagine why she'd even want to come back. No one wants her, not even Tati."

"Well, that's the strange part about the whole thing," Justin said. "Travis says Jordan *doesn't* want to rejoin the team, but her parents caused such a fuss that Mr. Reese got involved, and the whole thing blew up and now she *has* to go back. She has no choice."

Mel grew thoughtful. I could see her mind moving leaps and bounds ahead of all of us. "You know," she said a few seconds later. "That might be the best punishment of all."

"What?" I asked.

"Jordan doesn't want to come back to the team because she knows she's enemy number one now."

"I'm glad she took that spot from me," I said.

"No one will talk to her, not even Tati. She's made too much trouble. And she still hasn't made a qualifying time for the Division Championships, and we've only got three meets left."

"Don't forget the Last Chance meet," Erica said. It was the very last opportunity for a swimmer to make a division time after all the season's dual meets were finished.

"True," Mel said, "but she'll have to work hard to succeed, and we all know Jordan's a slacker. She'll come back, no friends, and finish the season without making it to championships. Sounds like a good plan to me."

"Even better," Justin said, "she'll have to watch Aerin break the 500 record."

"Hey," I said, "There's no guarantee that'll happen."

"Oh, be quiet," Mel said. "You're the only one who doesn't see that happening."

Justin seconded that, and Erica voiced her conviction that I'd beat Tati.

"I knew Aerin could do it all along," Charlie piped up in her little voice.

"Living well is the best revenge," Mel said, a gleam in her eye.

"I'm glad you guys are on my team," I said, touched.

"My mom's waiting for me," Charlie said and hoisted her bags over her shoulder. We said goodbye, and she trotted across the parking lot toward her mom's car.

"Let's go home," I said. "I'm starved and exhausted. I've got two pages of math problems and a history quiz to study for tomorrow."

End of discussion.

Chapter 67

Visiting my mother for the second time in that place was not as traumatic as the first. When I walked out the last time, I left behind the initial shock of seeing the facility with its barbed wire fences, austere brick buildings, and long, winding corridors. But it still hurt my heart to know my mother had spent the last two months behind its walls and had four months to go before she'd be free again.

She sat at a table in front of the room and jumped up when Maggie and I entered. Her short hair had grown out a bit and didn't have that fresh-cut look it had a month ago. Her skin was clear and pink, her eyes bright, and she walked better than she had in months, her limp almost imperceptible.

"Come here," she said, pulling me in for a hug. We clung together for at least a minute and then pulled back to examine each other. "You've grown an inch or two," she said.

I shrugged. "You've grown a pound or two."

She laughed. "I'm up fifteen pounds. Look! I almost can't button these jeans." She lifted the hem of her shirt and showed me how the button strained between her waist and her waistband. She was still thinner than normal, but better rounded than a few months ago. I was happy to see her looking well, and cheerful, too, her face alive and animated, her voice full of life. I hadn't seen her with so much energy and enthusiasm in a long time.

"How is everybody?" she asked Maggie as we settled into the seats around the table. Around us, other families reunited with their loved one and the noise in the room grew to a steady din punctuated with laughter, high-pitched squeals, and a few sobs. I minded my own business, focusing on Mom, drinking her in. These visits were brief and far between. I savored every moment.

Maggie filled Mom in on all the happenings at home: Uncle Pat's taking a second job as a security guard for the school district, the kids' sports and school activities, and other family news. Mom listened, interested in everything, from Paige's Girl Scout cookie drive to Salty's latest vet visit. Mom and Maggie held hands the entire time, and when Maggie finished, she pulled her hand away and sat back in her chair.

"Enough about me," she said. "How are you?"

Mom's smile almost lit up the room. "I'm great," she said. "Ninety days clean. Look." She paused to dig something out of her front pocket. "A medallion." She placed it on the table, and it shone under the overhead lights.

I picked it up. "I'm proud of you, Mom," I said. "That's great."

She took it back and kneaded it between her thumb and forefinger while she continued to talk. "I get credit for the time I spent in detox waiting for my trial. It's a start."

"It's a good start," Maggie said. "I'm thrilled to see you looking so well."

"What else are you doing?" I asked. "You mentioned teaching swim lessons and helping some of the women with the GED exam."

"That's right," she said. "Two have already passed. And I'm putting together a swim team, can you believe that?"

"No!" I said. She was too much.

"We needed something constructive to do in the evenings besides television, so I've got about ten or twelve of the women coming down to the pool to work on their technique. We race each other. It's all fun. No pressure."

"It's therapeutic," I said.

"Yes," she said. "It *is* therapeutic. Speaking of which, are you still in therapy?"

I laughed. "I've moved on."

"You're still swimming, aren't you? You haven't stopped?" Her shocked expression was priceless.

"No, Mom, in fact, quite the opposite. I got my act together. I decided to stop licking my wounds and go all out." I told her the whole story about Jordan outing me and the team's response, but left out part two of her attack. "So I'm an official challenger for breaking the 500 record and winning the scholarship. What do you think?"

"I think it's wonderful," she said. "I knew you wouldn't be able to let that opportunity slip by you."

"I flip-flopped so many times, not wanting to step on any one's toes. After everything that happened with Jordan and the other girls on the team, I decided to do my best. It's between Tatiana and me. May the best swimmer win."

"That's a much better outlook than the last time we spoke. How many meets are left?"

"Just two, but they're our biggest competitors. Then it's the Division Championships, with two more chances to break the record – preliminaries and finals - and after that the State Championships, with another two chances to break it if I haven't already."

"So eight more chances," Mom said. "And how close are you?"

"My best time so far is one second off." Saying that sent a thrill of excitement coursing through my veins. I was so close, but Tati was right on my heels, and it could still go either way. I could take nothing for granted.

"You'll make it. And won't it be nice to have that scholarship in place when we plan next year?"

I nodded. Although I wanted to beat Tatiana, break the record, and put my name on that leaderboard, I had to admit the scholarship was a tempting incentive to take on the challenge.

Mom changed the subject. "So tell me about your social life. Is everything okay with the other girls, your friends? Mel and Erica?"

I nodded. "We're cool."

"And Justin? How's he?"

My cheeks pinked. Before I could answer, she grinned and said, "That blush tells me Justin is just fine. Look at our girl, Maggie," she turned toward Aunt Mags. "I think she's in love."

"Get out!" I squealed. "I'm not in love."

"First love. Remember that, Mags?" Mom mused.

They laughed, and my cheeks grew warmer. "Stop," I said.

"I'm sorry," Mom said. "I don't mean to embarrass you. I think it's great."

Our time was almost up, and soon Maggie and I would have to leave. "How's your father?" Mom asked. "Is everything all right with Dawn and the baby?"

"They're doing okay. Dawn is on bed rest if you can imagine that, but she's doing all right."

"That's good to hear. The baby will be born soon after I get out of here."

February seemed so far away. I couldn't imagine it.

"Any thoughts on what you plan to do then?" Maggie asked.

Mom shrugged and looked thoughtful. "I'm learning to live one day at a time, but we are encouraged to think ahead to our discharge. I guess I'll go home, to Manhattan, find a new job, get into some meetings."

"What about Aerin?"

"I'm going with Mom," I said. "That hasn't changed."

"But you're doing so well in Two Rivers," Maggie said. "Are you sure you want to uproot yourself and start again?"

No, I didn't, but my first loyalties were with my mother. Before I could answer, Maggie turned to Mom.

"You can always come to Two Rivers, Devon," she said. "Pat and I will help you get established, find an apartment, a job. That way you and Aerin can be together and she won't have to make any changes."

"Great idea, Maggie," I said, excited about the possibility.

"That's kind of you, Mags, but I'm not a country girl," Mom said.

"It's something to think about, Mom," I said. "It might be a good idea to get a fresh start."

"I don't know," she said, unconvinced.

"You've got plenty of time to make plans," Maggie said. "No rush."

"No rush, Mom," I agreed, "but think about it. Could be a win-win."

"Okay," she said. "I'll discuss it with my counselor."

"Speaking of the city," I said, remembering I needed to ask my mother something important. "Some friends and I want to take a trip into Manhattan, see a show, grab some lunch. Is it okay if we stop by the apartment so I can pick up a few things?"

"What do you need?"

"I want the competition suits and caps I won at last year's championship meet." I won the 200 and 500 free, and the 200 and 400 free relays and came home with a bag of high-tech equipment, including the best swimsuit available for a competitive swimmer. I wanted that suit and the caps and goggles that came with it when I went to the Division and New York State Championships.

"Good idea," Mom said. "Just let Maribel know you're coming." Maribel, a friend of Mom's, was subletting our apartment. "And give Sam a call. He'll be able to get you cheap seats to the Broadway show of your choice." Sam was another friend who had a job working with a ticket wholesaler. "When are you going?"

"I'm not sure. In a couple of weeks. It's just me, Mel, and Erica." I told her a little more about our plans. When the guard announced the end of visiting hours, she was beaming with happiness for me.

"I'm so glad to see you've made some friends, and you're having a good time. It looks like everything is working out for you."

I had to agree. "Staying with Maggie was a good move."

Maggie and Mom hugged goodbye. We all stood up, and Mom pulled me in for her embrace, stroking my back and planting little kisses all over my face. There were no tears.

"Don't forget to write," I said.

"Don't forget to write back," she responded. I was not as dedicated to letter writing as she was, but then school and swimming consumed my life. "Send me the dates of the championship meets. Maybe I can pull some strings around here and arrange to follow them online. At the very least I'll be able to see your stats."

People started filing out of the room and the other inmates lined up to return to their quarters. We were among the last to part. We held each other for a long minute, not saying a word. When the guard gestured it was time to go, she released me and followed him to the door. Maggie and I went the other way with another guard, and were soon on our way home.

Week Eleven:

Team in Turmoil

Chapter 68

Monday morning came early. Justin and Mel picked me up at 5:15 and in spite of the fact that we'd dressed for the pre-dawn temperatures – heavy sweat pants and shirts, hats, and gloves - we shook from the cold. The Jeep's heater didn't start blasting hot air until we turned into the school's parking lot. We leaped out as soon as we parked and ran for the doors to the athletic center.

I sensed the buzz before I entered the locker room, Mel on my heels.

"Something's up," she said as I pushed open the door.

All the usual morning swimmers, including Tati and Erica, congregated inside, peeling off their sweats and grabbing their towels, caps and goggles. Tati looked grim, her face taut with tension. She made eye contact with no one. She was the first one out to the pool deck and once she'd left there was a collective exhale as we all started breathing normally again.

"What's up with her?" Mel asked.

"Jordan's coming back today," Erica said, "and she and Tati are still not speaking."

"I wouldn't speak to her either," Mel said, tugging on her cap.

"Think Jordan will show for morning practice?" I asked as I

stuffed my bags into a locker.

"Fifty-fifty," Erica said. "Even on her best day, she's inconsistent."

"If I were Jordan I'd stay away from this pool as much as possible," Mel said.

We were the last ones in the locker room; everyone else had hit the pool deck. We grabbed the rest of our gear and headed for the door. Before we exited, the outer door to the lobby opened with a rush of air, and someone came in. Jordan. We stared at her, not knowing what to say. She didn't say anything either. She didn't even look at us. She pulled open a locker and started unloading her gear.

"Come on," Mel whispered and pushed us out the door. No time for talking.

Coach was on deck with his clipboard, and the girls were in the pool. Mel, Erica, and I lined up for the blocks, ready to dive in. Before Erica could push off Jordan came on deck, pulling the bottom of her two-sizes-too-small suit over her rump, her eyes downcast as she headed for the blocks. Everyone else was in the middle of the set, oblivious to her appearance.

"Go!" Mel ordered Erica, and Erica made her start, plunging into the water. I was right behind, and took off, hitting my stride almost in seconds. I didn't stop until I finished, coming up for air at the pool's edge where Erica and Mel joined me. Tati was also done, and rested in the next lane, catching her breath. In the other lanes, swimmers finished up. A few of the guys backstroked their way to the end, cooling down from the grueling set. Jordan was in lane six by herself, struggling to make the intervals.

"She's not in shape," Erica said.

"She's a slacker," Mel said. "It's a little late to make a statement now."

"She won't be able to make up for all the time she wasted earlier in the season," Erica said. "You need to make your cut times early and keep moving."

We watched her swim a length while we recovered. Mel was first out of the pool. Erica and I followed. Tati was already at the bleachers, toweling dry.

"How are you doing, Tati?" Mel asked. "Weekend okay?"

Tati glanced at her and shrugged. "It was all right."

"I heard you guys went to the drive-in."

"Who told you that?"

"Justin."

"He was there. It was the last night for the drive-in. They're closing for the season," Tati said.

I hadn't been to the drive-in. Guess I wouldn't be going anytime soon.

The question we all wanted to ask but none of us dared was, "How are things with Jordan?" If Coach heard us talking about their rift or anything about Jordan he'd bench us, and no one wanted to sit on the bench this week; we had our two biggest meets. The Bears were tomorrow, and the Boxers meet was on Friday. Our dual meet schedule would be behind us, and we'd start tapering for the Division Championships.

We lingered, drying off and squeezing the excess water from our hair, waiting for Jordan to finish her set and get out of the pool. The smart thing would have been to hightail it to the locker room, change, and leave before she finished, but the friction between her and Tati enthralled us. Even the boys lingered, waiting for something to happen. Jordan was now the lone swimmer in the pool while the rest of us took our sweet time toweling dry and picking up our gear.

"Let's get a move on, kids," Coach said from behind us. "Don't you have class in twenty minutes?"

Some of the boys grabbed their stuff and headed out, Justin at the lead. He glanced over his shoulder at me with a quizzical look, and I gave him one right back. The other girls sauntered to the locker room, buzzing amongst themselves. Jordan now sat on the pool's edge catching her breath.

"I've got to hand it to her," Mel whispered to Erica and me. "It took a lot of guts for her to show up this morning."

"She had no choice," Erica said.

"Are you guys done?" Tati asked. "I want to speak to Coach alone for a minute."

"Well, pardon me," Mel said, picking up her cap and goggles and shuffling into her flip-flops. "I guess we'll just have to get out of your way."

"Girls!" shouted Coach from across the pool. He tapped his wristwatch and pointed at the locker room door. We moseyed off the pool deck.

"What's happening?" asked Taylor as soon as the door to the locker room closed behind us.

"Tati's out there with Jordan and Coach, no one else," Erica said.

"Is there going to be a fight?" asked Charlie.

"I doubt it," Mel said.

"If I were Tati I'd smack her," said Taylor.

"That's not going to happen," Erica said.

"Nothing's going to happen. Now get dressed and get out of here, or you'll be late for first period," Mel ordered.

They heeded her advice after noticing the time. Again, we were last to leave, waiting for Tati or Jordan to come in.

The seconds ticked on and we were in danger of being late for class. Erica picked up her bags and made for the door. I was right behind her, but before she could open it, Mel said, "Wait a minute. I hear someone coming." Erica and I turned back, dropping our stuff on the tile floor, pretending we weren't just about ready to walk out. The door from the pool deck opened, and Tati walked in.

"You guys are still here?" she asked, annoyance flashing across her face.

"We're almost ready to leave," Mel said. "Are you okay?"

"Of course I'm okay," she said, whipping off her cap, her short brown curls set loose and framing her face. She looked tired, her eyes bloodshot. A fine line of pimples dotted her forehead. She grabbed her stuff from her locker and headed to a changing stall. "Move along or you're going to be late for first period."

The three of us looked at each other, unsure whether or not to leave while Jordan could enter at any moment. Before we could decide, the door from the pool deck opened again and Jordan joined us. She too looked taken aback at our gaping at her.

"What are you waiting for?" she asked. "Aren't you going to eat breakfast or something?" She headed for her locker and flung it open, rooting through her belongings. She pulled out a banana and peeled it. "It's almost 7:30," she said, taking a bite.

"We're out of here," Mel said, glancing at the changing stall where Tati had disappeared. If a fight was about to eupt, we'd miss it. We hoisted our bags onto our shoulders and moved toward the door. Before we could make our exit, the curtain over Tati's changing stall flew open and out she came, dressed in jeans and a sweatshirt, her hair wrapped in a towel. She ignored all of us, including Jordan, as she went to her locker. Jordan stood a few feet away, a forlorn expression on her face.

"Well, you guys have a great day," Mel said before slipping through the door. I was halfway out behind her when I heard a loud crash followed by raised voices. I ducked back in. Jordan had her hand on the door to Tati's locker, and slammed it shut. They stood inches apart and did not look up as Mel and Erica reentered the locker room and stood beside me.

"I can't believe you did that to me," Tati yelled at Jordan. "Do you have any idea how much trouble I'm in?"

"Why are you in trouble?" Jordan yelled back. "You didn't do anything. Do you have any idea how much trouble *I'm* in?"

"Are you an idiot? Everyone thinks I put you up to it – Coach, my parents, Mr. Sorenson and Mr. Maxwell. *Everyone's* talking about us, and they're not saying nice things. You embarrassed the team, the school, and me. I don't know why you felt you had to cut Aerin down, anyway. She never did anything to you."

"I did it for you, Tati, so you could win the Singer challenge. Aerin Keane is about to take it away from you. I needed her to get out of the way."

"I can handle Aerin Keane," Tati said. "You need to back off. All you've done is cause drama and trouble."

"I thought I could help you." Jordan's lower lip trembled.

"I don't need your help," Tati shouted, her face red. She picked up her bags. "I can win the challenge on my own, and if I can't, then Aerin deserves to win."

Jordan's face fell, and tears filled her eyes.

"Do you have any idea how difficult this season is for me?" Tati continued. "Everyone, and I mean *everyone* – the team, the school, and the town – expects me to break the record. I've been under immense pressure for two years, Jordan, and I'm working as hard as I can, but the season is ending soon, and I'm still struggling. I'm tired, and I don't care about it anymore. It has nothing to do with Aerin. I'm glad she's here because she's taken some of the focus off of me. She's given me a little push, some much-needed competition, but she's better, faster, and stronger than I am, and I don't think I can beat her now that she's determined to break the record."

"Don't say that, Tati, of course, you can beat her."

"Stop, Jordan. You put as much pressure on me as my father, Coach, and all those reporters who follow every meet like it's an Olympic event. It's high school swimming. Does it really matter?"

"Yes, it matters," Jordan said. "You'll break all the records. Your name will be all over the board. You'll win the scholarship."

"I don't care about all that," Tati said. "I'll get into any Division I school I choose. My father can pay the tuition. My name is all over the boards anyway. One more spot won't make a difference."

"But Tati, it's the Singer challenge. Even she wants to see you win."

Tati snorted. "Add her to the list. You seem more invested in it than I am. Why do you care so much, anyway? It's not about you."

"You're my best friend, Tati. I want you to win, to be the best."

"Your kind of friendship I don't need," Tati said, unmoved by Jordan's tear-streaked face. "We're done, Jordan. I don't want to talk to you anymore." She flung her bags over her shoulders and turned to head out, noticing us for the first time huddled by the door.

"Was that what you've been waiting for?" she asked. "Show's over. Now get out of my way. I'm late for class."

We parted to let her through, and she pushed through the door past us. Jordan still stood by the lockers, crying, her back to us, shoulders heaving. Mel, Erica and I looked at each other, wondering what to do. Mel broke the silence.

"Are you going to be okay, Jordan?"

Jordan whipped around, her cold blue eyes flashing. "Why do you care? Get out of here, Mel, and take your girlfriends with you."

We couldn't get out fast enough and stumbled over each other to rush through the door. Kids on their way to gym and swim classes crowded the halls. We pushed against the tide of incoming students to get to our classes.

"That was awkward," Mel said.

"Do you think Tati meant it?" Erica asked. "Are they really through?"

"If I were Tati I'd never speak to her again," Mel said. "Jordan caused her a lot of trouble, and it wasn't even necessary. I don't think Tati cares about beating Allison Singer's record anymore, at least not as much as Jordan does."

"I bet Tati's father cares," Erica said.

"He must have broken a few blood vessels when he heard what Jordan did and how she dragged Tati into it."

"I thought they came up with the plan together," I said.

"Why do you say that?" Mel asked.

"Jordan went to a lot of trouble to discredit me. Maybe Tati helped."

"Tati doesn't work that way," Mel said.

"Jordan still owes you an apology," Erica said.

"I'm not holding my breath," I said. With that, the bell rang to signal the start of first period. We ended our conversation and split up to head to class.

The school was humming with news of Tati and Jordan's blow out before the end of first period. Mel, Erica, and I had made a pact to keep quiet about the whole thing to prevent further damage to the team, but someone found out and, like wildfire, news of their argument was common knowledge. It had to have been Jordan. I doubted Tatiana would have broadcast that news. I passed her in the halls between classes, her head down, a dour expression on her usually cheerful face. We had two classes together, and in both she took a seat at the rear of the room and focused on the teacher and the work. She ignored anyone who tried to get her attention until they gave up, reduced to speculating with their friends about what happened between her and Jordan.

I kept an eye on her, replaying what she said in the locker room. Did she really not care about the Singer challenge? I found that hard to believe; she'd been focused on it for years. Not a day went by without someone mentioning it in school, at practice, in the newspaper, on Channel Six, or on social media. But I could understand if she had decided to pull back. I'd been in that spot before, many times. It's one thing to put pressure on myself to meet a goal or challenge, but when everyone else expects me to succeed the pressure intensifies. It's not a good place to be.

And did she really believe I was faster stronger, better than she was? I considered her my equal, but on my best day I *was* faster, better, stronger, no doubt. I planned to prove that over the next week or so.

By the time afternoon practice came around, everyone on the team and beyond knew Jordan and Tati were finished. As we assembled on the bleachers for practice, most of the girls huddled around Tati, although she seemed like she wanted everyone to leave her alone. Coach gave us our practice set – an easy one because of the Bears meet the next day – and we dove in with relief. The tension on the pool deck was thick, and Jordan hadn't even arrived. I was well into the set when she showed up and slipped into the water. We finished practice and exited the pool deck in twos and threes, no one speaking to Jordan, who finished her set alone.

We showered and changed quickly, eager to go home. The chatter was much quieter than usual. As much as the team had divided because of the tension between Jordan and me, the rift between Jordan and Tati divided it even more.

Not many sided with Jordan. She was *persona non grata* now. But Tati's detachment from everyone else left us in limbo. She was, after all, our leader, and her mood had a trickle-down effect. We were tense, anxious, and angry. If anyone asked me, I'd say tomorrow's meet against the Bears was up for grabs. Our winning record was about to be put to the test.

Chapter 69

On Tuesday, the school continued to buzz with rumors about what happened in the locker room with Tati and Jordan, the stories going so far as to say they'd had an actual fist fight, and Tati had broken Jordan's nose. No one had proof, and Jordan's nose looked fine, but that didn't stop people from spreading the rumor. Tati still wasn't talking to anyone, and Jordan had allied herself with some of her lesser known minions from on and off the team to put on a good front. She took down her web page as ordered, but I still waited for a formal apology from her that I suspected would never come. And she still had to write the essay on cyberbullying for the school website.

The news in that morning's *Two Rivers Times* was all about the Blazers' undefeated season, the face-off with the also undefeated Bears in the afternoon, speculation about Tatiana and the Singer Challenge, and projections for the Division Championship. Mel said that when the competition got that fierce at the end of the season, large crowds turned out for the meets. Bears territory was only fifteen minutes away, and their entire fan base showed up to cheer for them. It was a home meet for us, so we had a slight advantage, but after that all bets were off. The Bears had a powerhouse swimmer in every event backed up with a couple of Chinese swimmers leaving their marks on the season.

In school, I faced a math test and a super hard physics lab right before we assembled for the meet, which added to my stress level.

Throughout the course of the day, I was the recipient of many "Go get 'ems" and "Go Blazers" when I passed through the corridors between classes or settled into my seat in a classroom. We all dressed in team gear – official Trailblazers sweat pants and shirts with "Blazers Swimming" embossed on the back – so everyone in the school knew who we were. I had not experienced such support at any other school I'd attended. Two Rivers' teams supported each other, and kids from the other extracurriculars also got in on it and passed along encouragement and well wishes. By the end of last period, their show of support raised my spirits and buoyed my confidence, but the pressure of bringing in a big win for them put my stomach into nonstop flips.

When I arrived in the locker room, most of the girls were already there. They changed into their suits and grabbed their gear out of their bags before stuffing them into lockers with much less chatter than usual.

"Everyone's so serious," I whispered to Mel.

"It's our biggest meet of the season," she said. "The other teams in the division are no match for us, but the Bears are as good as we are and sometimes better. Even if we do everything right, they can still win. Our rivalry has been going on forever, and this is the meet Coach wants to win more than any other."

"Just what I need – more pressure," I moaned.

"The pressure will be on all of us, and I'm not so sure we're ready to meet it with all the commotion that's been going on around here."

"Who won last year?"

"We did. It bounces back and forth. Justin says they're out for blood today because it's their last meet of the season and they'll try to break the record in the 500."

"Can they?" I asked.

She nodded. "If someone from the Bears breaks that record the Blazers will look like a bunch of losers."

"I won't let that happen."

She smiled. "Maybe today's the day you knock that beast down."

Chapter 70

Mel was right. Loyal fans packed the viewing stands. One end was a sea of navy and white – Blazer's colors – and the other was awash in red and white, Bears' colors. I scanned the crowd until I found Aunt Maggie, Uncle Pat, and all their kids clustered together in the top row, the well-used banner that read "Go Aerin!" held above the heads of the twins. I waved, and they shouted their encouragement back down to me.

Mel and Justin's parents stood beside them. Erica's mom and dad sat in the front row, and midsection Charlie's mom was chatting with another swim mom I didn't recognize. I waved at all of them and then joined the rest of the team in the bleachers for Coach's final instructions.

We sat in groups, most of the girls gathered around Tati, the remaining clustered around me.

"This is not good," Mel whispered, looking around at the two groups.

"Coach said to cut out the Team Tati, Team Aerin thing," Erica said.

"This is ridiculous," I said.

"Couldn't happen on a worse day," Mel mumbled. We looked

across the pool where the Bears crowded around their coach for last minute instructions. They were a big team, the division's largest, forty girls, with three and sometimes four swimmers excelling in each event. They looked like a cohesive unit, not torn apart by backbiting, petty arguments, and drama trauma. I looked at my teammates, many of whom had tuned out of Coach's pep talk, and sat there studying their nails, fidgeting with their gear, or watching the clock.

Across the way, the Bears broke from their huddle and started an earsplitting cheer that rocked the pool deck. Even our bleachers vibrated.

Coach wrapped up his talk. We drew in together for a team hug and then Tati and Mel led us into our cheer, which did not reach the decibels of the Bears' but rocked the pool deck.

"Here we go," Mel said, and the girls in the 200 medley relay headed for the blocks.

We lost that event, coming in second and fourth. Charlie did the breaststroke leg of the second place team and passed me on her way back to the bleachers, her troubled eyes brimming with tears.

"This is going to be a tough one, Charlie," I said. "You did your best. Keep your head up." She gave me a high five and continued her way to the bleachers.

The 200 was next, and I took my spot in lane six. Tati was in lane four. I stretched out my arms and legs while we waited for the officials to get their act together to start the race, making sure my cap and goggles were on tight. When I was sure my gear was secure, I glanced at Tati, who made the same adjustments to her gear.

One of the Bears' Chinese exchange students stood between us, a long thin girl I had not yet challenged. She turned my way and gave me the onceover before turning her attention back to the water and positioning her feet on the block. Tati and I locked eyes, and she gave me a little nod. Beyond her was the Bears' top distance swimmer, her body poised for the start. She looked strong and powerful, like Erica, and I wished I'd scoped out my competition before the meet. Was she faster than Tati? Than me? I was about to find out.

The official announced the start, and when the buzzer buzzed the six of us flew off the blocks and hit the water. I surfaced and got right down to it, pushing through it as hard and as fast as I could, not looking at the swimmers around me. I saw no one and figured I had the lead. My charge was to keep it and win the race in record time. I had still to perform my best in this event.

I hit the wall on the first turn and headed back to close the first fifty yards. The Chinese swimmer crept up beside me and I hustled a little harder, my legs a nonstop kicking machine slicing through the water.

My chest started to feel tight, but I pushed on, ignoring the discomfort. I reached the wall with the Chinese swimmer on my heels.

On the left, two other bodies hit the wall – Tati and her competition – and I pushed on, my mind a blank, focused only on winning by being the first to make each turn. The long, lean swimmer beside me was gaining ground, and we hit the wall again at the same time She pushed off a little harder than I did and gained the lead; I was now at her heels. *Unacceptable.*

I endured, my arms plowing through the water, my legs kicking, kicking, kicking, to the wall again, completing the first 100 yards.

Tati and the other swimmer stayed with me, and I took a deep breath before spurring on for the next 50. The four of us, now locked in battle, raced for the turn stroke for stroke. The crowd roared, and I heard Mel and Erica cheering for me. Coach ran back and forth between them, screaming at us to *"Go! Go! Go!"*

We finished the lap again in tandem and pushed off the wall for the last fifty yards. My heart pounded as I strained to control my breathing and pump through the water. It was the hardest I'd worked all season, and it felt great. The extra training with Justin had paid off as my arms and legs did their necessary work without my brain having to tell them what to do. I was on autopilot, focused on the finish. The wall came into view and I added a little more *oomph* to my kick, and reached longer and faster with my arms.

The four of us approached the finish line dead even. I took the extra stroke to push toward the finish and hit the wall. Struggling to catch my breath, I looked up at the clock, and couldn't believe my eyes. I finished fourth. The Chinese swimmer and the Bears' best took first and second. Tati was third.

I clung to the wall, struggling to catch my breath, still stunned. I was so sure I was in the lead. That one last stroke should have pushed me ahead; instead, it slowed me down. A rookie mistake that cost me the race.

I climbed out of the pool, ripped my cap and goggles off my head and followed Tati to where Coach waited for us, shaking his head as he scribbled on his clipboard. He didn't look up until he'd finished writing. "Bad moves, girls," he said. "That extra stroke cost you, Aerin, and gliding to the finish cost you, Tatiana. Haven't I told you not to overthink? It was a tight race, but you could have prevailed. Next time, don't think. You're facing the same two swimmers in the 500. Get prepared." He turned away to catch the start of the 200 IM.

We lost that one too, but scored second and third, so it wasn't a total train wreck. Mel was up next in the 50. She looked about to pass out as she prepped for her race, swinging her arms in circles as she hopped from one foot to another. She jumped onto the block, and a moment later propelled herself into the race. It was finished in under 26 seconds. Mel took second place with a personal best of 26:01. She leaped out of the pool with a smile plastered across her face, high fived Coach and plopped down beside me on the bench.

"Good job, Mel," I said, flinging an arm around her and pulling her close. She'd been working so hard on breaking 25 seconds, and that was the closest she'd come.

Her chest heaved. She couldn't speak. She waved up at her

parents who raised their arms in victory.

"I'll get it next time," she said when she caught her breath.

Our divers came up next, and things started to take a turn for the better. Our dive team was the best in the division, and took first, second, and fourth place. Still, we were behind 40-37.

We won our first swim event in the fly. Erica launched off the blocks into the lead and kept it, her finish time a personal best. In the 100 free, Mel placed second again, also with a personal best. We took third and fourth place too.

Tati and I lined up for the 500, performed our pre-race stretches, and took the blocks. I blocked out the swimmers on either side, and focused on the shimmering surface of the water. This time, I'd be a machine, no thinking, my arms and legs doing what they did best until the race ended. It was how I always raced, and a strategy that served me well.

The buzzer buzzed, and I took off, executing a perfect start, entry, and streamline, surfacing almost halfway across the pool, attacking the water with strength and ferocity I thought I'd left in the city. The thrill of it amazed me, and I realized how much I'd missed that sense of competitiveness, that drive that propelled me through the water and pushed me off the wall through 18 turns until I heard the signal that the first swimmer was about to start the final turn. I shoved off the wall, in my zone, my eyes focused on Mel, who showed the lap counter for the last time: 19. I ventured a look alongside me and saw I was clear on both sides.

I came to the last turn and ricocheted off the wall, unmindful of the roar of the crowd and the slapping of my arms and legs against the water, until the finish was in reach and I rocketed toward it, slamming into it with both arms outstretched. As I came up for air, the crowd was rocking and my teammates screamed my name. I looked up at the clock. First place, and the season's best time: 4:54.10.

Tati finished third, and I passed her on my way to see Coach.

He pulled me in for a quick hug and said. "That's more like it." We high fived, and I made my way to the bleachers to accept the cheers and congratulations from my teammates.

Everyone was happy, even the Team Tati members. Witnessing a new personal best is special and thrilling. Recent events didn't detract from the significance of the achievement. Moments later, Tati joined us and accepted congrats for her third place finish. She left us to get a drink of water and came back with two. She offered one to me.

"I thought you'd be thirsty," she said.

I accepted with gratitude, puzzled by the gesture.

"That was awesome, Aerin," Mel said as Tati sauntered away. "I wasn't sure what to expect with the Bears' bringing out their big guns for the 500. You're less than two seconds from breaking the record, and you've got five more tries. I think this is going to happen, girls." She looked at the girls grouped around us. "We're going to see some history in the making." They looked at her like she was nuts – which she was – but I appreciated her confidence in my abilities.

First place in the 200 free relay went to the Bears, but we took second and third and scored more, gaining on their lead. Taylor took second in the backstroke and Ashley came in fourth, a not so good event for us. Charlie was up next in the breast, and we gathered at the turn to cheer her on. She looked a little green around the edges, and I prayed she wouldn't throw up. It was her first time against a double set of powerhouses in her event. Jordan was also in the race but was no threat to Charlie, who had a poor start but made up for it in the first half, and paced herself to stay in third place. She finished as expected and walked back to the bleachers with her head high.

"I did it," she said, and I hugged her.

"Yes, you did, and you'll do it again."

We were only five points behind when the 400 free relay came up. If we won and took second or third place too, we'd win the meet. We headed for the blocks with high expectations. All four relay teams were the best in the division, but the Blazers had a bit of an edge over the Bears. If we forgot our exhaustion and focused on winning, the race would be ours.

The crowd went wild from the start. Both teams rallied on the pool's edges to cheer on their swimmers. Tati had the lead leg, followed by Mel, then Erica, and me in anchor position. One by one, my teammates shot off the blocks and completed their 100 yards, maintaining a slight lead over the "A" team for the Bears. Our "B" team was right behind them. I screamed and cheered along with the others as I prepared for my leg. When Erica reached the wall, I dove in, plunging through the water like an engine, concentrating on the finish, thinking of nothing else as I ricocheted off the wall to complete my final 25 yards. The water churned around me, and I couldn't see anyone with me or ahead. I went by faith alone, believing I had the lead and would finish first.

And I did, but with the last swimmer from the Bears' "A" team coming up just a second and a half after me, and their "B" team finishing third.

The Bears crushed us, our first defeat of the season.

We clustered on the bleachers while the Bears' celebrated their win, some of us crying unashamedly while others looked stunned. When the Bears quieted down, we congratulated them on their win, shaking hands and faking smiles.

Coach drew us around him. "It was a tough meet," he said, "but you did your best, and I'm proud of you."

"We spoiled our perfect record, Coach," Mel said, her eyes wet with tears. "We let you down."

"No one has let me down, Melanie. We can't expect to beat the Bears. They're our toughest competitor. Sometimes we win. Sometimes we lose. Today, every one of you rose to the competition, and that's what's important, not whether we won or lost."

"Winning is better," Charlie said, her lower lip trembling.

Coach pulled her in for a hug. "You've got plenty of meets

ahead of you to win, Charlie."

We wrapped our arms around each other for a group hug. Coach broke away first.

"The season's not over. We've got the Boxers waiting for us on Friday, and the Last Chance Meet next week for those who have not yet qualified for the Division Championships." He zeroed in on Jordan, who squirmed under his attention. "We've got records to beat." This time, he looked right at Tatiana and then at me. "And a title to win for the fourth time. What do you say?"

He raised his right arm, and we all did the same, shouting in unison, "Go Blazers!"

"Now give me five hundred before hitting the locker room."

We groaned in harmony, but a minute later were stroking through the water for our cool down.

Chapter 71

The next day during English class we went down to the College and Career Center. I spotted Mrs. Cashman talking with another student and waited to get her attention. She met my eyes and smiled, then gestured for me to come over as the other student said goodbye.

"Aerin, is that right?" she asked, smiling.

"Yes," I said. "I've talked with my parents, and we want to continue with our plan for me to attend a Division I school."

"Any one in particular?" she asked.

"We're looking at Stanford, Cal, and Georgia, among others."

"Wow," she said, her eyes widening. "Those are some top-notch schools and not easy to get into."

"I've received letters from some of their coaches."

"I've been following your performance on the swim team, and I'm not surprised," she said. "Do you have the grades to get into these schools?"

"I've been working on it."

"SAT scores?"

"Good enough." I'd taken the test again and scored in the top percentile.

"Finances?"

"They're offering scholarships and my parents have a college fund for me."

"Sounds like you've got a plan," she said. "Let me know when you're ready to write your application essay and I'll help." She turned away to help the next student.

With almost thirty minutes left in the period, I headed for a table in the back to start my homework. I dropped my book bag on an empty chair and pulled out my French textbook.

"Hello," a small voice said to my left. Tatiana sat at the next table, cell phone cradled in her hand.

"Hey," I said. "I didn't see you sitting there." I moved my stuff and took the seat across from her. "What's up?"

She shrugged. "My class had to come down so here I am."

"You're not looking at any schools?"

"It's already decided."

I should have known she'd have a done deal. "Where are you going?"

"Michigan."

"Michigan? I thought you'd go to a Cali school."

"My father went there. He's on the alumni committee."

"So it's not just about swimming."

She shrugged again. "For me it is."

"Is that where *you* want to go?" I asked.

She laughed. "Aerin, what I want is not always part of the equation." She put her phone down and leaned toward me. "But it's okay. It's a top Division I school with a great coach." She glanced down at the brochures I'd spread on the table. "California? Is that your goal?"

"My parents and I have been planning for a long time."

"Any bites?"

"From Stanford and Cal. Also Georgia, Texas, and Virginia."

"No Michigan?"

I shook my head. "Not yet, anyway."

"It might not be a bad idea for us to go together. At least we'd have a friend on the team."

I'd never thought of her as a friend before. She was just a teammate. It was the longest conversation we'd ever had. "Well, we'll see," I said.

"I can ask my father to put in a good word for you. He's close with the coach."

The idea of Calvin Reese having any influence in my life gave me the chills. "No thanks," I said. "Michigan's not on our radar anyway."

"Good luck with the Cali schools. What I wouldn't give to head out there."

"Maybe *you* should come with *me*," I suggested.

She laughed. "Not if Daddy is paying my tuition."

"Gotcha," I said.

"I heard you swam for Mike Starling at Manhattan Swim Club."

"Nine years."

Her eyes widened. "How old were you when you started?"

"Eight. You?"

"Ten. I've always loved it. It's my life now."

"Mine too."

"So," she said, picking up her phone and fidgeting with the buttons. "You're going for the Singer Challenge?"

I should have figured the conversation would come to that. I laid my cards on the table. "I am."

"Well," she said, glancing at her phone, "just between us, I think you should. It's not a sure thing I'll make it, and if I don't, I'd like to see you do it."

I never expected to hear that from her, but it made sense.

"I agree. I hope you win if I don't."

"*Someone* has to beat that record," she said, looking up with those rich brown eyes. "I mean, come on, it was set more than twenty years ago."

"Allison Singer must be sick and tired of following the Blazer's swim seasons."

She laughed. "I bet you're right."

It was good to laugh with Tatiana over something this serious. The deep root of tension that ran between us had somewhat dissolved, and we were on firm ground. If not for our rivalry we could be friends.

"I owe you an apology," she said.

"For what?"

"For everything Jordan did."

I shrugged. "You didn't do anything. She did."

"I didn't stop her."

"You knew what she was up to?" I asked.

"Sort of. At first, when you joined the team, I didn't think too much of you. Then Jordan noticed Coach watching you, and she started to watch too. She tried to warn me you were stiff competition, but I didn't want to listen to her warnings. When she tried to sabotage you, I should have stopped her."

I laughed. "You think you can control Jordan?"

"I guess not," she said. "She went above and beyond this time."

"She's done this kind of stuff before?"

"It's her M.O., basic Jordan operation."

"Some people might consider her a good friend."

"Not me. Jordan and I have been best buds since grade school, but we hang around out of habit now, a bad habit. It was the last straw. I don't like what she did to you, and I don't appreciate her dragging me into it."

"So you weren't behind it?"

"Come on, Aerin, your life is like mine. Would you have time for such tricks?"

"I guess not," I mumbled, thinking about how my whole life revolved around swimming, school, and trying to get enough sleep. I couldn't imagine spending hours on the internet digging up dirt on someone.

"It was Jordan's idea. I told her not to do anything, but she thought she could intimidate you into backing off the 500."

"Well, it didn't work," I said.

"I told her it wouldn't, but you can't stop Jordan once she gets started. I'm sorry for all the pain she caused you and your mother."

At the mention of my mother, I looked up to meet her eyes.

"How is your mother?" she asked.

I shrugged. "She's okay."

"The whole thing must be so hard on you, and we made it more difficult."

"Don't sweat it," I said. "I'm okay."

"Well. If I can do anything to help –"

"No," I interrupted. "Nobody can help. In a few months, it will all be over, and she'll come home. We'll get a fresh start."

"I'm glad you've got a handle on it. If it were me, I'd be a wreck."

"Oh, I'm a wreck, but it gets better every day."

We sat in silence for a moment and then I just had to ask. "You're really finished with Jordan?"

"It's not easy," she said, "but in a few months we'll be going off to college, and there will be a natural break. I just accelerated it."

"Where's she going to school?"

"She doesn't know yet."

"Will she swim?"

"Jordan?" she laughed.

I shrugged. "She could make a Division III team."

"No. She's looking at the party schools. She's not going to swim."

"So this is her last shot."

"And she hasn't made a cut time for the Division Championships."

"She still has the Last Chance meet."

"Even that might not be enough for her. She's slacked off all season, too busy minding everybody else's business."

"Enough about her. She's just a bad memory."

"I'm glad we cleared the air. We're going to States together, and we need to be a cohesive unit. We can't have any animosity between us."

She was right. We would represent Two Rivers in the 200 and 500 free and two relay teams. We had to be in sync in *and* out of the pool.

"One more thing," she said. "I think we should do something special for Coach since it's our last season. I'd like to get together with the rest of the seniors to brainstorm some ideas."

"The best gift we could give him is one of us shattering that Singer record."

She laughed. "That will definitely happen. I was thinking something more personal from the team."

"Should we get together at lunch? We all have the same lunch period."

"Good idea. I'll meet you in the cafeteria."

Chapter 72

I was the last to arrive at our lunch table and plopped down next to Erica, who was unwrapping an egg salad sandwich with a look of disgust on her face.

"I hate eggs," she said.

"Funny thing for a farmer's daughter to say," said Mel, after taking a sip from her carton of chocolate milk. "Don't you guys have hundreds of chickens?"

"Yes, and guess who has to help collect the eggs?"

"Don't let your father hear you say that," Kelsey said. "You're trashing the source of his livelihood."

"Let me vent," she said. "I had to hop out of my warm bed to go out and gather eggs."

"Poor you," Mel said. She popped a carrot stick in her mouth and started crunching.

"Company's coming," I said, wanting to warn them before Tatiana joined us.

Mel perked up with interest. "Someone I know?"

"Yes, you know her very well. It's Tati."

Her eyes narrowed. "Why would Tati deign to join us for lunch?" She thought for a second then snapped her fingers. "Oh, yeah, she's on the outs with Jordan. Otherwise, no reason to slum with the second string."

"That's not it at all. She wants to talk to the seniors on the team about an idea." I spotted her making her way across the cafeteria, lunch tray in both hands, heading right for us. I waved her over, and a few seconds later she squeezed in beside me.

"Hey guys," she said as she settled in.

"What's up Tati?" Mel asked as she peeled the skin off a banana. It was her second one. "Aerin says you have some idea to spin for us."

"That's right," Tati said, glancing at me. I motioned for her to go on. "It's about Coach."

"What about him?" Mel asked, her full attention on Tati.

"It's our last year -" Tati started.

"We know that," Mel interrupted.

"Let her speak," I said, annoyed. "Go on, Tati."

"Well, I thought it would be fun if the team got him something special, a parting gift, something to remember us by."

"If we win the division title for the fourth time in a row he'll never forget us," Erica said.

"Well, of course, winning the title would be the best gift ever, but I was thinking of something a little more personal."

"Such as?" Mel asked.

"I don't know, maybe a piece of jewelry, something he can wear."

"I've never seen Coach wear any jewelry other than his wedding ring," Kelsey said.

"He doesn't strike me as a jewelry kind of guy," Mel said.

"How about a watch?" I suggested.

"He's got a ton of watches," Mel said, "all kinds."

"He doesn't have one engraved from the team," I said.

That shut them all up. It was an excellent idea.

"We could get him a dress watch, something not for

swimming," Tati said.

"Or we could get him the best Coach's watch around," Mel said.

"How will we pay for it?" asked Kelsey.

"We'll take up a collection," Tati said. "There are twenty-eight of us. If we all chip in ten bucks a piece, we'll have plenty of money."

"Sounds good to me," I said, liking the thought of the whole team presenting him with something special.

"I'm glad that's settled," Tati said, diving into her turkey sandwich.

"Are you going to the game on Friday night?" Mel asked her. "The guys are playing the Bears, as tough a match for them as it is for us."

"Of course. Are you?"

"Wouldn't miss it. We'll save you a seat."

"Thanks," she said, smiling. "That's nice of you."

Mel shrugged. The bell rang, and we all moved toward the cafeteria's exit.

"I'll see you guys at practice," Tati said and disappeared into the crowd.

"That was kind of you," I told Mel.

"She's all right," Mel said. "And now that she's finished with Jordan, I like her a little more."

"If we put our differences behind us the team will be stronger," I said. "Especially when we go to States. Only four of us are going. We'll travel together, practice together, and share a hotel room. A lot of bonding time. It will be to our advantage to go as friends."

The day of our last dual meet started with two quarterly exams and a paper due. I woke that morning exhausted from a late night of studying. I slept right through my alarm and Aunt Maggie had to come in to wake me up.

"What time is it?" I asked, rubbing the sleep out of my eyes.

"It's quarter to seven. Better get a move on."

I jumped out of bed, threw on my clothes and grabbed my bags, all prepped and packed the night before, smart thinking. Mags had an egg and cheese sandwich waiting for me with a tall glass of OJ and a banana. I chugged the juice and then ran out with the rest of my breakfast when Justin's Jeep announced itself.

"We'll see you at the meet!" Maggie shouted after me.

"Come on!" Mel called from the backseat of the Jeep. "We're gonna be late!"

They too had overslept. Justin gave me a sleepy smile. "Good morning." He looked so adorable I couldn't speak, and just smiled.

"Way to start the day!" Mel complained from the rear. "Like it's *not* the most important day of the week with a big meet this afternoon. Now my whole day is unbalanced." She sipped from an extra-large cup of coffee.

"Chill out," Justin said. "We're okay. We're on time, you did all the studying you needed to do, and you guys are going to kill the Boxers. No worries."

"I hate quarterly exams," she said. "Why do they have to have them the last week of dual meets? Aren't we stressed out enough?"

"You're putting athletics ahead of academics," I said.

Justin laughed. "Well, at least, you can look forward to Senior Night."

I'd forgotten about Senior Night. It was the seniors' last meet in our own pool. Per tradition, the underclassmen and the Boosters planned something special to recognize our achievements and send us off with fanfare. It couldn't happen on a worse night.

"As much as I love Senior Night," Mel said, "it stinks to have it when we're up against the Boxers and pressured to *win, win, win.*" She'd read my mind. "Poor planning."

By the time we arrived at the high school, she'd finished venting. We made it just minutes before the final bell and split up to get to our classrooms. By lunch, I'd made it through my College

History and French exams and proofread the final draft of a five-page essay for College English one last time.

"I see you survived," I said to Mel as I dropped into my seat in the cafeteria. She'd bought her lunch today – no time to pack one – and chewed on a tuna fish sandwich.

"I guess you could say that. How's your day going?"

"Fine." I dove into the egg and cheese sandwich Mags had packed for me. I hadn't had a moment to eat it all morning, and now it was cold and rubbery, but I didn't care. I was starving.

Kelsey had her face in her notebook, studying our stats.

"How do we look for this afternoon?" I asked. She didn't respond. "Kels?"

She blinked and looked up at me. "You said something?"

"She's had her head in that book all morning," Mel said. "You'd think she was taking a test on it."

"You're scaring me, Kels. What do you see?" I asked. We'd just lost our most challenging meet and ruined our undefeated record. All of us were a little edgy.

"They're having a good season, ten wins. A couple of youngsters on their team are dropping time like crazy."

"What events?" Mel asked, looking worried.

"Not yours," Kelsey said. "You should be okay. It's the distance swimmers who are starting to look good."

"Times?" I asked. The last thing I wanted today was to hustle in the pool.

"Under five minutes for the 500. Just over two for the 200."

"Crap." I pushed against the back of the booth.

"No," she said. "That's good. It will drive you to beat your own time and maybe break the record."

"Let's not talk about the record, okay? I'm not thinking about that today."

"Today's your last chance to pop that record before championships," Mel said. "You better start thinking about it."

"I know," I sighed. "I just want to get through all these tests and papers before I start thinking about that stupid record."

"I bet Tati's thinking about it," Erica said.

"Where is she anyway? Not joining us for lunch?" Mel surveyed the cafeteria. No sign of Tati. Jordan was also not present, preferring to take her lunch break in the library now that she was *persona non grata* with Tati and the rest of her crew. I'd heard things between her and Travis had cooled off too.

"Tati said she was going to talk to Coach at lunch time," I said.

"Told you!" said a triumphant Erica. "They're strategizing."

"You should be strategizing too," Mel said.

"Don't worry, Mel. I've got it all under control." Justin and I had plans to prep for my physics final tomorrow followed by a training session in the Y pool.

"Glad to hear it," Mel said. "Now that you're all buddy-buddy with Tati don't get soft on me. Killer instinct, remember?"

"I won't let you down, Mel."

Chapter 73

In spite of the fact that we were on edge about winning today's meet, the mood in the locker room was cheerful as we changed into our suits and gathered our gear. Senior Night gave the meet a festive air, and we couldn't help but feel excited.

The seniors left the locker room last by orders of our junior class members. When we stepped onto the pool deck, we saw that our teammates had been very busy. Blue and white balloons fluttered everywhere, all across the deck and in the stands, and they'd strung streamers in the school's colors wherever they could hang them.

Hand-painted posters, one for each senior, hung on the wall. We each took a moment to study our own. Charlie and the freshmen had done mine, which had a drawing of me - a good likeness - holding a trophy with "First Place" written across it. In the background was a scoreboard emblazoned with the numbers 4:52:49. Beneath it, the likeness of a fifty thousand dollar bill. Hilarious.

Coach gave us a few minutes to check out each other's posters and wave to family, friends, and fans in the stands before he ordered us into the pool for warm-up.

It turned out we didn't have much to worry about. The Boxers weren't having a good meet, and the excitement of Senior Night energized us. We were ahead by the time the festivities started, coming in first or second in every event and placing in two of the top three spots in most of them. Their divers were stronger than ours, and they had one more than we did, but that still didn't put them on top. Score: 45-33.

After the diving came the senior sendoff. Mel, Erica, Tatiana, and I sat on the bench with the other seniors: Jamie, Jordan, Cassie, and Taylor. Coach started the preliminaries, welcoming everyone. He congratulated the eleven seniors on the Boxers team and presented each girl with a small bouquet of flowers, a gift from our team courtesy of the Boosters.

We sat on the bench trying not to look anxious while we waited for him to announce the first senior. He presented us according to how many years we had on the team, so because I was the newest member I was first. The tradition was for an underclassman, someone who had a close relationship to the senior and looked up to her, to write and present a tribute to that girl. Charlie volunteered to write my tribute and stood at the end of the pool deck with the announcer's microphone in one hand, and the sheet of paper she'd written her speech on in the other. Both hands trembled.

"Tonight I have the privilege to introduce a new swimmer to our team, as new as I am because it's my first season swimming varsity," she began, her sweet voice a little shaky. "But this girl is not new to varsity swimming. In fact, she's been swimming competitively for nine years in both club and varsity. When she started here she was an unknown, but we soon came to know her as a swimmer who works hard in and out of the pool, someone willing to help others improve their technique or make their best time. She is the bravest person I know, and taught me not to back down to those who try to intimidate me or make me doubt myself. She has proven to be a leader and has helped us win in every meet. She's my Big Sister, and made me feel welcome and wanted when I first started out, even though she was also the new girl on the team. I believe this girl will go farther in our sport than any of us sitting here today. My senior is Aerin Keane, the greatest swimmer I know."

As Charlie spoke, tears welled in my eyes. Her words moved me. I'd had no idea of the impact I'd made on her as her Big Sister. I walked toward her to rousing applause from the stands and everyone on the pool deck. We embraced, and she clung to me, crying.

"Thanks, Charlie," I said, smiling through my tears.

"I wrote it myself," she said. "I meant every word."

I ruffled her hair and hugged her again.

Coach introduced Jordan next because she had joined the team in ninth grade. Her presenter, a freshman, had few words to say about her and did so in a rush. Erica was next, followed by Mel, and at last, Tatiana. All of them received tearful, glowing tributes. When the ceremony ended, the parents came down to congratulate their daughters. I hadn't thought to invite my father – it was a weeknight, after all – and Mom was not in a position to make it. For a moment, I felt sad I had no one to share this special time with, but seconds later Aunt Maggie and Uncle Pat approached me and my heart filled with happiness. We came together in a three-person hug.

"None of it would be possible without you two," I managed to say through my tears.

Mags had tears, too. "We've loved every minute of it," she said. "We are so proud of you."

After posing for dozens of pictures, the seniors stood in front of the crowd, waving at our friends and families in the stands. Then Mrs. Reese and Dr. Ford presented us each with a gift from the Boosters. I opened the fancy jewel box and found a silver charm of a freestyle swimmer. The seniors huddled to compare their gifts. Tatiana and Mel also had a freestyle swimmer charm. Erica's was a flyer, Taylor's was a backstroker, and Jordan's was a breaststroker. Jamie and Cassie had divers. I couldn't stop staring at mine, the nicest gift I'd ever received from a swim team.

All of the accolades, the gifts, and the applause increased the team's excitement, and we went into the second half of the meet with more energy and enthusiasm than we did in the first. Erica won the fly, and Mel came in second in the 100 free, finishing in her best time ever: 57:02. She was all smiles when she got out of the pool.

"Look at that!" she said pointing up at the clock. We high fived, and I moved onto the blocks for the 500. "Your turn, Aerin. Put up your best time. 4:52!"

I jumped onto the block in lane six, pulling my cap into place. I glanced at Tati in lane four, doing the same. Between us was the Boxer's best distance swimmer, a girl both Tati and I had beaten at the season opener and the away meet. This race would be between my teammate and me.

We dove off the blocks and hit the pool, pounding the water as we went head to toe one lap after another. Mel counted my laps as usual, shrieking, "Go! Go! Go!" at every turn. Tatiana was with me all the way, not letting up, not giving me any room to take the advantage. As we headed into the final 100 yards, my lungs burned and my legs cramped, but still I went all out, thrusting my discomfort out of my mind, fixated on the black line at the bottom of the pool and my turns. At last, Tati faltered as we made it into the final turn and I took my shot, ricocheting off the wall with all the force I had left, then swimming on autopilot as my lungs continued to burn and my arms and legs ached until I hit the wall first. 4:52.59. Less than one hundredth of a second from breaking the Singer record.

I held onto the wall for dear life as I gulped in air, trying to catch my breath and slow my racing heart. Tatiana popped up two lanes away and whipped off her goggles, looking up at the clock. 4:53:10, her best time ever. She turned away and climbed out of the pool. I followed, and we met up with Coach.

"That was incredible," he said, high fiving both of us. "I thought one of you had it. You slipped a little on the final turn, Tati, taking that extra stroke, which gave Aerin the advantage. Good pick up, Aerin. You had a little more gas in your tank than you let on.

Now, get a drink of water and catch your breath before the 200 free relay."

Tati and I sucked down a cup of water as some of the girls descended upon us with congratulations and high fives. Mel was the loudest.

"Holy smokes!" she said, throwing her arms around me. "I thought you had it."

I pushed her way. "I'm trying to breathe here," I gasped.

"Oops, sorry," she said, her eyes shining, her face almost about to break from her insane smile. "You popped 4:52. You're almost there!"

My heart rate had resumed its normal rhythm, and I was able to speak. "It almost killed me." I looked at Tati, surrounded by her fan club, still looking a little green around the edges. It looked like it almost killed her too.

We hadn't fully recovered before it was time for the relay. Erica was in the lead, followed by me, Tati, and Mel. There were four relay teams, and we were in lane four.

"We've got this," Mel said.

And we did. The Boxers were no match for us in the second half. We took either first or second in every event, as well as a few other scoring positions. Our relay team won the 400 free relay. We cooled down while they slunk home.

I caught up to Mel at the end of my set.

"Why did we worry about them?" I asked.

"They beat us half the time, but they were a little off their game tonight. Their top swimmer injured her shoulder and sat out the meet. Another top girl is out sick with the flu. One is on academic suspension. Their second string wasn't prepared to fill in."

"We would have won anyway, even if their best girls were in the water," I said, shaking the water out of my ears.

"I told you to wear ear plugs," Mel said as she plucked hers out.

"The water doesn't usually bother my ears."

"Lucky you. I get swimmer's ear at least once a season. I've been using this stinky alcohol-vinegar stuff my mom mixed up to ward it off and it looks like it's working."

"Keep it up. We don't need you out sick."

Our dual meets for the season had ended, and we looked like a sure thing for the division title. It was important no one got sick, and no one was injured. We had two weeks to train and taper for the big meet and then two more until States.

The next day was the Last Chance meet. Many of our swimmers had qualified for the Division Championships, but Jordan had yet to qualify for any event in the Division Championships, and was the only senior to accompany the rest of the girls to the meet at the Boxers' pool. Those already qualified attended our usual after school practice. We went through our tapering sets and lengthy stretching routines while we waited for Coach to call from the meet to tell us who made it.

The news came right before we left the pool. Coach D answered the phone and listened, her expression giving nothing away. After the call ended, she reported to us. "Six girls made a cut time: Janet, Amanda, Danielle, Marissa, and Allie."

"That's five," said Mel. "Who's the sixth?"

Coach D sucked in her breath before announcing, "Jordan Hastings made a cut time in the breaststroke."

Mixed reactions. Some of the girls cheered for Jordan. She still had a few loyal followers who didn't know any better. Most of us groaned, sentenced to two more weeks of Jordan at practice.

"How close?" Mel asked. "Please tell me she just *squeezed* by the cut time."

Coach D nodded. "She made it by two-tenths of a second."

"Well, I've got to hand it to her," Mel said. "She did it. She must be ecstatic."

"Coach and I are thrilled that more than half the team will represent Two Rivers at the Division Championships," Coach D said.

"Go Blazers!" Erica shouted and fist pumped. We joined her in a cheer, our feelings about Jordan cast aside. Our team looked good, and that was all that mattered.

~

After finals week and our toughest meets of the season, we wanted some fun. Justin and Mel picked me up Friday night for the football game. The Blazers faced the Bears, fierce competition in *and* out of the pool. We met Erica, Kelsey, Charlie, Tati, and several members of the girls' and boys' swim teams for a little pregaming in the parking lot. Justin had a mini grill in the back of his Jeep and cooked up some hot dogs. Kelsey brought a cooler full of soda. Mel had packed the makings for S'mores, and everyone had at least two or three.

With our bellies full we claimed our seats in the stands, spreading out blankets all around. It was a chilly evening. Everyone wore their Blazers' gear, most of the swimmers in team sweatshirts to show our solidarity with the football team.

The game was close. Our quarterback filling in for Travis was an even match for the Bears', and the game swung from side to side until the final quarter, when the Blazers took advantage of a Bears' fumble and made a 25-yard touchdown, pulling ahead to win the game. The stands rocked as we celebrated our victory, made sweeter by the humiliation of our loss last week to the Bears' swim team.

"We'll get them at championships," Mel said, vowing to beat the Bears in the end.

"And States," I said.

We shook on it.

WEEK TWELVE:

Taper

Chapter 74

Tapering for the Division Championships meant two weeks of scaling back on our yardage, allowing our muscles to recuperate from the strain and stress of the season. Only the swimmers competing in the meet attended, the season having ended for those who failed to make the cut at the Last Chance meet.

"I'm glad we're not swimming as hard as we usually do," Charlie said during Monday practice. We'd just finished a set and were taking a break.

"Me too," I said. "The idea is to cut down on our workouts to let our bodies rest, so when we get to championships we'll perform better."

"Does it work?"

"Most of the time. Some people don't taper well."

"What does that mean?"

"It means when they get to the meet they're not rested and don't perform well. Most swimmers will drop a lot of time at a championship meet."

"Do you?"

I smiled. I had always tapered well. "Yes, Charlie. I've made all of my best times at high-pressure meets."

"I hope I do," she said, brow furrowed with worry.

"Don't worry about it. You'll do fine. I'm so proud of you for coming this far. Qualifying for championships your first year out is amazing."

"I couldn't have done it without you," she said.

"Don't delude yourself. You don't need me."

She smiled. "I'm not deluded. You've been a great Big Sister."

"And you're an awesome Little Sister."

"What's got you two all touchy-feely?" asked Mel as she swam to us, her set completed.

"Nothing," I said. "Talking about tapering. Do you taper well?"

She shook her head. "No, but Coach and I are working on something to see if I can't be better prepared."

"What about Tati?" I asked.

She thought a moment. "Let's say Tati is a well-oiled machine when it comes to championship meets. Why? You worried?"

"Nope. I'm just up against the unknown," I said. "It's our first time competing against each other in a major meet."

"You beat her at the Long Island meet," she reminded me. "You had some tough competition there."

"Don't forget the Chinese swimmers," Charlie piped in.

"Come on guys," I groaned, "that's no way to pump me up, talking about all the competition."

Mel splashed me. "Don't tell me the great Aerin Keane is going to let these girls get under her skin."

"Didn't you already beat most of them?" Charlie asked.

"Trust me," Mel said. "You have no worries."

I wished I'd shared Mel's confidence. I'd learned the hard way that false pride and overconfidence could derail a swimmer in an important event. As a middle-schooler swimming varsity, I was the top seed in both of my events my first championship meet. The night before, I ate a big meal - a double cheeseburger with bacon and fries – and paid for it the next day when I swam like a slug, finishing third and then fourth in my events. My relay team came in second. No one was more disappointed in my performance than I was, and it was all my fault. I should've skipped the burger.

I learned to think about my actions during taper, being extra careful about what I ate, and getting a good night's sleep. I practiced meditation techniques and took time to stretch several times a day. I drank gallons of water and washed my hands often to avoid catching a cold, or worse, the flu. These measures I controlled. Other things involved with finishing well at the big meet I *couldn't* control: how well my opponents tapered, how they controlled themselves, their thought processes. I had to focus on my own performance and not worry about my competitors.

The first week of tapering ground on. The best thing about it was no morning practice, so we slept in. Rising after dawn had all of us in better spirits and improved our taper.

At lunch on Thursday, Erica had news. "My parents said I can go into the city with you guys this weekend."

"Super," Mel said. "So did mine. Is it a go, Aerin?"

"Definitely," I said," I can't wait to show you guys around. And if you don't mind, I'd like to make a pit stop at my apartment while we're there."

"I almost forgot you lived in the city," Mel said.

"Sometimes even I forget," I said. At times it felt like my city life was light years behind me.

"Why do you want to go to your apartment?" Erica asked. She'd finished eating and was inspecting herself in a hand mirror she kept in her book bag.

"I want to pick up a few things to bring to the championship meets."

"What kind of things?" Mel asked, eyes narrowing.

"You know, caps, goggles, suits."

"What kind of gear do you have?" she asked.

"The usual," I said, not wanting to go into details. She'd find out soon enough.

"Better than the stuff Coach is getting?"

Coach had ordered new high-tech suits and gear for those of us going to the Division Championships – all excellent stuff – but what I had was better, the best you could buy. Or win. I'd checked the division rules, and nothing said I couldn't use my gear as long as it met their regulations. It did. I just didn't want to alert anyone to the fact that I had top of the line equipment. I suspected Tatiana had it too, and I wanted to give myself every possible advantage to break the record before she did.

"It's good stuff, Mel," was all I would say.

Chapter 75

I followed Mom's instructions and called Maribel at our apartment to tell her my plans. She was a good friend of Mom's – they'd worked together in the ER for years – and needed a place to stay at the same time we needed someone to sublet our apartment. She moved in the day after we left. She said of course she didn't mind my stopping by to pick up a few things while I was in the city, although she'd be at work and would miss me. I still had the key, I assured her, and would be in and out in minutes. She asked after my mom, and I filled her in on her progress. My next call was to our friend Brian who found us mezzanine seats for *Wicked* at a deep discount in under two minutes.

Practice ended at ten a.m. on Saturday. Justin drove us to the train station, and we landed in Penn Station just after noon.

"Hungry?" I asked as we emerged onto the streets of Manhattan. My appetite hadn't caught on to my new training regime and I was still hungry all the time. My stomach had growled with emptiness the whole ride.

Mel and Erica were too busy gawking at the crowded streets to respond.

"This way," I said and led them to a deli on the corner that served the best corned beef in the city. Once we'd filled our bellies, we tackled the streets.

"What's next?" Mel asked, slurping down the last of her soda.

"We walk," I said. "We're heading uptown. I know a few cool shops we can poke around in, then we'll cut through Central Park to my apartment. After that, we'll head to Broadway and find the theater."

"I'm glad you know what you're doing," said Erica. She looked like a country bumpkin lost in the big city the minute we exited the train station.

"Hold my hand," I said. "I won't let you get lost. I promise."

She smirked. "I'm not that bad." She turned to Mel. "Am I?"

"You should have seen the look on your face when you emerged from the subway," Mel said. She imitated Erica's overwhelmed expression. "Priceless."

I laughed too, but Erica didn't think it was funny.

"Hey, it's my first time," she said.

"And everybody knows it." Mel laughed.

We started out on Seventh Avenue, through the Garment District, stopping at a few trendy shops I'd frequented with my mom, trying on a few things and buying nothing. It was just fun to look and dream. None of us had much cash. An hour later, we stood in the middle of Times Square. If Erica looked like a fish out of water at Penn Station, she looked like a deer in the headlights in Times Square. Her mouth hung open almost to her knees as she observed the characters traipsing through, her head swiveling right, left, up, and down as she took in all the lights. Times Square was visual commotion, and she didn't know where to focus.

"Just keep walking," I said.

Mel stopped every few feet to snap pictures.

It was a crazy day in Times Square but no crazier than usual. I didn't know what was more entertaining: the crowd or the two gawking girls from upstate.

"I can't believe you live here," Erica said.

"I don't live *here*," I said. "I'm in Midtown, near the park."

"How far is it?" Erica whined. We'd already gone about twelve blocks.

"Don't tell me you're tired," I said. "You're in better shape than anyone else on the team." Over the last two months, Erica had become lean, but she was all muscle, her shoulders thicker than most guys'.

"Hey, I've been up since five," she said, "milking cows and gathering eggs while you were still dreaming. A farmer's work never stops."

"You slept on the train," I pointed out.

"Dozed, not slept," she corrected.

All of our banter helped pass the time. We veered east and approached Fifth Avenue and 50th Street, the intersection for St. Patrick's Cathedral. I didn't say anything, wanting to catch their reactions when they first laid eyes on it. I led the way and stopped as soon as I saw it. Mel and Erica, still bickering, plowed right into me.

"What the - ?" Mel said and then squealed, "Is that St. Patrick's?"

Erica stood in wonder, staring at the edifice.

"Come on," I said, once again leading the way. "Let's go inside."

We crossed the street and worked our way past the crowds to the doors of the church, slipping in as a group of Japanese tourists exited. The church was filled with people worshiping, taking photos, and examining the architecture. We walked down the aisle a few feet and then slipped into a pew. Mel made the sign of the cross and sat back, taking it all in.

"Have you been here before?" I asked.

"Once, but it was a long time ago."

"I've never been here," Erica said. "This place is gorgeous."

We watched the people coming and going, pointing out different points in the architecture to one another, the vaulted ceilings, the statuary, the organ's pipes.

After ten minutes or so, I gestured toward the door. Before we left, we knelt and said a quick prayer of thanks for this sacred space.

"And please let us win the division title," Mel added at the end.

Erica laughed, and I elbowed Mel in the ribs.

"Do you think that's appropriate?"

"Hey," she said. "We're in church. When would it be more appropriate? Besides, we need all the help we can get."

We headed uptown again. We weren't far from my apartment, and I was excited to see it after all these weeks away. But I suspected it would be weird to see someone else living in my space, even if it was Maribel.

Erica stopped to buy a bag of fresh roasted peanuts from a street vendor. As we continued our walk up Fifth Avenue, we broke open the warm nuts and crunched on them.

"Let's take a walk through Central Park and then we'll head to my place," I said.

"More walking?" Erica groaned.

"I want to see the park, then we'll go to my apartment. It's just a couple of blocks more. I promise."

In minutes, we entered the park. I just wanted to see and smell the place because the closer we got to it the more I realized I missed it. The park was always a haven for my family. We'd spent most of our free time there, visiting the zoo, watching street performers, concerts, and theater, picnicking on the grass under the city sky. Living in Two Rivers was peaceful, the air clean and fresh, the trees and grass more vibrant, but the park had an energy the town didn't. I needed a dose of it right now.

Mel and Erica seemed to sense my feelings and kept quiet, or maybe they were just tired of walking and complaining about it. If they only knew I walked as many blocks most days in my swim-school-swim routine in the city.

We backtracked to East 57th Street and Lexington Avenue and minutes later stood in front of my building.

"Here we are," I said. The afternoon had turned warm, and both Mel and Erica were flushed from their exertion. They'd removed their sweatshirts and tied them around their waists. They collapsed against the side of the building in exhaustion while I fished around in my bag for my keys.

"Water," Mel gasped.

"In a minute," I said. "And relax. We're taking a cab to the theater. No more walking."

Before I could enter the lobby, the door opened, and Phil, the doorman, stepped out. He rushed toward me, a huge grin on his face. "Aerin!" he said. "What are you doing here?"

"Hi Phil," I said, happy to see the always present doorman who had welcomed me in and escorted me out of my building ever since I could remember. He even went to a few of my swim meets, the big ones. Funny, I hadn't thought of him once since I'd left, but seeing him made me realize I missed him very much. "I'm visiting the city with my friends." I introduced Mel and Erica. "I thought I'd stop by and pick up a few things."

"How's life upstate?" he asked.

I gave him a few details about life in Two Rivers and my swim season.

"And how's your mom?" he asked. He'd always had a soft spot for her, stepping out to get her taxis without her asking, and carrying her packages upstairs.

"She's doing very well, Phil," I said.

"Do you have your key?" he asked.

I waved it in front of his face. "Sure do."

"Let me get the elevator for you." He held the door open for us and pressed the button for the elevator.

"You have a *doorman*?" Erica whispered.

We got off on the sixth floor. Our apartment was in the front of the building on the right. My parents had rented it soon after they got married and Mom had hung on to it after the divorce although she often wished we lived somewhere less expensive. She never had time to find us another place, and here we stayed.

I let my friends in and followed them down a short hall that led to our living room. The place was neat, dust-free, everything in order. A vase filled with fresh flowers stood on the coffee table giving off a pleasant fragrance of lilies, Maribel's favorite. I switched on the lights even though the oversized pair of windows at the front of the room let in plenty of sunlight. I pulled the blinds and looked out at the street. Everything was so familiar and yet so strange. I felt a little tug in my gut, a yearning to return. That was not about to happen anytime soon, and I put it down. I was here for a purpose.

"Kitchen's here," I said and walked them into the galley kitchen with barely enough room for the three of us. I opened the refrigerator and pulled out a pitcher of filtered water with thin slices of lemon floating in it. I poured three glasses. Maribel wouldn't mind. I'd refill the pitcher before we left. We sucked down the water in seconds, and Mel and Erica pushed their empty glasses toward me for refills. We emptied the pitcher and sated our thirst.

"Where's the bathroom?" Mel asked.

We took turns refreshing ourselves and met in the living room again.

"So, this is your place," Mel said, looking around.

I plopped down on the sofa. "Yup."

Mel's eyes were everywhere as she tried to take in the room. Several windows gave a sweeping view of Midtown and she gravitated to one and looked down on the city.

Erica wandered around the room, checking it all out, and stopped when she faced the furthest wall. I called it "Mom's Wall of Fame."

"Wow," she said, "look at this Mel."

My mother had arranged all of our trophies, ribbons, and prizes on the wall, Mom's on the left, and mine on the right. Framed copies of newspaper articles detailing our triumphs filled the open spaces. Her spoils filled a much larger area than mine did.

"Check it out!" Mel exclaimed. "I don't think you can fit anything else on this wall."

"Your mom was good," Erica said. "Look at all the plaques, Mel."

My mother had won titles in club, varsity, college, and –

"Your mom went to the Olympic Trials?" Erica shrieked.

Mel bolted toward the framed news story that told of Mom's experience at the trials. She read the story aloud, then stared at the wall, taking in all of Mom's achievements.

"And I thought having a doctor for a mom was cool," she said at last. "This is incredible. Look here Erica." She pointed out one win after another, NCAA, Nationals.

I basked in my mother's successes. No one knew better how much work went into it than the three of us, all swimmers training to do the same thing.

"And these are all yours?" Mel asked, moving over to examine my side of the wall.

I got up from the couch and joined her, standing between her and Erica. I showed them how everything was arranged chronologically, telling my life's story. It all ended when my mom's problems started.

"How come you stopped here?" Erica asked, pointing to a trophy dated almost a year ago.

"That's when things started to fall apart around here. I lost my focus. I didn't care about winning anymore, so there's nothing new to put on the wall." It made me sad. I didn't want it to end like that.

"No problem," Mel said. "You're going to start picking up trophies and titles again. You can also invade the next wall, start hanging stuff there."

"I hope you're right," I said, liking her idea.

She turned away from the "Wall of Fame" and took another

tour of the room. "It must be weird to see a stranger living in your place," she said.

I shrugged. "My mom's friend is keeping the place safe for us. We're helping her out. A win-win."

"Does she sleep in your room?" Erica asked. "That would be *really* weird."

"No, I think she sleeps in my mom's room," I said, but I sprang off the couch and headed for my room to check. I found the door closed, a positive sign. Holding my breath, I opened it slowly, Mel and Erica right behind me.

Inside, my room was just as I'd left it but it looked like Maribel came in once in a while to dust.

"This is your room?" Erica asked, pushing past me to enter. Mel followed.

I stood back and let them examine every inch of my space. I had a four-poster bed covered with a hand-sewn quilt my grandmother had made. She'd cut pieces from the dozens of T-shirts I'd gotten at swim events and stitched them together. Posters and framed artwork of the wild animals I loved - giraffes, lions, tigers, chimpanzees - decorated three of my walls, along with posters of my favorite swimmers: Michael Phelps, Natalie Coughlin, Dara Torres, Peter Vanderkaay, and a few others. The fourth wall held my TV and a bookcase.

"It's very different from your room at the Flynn's," Mel said.

"It took years to get my room the way I want it," I said, plopping down on my bed and stretching out. So good to be home again. "The room at Maggie's is temporary."

Mel dropped into a Papasan chair in the corner, and Erica took the seat at my desk.

"So no chance you'll be staying in Two Rivers?" Erica asked.

I shook my head. "Once my mom gets out she's coming back here. And I think I'm coming back too." As soon as I said the words, a wave of sadness rolled through me. I'd promised myself I wouldn't get attached to Two Rivers, yet I'd grown to care for my new friends. I liked the tight-knit small town life, the school spirit, the "everyone cares" mentality. It wouldn't be easy for me to return to the fast-paced anonymity of city life.

"You're not going anywhere," Mel said.

I ignored her assumption and hopped off the bed. "We need to get moving. The show's in an hour." I opened my closet door and rummaged around for the gear I'd come to retrieve. I pulled out boxes and laid them on the bed.

"Look at all that stuff," Mel said and joined me at the bedside while I pulled swimsuits out of the boxes. Most of them still had tags. Erica came over to inspect too.

"Where did you get all those suits?" she asked as she picked up an open back kneeskin in black with blue racing stripes. I grabbed it from her.

"Just what I was looking for," I said. "I won it at my last championship meet."

"You won *that*?" Mel asked.

I nodded. "These are the prizes that don't get hung on the wall. I win them at one championship meet and wear them at the next."

"Does it make a difference?" Erica asked.

"She wears one and then wins another one," Mel said. "I'd say it does."

"It works for me," I said.

"Tati has suits like these," Erica said.

"I figured. That's why we're here."

"Too bad we're not the same size," Erica said. She was at least two sizes larger than I was.

"But we are," Mel said. "Hint, hint. Got any extras?"

I pulled out another one just like the first. "How's this?"

"You're serious?" she asked, reaching for it.

"Why not? I can only wear one at a time."

She held the suit up against herself. "I've never worn a

kneeskin."

"You'll get used to it. But you need to practice putting it on. It's not easy. It's like a second skin."

"What else you got?" Erica asked.

I pulled out top-name goggles and caps, enough for each of us. "Is this stuff better than what Coach gets?"

"Coach gets top-notch stuff," Mel said, "but not top of the line. I think these are a step up." She pulled the goggles on and adjusted them to fit.

"We can borrow these?" Erica asked.

"You can have them," I said. I grabbed another suit, cap, and a pair of goggles in case I had issues with the others, and packed up the remaining gear to store back in the closet. We collected our stuff and left my room.

Before leaving the apartment, I refilled the water pitcher and made sure everything else was just as we found it. I left a note for Maribel: "Sorry I missed you. Thanks for taking care of my place."

Phil waved down a cab in seconds, and we made it to the theater with minutes to spare. We found our seats, and it was show time.

Week Thirteen:

Division Championships

Chapter 76

Everyone's nerves were on edge the final week before the Division Championships. All the teams had met up at the season's start at the Boxer's Country Open, but that was before swimmers made cut times, set new records, and won or lost meets. Over the course of the last two months winners emerged, both teams and individuals.

All the adults in our lives - our coaches, parents, teachers - said "Winning isn't everything."

They said "It's the fun that counts, the friendships, the personal bests."

Those of us at the top, swimmers like Tati, Mel, Erica and I, knew this was not true. We had worked too hard to get this far. Failing to set our personal bests and win the division title for the fourth year in a row was not acceptable.

We didn't talk about the Singer Challenge at practice anymore. Everyone understood Tati and I were under enough pressure. Instead, we focused on the team effort. Kelsey had organized a spreadsheet of all the teams in the division, their wins, losses, best times, etc. She figured we had a good chance of meeting our goals, but a few swimmers in the competition could mess things up for us, and we had to watch out for the Bears to make sure they didn't take our title away.

The buzz around school was all about the football team's upcoming game, their last game of the season against the Falcons. Our team had a 5-2 season and looked certain to make the playoffs. We were glad the spotlight was on them. We put enough pressure on ourselves and didn't need anymore.

On Thursday night, I was on my own to walk home. Justin had to work, and Erica and Mel had a Glee Club meeting right after practice and wouldn't leave the building until much later. Aunt Maggie and the kids were at an away soccer game for Paige. I didn't mind. It was a short walk, and I'd use the time to think a few things through and take in some fresh October night air.

I said goodnight to the remaining girls in the locker room, Tatiana and a few of her friends, and left. As I exited the building, the parking lot was almost cloaked in darkness. One of the streetlamps was out. It seemed spooky, but I steeled myself and headed for home. Halfway through the parking lot, someone called my name.

"Is that you Aerin Keane?"

The voice sounded familiar. It was a man's voice, a teacher maybe, or someone's dad. I wasn't sure and didn't care to find out. My mother taught me not to speak to strange men. I ignored it and kept walking, my head down, shoulders hunched, but he called to me again. I turned. Tati's father, Calvin Reese, stood next to his fancy Lexus smoking a cigarette.

"Hi Mr. Reese," I said, quickening my pace. No way was I going to stop. The guy gave me the creeps.

"Tatiana almost out?" He exhaled a long plume of smoke. I wrinkled my nose.

"She's right behind me." I kept moving.

"Need a ride home?"

"No thanks, I'm okay."

"It's cold out here."

"I'm all right."

"Wait up," he said. "I want to talk to you." He stamped out his cigarette on the pavement.

I stopped, turned, and to my surprise he jogged over to me. Trapped, I dropped my bags on the blacktop and waited. He was winded when he reached me.

"Man," he said, "I've got to start working out."

I smiled and waited for him to catch his breath.

"Practice going okay?" he asked.

"Yeah, it's good."

"You're having a terrific season."

"Yeah," I said. "It's good." I looked everywhere but at him. Where was Tati? She should have come out by now.

"You know," he said, "Tatiana's been swimming at this school a long time."

I nodded.

"Six years," he continued. "She's had her eye on breaking that Singer challenge for quite a while."

I nodded again, wondering when he'd get to the point.

"Everyone is hoping she'll break it, since it's her last year and all." He didn't meet my eyes either. He kept glancing around to see if anyone else was coming. There were a few cars parked by the gymnasium doors - parents waiting to pick up their athletes - but nobody was close enough to hear or see us. "It would be a shame if she didn't make it. It would be a bigger shame if another swimmer beat her to it."

His eyes were cold, hard. I remembered what Aunt Maggie said about his shady business dealings, and felt like one of his business competitors about to get squashed.

"It's not about the money," he went on. "We don't need it. For us, it's about the glory. Tatiana holds the record in every event she swims, except for this one, and it's in her grasp. I aim to see no one takes it away from her." He paused, waiting for my response.

"We have a saying about that out on the pool deck, Mr. Reese," I said. "May the best swimmer win."

He laughed. "Yeah, I've heard that before. Well, we both know Tatiana is the best swimmer, don't we? We also know she deserves to break that record, to win that honor, don't we? After all, you're not *really* a member of this team, this school, this town. You're just passing through. You're here for a few months, a year maybe, and then you're going back to wherever you came from with your infamous mother. By the way, when is she getting out of jail?"

This sick, twisted conversation made me want to puke, but when he mentioned my mother that fire I'd been fanning all season flared and I burned with the desire to break that record and put an end to his dreams of "glory" for Tati.

"My mother is none of your business," I said. "You have no right to speak to me like that, to try to intimidate me."

He put his hands up. "Whoa," he said, backtracking. "I would never try to intimidate you. That's not my way."

Yeah, right.

"I'm just giving you my thoughts on a couple of things, that's all."

"Well, thanks a lot, I appreciate you telling me your thoughts, but I need to get home. It's late, and I've got homework." I picked up my bags.

"Hold on, hold on," he said. "I'll give you a ride. You don't have to walk home in the dark. I'm driving a few of Tati's friends home, too. It's not out of my way."

"I'm good," I said starting to walk away.

"Come back here," he ordered, his voice harsh.

I hesitated.

"Come back here," he repeated, harsher. I turned back. Some of the cars had left the entrance to the gymnasium. We were the only ones out here. Where was Tati?

"I'm a businessman, Aerin, and when I want something I'm willing to make a deal. I'd like to make a deal with you."

Puzzled, I waited for him to explain what he meant. I heard voices exiting the building. Tati and a few of our teammates were walking out, laughing. Relief flooded through me. This ugly conversation would end in just a few minutes.

He heard the voices too and pulled in closer to me, his face taut with tension. In a low voice, he said, "I'm not fooling myself. I know you can beat Tati. Heck, you probably will. It would be foolish of me to let that happen. I have a proposal." He gave a quick glance behind him. Tati and her entourage were twenty yards away.

"You can use the money, Aerin," he continued. "Your mother's got a lot of legal trouble. She lost her job and may lose her license. And your father has a new family and an expensive home in Westchester. College is coming. I can help with all of that. It's easy. Let Tatiana break the record, and I'll give you the prize money."

Stunned is not a strong enough word to explain how I felt about what he just said. Throw the race? *Let* Tati win? He was nuts.

"I don't think so, Mr. Reese, that would be cheating. I don't cheat."

"But you lie," he said. "That's not much different, is it?"

"I'm leaving," I said. "I'll forget we ever had this conversation." I whipped around and started walking.

"Don't forget this conversation," he hissed. "And if you tell anyone else about it remember: it's your word against mine. I run this town, and you're no one, so don't expect anyone to believe you. We all know you've lied before."

Tears stung my eyes. I quickened my pace. Behind me, Tatiana and her friends reached her father with big hellos.

"Who are you talking to?" Tati asked.

"No one," her father said. "Just some kid passing through. I wanted to make sure she wasn't up to no good."

Car doors opened and then closed as they filled the Lexus.

Seconds later, they left the parking lot, heading the other way.

I made it home in record time, thinking about his horrible, hurtful comments and his insane offer to give me fifty thousand dollars to blow the race. He was nuts, he was not a nice man, yet the thought of all that money was tempting. I'd spent most of my season underplaying my hand. I could back off and lose to Tati. No one would know. I could use that money to pay for my education. It would be an enormous relief to my parents. And who cared if I won that Singer challenge anyway? He was right. I *was* just passing through. I hadn't earned the right to that title or that prize. That belonged to Tati.

"Let the best swimmer win." The voices in my head were loud. Coach, Mom, Dad, Maggie, Mel, Justin. Everyone said it: let the best swimmer win.

My head hurt just thinking about it. I rejected, accepted, and rejected his "deal" all the way home. When I finally reached Maggie's front door, I was a wreck.

Chapter 77

The family came home shortly after I did, triumphant with Paige's winning goal in a soccer match, all of them complaining they were starving. Aunt Maggie had prepared beef stew in the crock-pot and had homemade biscuits on the table. Within minutes, we were all seated and digging in.

Around me, the Flynn children chattered about their days, each trying to up the other. Most nights I found their banter comforting. It provided a glimpse of family life I rarely witnessed. But tonight I tuned out, lost in thoughts about Calvin Reese's proposal.

I was still shocked he'd spoken to me at all, and said so many hateful things that both angered and hurt me. I thought I had come far in becoming a valuable teammate, classmate, and member of the high school. It pained me he thought of me this way, and I wondered how many others thought the same. His comments about my mother were despicable. He didn't even know her. He didn't know us! He had no business saying her name or asking after her in such a cruel way.

Worse was his assumption that he could pay me to throw the race and let Tatiana win. He didn't understand his swimmer daughter very well. No swimmer would sink to that level, at least, no swimmer that I knew.

On the other hand, his offer was tempting, and it shamed me that I would even contemplate it.

I couldn't do it. I would hate myself if I sank to his level.

"Earth to Aerin," Uncle Pat said.

I shook myself out of my reverie. "Yes?"

"You look like you've got a lot on your mind," he said. "Worried about Saturday's meet?"

"A little," I said.

"From what I hear Two Rivers is poised to win the division title again and hang on to most of its individual titles as well."

"Where'd you hear that?" I picked up my third biscuit and slathered it with butter.

"At the soccer game. Some of the parents have kids participating in the big swim meet. They said it looked like Tatiana Reese might break that old 500 record too."

"No surprise," I said. "Tati's a star swimmer."

"Well, I set them straight," he said. "I told them all bets were off on Tatiana, that I had some insider knowledge there could be a major upset."

"You didn't," I said, my spirits sinking. With the way news traveled around here everyone would be looking at me on Saturday instead of Tati.

"Of course, I did," he said. "I'm so proud of you, Aerin. You've turned things around. You're back in action, making up for lost time, swimming your best. Your mother is proud of you too."

Maggie and Pat kept my mother up to date on how I was doing via email. In her last letter she was gushing about Maggie's last bit of news telling her about my latest win. They meant well, but that just added to the pressure.

"Uncle Pat, it's not a sure thing," I said. "Tatiana is an excellent swimmer, and she's been training for this event most of her life. I wouldn't put any money on my breaking the record. If it happens, it will be because I'm having a better day than she is."

"Don't underestimate yourself," he said. "I also heard that Calvin Reese is worried about you. He's told a few people he's not sure Tatiana can beat you. That's serious because Calvin has never conceded that anyone is better than his daughter."

"Up till now no one has been," Maggie chimed in.

"We're going to find out on Saturday," Pat said, scraping his bowl.

"Speaking of Calvin," Aunt Maggie said as she began piling the dirty dishes up to carry them into the kitchen, "Cory Janson is suing him."

"Over what?" Uncle Pat was all ears.

"He rented Cory some office space for his insurance business, and not six months later raised his rent even though they had a contract for a year. Then when Cory had problems with the electricity, he refused to call in an electrician, and Cory had to close his business for three days because he had no power. The last insult was when Calvin violated their contract by not allowing Cory's customers to use the building's parking lot without paying an additional fee. Cory said it was the last straw. He hired Diana Marino to take him to court."

"I'd hate to have to pay Calvin's legal fees," Pat said. "He's in court several times a year for one thing or another."

"He's a snake," Maggie said. She had my full attention. "A cheater and a liar. You can't trust a word he says. He manipulates everything to his benefit and bullies people into getting his way. He's been like that ever since he was a little boy." Maggie's face turned pink, her eyes narrowed. I'd never seen her so angry.

"Now, Maggie, don't let him get your blood pressure up," Pat said.

"Well, it's a good thing some people are brave enough to stand up to him. He's been running this town for too long." She carried the dinner dishes out to the kitchen.

"He keeps things interesting around here. I can say that much about him," Pat said. "What's his daughter like? I heard she was a lovely girl."

I nodded. "She is," I said. "She's nothing like her father."

"That's good," he said. "So, anything else on your mind? You were pretty far away from us a while ago."

I shook my head. "No, I'm okay. Just a little tense about the meet."

"It should be a piece of cake for you. You've faced stronger competition with the Manhattan Swim Club and come out on top."

That was true. Two Rivers and its league were good but not the best by far. I'd swum against faster teams, faster girls. Still, I never took anything for granted.

"We'll see," I said and got up to help Aunt Maggie with the dishes.

Friday night was Shave Night. During the season, we all stopped shaving our legs and we were hairy like boys. It was gross, but it gave us drag and slowed us down in the pool. Consensus was that shaving before a big meet cut drag and made us sleeker and faster. For most swimmers, it worked, but for me, not so much. I still participated, and after practice we all met in the locker room for the big shave down.

Tatiana and Mel came with razors and shaving cream. We lathered up and stripped the hair from our legs, laughing at how much came off, some of the younger girls shrieking with excitement.

"Will I really go faster?" Charlie asked as she concentrated on making straight lines with the razor through the thick white shaving cream.

"Probably," Mel said, "but remember: every girl on every other team is doing the same thing tonight, so we all have the same advantage."

"Then why do it?" she asked.

"I don't know," Mel said. "It's tradition."

"I think we should shave all season long," Tati said. "It's gross being all hairy. I can't wear skirts or let anyone see my legs. I hate it."

"Does shaving make you go faster?" Charlie asked her.

"I hate to admit it, but it does," she said, rinsing her razor blade clean in a stream of warm water.

It figures, I thought as I wiped dry my first leg.

Some girls shaved their arms, and when it was their turn, the guys shaved their arms, chests, and *heads*. Tonight, no one was doing anything *that* crazy.

"What happened to Jordan?" I asked, noticing that our Little Mermaid was absent.

"She said she was swamped with homework and staying home to shave on her own," Erica said.

"Jordan's hitting the books?" a disbelieving Mel asked. She finished with her right leg and wiped it clean with a towel, inspecting for any stray hairs.

"Since she's failing two classes and her parents grounded her for what she did to Aerin," Erica explained. The hair on her legs was thick, dark, and downy. If there were an award for hairiest Blazer, she'd win it.

"How do you know?" Mel started working on her left leg and squirted a thick stream of shave cream from thigh to ankle.

"I'm in both of those classes," Erica explained, "remember? She told me."

Shave cream clogged my razor and I jockeyed for a place at a sink to rinse it off. A party atmosphere filled the locker room. Some of the girls had never been to a shave party, and, overexcited, they chased each other around the locker room squirting shave cream and making a mess.

"Hey!" Mel shouted as three or four of them ran around us. One slipped and crashed into a bank of lockers to break her fall, a surprised expression on her face. "Yeah," Mel said, ever the captain. "That stuff is slippery, so knock it off. No running!"

They quieted down for a moment. In seconds, the room was full of chatter about boys and that night's football game. We didn't talk about tomorrow's meet.

"So no Jordan at the football game, either," Mel said, giving Erica a questioning glance. Erica shook her head. "That's a first," Mel said. "I didn't think the boys could play without Jordan cheering for them."

"Well, Travis isn't playing anymore," I said. "So maybe she's not that interested."

"That's not it," Erica said, all knowing. "Travis is breaking up with her."

"What?" Mel screeched. Talk in the locker room came to a stop as everyone looked at us. "What are you gawking at? Get back to shaving." The other girls got back to work, their chatter resumed.

Mel pulled in closer to Erica and me. "Okay, fill me in, Miss Know-it-All," she said to Erica. "I haven't heard a word about it."

"It's true," Erica said, preening because she knew more than anyone. I guess it paid to be in class with Jordan. "She told me herself. We're lab partners and she was distracted during lab today. I asked her what was wrong, and she started crying. She ran out of the lab, and Mr. Martinez told me to go after her. She was bawling in the bathroom. After about five minutes, she said Travis was talking about breaking up. It hit her pretty hard."

"That's a shame," Mel said. "A lot of things aren't working out for Jordan these days."

"It's not like she doesn't deserve it," I said, still smarting from the damage she'd inflicted on me.

"I'm not saying that," Mel said. "She's earned her fair share of misery after all the pain she's caused the team. I'm not surprised Travis wants out. He deserves better."

"There will be a lot of happy girls around here when news of their breakup gets around," Erica said.

We finished shaving and dried off and lotioned our legs.

"Wrap it up, girls," Mel said, raising her voice above the din. "This party is shutting down in ten minutes."

Erica and I helped Tati and Mel put the locker room back together after the other girls packed up and left.

"That was fun," Tati said.

"Last time," Mel observed, now somber. She looked around the locker room. "Tonight was our last time here with the team."

Tati also looked sad. "I hadn't thought of that," she said, plopping down on a bench with a sigh. "We've had some good times here."

"It's been a long road," Mel said, sitting next to her.

Erica also looked grim. "I can't believe it's almost over."

The three of them looked about ready to cry.

"Come on, you guys," I said, lightening up the mood. "I'm starved. Aunt Maggie made shepherd's pie for dinner and I don't want to be late."

That broke their solemn mood.

"We wouldn't want that to happen, would we girls?" Mel asked. She got up and threw the rest of her belongings into her swim bag.

"Let's go home," Tati said, hoisting her bag over her shoulder.

She was the last to leave, and as she made her way to the door I heard her whisper, "It was a blast," to the empty room before she turned out the lights, backed out, and shut the door behind us.

Chapter 78

I woke before daybreak on championships morning, lucky I'd slept at all. Worry about winning the 500, breaking the record, and Calvin Reese's bribe gave me plenty of reasons to toss and turn. Still, I felt refreshed and ready to go.

The house was quiet, everyone else still asleep as I finished my morning stretch in silence. A gentle tap on the door pulled me from that peaceful zone.

"Can I come in?" Maggie asked.

I told her to enter and she closed the door behind her.

"I hope I didn't wake you," I whispered as I rose from the floor.

She shook her head. "I couldn't sleep. Too wired thinking about the meet."

"It means a lot to me that you're all going." I bent down to make my bed. She moved to help from the other side. "It's a long day. I understand if you have to leave after my events."

The Division Championships were held over two days. The first was the preliminaries, when hundreds of girls competed to make the next day's finals, where only the top sixteen in each event would race.

"We're going to try to stick it out. The kids are excited. I want them to see what it's all about. Paige and Danny start their first club season next month, and we'll be going to meets all the time."

"I'll be here to help."

"Have you decided whether or not you're joining the Marlins when varsity season ends?"

"Mel and Erica decided for me. No way they'll let me out of it. It's okay. I need to stay in shape if I'm going to swim in college. Plus, I've been swimming eleven months of the year for most of my life. Now that I'm back in the routine I don't want to stop."

"I'm glad to hear that," she said. "Paige will be so happy to have you on the team."

"I hear it's a good team."

"It is," she said. "It's what makes the Blazers so good. All of these young kids grow up to be varsity swimmers, and some of them go on to college teams, like you, Mel, Erica, and Tatiana."

"That's how it works," I said. We'd finished making the bed and sat side by side on the pink comforter.

"Do you need a ride to the high school?"

I shook my head. "Mel and Erica are picking me up."

"Can I make you some breakfast?"

"I thought you'd never ask. I'm famished."

"What do champion swimmers eat before a big meet? I don't want to feed you the wrong stuff."

"Let's keep it light: fruit and cereal. I'm in the second event and don't want to get bogged down."

After breakfast, I went back to my room to pack for the day. I brought two of everything: two suits, two pairs of goggles, two caps, and two pairs of flip-flops. I needed to prepare for any equipment breakdown. I threw in an old pair of leggings and a couple of swimsuits better sent to the trash can because Mel had informed me it was a meet tradition to dress in funky swimsuits and leggings for the warm up at the start of the meet. Sounded like fun. I also packed two towels, a chamois, and my shower kit. The smart swimmers also packed their books so they could study during the many hours of down time between events. These I packed in a separate backpack so nothing would get wet. Coach would make sure we had plenty of water and snacks, so I didn't have to worry about packing any food or drink.

Once I had everything together, I showered, letting the hot water relax my tense shoulders and arms. The tapering had gone well, but I was still a little tight. I did some stretching exercises while the water streamed over me.

Then came put-on-my-suit time, the most difficult part of getting ready, because the suit was two-sizes-too-small and a battle to pull up over my hips and shoulders. Any other time my mother helped, but since she wasn't available and I was too embarrassed to ask for Aunt Maggie's assistance, I struggled alone, inch by body-hugging inch. I pulled it on like a second skin, careful not to tear it, until, twenty minutes later, breathless and in a light sweat, I stood before my mirror encased in nylon and spandex. I tugged at its edges and seams for maximum comfort. I felt like a sausage, but the suit would act as a wick, absorb no moisture, and allow me to glide through the water with no drag. Most of the other swimmers would have a similar suit, but not as technologically advanced as this one, although I expected Tatiana would also be wearing the best.

I covered the swimsuit with my warm-up suit and took care of my hair, securing it on top of my head in a tight swimmer's bun. The last thing I needed was my hair to get in my way. Once I was ready to go, I stood in front of the mirror and stared at myself, searching deep into my eyes, looking for the well of strength and competitiveness that lay deep inside me. I had used these mental techniques throughout my swimming career to psych up for the big meets, but I'd buried them deep, not wanting to stir these emotions because my goal was to lay low. Over the last few weeks, as I sought to become more of a competitor, to win, I'd been releasing them bit by bit. Today was the day to unleash them full force.

I stood tall and spoke aloud the words Mike Starling had taught me many years ago. *You are a winner. This is your race. Do not be afraid.* After repeating my mantra until I'd eliminated all distraction, I bowed my head, closed my eyes, and joined my hands together in prayer.

"Dear God," I whispered, "I've been distant these last few months and only speak to you when I'm looking for something or complaining about something else. Please forgive me. I know you love me and want the best for me. As I go about my events today, please fill me with your spirit and give me strength to compete at my very best, using the gifts you have given me. Amen." I waited a moment for a response, and soon a calming peace spread through me, and I knew I had connected.

I backed away from the mirror and examined my appearance one last time to make sure everything was as it should be. I heard Erica's Honda pull up outside and grabbed my bags. The meet was on.

Chapter 79

The Boxer's hosted the championship meet because they had the biggest pool – eight lanes – and spectator seating for hundreds. Coach gave us last minute instructions and a pep talk on the bus ride, and we listened in silence, some of us too stressed about the upcoming competition to say much, others intent on preparing for the races ahead. Mel, Erica, Tatiana and I were in the latter category. I continued my Coach Mike mantra all the way over – *You are a winner. This is your race. Do not be afraid.* - envisioning each of my races from start to finish, seeing myself win, visualizing the clock lit up with my best times.

We entered the natatorium, the first team to arrive. Coach wanted us all in the pool for warm-up before it got crowded. We had just enough time to claim our space on the bleachers, drop our gear, and shed our warm-up suits before the second team arrived. Just as Mel had said, most of the girls wore old, tattered, and stretched out swimwear on top of their competition suits. Some added a third layer of fabric to create drag. I slipped mine on, and Mel laughed at the holes in the seat of my suit.

"When did you get that one?" she asked. "Ninth grade?"

"Nope," I said. "Eighth."

She shook her head, a goofy grin on her face. Her drag suits looked as old as mine, minus the holes.

"I won't even ask how you got the holes."

"Good, because I won't tell you."

Most of the girls also wore leggings in crazy colors and patterns. Mine were multi-colored polka dots, Tati's were red and white striped, Erica's were a cheetah print, and Mel's were psychedelic. The whole thing gave the event a carnival-like feel. It helped defuse the tension and relax us for what lay ahead, and I was grateful for the distraction.

We lined up, and Coach started us off the blocks. In just minutes, we swam through the water in tidy formation while our divers warmed up on the boards.

When we emerged from the water, most of the other teams had arrived. The noise inside the natatorium was deafening. We dried off and donned our warm-up suits. The air temperature on the pool deck was cool and no one wanted to catch a chill. Mel handed out bananas, and we settled in the bleachers to watch our competition warm-up. Some of the girls took out their books and started on homework. A few stretched out on the bleachers with their iPods turned on and earbuds inserted to drown out the noise and chill out. Some of the younger ones took pictures of everyone with their cell phones. Coach joined the rest of the coaches and the officials for a pre-meet conference.

Behind us, the stands filled with spectators: anxious parents and siblings, excited friends and classmates, hopeful college recruiters. I looked around for my Dad and the girls, hoping they'd come to surprise me, but I didn't see them. He'd explained he could only get away one day, and he'd rather see me in the finals.

"I can't believe we made it," Erica said, looking around. "It's our last meet."

"We've got one more," Mel said. "States."

"That's different," Erica said. "It's our last meet with the girls we've been competing with over the last six years."

"It's sad," Tati said.

I'd swam on three high school teams as the new girl without any shared history with my teammates, and couldn't relate to the depth of emotion these girls had for the magnitude of this meet. Yet I understood that it was bittersweet for them. Although all of us would swim in college, we would not swim together again like this. In the past, this never bothered me, but now I felt a loss. I'd grown to care for and appreciate these girls, and would miss them. I started to choke up, but before I could shed any tears, Mel defused the moment.

"Where's Jordan?"

I looked around for the Little Mermaid but didn't see her anywhere on deck. She'd been keeping to herself all morning, riding on the back of the bus plugged into her iPod, and sitting off to the side on the bleachers, throwing us surreptitious glances every once in a while, waiting for the ice to break so she could rejoin our group. That wasn't happening. The four of us were tight now and wouldn't allow her to infect us with any more of her negativity. We planned to win and she couldn't help us, so we kept our distance.

"Knowing Jordan she's hiding in the bathroom," Mel said.

"Look!" Erica said, jumping up. "It's time for the wave. Come on!"

We joined the hundreds of swimmers around the pool's perimeter and started a wave, all of us raising our arms overhead with a big whoop. It lightened the mood for a few seconds before the start of the heavy competition. It went around four or five times and faded to a close. We returned to our spots to get ready for the first event.

It was a tough meet. Competition from the Bears and the Boxers was fierce, and many of the other teams had outstanding individual swimmers too. Plus, the Chinese exchange students added to our worries. We were all grouped by our individual best times, but in the preliminaries we competed in circle seeding, so we didn't always come up against the best swimmers in our events. It was a mish-mash of talent. When it came to the 200 free, I was the top seed, swimming against girls I didn't remember from the dual meets. I won my heat and seeded third in the finals. Tatiana finished her heat as the top seed, and a Chinese swimmer was second. Back on deck, Tati and I agreed to shut her out of the top spot.

"It's going to be me and you, top two," she said.

"Or me and *you*," I corrected. I had no plans to come in second.

"Oh yeah?" she asked, eyebrow arched. "You want the 200?"

"I want it all," I challenged, meaning it.

"So do I," she said.

"This is going to be a long weekend."

The events moved like clockwork and the lineup for tomorrow's finals took shape. Mel and Erica both made it in their events - the 50 free and the 200 IM - and our divers did an outstanding job, each one making it into the finals for their event.

Only the top sixteen in each event would compete tomorrow. Everyone else would go home, their season complete. Then the top swimmers from the division would continue on to States. Some swimmers were still trying to make cut times. Emotions ran high as some achieved their goals while others failed, not only to make the state qualifying times but the division finals. Championship meets were always full of tension and heartache to go along with the victories and personal bests. Scoring points was essential to bring home a title, but the individual swimmer's achievements helped them get into the college swim programs of their choice – or not. Several of my teammates failed to make the finals, and red eyes and tear-streaked faces surrounded me. Tears of joy and sadness were heard all around the pool deck.

Charlie glued herself to my side during the entire meet, almost sick with worry about her performance in the breaststroke. We had already made the finals for the 200 medley relay with Charlie doing the breast leg, but she was terrified of failing to make the top sixteen in her event.

"You have to be in the top eight to score in the final," I explained to her. She nodded. "You don't want to come in ninth or lower, Charlie, you need to finish eighth or better. You can do it."

"How do you know?" she asked, her lower lip trembling.

"Your previous times tell me that you can finish better than the top four in your event. And that's great because you're so young. You have several years to improve. Keep working hard and maybe you'll be the division champ one day."

"Really?" she looked doubtful.

"Really," I said. "Quit worrying. Keep telling yourself *'You are a winner. This is your race. Do not be afraid.'* Believe it. It's true."

She took a deep breath. "You are a winner. This is your race. Do not be afraid." She repeated it three times.

"Feel better?" I asked when she paused to take a break.

She nodded, her smile mega-watt.

"Keep saying it, but quietly, especially when you're waiting on the block."

"Is that what you do?" she asked, eyes round with wonder.

I nodded. "It keeps me grounded."

"It keeps me grounded, too."

If I had no other success today, the fact that I helped Charlie throw off her pre-race jitters would be satisfaction enough.

We had a while to wait for the breaststroke – the second to last of 12 events - and several other pivotal races came before it. Mel made the top eight in the 100 free coming in fifth, and Erica finished third in the fly, putting them both in the finals. High fives and hugs all across our bleachers when they returned from their races. All of our seniors had made the finals so far, with Tati and I still to go in the 500 free and Jordan waiting for the breast with Charlie.

"Do you think Jordan will make the finals?" a worried Charlie whispered to me.

"Doubtful," I said. "She's seeded twelfth. She doesn't even come close to you so I wouldn't worry about her. There's nothing she can do to get in your way."

It was soon time for the 500 free, and Tati and I walked to the blocks together. We were in different heats but the same lane. She'd swim first. Good news for me because I'd see her finish time before my race.

"Before the event starts I have something to say to you," she said while we waited for the first heat to begin. On guard, I gave her my full attention. "I'm happy you came to Two Rivers," she said. "Without you, I had little to motivate me to break the Singer record, besides my father. I haven't had a lot of competition these last few years so you kind of woke me up, made me think about what I was doing and why, and motivated me to do my best. Either of us can break that old record, and if you do, I want you to know I'll be happy for you. You've earned it."

Her generosity stunned me. I was at a loss for words.

"Whatever else it is, it will be a good race," she said and tugged on her cap.

I pulled on mine, trying to think of how to respond. "You're a formidable opponent, Tati," I said. "If it weren't for you I'd still be hiding, not reaching my potential, and messing up the rest of my life. I'm sorry for all the trouble I caused. I should have been honest about who I was and what I do. I had no idea at the start of the season I'd be standing here right now wanting to win this race with my best time ever, more than I've wanted to win any other event. Thanks for waking *me* up."

We fist-bumped and the moment was over. We watched the heats ahead of us, noting the finish times, seeing that none came even close to what we were about to do.

I looked up at the stands and searched for Aunt Maggie, Uncle Pat, and the kids. I found them up at the top, holding a gigantic sign that read "Go Aerin! 4:52.49!" I laughed and waved. They waved back with their free hands and shouted down cheers.

Justin, Travis, and Sean sat in the middle of the crowd by the blocks. I stared at Justin, sending him a telepathic message to look at me. He must have gotten it because a few seconds later he turned my way and spotted me. He jumped up and shouted, "Hey Aerin! Make some waves!" I laughed and blew him a kiss. He looked around as if to see who it was for and then caught it, wrapping his hand around it and clutching it to his chest.

My gaze wandered through the crowd, recognizing classmates, parents, and teachers. Mrs. Cashman from the College and Career Center sat with Mr. Ferrara, my physics teacher, and a few of the other science teachers. I'd wager the heavy representation of Two Rivers fans were here to see who broke the Singer challenge. The 500 record holder herself sat front row center.

Next to her was Calvin Reese, a grim expression on his face. Tati was about to start her race, but he wasn't looking at her, he was looking at *me*, his steely gaze boring into mine. I almost flinched, but instead mustered my courage and stared back, telling him he didn't intimidate me. The starter blew his whistle, and the line moved forward for the next heat. Our locked eyes separated as we both turned to watch Tati prepare for her race.

She hopped onto the blocks in her graceful way, pulling down at the edges of her two-sizes-too-small swimsuit. She gave her cap and goggles a final tug, and got into position. The natatorium grew quiet for the start. Seconds later the buzzer went off and so did the swimmers. The crowd erupted in a massive cheer, and the race was on, twenty fast laps, Tati in the lead from the opening shot. I kept an eye on the clock, calculating each leg of the event, looking for any signs of weakness or mistakes. She was flawless, gliding through the water like an eel, feet kicking non-stop, arms in perfect symmetry. What a thrill to watch her. Any competitive spirit I'd been holding back sprang to life and I felt the urge to win, to conquer my opponent, as strong as I'd ever felt it. It did not matter what else happened in this race or at this meet. This event was between Tati and me, our shot at shattering a record that had been unbreakable for twenty-one years. I would do all I could to make sure I was the one who broke it.

Tati came in first as expected, her time 4:55.22, two and a half seconds away from breaking the record, not her personal best, and ten seconds faster than the second place finisher. Now it was my turn.

The crowd had little time to digest what Tati had done before the swimmers in the final heat climbed on the blocks. I took my time, shaking my arms to release the tension, pulling my suit, cap, and goggles into place one final time. I silently recited my mantra. *You are a winner. This is your race. Do not be afraid.*

After the start, I broke through the water's surface and streamlined halfway across before surfacing and setting my pace. Tati had averaged twenty-nine seconds for each leg of her race, and I needed to do just a little better than that. Any other time it would be no problem, but given the months I'd been slacking off it wasn't so easy. I steeled my resolve and kept swimming.

By my calculations, I was on top, ahead of everyone, making excellent time without overexerting, just as Mike Starling had taught me to win the 500 free.

Then, on the second to last turn, I came out a little on the wild side and slipped off the wall.

At that moment, I understood that Tati had won the race. I tried to make up the difference, but as I knew all too well, one little slip when you're *that* close to a monster swimmer like Tatiana is the difference between winning and losing. At the finish, I looked up at the clock. My suspicions were right: 4:56.02, almost a full second behind Tati.

She was the top seed in tomorrow's final 500 free, and I was a close number two.

Chapter 80

"Tough break," Mel said once I'd climbed out of the pool and made my way to our bleachers.

I peeled off my cap and shook my hair out. "You think?"

"Too bad you slipped on that last turn. You had her up till then."

"I know, Mel, I don't need a play by play."

"Sorry," she said, getting snippy.

"No, I'm sorry," I said. It wasn't her fault. "And thanks for counting my laps and being head cheerleader." Each time I surfaced for a quick breath before a turn, I heard Mel's booming voice cheering for me.

"Hey, it's my job," she said.

We walked back to the bleachers. I still hadn't recovered from my event and was huffing and puffing a little bit. Coach met us halfway. "Good job, Aerin," he said, high fiving me.

"Really?"

"You're right where I want you to be."

"In second place?"

"We're seeded first and second. Something big is going to happen tomorrow."

"I'm sure it will," I said, just wanting to pack up and go home.

I had time for a quick drink of water before we had to line up for the 200 free relay. We placed third, behind the Bears and the Boxers.

"Is that where Coach wants us to be in that race?" I asked Mel as we recovered on the bleachers.

"He has a strategy," she said.

"Does anyone know what it is?"

"No."

"Does he?"

"I hope so," she grumbled.

In the backstroke, we cheered for Taylor and Franky, who made it to the finals, seeded fifth and sixth.

When Charlie started heading for the blocks for her event, Mel and I walked her over.

"Jordan's in my heat," she said. The poor kid was trembling.

"So?" Mel asked. "That shouldn't mean anything to you."

"Forget about her. Do what you know how to do. You'll be okay, Charlie," I said.

She didn't look convinced.

"What did I tell you?" I asked, stooping down to meet her eye to eye.

"You are a winner. This is your race. Do not be afraid," she whispered.

"Keep saying it," I said as she went on ahead of us to take her place.

"What's that all about?" asked a puzzled Mel.

"Just a little trick I taught Charlie."

"Teach me. I need all the help I can get."

Charlie was in lane seven, close to the edge, so Mel and I positioned ourselves by the turn to cheer her on.

"She looks so small compared to the others," Mel said.

"She is small, but she's strong," I said, keeping my eyes glued to her. "Go, Charlie!" I hollered.

Jordan had the advantage of starting in lane four. I didn't think it would help her much against Charlie, but I kept an eye on her as well. They both had good starts, leading the pack, and it was close all the way. At the finish, though, Charlie came out ahead, placing first. Jordan was touched out by a Boxer. When all the heats concluded, it turned out Charlie was the fourth seed in the finals and Jordan, by some miracle, had made it too, placing eighth.

"She just managed to squeeze in," said a disbelieving Mel.

"I didn't think she could do that," I said.

"She was a pretty good swimmer early on, but she got caught up in all the drama and lost her momentum."

"Guess we'll have to deal with her tomorrow."

We ended the meet with the 400 free relay, and two of our teams made it to the finals. Mel, Erica, Tatiana and I were in the "A" relay, top seed.

"We are looking good!" a triumphant Erica proclaimed.

"Can it, Erica," Mel said. "It's not in the bag yet. You'll jinx us."

"You don't believe that, do you?" asked Tati.

"Let's just say I'm cautious."

"Well, we *do* look good," I said.

"So do a lot of other people."

That was true. For every Blazer who had a great day, a competitor from another team had just as great a day.

Kelsey joined us. "It's tight at the top," she said. She'd been at Coach's side all day helping him keep score and track times.

"How tight?" Mel asked.

"Ten to twenty points tight."

"Who?" Tati asked.

"Bears, then Blazers, then Boxers."

"Bears are ahead?" Mel asked.

Kelsey nodded.

"See?" Mel asked. "Don't be overconfident. We haven't won

yet."

"I'm tired," Charlie said, leaning against me. I reached down to tousle her damp hair.

"We have to cool down," Tati told her, "then we can change and get on home."

Minutes later, Coach had us doing a 500-yard cool down. We were the last to leave the natatorium. On the bus back to the high school, he gave last-minute instructions.

"Get to bed early, girls. Tomorrow is another big day. Eat plenty of carbs tonight and a good breakfast, and hydrate, hydrate, hydrate. The bus is leaving at ten o'clock, and we warm up at eleven. Those of you not swimming are encouraged to cheer us on from the stands. This is still a team effort."

Back at the high school, we staggered off the bus, tired and hungry, eager to eat, shower, and relax. Mel and Erica drove me home. Aunt Maggie and the rest of the Flynn's had arrived an hour before. The house already smelled like dinner.

"I'm starved," I said, entering the kitchen. Maggie was stirring a pot on the stovetop. "What smells so good?"

"Meat sauce. I'm making spaghetti and heating up garlic bread. Paige made a tossed salad."

A sheet pan of brownies cooled on the counter.

"Perfect," I said, reaching for one.

She slapped my hand away. "Those are for later," she said. "Food first."

"Okay," I said, "Do I have time for a shower?"

She looked up at the clock. "Five minutes."

I scooted out of there to shower and dress.

I dropped all my bags on the floor in my room and plopped down on the bed for just a second to rest. I landed on something that wasn't my comforter and reached for it. Maggie had left my mail on my bed. I sifted through the letters from college recruiters and admissions counselors and found a letter from my mom. I tore the envelope open.

Hey, beautiful. I timed it so you'd get this letter on Saturday, right before the big meet. How'd I do? The purpose is to wish you all the luck in the world, but also to say that you don't need luck because you have the talent, skill, and determination to win your events and to break that old record everyone's talking about. On the other hand, I know how hard it is to pull it off in spite of your talents, and I don't want to pressure you. You're always the best in my book despite what it says on the scoreboards. I wish I could be there to cheer you on, but not this time. I'll be cheering for you from within these walls. I recruited a cheerleading squad. All of my swim students are now hooked on the sport and can't wait to observe their first swim meet. We cashed in the chips we earned from doing community service for the privilege of tracking the results of your meet online. I'll be with you in spirit and virtually following along. Have a great day! Love, Mom

Leave it to Mom to find a way to follow my meet. I read the letter twice, then tucked it back into its envelope and filed it away with the others. The stack was growing taller and had outgrown the rubber band that held it together. I replaced it with a larger one. I riffled through the college mail and stacked that on my dresser, too. Once swim season ended, I'd go through the letters and packets, weeding out the definite no's and categorizing the remaining ones according to my interests. I'd present the top ten to my dad and we'd decide which schools to apply to. Most had an application deadline of February 1st. Plenty of time.

I slipped into the shower, changed, and was the last to sit at the table. Maggie had prepared a feast and I dug in with everyone else.

Chapter 81

The championship finals were not as long as the preliminaries. More than half of yesterday's swimmers didn't make the final cut. Each event consisted of two heats. The first was a consolation heat for the swimmers who placed ninth through sixteenth. It was an opportunity to better their times and perhaps make a state cut time, although that was a longshot. The second heat was for the top eight finishers to decide who would be the season's champions.

All of the fun and games from the day before - the carnival-like atmosphere, funky leggings, tattered swimsuits, and the wave - were over. Everyone wore her serious gear and her game face, her expression set to match the significance of the day. Some of us had a lot riding on this meet. We stuck together in the bleachers, did our warm-ups as ordered, hydrated, and tried to keep each other calm.

Ten of us made the finals – Tatiana, Mel, Erica, Charlie, Jordan, Taylor, Franky, and me on the swim side, Cassandra and Kim in diving. Of the eight, Charlie was the most nervous, her face a sickly shade of green. She sipped at her water and knocked her knees together as she sat on the bench beside me.

"Are you going to be all right?" I asked.

"No," she said in a tiny voice. "I'm not."

"You've been to championship meets before, Charlie. You've been to Junior Olympics. This meet is like that, just another meet."

"I'm the smallest one here," she said.

I checked out the rest of the girls on the pool deck. She was right. She was such a powerhouse I tended to forget she was only thirteen, not even five feet tall, and under a hundred pounds. "That means nothing," I said. "You've already beaten most of these girls. You can do it again."

Jordan passed by, plugged into her iPod, on her way to where I don't know. We were supposed to stay put.

Charlie watched her pass and I swear her face turned a deeper shade of green. "I think I'm going to be sick."

"No, you're not," I said, trying to gain control of the situation. She really did look like she might get sick. That would be a disaster. Then the light bulb went off. "Did Jordan say something to you?"

She shook her head in denial.

"Charlie?" I pressed. "You can tell me."

Her eyes welled with tears.

"What did she say?"

She sniffled, her lower lip trembling. "She told me I didn't belong here. She said it was just a fluke, that I had no chance of winning my event."

After all we'd been through these last few weeks, Jordan was still bullying Charlie. I was furious, but now wasn't the time or place for me to confront our champion mean girl.

"Listen," I said, grabbing her hands. "I've told you before. Jordan's playing mind games. She knows you're a better swimmer and will beat her. She can't let that happen because she's a senior and you're in the eighth grade. She's just trying to scare you so you'll blow the race. It won't work. You've beaten her in every event all season, and you'll beat her today. That's all you have to do. Beat Jordan. Don't worry about anyone else. Okay?"

Her tear-filled eyes looked up at me with such hope. "I did beat her in every event, didn't I?"

"And you'll do it again today. Now pull yourself together. Drink some water, plug in your iPod and listen to whatever you've got on your playlist. Take it easy. I'll tell you when you need to get up."

She took my advice and laid down on the bleachers, using her sweatshirt as a pillow and covering herself with a dry towel.

Pleased I'd averted a disaster, I rejoined Mel and Erica, who stretched out on the pool deck. I laid down my mat and went through my routine.

The noise level in the natatorium grew as the stands filled in. I searched for our cheering section and quickly found our friends and families, dressed in Blazers colors and holding signs encouraging us to do our best. In the middle was my father, sitting next to Maggie and her brood. Avery and Emily flanked him. Emily looked bored. Avery was busy eating popcorn. I waved my arm to catch their attention. My father saw me and waved back wildly. He gave me a thumbs-up and I went back to my stretches.

Once the opening formalities ended, the relay teams lined up for the first event, the 200 medley relay. We had two teams in the race, one in each heat, and I wasn't on either of them. I grabbed a spot on the pool's edge to cheer on my teammates. In the first heat, we finished tenth, not bad. Our "A" relay team was up next. The race ended in 1:50.13, Blazers in first place.

The first of my events was next, the 200 free. I was in lane four. Tati had lane five. Taking deep breaths, I limbered up my arms, stretching as wide as I could. Coach Mike's mantra – *You are a winner. This is your race. Do not be afraid* - ran through my head on auto repeat. I didn't even think about it anymore. I adjusted my cap and goggles and prepared for the start.

As soon as I hit the water, I knew I'd win. I surfaced last, a full arm's length ahead of Tati and just kept going, doing everything right this time. It was a quick 200. As I finished with a hard slap against the pad, I saw Tati come in second, and the Chinese swimmer finish third. Catching my breath, I whipped off my goggles and found my time on the scoreboard: 1:55.23, first place and my season's best. Tati finished 1:55.73, a half second behind me. She reached over, and we shook hands.

"Great race," she said, then turned to say the same to the girl on her right.

The Blazers had won the second event of the day, and I was the season's 200 free champion.

Coach was waiting for us as we climbed out of the pool, giving us both hugs and patting us on the back.

"Excellent job, girls, what a great start. Take a break. You've earned it."

Back on the bleachers, our teammates showered us with congratulations. We posed for pictures and celebrated our victory. Everyone seemed happy for me, including Tatiana.

"What a relief," she said as we plopped down on the bench with cups of water. She sucked hers down in two seconds. "I'm glad that's over."

"We're not done yet," I said, alluding to the 500.

"That was just a warm-up. It won't happen again."

"We'll see." We'd grown to be friends as well as teammates these last few weeks, bonding during the taper, the shave down, and the preliminaries. I found I *liked* Tatiana. Too bad I'd beat her in the 500 and break the record.

The meet went on, and we cheered for our team from the sidelines. The Blazers would not win every event – we didn't expect to – and the losing started with the 200 IM. Erica was our only swimmer and placed sixth. Still, she was all smiles when she got out of the pool.

"That was my best time this season!" she said, but she still hadn't made a state cut time. She'd need to do that in the fly to qualify for an individual event. Otherwise, she'd only swim in the 200 and 400 free relays.

Mel also failed to make a state cut time in the 50 free but placed seventh with a personal best of 25:95.

"I broke through 26!" she cried when we surrounded her for a group hug. After seeing her struggle to hit the 25's all season we were happy to see she'd made her personal goal at last.

We settled down for the diving finals, rooting for our divers, Jamie and Cassandra. We would not dominate in that event – the competition was thick, four of the top girls were going to States – but they put on a great show. I tried to focus on the flips, turns, and twists, but I was jumpy, my mind wandering to my upcoming events.

Tatiana sat behind me, stretched out on the bleachers as though she didn't have a care in the world. I was almost sick to my stomach worrying about the outcome of the 500, and she sat there like it was any other day.

The rest of our team was in the stands, hanging out, eating hot dogs and popcorn, chatting with the boys. I wanted to be with them.

"Get a hold of yourself," I muttered. "It's not like you haven't done this before."

The only thing different about this event was the Singer challenge. Aside from that, it was just another 500-yard freestyle race, and I'd won more than my share in the past. The prize money and celebrity attached to winning the challenge haunted me. I saw dollar signs. I imagined my name on the leaderboard, replacing Allison Singer's, a name that had stood there since 1989. Why did it mean so much to me? Why did I care?

A conversation with my father replayed itself. "It's something you have to do. You're a champion, Aerin, everything about you screams winner. If you set your mind to breaking that record, you'll break it."

I found him again in the stands. He was talking to Maggie and didn't notice me watching him. Emily and Avery played with the twins, oblivious to what was going on.

The diving competition ended with our divers finishing in fifth and sixth place.

We all hit the water for a quick warm up.

After diving came the fly and 100 free, Erica's and Mel's big events. They each had a chance at making a state time – a long shot, but still a chance. The most they could hope for was to beat their own best time. Yet deep inside I knew each one hoped a major upset would give them a chance to win or move on to the next level.

I dried off, put on my sweats, and took my place at the pool's edge to cheer them on.

Mel finished the 100 in seventh place.

Erica was touched out of first by a Bear, and came in second.

"Good job," I told them as I tugged my cap into place in preparation for the 500.

Erica gave me a high five and headed for the bleachers.

"You're up," Mel said. "Go get 'em. I'll see you on the turns." She was counting laps for me again.

Tati waited for me, and I joined her for the walk to the blocks. "I feel like I'm walking to the electric chair," I said.

"I *will* walk to the electric chair if I don't win this event," she countered.

She was probably right.

I shut out everything as we waited our turn to start. The first heat would take less than six minutes. I watched the swimmers without seeing them, the messages running through my head drowning out the noise of the race, the screaming crowd, the thrashing water. I drifted into another plane, a familiar one I hadn't visited for a long time, where it was just me and the race.

I blocked out everything except Coach Mike's mantra, playing nonstop in my head, and the voices of my parents, Aunt Maggie, Mel, and Justin convincing me I could win the race and break the record. I felt it in my arms, in my legs, my hands, and feet. The urge to win, to do my best, infused me, familiar reactions that had led me to victory many times. Would it be enough to drive me beyond my best performance this season?

To my left Tatiana stood lost in her own mind games, stretching and warming up, locked in racer mode. She too focused on the race in front of us, but I could tell she didn't see it either. We were so much alike it scared me. She was the most challenging competitor I'd ever faced.

I glanced up in the stands for one final look at my support team. My father talked with the Flynns, not paying attention to the current race. Justin and his friends also ignored the race, looking down at their phones, eating, and chatting. My gaze wandered over the crowd and settled on the front row, where Calvin Reese and Allison Singer sat together once more. She focused on the current event and the clock. But Calvin Reese was looking at the swimmers waiting for the big event and in seconds, his laser-like eyes found mine. My skin prickled under the intensity of his gaze, but I brushed it off, understanding that it was just another of his intimidation tactics. We stared each other down. I thought about our encounter in the parking lot, his bribe. "Let Tatiana break the record and I'll give you the prize money." Then I remembered what Maggie had said about him. "He's a snake. A cheater and a liar. You can't trust a word he says."

"No way, Mr. Reese," I whispered. "The best swimmer wins."

And with that, the first heat was over, and we transitioned for the main event. I checked the clock. No one had come even close to what Tati and I could accomplish.

As we took the blocks, the crowd came to its feet, expecting a historic race. Again, I blocked everything out, quieted my mind, and focused on the now placid surface of the water. In less than five minutes, the race would end, and Two Rivers and the division would have their champion and their record breaker. With everything I had, I'd make sure it was me.

~

It would be the fastest 500 of my life.

Tati and I swam neck and neck, side by side, from the second we launched off the blocks. The roar of the crowd was so loud I heard it under water. The pool felt like it was rocking, but that was just the force of the water hitting back at me with every stroke of my competitors.

I drove everything out of my mind and focused on my body as it pushed through the water, mindful of the position of my arms and hands, the precision of my kicks, and the rhythm of my breathing. I took everything I'd learned from every coach I'd trained with and every race I'd swam and used it.

At the end of twenty laps, I pounded the pad and emerged from the water, ripping off my goggles. Tati was right beside me, doing the same. We gaped at each other for a moment before turning our eyes to the clock. The roar of the crowd died down as the other swimmers completed their laps and the race ended.

The clock said it all. Tati and I both had our best times ever - she clocked in at 4:52:55, I finished at 4:52.57 - but neither of us had broken the Singer record.

Tatiana was the division champion.

I was in second place.

I let it sink in while I caught my breath, dazed, disbelieving. After swimming the hardest I ever had in my life, I'd failed at both of my goals. I was disappointed and relieved.

I reached over the lines toward Tati, and she met me halfway. We grabbed each other, embracing as we let the tension leave our bodies. She was crying. I was too numb to cry. An official yelled at us to get out of the pool for the next event. We clung together a moment longer, then pulled apart, Tatiana wiping her tears away. It hit us at the very same second.

"States!" we said, and high fived.

The competition wasn't over.

Chapter 82

Minutes later, we were back on the block for the 200 free relay. Erica had the lead leg, followed by me, Tati, and then Mel. It was how we always ran this race but with Tati and I having gone all out just minutes before in the race of our lives, we were worthless. Tati looked sluggish, and I was like a beached whale. We came in sixth.

The Blazers, Bears, and Boxers split the next events, all three teams struggling to get on top and switching places with every race. As we got closer to the breast, Charlie turned greener than she had ever looked and clutched at her belly. I wrapped my arms around her, and she cowered beneath me.

"You okay, Charlie?" I asked.

She shook her head. "I'm scared."

"Don't start that again," I said. "It's not much different from yesterday, and you finished great. After this, you won't have to swim another varsity event for almost a year."

She broke away from me and smiled. "That's true. Although there's still the Marlins."

"You've got nothing to worry about in club either. Just do what you know how to do and you'll be okay."

It was time for her to line up for the event. She pulled off her warm-up suit, and I helped her yank on her cap. Coach gestured for her to speak to him and she walked toward him as if she was heading to the guillotine.

"Poor kid," Mel said. "I remember my first championship meet. I almost puked too."

"She'll be all right. Let's watch the race from up in the stands," Erica said.

We climbed into the stands and sat with Justin and his friends.

"Good job, Apple," he said.

"I lost."

"Best time all season."

"No arguing there."

The results of the first heat were unremarkable, no upsets. We chatted while the swimmers readied on deck for the final heat. Charlie was supposed to be in lane six and Jordan was in lane eight, but instead of getting on the blocks, they looked like they were arguing. Jordan's face twisted into that hideous grimace she wore so well, and Charlie looked like she was up against a giant.

"What's going on?" I stood to get a better look. "Check that out," I told Mel. "Something's going on with Charlie and Jordan."

Mel rose to watch our breaststrokers. "What's Jordan doing? She'd be crazy to mess with this race after everything we've been through all season."

"Jordan *is* crazy," said Justin, also on his feet. "I wouldn't put anything past her."

No one on deck paid them any attention. Jordan was pointing to lane eight gesturing at Charlie to get up on the block. Charlie pointed to lane six and shook her head. They argued for a few more seconds, and then Jordan climbed onto the block in lane six. Charlie looked around, confused, searching for someone to help, but no one came to her aid.

"Where's Coach?" Mel asked. We spotted him on deck at the opposite end of where Charlie and Jordan had their dispute.

"Coach!" Mel shouted, but with all the noise in the natatorium he didn't hear her, and kept talking to some other coach. "Come on," she said, pushing her way through the crowd. "They're going to run the race with Jordan in the wrong lane and without Charlie. We have to get down there." She was out of the stands and climbing down to the pool deck. Erica and I followed.

Too late. The starter called for silence and then announced the race. Charlie, in tears, tried to run across the deck to Coach, who still had no idea what was going on. An official stopped her, not allowing her to pass by, and gave her a tongue-lashing.

"Take your mark!" the started announced and the buzzer buzzed. The race was on.

Charlie broke away from the official and ran to Coach, who almost choked when he saw her. They had a heated exchange. Coach turned to an official and spoke with him, gesturing at the pool and the swimmers in the race, lane eight empty.

"This is so bad," Mel said.

"This has never happened before," Erica said.

"Poor Charlie," I said. The eighth grader was in a heap on the floor, devastated that she had missed her event. Jordan was churning away in lane six, in last place.

"What a disaster," Erica muttered.

They didn't stop the race. They couldn't. It was over in 1:09.92. Jordan came in last, missing her seedtime by a full four seconds.

"Serves her right," Mel said, seething.

"Let's see what happens," I said.

Coach clustered with all of the officials and a few other coaches, having a big debate, angry faces all around. The meet was on hold while the officials figured out what to do.

"I wish I could hear what they're saying," Erica said.

Jordan and Charlie approached Coach, both of them crying. Coach broke away from the discussion and ushered them to the sidelines to wait for the official's determination.

In the bleachers, Jordan's parents, Charlie's mom, and Calvin Reese tried to get Coach's attention, but he ignored them.

A slow murmur grew in the stands as people figured out what had happened, and soon it became a dull roar.

Five minutes passed before the officials walked over to Coach, Jordan, and Charlie and started asking questions.

"I can't see anything, can you?" Mel asked, standing on tiptoe. I shook my head. The adults blocked our view of the girls. "What do you think is going to happen?"

"I don't know. I've never seen anything like it."

Moments later the conference broke up. The officials went one way, and Coach and our teammates went another. The head official made the announcement.

"In the 100-yard breaststroke, swimmers in lanes six and eight are disqualified."

The crowd erupted as fans and parents expressed their opinions about the call.

"Bummer," Mel said.

"Jordan deserves it," Erica said.

"Charlie doesn't," I said, looking for the tiny swimmer. I didn't see her or Jordan anywhere on deck. "Where is she?"

"Coach took them out," said Justin.

"Let's just wait for her to come back," Mel said. "We need to get ready for the 400 free relay."

We got in line for our event, the timers and officials taking extra care to make sure all swimmers were present and in the right lanes. I didn't even watch the first heat, I was so focused on finding Charlie, wondering if she was all right. I looked up into the stands for her mother and didn't see her, which made me feel a little better. Perhaps she was consoling her daughter, whom I knew needed lots of consolation. As much as she worried about her event, I doubted disqualification ever crossed her mind.

"Hey," Mel said, pulling our relay team into a huddle. "We need to win this one."

"We need to win it for Charlie," I seconded.

"For Charlie," Erica said.

"For Charlie," said Tati. We clasped hands and shouted to the rafters, "Blazers relay!" four or five times. On the bleachers and in the stands, the rest of our teammates joined in for the last refrains. Buoyed by team spirit, we took our places behind the blocks and prepared for the event.

No one could beat us. We were too pumped with supporting Charlie, trying to make her personal loss up to her in a show of team strength. We won, with a meet record time of 3:45.33.

Drained after our victory, we dried off, accepted the congratulations of our teammates, and looked for Charlie. Still no sign of her.

"Maybe she went home," Erica said.

"I don't see her mom," I said.

"Coach wouldn't send her home," Mel said. "He's probably got them in some office somewhere."

We waited while the officials tallied up the meet results.

"I think we got it," Kelsey said, chewing on a pencil as she perused her score pad.

"Seriously?" Mel asked.

"I'm 99.9 percent sure," she said and crossed her fingers. The rest of us crossed ours too. We'd been going back and forth all day, trading places with the Bears and the Boxers. We were counting on Jordan and Charlie to bring in points for the breaststroke, but they'd brought in zero. We weren't a sure thing for the 400 relay, but our top spot brought in forty points, so maybe it made up the difference. I was no good at following scores and said a little prayer.

"There they are," Tati said. Coach and Charlie walked onto the pool deck. She walked in front of him, her head down. Coach had a blank expression and walked toward us without acknowledging the coaches who spoke to him along the way.

"Are you okay, Charlie?" I asked as soon as she was within hearing distance. She nodded, her lower lip trembling, as she reached for her warm up suit. "Let me help." I took the jacket from her and helped her put it on, then handed her the pants. The rest of the team encircled us, shielding her from the curious stares of the other swimmers.

"What happened?" Mel asked. "Did Jordan say you were in the wrong lane?"

Charlie nodded. "I tried to tell her I wasn't, but she wouldn't listen."

"This is important, Charlie," Mel said. "What did she say? Was it a mistake or was she trying to throw the race?"

"Throw the race?" Charlie asked, not understanding.

"Was she trying to get you disqualified? Or did she just have the lanes mixed up, you know, by accident?" I tried to clarify the question.

"She said it was a mistake," Charlie said.

"Why would she try to disqualify Charlie?" Tati asked. "She'd have to disqualify herself too. That doesn't make any sense."

"Jordan doesn't make sense most of the time, Tati," Mel said.

Tati shrugged.

"It could have been a legitimate mistake," Erica said. "I've gotten confused before a big race too."

"Too bad none of the officials or timers were paying attention," Tati said.

"We should find her," Mel said.

"How can we do that?" I asked. "They're getting ready to announce the winners, and we need to be here. Coach will kill us if we're not around."

"We've got time," Mel said. She gestured to where the coaches assembled around the computers and officials analyzing the meet results. She started walking, heading for the door from which Coach and Charlie had emerged. Tati and I looked at each other.

"Come on," she said, following Mel.

"You stay here with Erica," I told Charlie. I grabbed my phone. "Text me if they start the announcements before we get back."

Chapter 83

The three of us entered a dim, quiet corridor. It was cool, and I shivered, wishing I had on more than a damp swimsuit and my warm-up jacket.

"Let's go this way," Mel said, turning left, into the school. Walking through an unfamiliar high school was a little creepy, especially since it was Sunday. Few lights were on, and no one was around.

"Do you know where you're going?" Tati asked.

"No, I'm just following my gut," Mel said.

"She could be anywhere," I said, checking my phone to make sure I hadn't gotten a text from Charlie. The further we walked into the depths of the school, the farther we'd be from the natatorium when the text came that we needed to get back on deck *now*. "This is pointless. We won't find her, and Coach will kill us for being AWOL."

Mel ignored me and turned down another corridor. This one looked like classrooms, their doors closed for the weekend. We tiptoed through, my nerves on edge as I waited to run into a security guard or custodian. We'd be in big trouble if someone caught us roaming the school.

Mel stopped walking. "Look," she whispered, and pointed toward a door at the end of the hall that was ajar, emitting a thin shaft of light. "Quiet."

We walked without breathing, sneaking up on the classroom. Mel pushed the door with her left arm, and it creaked open.

"Who's there?" a voice asked.

"It's us," Mel said and entered the room, Tati and me on her heels. My eyes adjusted to the change in light. Jordan sat on the floor in a corner, her arms wrapped around herself in a tight ball.

"Get out of here," she said, her voice harsh and nasal like she'd been crying her eyes out.

"Sorry to spoil your pity party but you need to come back. They're announcing the winners any minute," Mel said.

"What do I care? You saw what happened. I blew my race. I'm an idiot."

"Stop being so dramatic," Tatiana said. "So you were DQ'd. Big deal."

"Easy for you to say, Tati. When have you ever DQ'd?"

"I've DQ'd," Tati said.

"Yeah, *in sixth grade*. You haven't been disqualified in ages, and never at a championship meet. That was my last varsity race, and I blew it."

"You're right, Jordan, you blew it," Mel said, crouching down beside her. "But this isn't about you. It's about the team. In two minutes, they're announcing the meet winners and the division champions. If it's us, we need to climb on that podium and receive our award. So get up and come with us."

"Come on, Jordan," Tati said.

Jordan remained seated, and looked up at us with tear-filled, red-rimmed eyes, her face blotchy. She wore only her damp swimsuit, and the room had a definite chill.

I pulled off my warm-up jacket. "Here," I said.

She looked at me with surprise. "You're giving me your jacket?"

I shrugged. "It's cold in here, and you're turning blue."

She wrapped it around herself, and then rose to her feet. "Thanks," she said and zipped it up. "You guys think we won?"

"Yeah," Mel said. "But we could have used some help from you. What happened out there?"

We exited the classroom and began the long walk down the corridor back to the natatorium.

"I messed up," Jordan said. "I mixed up the lanes."

Mel grabbed her arm and stopped her, confronting her face to face. "Truth?"

Jordan didn't squirm and looked Mel straight in the eye. "Yeah. It was a mistake."

Tati and I exchanged a skeptical glance.

Mel pressed her. "Just to be clear, Jordan, for the sake of the team, I have to ask you. Did you try to mess things up for Charlie?"

Jordan shook her head. "Why would I do that Mel? That would be shooting myself in the foot, which is exactly what happened."

Mel let her go, and we resumed walking.

The noise in the natatorium had reached a crescendo as the crowd waited for the meet results. Fifteen minutes had passed since we'd left to find Jordan, and when we reached our bleachers everyone was in a panic.

"Where were you?" Kelsey asked. "Coach is wild."

"He's about to blow a gasket," Erica said.

"Everything's under control," Mel said. "We're all here now." She examined the team. "Why aren't you guys ready to get on the podium? Put on your warmup suits. Do I have to tell you to do everything? Where would you guys be without me?"

We donned our suits and finger-combed our hair to look good for the cameras. We weren't one hundred percent sure we'd won, but we needed to prepare for the attention if we did.

Coach raced toward us, a relieved but irate expression on his face. "Thanks for finding Jordan," he said, "but the disappearing act was a major misdemeanor. We'll discuss that later. You girls need to get ready for the award ceremony."

The officials stepped up to the microphone, and the natatorium grew quiet as the crowd realized they were about to announce the winners. The top eight performers or teams in each event would stand on the podium. Each would receive a medallion noting her achievement and pose for pictures.

The first of the Blazers recognized was our 200 medley relay team, who came in first. Tatiana and I were next for winning first and second place in the 200 free. As I accepted my medallion I looked up at my father and the rest of my fan club and waited while he took a few pictures and cheered for me.

"Way to go, Aerin," he shouted.

Emily and Avery waved Blazers flags at me and shouted their congratulations.

Aunt Maggie, Uncle Pat, and their kids added their cheers.

Erica was my next teammate to stand on the podium for finishing sixth in the IM.

Mel, seventh in the 50 free, got up behind her. Of all of us, I was most proud of her for working so hard all season and meeting her goal. She beamed, accepted her medallion, and posed for pictures. Justin and his friends leaned over the rail, shouting her name. Very well deserved.

Jamie and Cassandra received their recognition for their diving performances.

Then Tatiana and I took our spots for the 500 to a thundering round of applause. My father, the girls, and the Flynn's applauded loudest of all. I glanced at Allison Singer, who clapped her hands like crazy. Calvin Reese stood with his arms folded across his chest, scowling. Tati's mother stood beside him, wiping tears from her eyes.

We accepted the rest of our recognition for placing third in the 200 free relay and first in the 400.

The last awards went to the meet champions, Division

Champions, and Swimmer of the Year. We held hands while we waited to hear who won.

"This year's meet champions are the Two Rivers Trailblazers!" the announcer proclaimed, and we raced for the podium, shrieking with excitement. After all the hoopla, the announcer told us not to move.

"This year, for the fourth consecutive time, the Division Champions are the Two Rivers Trailblazers!" he shouted. Our excitement rose to new levels as we jumped up and down, screaming, hugging each other. We did it! We won the division title for the fourth consecutive year.

The announcer waited for the roar of the crowd to die down before speaking into the microphone again. "Each year, we recognize one swimmer who has exemplified the spirit of the sport and has reached new personal heights. This year, the Swimmer of the Year is Tatiana Reese."

Once more, our team erupted in cheers as Tatiana came forward to accept her award, an engraved plaque, and shook hands with the heads of the division. In seconds, her parents joined her. Mrs. Reese hugged her while Calvin Reese shook hands with all the officials and coaches. At last, he threw his arms around Tati and gave her a bear hug, pulling her up off her feet. Tati looked like she couldn't breathe. When he let her go, her face was flushed. Photographers and reporters from the local media swamped them, and Tati disappeared from our sight.

"Well, no surprise," Mel said, heading back to the bleachers. Everyone followed, and we started gathering our stuff.

"She earned it," I said.

"You're right," Mel said, "but I would have liked to see someone else get it. It's been her the last three years."

"Next year it will be someone else."

She laughed. "No kidding."

The meet was over. We'd done our best, and we'd won. We

were too ecstatic to be tired. After showering and dressing, we congregated at Tatiana's house for a post-meet feast of Italian specialties – antipasto, three different kinds of pasta, roast chicken, meatballs, and loaf after loaf of bread. We ended with a tableful of pastries. I thought I'd bust.

"Tonight we feast," Mel said, "for tomorrow we are back in the pool to prep for States."

"I thought we had tomorrow off," I said, licking cannoli filling off my fingers.

"You're right, we do. I'm sleeping till noon."

"I'm sleeping till after noon."

"Maybe my mom will fill in for me so I don't have to get up for the chickens," Erica said.

"I hope so," Mel said. "We kicked butt today. That deserves a day off from chores."

"You tell her," Erica said.

"I will," Mel said.

We crashed out on the floor in the Reese's family room. The TV played a movie no one watched. A few of the girls were half-asleep. The rest laid around talking or working their phones.

"Oh yeah, we look like a bunch of champs," Mel said.

"Chumps is more like it," I said.

"Most of them will go home tonight and not swim for weeks, some not for months."

"But not us," Erica groaned. "We still have two weeks to go."

"And then club starts," Mel reminded us.

Such was the life of a swimmer.

We wouldn't have it any other way.

Week Fourteen:

States

Chapter 84

The next two weeks were an abbreviated version of the ones before. The four of us practiced after school, a modified version of dry land and tapering with lots of stretching and sessions with the trainer. Coach harped on us every day about our diet and sleep habits. Outside of school and practice, he wanted us to lay low, to protect ourselves from injury, and prevent infection. One person with a cold could blow our whole performance.

"Is he always like that?" I asked Mel.

"I wouldn't know. I never made it to States before."

I turned to Tati, who had competed at the big meet the last two seasons. and she nodded. "He's super intense about States," she said. "It's a big deal."

Just when we thought the pressure couldn't get any worse.

I followed orders and kept a low profile, begging off on visiting my father for his weekend because Avery had the sniffles.

"I can't afford to get sick," I told him. He understood but was disappointed. They planned to paint the nursery that weekend, and he needed my help. "No painting for me," I said. "I can't risk injuring my shoulder. Wait until after the meet and I'll help however you need me. You've got plenty of time before the baby comes."

He said he'd think about it. Dawn had ordered furniture, and they needed to paint the room before delivery. She was getting antsy with the bed rest and anxious to prepare for the baby.

"What colors?" I asked, hoping he'd let down his guard and clue me in as to whether I was expecting a brother or sister.

"She picked out a beige, peach and green motif," he said.

"Yuck."

"It's gender neutral. She's had enough of the 'pink for girls, blue for boys' color scheme. She wants something different."

"That's different."

"It looks better than it sounds."

"I'll see you in two weeks."

"Wrong. You'll see me at the meet next weekend."

"You're coming?"

"I wouldn't miss it for the world."

"But it's upstate, *way* upstate. It's a million miles away."

"I'm flying in. Alone. Geneviève is staying with Dawn and the girls."

I was so used to being last on his list of priorities I was stunned he'd set aside time for me, and clung to the phone, wordless.

"Your silence is worrying me," he said.

"Sorry, Dad. I'm a little shocked."

"You shouldn't be. Of course I wouldn't miss my daughter's biggest varsity swim meet. I'm ashamed you'd think I would."

"No," I said, "don't feel that way – "

He interrupted. "Look Aerin, I haven't been fair to you, and I suppose I've earned your skepticism. We never get to talk, and there's a lot I need to say. I'm proud of you, honey, the way you've turned yourself around, all that you've accomplished these last few months. My life is moving at lightning speed, and I haven't given you the attention you deserve. That stops right now. I promise to be a better father. I cleared my schedule, and I'm flying up to the meet on Friday morning. I'm staying at the same hotel as you and your team.

Maybe we can have dinner together."

"Yeah," I said. "I'd like that."

Justin popped in two or three nights a week to help me with my physics homework and prep for tests. I now had the highest grade in the class, and my GPA was the best it had ever been.

He ran me through my study cards a few times for a quiz the next day, and later we lay stretched out on the floor in the family room watching TV. Aunt Mags was upstairs putting her children to bed, and Uncle Pat was at a church meeting. A bucket of freshly popped popcorn drenched with melted butter nestled between us and we bumped fingers each time we reached in for a handful.

"So, how's practice going?" he asked between bites.

"You should know. You've been to States before."

"Last year I was the only one."

I sat up to get a better view of him. "That must have been awkward."

He nodded. "It was just Coach and me at practice and on the bus. I had my own hotel room. It was creepy being all by myself."

"Didn't your family go up?"

"Yeah, but they stayed somewhere else because the hotel I stayed in was booked."

"Thank God I'm going up with Mel, Erica, and Tati."

"It's intense. It will be good to have someone to talk to, someone else to cheer on." He munched on another fistful of popcorn, then asked, "Are you nervous?"

I shrugged. "No. It's just another big meet. I can't get too rattled."

"It's your last chance to break the Singer record."

"I know. I'm not focused on that right now. I'll go crazy."

"It's all everyone is talking about around town."

"It's a little out of hand," I said.

Some reporters from the local media had interviewed Tati and me and featured us in a full-page newspaper article and a spot on the local TV station. The New York City media and a few sports outlets picked up the story too, including ESPN and USA Swimming. Our story was all over the internet. We even had a hashtag: #500. The attention had both of us biting our nails, but we'd agreed to put on a cool-as-cucumbers front to downplay the media frenzy.

"I'll say," Justin continued. "People are placing bets on who wins."

"People are betting money on the race?" The thought made me sick.

"Yup."

I had to ask. "Who's got the best odds?"

"Sure you want to know?"

Not really, but I nodded anyway.

Justin flopped onto his back, the popcorn forgotten. "Tati."

"Well, she is the hometown favorite," I said, not surprised, and grateful the pressure was on her, not me.

"Depends on who you ask," he said. "I'm betting on you."

I punched him lightly on his firm bicep. "You didn't wager money on me, did you?"

"Ow!" he cried, rubbing his arm.

"That didn't hurt."

He smiled and winked. "Yeah, it did, but just a little bit. And yeah, I did bet on you, but only twenty bucks."

"Twenty bucks?" What craziness. "Who else bet on me?"

"I'm not telling! You'll only worry."

"Of course I'm worried. I don't want people to lose money because of me. And isn't that illegal?"

"I don't know. Probably."

"The whole thing's sick."

"Aerin, don't you know this is the biggest thing that's happened in this town for ages? People are excited. Twice as many kids signed up for the swim club than this time last year. Everyone wants to be a swimmer. Two Rivers is in the national news. The competition has put this town on the map."

I had no idea any of this was happening, once again under water most of the time and oblivious to everything else. "You're scaring me."

He pulled me down on the carpet beside him. He stroked my hair and pushed a strand behind my ear. "Don't be scared," he whispered. "You're going to do great."

"I never expected it would be like this," I whispered back. "All these people. All this attention. It's crazy."

"You've got that right." He started stroking my back. It helped release some of my tension. "It's more than you wanted when you joined the team, but just think of the opportunity. It's a once in a lifetime break. You've got every coach in the country following you, and whether you destroy that record or not, you're going to whatever school you choose. This is big, Aerin, real big. And you're ready for it. You've been training for it most of your life."

I snuggled into him, soothed by his words. He knew me so well and understood what I needed to hear. "Thanks," I said. "You've made me feel so much better."

He leaned down and kissed me on the top of my head. "Hey," he whispered. "That's my job."

Chapter 85

As the day of the state meet loomed closer, I found myself growing immune to its pressures. My experience had taught me that when the anxiety and tension that accompanies a big race becomes overwhelming, the best strategy is to mentally and emotionally detach from it. I went to practice, made it through the practice sets and lifting routines, listened to and absorbed Coach's motivational speeches, ate what he told me to eat, slept as much as possible, and focused on my schoolwork. Everything else was out of mind: the meet, the media, the Singer challenge. At this point, I was as good as I was going to be. No amount of worrying or stressing would change anything.

The four of us – Mel, Erica, Tati, and I - went right home after practice to study and rest. No socializing. No hanging out. No movies. Nothing. We laid low, preparing, waiting for it to be over, and for "normal" life to resume.

~

Like the Division Championships, the State Championship Meet was a two-day event. On the first day, we left the high school at five a.m. for the long ride upstate and slept on the bus. When we arrived, we went straight to the pool and jumped in for a quick warm up. My muscles were stiff from the long ride, but soon I felt loose and ready.

Mel and I finished our set first and climbed out to dry off.

"This place is huge," she said.

Tati joined us. "There are sixteen lanes," she said, pointing to the pool, which was two pools attached to each other, one with lane lines running horizontally and the other with lines running vertically. "In minutes, this place will be teeming with hundreds of swimmers, more than you've ever seen."

Mel's eyes bugged out.

"Hey," I said, grabbing her arm. "Don't go anywhere on me. Focus. We're going to concentrate on our individual events, our own performances, okay? Don't let the crowds get to you." I ushered her to our place in the bleachers. We put on our warm-up suits and settled in for the long wait to the start of the preliminaries. We used the time to relax, playing a few games of Rummy 500, keeping our minds off our nerves.

Tatiana and I were the only swimmers competing in the first half of the meet. The 200 free was the second event. We stood at the blocks and waited for the medley relay to conclude, both of us at opposite ends of the pool. In the throng of swimmers in the event, I lost track of her and missed her presence. She had a grounding effect on me. In this crowd of strangers, I felt very alone.

Mel and Erica stood with Coach and Coach D, studying something on his clipboard, most likely the psych sheet. I willed for one of them to look my way, but no one did. I started Coach Mike's mantra in my head - *You are a winner. This is your race. Do not be afraid.*

The 200 free was not the race I cared about, but it would set the tone for my performance in the 500, especially if I had a better finish than Tati. Whether or not I made the finals was irrelevant. I just needed to stay ahead of Tati. At the very least my finishing with a better time would rattle her confidence for the 500.

I waited for my heat, stretching out my arms and legs, trying to quell my nerves. The event was circle seeded, so all of the swimmers swam together. The finalists could come out in any heat. I checked the clock for the fastest times and saw nothing that suggested I didn't have a shot at the finals. By the time it was my turn to take to the blocks, I was more than ready. I finished my heat in 1:55.25, and easily in the top eight. I didn't see Tati's race and headed back to the bleachers.

"I think you made it," Mel said. "I think you're in the finals."

"Great," I said as I dried off with a chamois. "What about Tati?"

"Right behind you." She grinned. "1:55.95."

I plopped down on the bleachers, relieved to have set the pace. Tati would have to catch up with me.

As the meet wound on, the crowd in the bleachers began to fill up. In one corner, Tati and Erica's parents congregated, wearing our team colors and waving Blazers' flags and banners. Mel's parents and Maggie had yet to arrive. I looked for my father and found him sitting by himself, searching the pool deck for me. Our eyes connected and he stood up and waved. I gestured toward the exit and directed him to meet me there. Minutes later, he wrapped me in his arms and gave me a huge hug.

"Did you see the 200?" I asked.

"You bet," he said, planting a kiss on the top of my head. "You nailed it. You're playing it smart. Let it rip tomorrow and you'll finish at the top."

"That's not the race that worries me."

"Do well in the 200 and you're sure to do well in the 500."

"I don't care about placing or winning," I said. "I want to break the record."

He gave me an appraising look. "If you want to, you will."

"It's not that easy."

"Look, honey," he said, cupping my face in his hands. "You've been working hard. You have the desire. Believe in yourself. You're the only thing that stands in your way."

I'd heard that at least a million times, but he was right. I needed to get out of my own way, stop worrying, and start believing I could break 4:52.50 today.

"You better get back to your team before your coach realizes you're AWOL," he said.

I gave him another hug. "All of the Blazers' parents are there," I said, pointing in their direction. "Why don't you join them?"

He located them in the crowd and nodded. "Is that where Maggie will be?" Maggie was planning to come with Paige and stay overnight for the next day's finals. Uncle Pat and the younger kids stayed home because Maggie thought the long days would be too much for them. I couldn't blame her. They were almost too much for me.

"Yeah. Save her some seats."

He gave me a peck on the cheek and sauntered off.

Back in the bleachers, Coach had everyone in a huddle. I slipped in to hear what he had to say.

"Congratulations to Tati and Aerin for making the finals. We have some time to go before our next event. Have something to eat, take in some water, and try to relax. It's a long day, I know, but use your time productively. Get some homework done. I know some of you are working on research papers. It's as good a time as any to make progress on that assignment."

"Yeah, right," Mel said as he turned away. "I'll get started on that ten page paper about global warming right away."

"Let's play cards," Tati said.

"Good idea," Erica seconded.

We took our places and started another game.

∽

We stopped playing to watch the 50 free, Mel making note of the qualifying finishes, a wistful look on her face. She'd missed the opportunity to compete in her event at States for the final time, and could only hope to make the big meets in college.

When the diving preliminaries finished we did another warm-up in preparation for our upcoming events: the 500 free, and 200 free relays. We watched the results of the fly and 100 free, events Mel and Erica would have loved to swim.

We had a short intermission before the 500 and Tati and I had a few minutes for a pep talk from Coach.

"Remember: these are the preliminaries," he said. "Make sure you get into the finals. Don't try to do anything spectacular right now, okay?"

We nodded, understanding he was referring to the Singer challenge. Tati and I were both in the top eight right now – she was seeded third, and I was seeded fourth. The top swimmer hadn't broken 4:52 either. It was going to be a very exciting event.

He sent us on our way, and we took our positions, again separated by several lanes. I soon lost sight of her.

In the end, we both maintained our positions in the top eight for the finals. Neither of us beat our seedtimes, and we'd flip-flopped spots. I was now third, and she was fourth. Crazy.

Before we could sit down, they called us to line up for the 200 free relay. Mel was in the leadoff position, followed by Tati, then Erica, then me pulling up the rear. We had done it so many times we didn't need to talk about it. We went through our usual stretches, and adjusted our caps and goggles. The meet officials ran these races so tight we had just a few minutes to get ready. Once again, we made the finals, placing eighth. Tomorrow's events shaped up to be a full day.

I was starting to get tired. All of the sitting around interrupted by bursts of intense activity was taking its toll, but we had no time to rest as the 400 free relay loomed ahead.

We passed the time in between events searching the crowd in the stands for our family and friends. Mel's parents had arrived with Justin and Sean, Tati's boyfriend. Aunt Maggie and Paige had made it and sat with my father. They waved down to us and cheered. It was too close to the relay to visit with them so we prepared ourselves for the race. When it concluded, we found ourselves in the finals, in seventh place. Exhilarated, we went through our cool down, changed into warm, dry clothes, and hopped onto the bus to take us back to our hotel.

Our families met us there, and everyone went for dinner at an authentic Italian restaurant that served platters of steaming pasta drenched in tomato sauce and the most delicious garlic bread I'd ever eaten. I almost ate a whole loaf myself. I sat between Justin and my Dad, who met for the first time, and talked over me to discuss the Giants' prospects for making the Super Bowl.

"I can't believe we're here," Mel said. "Pinch me."

I pinched her.

"Ouch!" she said. "I meant that figuratively, not literally."

"Sorry," I said.

"I've waited six years to go to States, and we're here, and I'm swimming in two events tomorrow in the finals."

"Is it better than the Junior Olympics?"

"Oh yeah!" she said, diving back into the pasta bowl for another serving of spaghetti.

We lingered after dinner while the adults had coffee and tea. I was starting to fade, and my teammates were also ready to call it a night. I nudged my dad. "Can you drive us back to the hotel? We're about to go face first in the cannoli." Trays of cannoli graced the tables, but we had to refrain from dessert until after the meet, Coach's orders. Mel and Erica had wrapped two each in a napkin and slipped them into their coat pockets for the ride home tomorrow.

I hated to say good night to my dad but couldn't keep my eyes open. He walked me to my room and gave me a hug.

"Thanks for coming," I said, stifling a yawn.

"I wouldn't miss it for the world."

"I wish Mom was here."

"Me too."

"Did you get any video for her?"

"Already sent it."

"Thanks."

"You need to get into bed. The alarm is going to buzz early tomorrow, and it's going to be another long day."

"Not as long as today."

"More tension."

I let that sink in before responding. "I won't give in to the pressure," I said. "May the best swimmer win. That's what it comes down to."

"Good attitude. And remember, whether you break the record or not you're still my champion."

"Gee Dad, don't get all cornball on me now, it's a little too late, and I ate a little too much."

He laughed and mussed my hair. "Go to bed."

I reached up to plant a kiss on his cheek. "See you in the morning."

Chapter 86

I wish I could say I slept great and woke ready to conquer the world, but that's not what happened. I tossed and turned all night, sharing a bed with Mel. Tati and Erica were deep asleep in the next bed. The room was too hot, and I cracked open a window. Then it was too cold, and I shut the window and cranked up the heat. All the pasta and garlic bread had made me thirsty, and I was up twice for a drink of water, which made me have to pee and got me up again. I finally conked out around three, which gave me almost four hours of rest before the alarm went off. We washed, dressed, and packed quickly to meet our coaches downstairs for a power breakfast.

"You look exhausted," Coach said as soon as he laid eyes on me. "What happened?"

I didn't want to bore him with the story and said, "What do you mean? I'm fantastic." I stepped around him to pile some eggs and bacon on a plate and took a seat.

We were among the first to arrive at the natatorium and Coach had us in the pool at once for a quick warm up. I set my mind and muscles on autopilot, shut down everything else, and focused on what I had to do.

The other girls were tense too, not too talkative, minding their own business. I guess the reality of where we were and what we were about to do had hit them. It was a first for Mel and Erica, but Tati and I had been here before, and it would be our last time. She went about her stretches and pre-race preparations, a serene expression on her face as she bobbed her head to whatever played through her ear buds. Cool as a cucumber. Nothing seemed to rattle that girl.

The stands started filling in as the pool deck grew thick with swimmers, not close to as many as the day before because more than half had not qualified for the finals. Only the best remained. I counted my blessings I was one of them.

I waited for the arrival of my father and the rest of the Blazers' parents. Minutes before the meet started, they filed in as a group and took their seats, my father sitting next to Calvin Reese, the two of them smiling and talking like old friends. I wished I could hear their conversation. Later on, I'd tell my dad what I thought of his new buddy. Just minutes before the national anthem someone else joined the Blazers' cheering squad. Allison Singer took the open seat next to Calvin Reese. She shook hands with my father, who looked thrilled to meet her.

"Look at that," I said, nudging Mel.

"I didn't know she was coming," Mel said.

Tati, released from her ear buds, said, "My father told me she'd be here."

As organized and swift as yesterday's meet was, today's was even faster and more efficient because the number of swimmers had decreased. The 200 medley relay was over, and Tati and I were on deck for the 200 free. There were two heats. We were in the second. I waited nervously, looking anywhere but at the swimmers and the clock. This time, I didn't want to know how anyone else was doing. I just wanted to beat Tati, and she was four lanes to my left.

The first heat ended, and we took our places. I checked that my goggles and cap were on tight, and waited for the start. The buzzer buzzed and I took off, thinking about nothing except making my turns until I hit the wall for the final time. I placed fourth, 1:54.19, my best time ever. I looked at Tati's finish: sixth place at 156.57. Once again, I was on top.

I climbed out of the pool first and gave her a hand as she clambered out, breathless, her face a bright shade of red. I was a little delirious too but managed to hang on.

"Congratulations," she said between gasps.

"I couldn't do it without you." I meant it.

"One more time," she said, smiling up at me.

"That's right," I smiled back. It was hard to feel any animosity toward such an agreeable opponent.

As soon as we were on the pool deck, Coach wrapped us both in a big hug. "Way to go, girls," he said beaming. Our teammates and Coach D gathered around us with praise and congratulations. Tati and I just wanted to recover. We pushed our way past them and collapsed on the bleachers. Mel brought us each a cup of water and we sucked them down in seconds. Erica handed us towels and we dried off. Minutes later, we were dressed in our warm-up suits, watching the next races. We had quite a wait before the 500.

I used the time to connect with my father who was still sitting with Calvin Reese and Allison Singer. Maggie and Paige sat on his other side. I willed them to look at me, and it worked. A few minutes later, we made eye contact, and they shouted a few cheers down to me.

My father held up his cell phone and mouthed, "I sent your mother the video." I nodded in appreciation, so happy he had thought to share this special time with her. My heart ached, wishing she was here, but I realized I shouldn't dwell on her absence and was grateful she could participate in her own remote way. We'd have plenty of time to talk the next time I visited her.

Two rows behind my father and Maggie sat Justin and Sean. Justin looked down at me, his face wreathed in smiles. He held up a large white poster board with "Go Aerin! Two Rivers' Finest" written across it in Blazer blue block lettering. He stood up and raised it over his head, letting out a long, shrill whistle, earning the attention of at least two hundred people who sat around him, including Calvin Reese, who scowled at him and looked down at me. Our eyes locked for a moment but I chose to ignore him and his pitiful threats. I focused back on Justin and blew him a kiss. He blew one back.

"You guys make me sick," said Mel, who witnessed the whole thing. "And I thought *I* was his favorite swimmer."

"If it's any consolation," I said, "you're his favorite sister."

"No competition there," she said. "And I don't mind the poster. You are Two Rivers' finest."

"Thanks," I said, for the first time thinking it might be true.

As the minutes dragged on and the 500 loomed closer, the butterflies in my stomach started fluttering. I hadn't eaten since breakfast more than four hours ago, but I wasn't hungry. The thought of food made me nauseous, and I realized pre-race jitters were coming on strong. I needed to be alone. I stood up and walked a few feet away from my team and my coaches, eyes on the ground, avoiding looking at the pool, the races, the other swimmers, the spectators. I needed to get a grip, and the noise and commotion in the natatorium weren't helping. There was nowhere to be alone, so I paced where I was, repeating Coach Mike's mantra in my head. When I'd settled my nerves I rejoined Mel and Erica.

"You okay?" Mel asked. "You look a little green, like Charlie does before a big race."

"I'm okay," I said.

We were in the midst of the diving finals, but I hadn't noticed the shift from swimming to diving. This event would take a while.

"Want to go up in the stands?" she asked.

I shook my head. "No, I don't want to talk to anyone until my race is over."

"We can take a break in the locker room."

The thought of retreating to the sweaty, smelly locker room made my nausea return. "I'm okay. Let's stay here."

"Where's Tati?" Erica asked.

Tati was missing. I glanced up into the stands to see if she was sitting with her parents or Sean, but saw no sign of her. She wasn't with our coaches either. Coach was talking to a few other coaches about ten feet away, and Coach D was sitting on the bleachers with her laptop open, typing away, most likely reporting our progress to Mr. Maxwell, the Athletic Director. I interrupted her.

"Where's Tati?"

She looked up from the keyboard with a dazed expression. "She was right here a minute ago."

"We should look for her," said Mel.

"No need," Erica said, "She's right there."

I followed the path of her pointing finger. Tati was crouched down in an isolated corner a few feet away, staring at the ground, looking a little shaky.

"Is she all right?" Erica asked.

"Hey, Tati!" Mel called. She stood up to join her, but I stopped her.

"Leave her alone," I said, recognizing that Tati was trying to settle her nerves just as I had. "She's all right. Pre-race jitters."

"Tati doesn't get pre-race jitters," Mel countered, still concerned.

"She does today. She has a lot riding on this race, and she's feeling the pressure." I guided them back to the bleachers. "Let's watch the races."

Minutes later, Tati was sitting beside Mel, looking a little calmer.

"You okay?" Mel asked.

She nodded. "It's so overwhelming," she said, gesturing toward the pool. "And it's my last high school meet, yours too. I'm a little melancholy."

"Let's be melancholy later," Mel said. "We've got work to do."

The hundred free and fly passed in a blur, and Tati and I were again on the blocks. As the first heat commenced, we went through our usual pre-race prep, checking and double-checking our gear, stretching our limbs, loosening up. We made no eye contact, pretending we didn't know each other.

As the first heat ended and the cheering died down for the start of our race, a hush came over the natatorium. The news media had hyped the event, and I supposed most people were familiar with the story. An air of expectation surrounded us. I looked to the swimmer on my right who stared back at me, her lips trembling. I turned the other way and scanned the swimmers beyond Tati. Everyone looked tense.

"Final heat: 500 freestyle," the announcer said, breaking the hush.

The swimmers climbed onto the blocks. I positioned for the start and waited, staring down at the broad expanse of water in front of me. It was motionless, placid, like glass. Mel was at the opposite end of the lane, ready to count my laps, Erica beside her preparing to count Tati's.

My gaze shifted to Tati, and she turned to me at the same time, our eyes locking. She gave me an almost imperceptible smile. I kept my expression steady, not giving away any hint at what I was feeling, and turned away. We were not friends. We were not teammates. She was just another swimmer who stood in the way of my victory.

"Swimmers take your mark," the announcer instructed. A second later, the buzzer buzzed, and I was in the water, streamlining across the pool, surfacing at ten yards with no one visible on either side. All of my training and years of hard work kicked in. I zoned out, concentrating on kicking, breathing, and slicing my arms through the water. As I approached each turn, Mel screamed at me, "Go! Go! Go!" I didn't need her encouragement. It was *my* race, and I intended to take it. I forgot about Allison Singer, the fifty thousand dollar challenge, Calvin Reese and his ugly bribe, my mother wasting time in jail, my father juggling two families, and Tatiana, whom I could not see but sensed was right behind me.

As each lap ended and I got closer to the finish, my lungs grew heavier. My muscles ached until I felt nothing at all. When three-quarters of the laps were behind me and the finish loomed closer, I faltered on a turn and immediately glimpsed a shadow to my left. It loomed larger and I realized Tati had caught up to me. I didn't have the strength to go on, let alone go ahead, but dismissed my discomfort and quickened my stroke, kicking more furiously until I gained the advantage. Still, she was at my feet, threatening to overcome me at every turn. On the last turn, I pushed off the wall with all I had, closing my eyes, counting my strokes, knowing exactly when I'd be at the finish. I had no idea where she was and hoped I had enough power and breath to finish first.

The crowd was wild as I approached the wall and opened my eyes two strokes before the finish. I slammed into the pad with all my might and surfaced, my vision blurred. I was disoriented, choking, crying, a mess. I lost complete control, struggling to catch my breath, to return my body to some level of equilibrium.

When I came around, I saw the other swimmers had also finished the race. The natatorium was rocking, a thunderous sound. I tried to come to grips with the end of the race and looked up at the scoreboard. My eyes found Tati's finish time first: 4:49:56. I closed my eyes, disbelieving. Tati had broken the record and won the Allison Singer challenge.

She was crying too, struggling to regain her breath and composure, her face the reddest I'd ever seen it. She ducked under the lane line and swam toward me. I collapsed in her arms, my head buried in her shoulder as we clung to each other.

"You did it," she said. "You won."

I didn't understand what she was saying and pulled back, confused. She pointed up at the scoreboard. That's when I realized she had come in second. I shifted my gaze and found my own time:

4:46.49, three seconds ahead of her, and in first place. I had won the race, the New York State Championship title, broken the Singer challenge, and had my best personal time *ever*.

I stared at the scoreboard, stunned, as the other swimmers congratulated me, reaching out to shake my hand, some of them hugging me. Tatiana was all smiles, telling anyone who would listen, "She's on my team."

The noise in the natatorium was through the roof, the spectators in the stands on their feet as they cheered and clapped, proud to have witnessed such a momentous event. In the far corner where the Blazers' cheering squad grouped, my father and Aunt Maggie were engulfed by a throng of well-wishers and I couldn't see them.

At the poolside, an official blasted his whistle and ordered us out of the pool.

I pulled myself out and collided with Coach, who caught me in a huge bear hug. When Tatiana emerged beside me, he pulled her in too, and the three of us held on to each other for a minute, speechless. Coach had tears in his eyes. "So proud, so proud," he kept saying.

Behind him stood Coach D, a dazzling grin on her usual poker face, tears streaming down her cheeks.

When we parted, Mel and Erica stood by with towels. Mel draped an arm around my shoulders and hugged me.

"I knew you could do it," she said, her eyes shiny with tears.

Erica wrapped Tati in a towel. "Are you okay?" she asked.

"I'm fine," she said, sniffling. She wiped away her tears. "I am so glad that's over."

Mel walked me back to the bleachers, the rest of our team following. As we walked past the stands, people called out my name, congratulating me, some of them reaching out to shake my hand.

"This is nuts," I said to Mel. "These people are crazy."

"You ain't seen nothing yet," she said. "The media is all over this place. TV and newspaper reporters, local media and national affiliates. You're big news, Aerin. And dozens of recruiters are itching to talk to you."

"It's only a swimming event," I said as I plopped down.

She poured me a drink of water and handed it to me. "It is *the* biggest event in varsity swimming. Nothing like it has ever happened. Get used to it. You're a star."

"Don't get used to it *now*," Coach said. "You've got another race in less than two minutes. Drink up and then get on the blocks. The 200 free relay is up."

The meet must go on.

Five minutes later, we finished the relay in eighth place, but no one minded.

And when we finished last in the 400 free relay, we cheered.

No other team left the New York State Girls' Swimming and Diving Championships prouder or happier than the Two Rivers Trailblazers.

Week Fifteen:

Season Wrap-Up

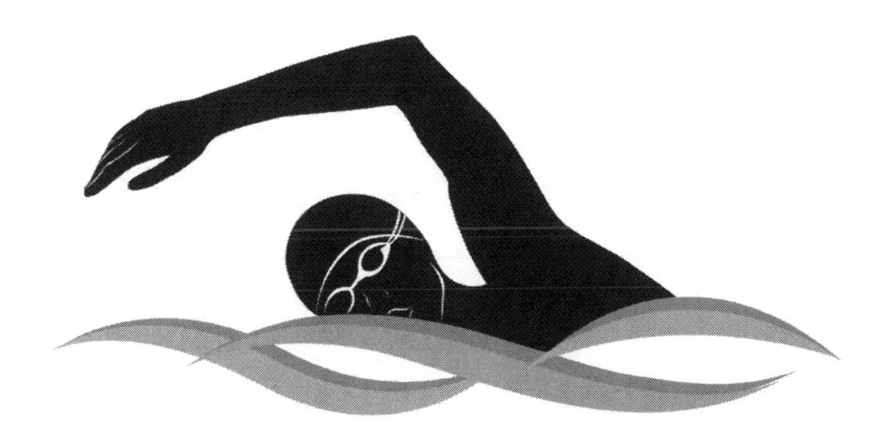

Chapter 87

The next few weeks flew by in a flurry of interviews with both reporters and recruiters. The pile of letters from coaches and admissions counselors on my desk doubled. Schools I never knew existed invited me to join their teams, and sports stations and magazines I'd never heard of called for interviews.

On my first day back at school, the principal made a big announcement on the school-wide sound system, and I couldn't pass through the corridors without someone high fiving me or asking me how it felt to win the Singer challenge. I was the most popular girl in school. Even Jordan sucked up to me.

In the beginning, all the attention was exciting, but it soon grew tedious and interfered with my schoolwork. I asked my dad to handle the media requests and email and letters from the recruiters. I forwarded him all that literature and told him to weed out the offers that didn't interest us. Once that burden was off my shoulders, I could breathe easier and get back to maintaining my GPA and friendships.

Thanksgiving came and I spent the holiday with Dad, Dawn, and the girls. Dawn was doing much better, and the doctor allowed her to get off the couch a few hours each day. She still had to take it easy so my father ordered a complete Thanksgiving Day dinner delivered to the house. In the past, they'd hosted a huge open house with all of Dawn's family and their friends, but this time it was just the six of us, including Geneviève, who enjoyed a turkey dinner with all the trimmings for the first time.

We skipped the Black Friday shopping frenzy for movies and games at home. Dawn did most of her shopping online, and I helped her pick out gifts for my father and Geneviève.

On Saturday, Dad and I made the trip upstate for my third visit with my mother. It was his first time seeing her in that place, and I could tell the whole experience unnerved him.

"But you're a lawyer," I reminded him. "You must do this all the time."

"Yeah, but this is personal," he said.

He hadn't seen her since her sentencing. Her hair had grown in a little bit but the pixie style – which was so adorable and took years off her face - startled him.

"You've cut your beautiful hair," he said after they embraced.

"It's the new me. Like it?" She pushed her bangs to the side and fluffed up the top.

"I do," he said, gazing at her in wonder. "And you've put on some weight."

"Uh, Dad," I said, "You're not supposed to say that to a woman."

"It's okay," Mom laughed. "I don't mind. I needed to gain a few pounds."

"You look great, Devon," he said.

We sat down and the conversation turned to me. My father showed my mother the videos of my races again, and we viewed them two or three times each, analyzing every stroke.

"So, what happens now?" Mom asked. "When do you get the scholarship money?"

"I spoke with Allison Singer," Dad said, "and she's setting up a trust for Aerin. Once she's enrolled in a school, we'll send the tuition bills to her representative, and they'll pay them from the trust."

"This is fabulous," Mom said, beaming. "You are on your way, sweetheart. Any idea where you want to go?"

I shook my head. "Not yet. Dad and I are going to look at all the offers and choose six or so for me to apply to, depending on what programs they offer. I'm looking for sports management or coaching. That will narrow things down. And it will all depend on how much money they offer me to swim. Once I'm accepted we'll visit the schools, meet the coaches and everyone, and then I'll decide."

"Well, whatever you choose, I'll support you. Don't worry about me. You go wherever you need to have the future you want, even if it's in California."

"It might be," I said and told her about the letter I received from the coach at Cal, which had been my first choice since the first day of considering college.

As usual, our visit ended too soon, and we parted amidst tears, happy and sad.

"In three months I'll be out of here," Mom reminded me. "I'll be on parole, but I can live wherever I want to in New York State. I think I'll take Maggie up on her offer and move to Two Rivers. That way you can continue at the high school and graduate with your friends. How's that sound?"

I threw my arms around her and squeezed her tight. "That's perfect," I said. I couldn't wait to tell Mel and Justin I wasn't going anywhere.

"Maribel wants to continue leasing the apartment, so I don't have to worry about that. Who knows? Maybe I will become a real country girl."

"I don't know about that," Dad said. "Devon Keane trading the city lights for country life?"

"Well, you never know," she said. "Like I said, I'm a new

woman. The change will do me good."

On the way home, my dad chuckled.

"What's so funny?" I asked.

"I'm thinking about your mother going country. Wouldn't it be funny if she married a farmer?"

That cracked me up too. "Yeah right," I said. "I'll believe it when I see it."

Chapter 88

Swim season ended each year with a team banquet, an elaborate event in a party hall with a huge buffet and a DJ. All the girls dressed up, not as fancy as they did for the church dance, but just a notch below. I was lucky I'd packed a little black dress for such occasions. I borrowed a pair of black spiked heels from Maggie. We could invite our families, so I went with my father. We sat with Mel and her parents, and Justin, who sat beside me and held my hand under the table.

His swim season was underway and he was in training. He went to the buffet table three times, filling his plate and then cleaning it.

"Don't count on any leftovers with that boy at the table," my dad said to Justin's mom.

She laughed. "Guess I'll get my money's worth. He eats enough for all of us."

"And I thought Aerin had a hollow leg."

"Dad!" I cried.

"We're in good company, Aerin, don't you worry. Everyone at this table understands, am I right?"

Mel's parents agreed, and they and my father got up to peruse the dessert table.

"I'm stuffed," Mel said.

"Me too."

"We need to start watching what we eat. If we don't, we'll start putting on the pounds."

Now that we were training much less than usual we'd burn hundreds of calories fewer each day and could plump up in no time.

"But not today," I said as Justin sat down with two plates full of yummy desserts.

After we had pigged out, it was time for the awards and recognition ceremony. We all sat in a party food stupor listening as Coach reviewed the highlights of our season, and recognized those swimmers who had received academic awards and varsity letters. Just about every girl got something. The swim team had an average GPA of 94.3, the highest of all athletic teams at the school. We all received a certificate recognizing this achievement.

As was custom, Coach saved the best awards for last: Rookie of the Year, Most Improved Performer, and Most Valuable Performer. For weeks we'd debated who would earn these titles. The coaches and the Athletic Director decided on the first two, and the girls voted for the recipient of the MVP. We'd cast our votes just days before, at our last team meeting of the season. We had no idea who would win. Some thought it would be me. Others rooted for Tati.

Coach stood at the podium and cleared his throat, looking a bit melancholy. The room grew quiet. "I've coached this team for more than twenty years, and I have to say this has been the most exciting, most rewarding season of my career. I have only you, my swimmers and your parents, to thank.

"With that, I have three final awards to give out. The first is for Rookie of the Year. This award goes to the athlete who has achieved more than was expected in her first season with the team. This year, it goes to a young swimmer who qualified to compete in the Division Championships and helped her team to the division title. That swimmer is Charlotte Donovan. Charlie is an eighth-grader who came to us after many years swimming on the Marlins club team. Not only is she an exemplary athlete and student, but also a good friend, as evidenced by the friendships she's made. I'm sure she will continue to be an asset in the future. Will Charlie please come to the podium to accept her award?"

With much cheering and applause, Charlie rose and approached Coach, who held out a plaque that read "*Charlotte Donovan, Rookie of the Year, Two Rivers Trailblazers Girls Varsity Swim and Dive Team.*"

Coach gave her a big hug, and she returned to her table, beaming.

Coach picked up the next award and examined it. "Our next award-winning athlete has shown significant improvement this season, exceeding her personal best and also showing leadership. This swimmer not only made it to the Division Championships where she finished her events with personal best times but also displayed her best at the New York State Championship meet. She is co-captain and has been a productive member for the past six years. Melanie Ford, please come up and accept the award as Most Improved Performer."

With a squeal, Mel shot out of her seat and raced toward the podium. "It's mine?" she asked as Coach handed her the plaque. He nodded, and she gave him a hug before they posed for pictures. She was back in her seat in a flash.

"Look!" she said, holding up the plaque. "It's the first time I've ever gotten anything besides academic awards and varsity letters."

"After six years I'd say you earned it," Justin said.

"Good job, Mel," I said, proud of her.

"And now, our final award is for Most Valuable Performer. This award goes to the swimmer who has made the greatest contribution to the team regarding leadership and scoring. It's also a reflection of who the girls look up to and wish to emulate. We arrive at the decision two ways. The first is a vote from each girl. Then Coach D and I measure the performance of the top athletes with the top vote getters. Most years it's easy to determine the MVP because she tends to rise to the top both in scoring and popularity. This year, however, it wasn't so easy because we have two outstanding performers who have each earned the respect of her teammates."

Under the table, Justin squeezed my hand, and my heart beat sped up. I had no expectation that I would be the MVP. That award belonged to Tatiana. If Coach called me to come up to the podium, I'd pass out.

"In the end, though, we measured all factors, and decided the MVP is a swimmer who has been on the team six years." Justin's grip on my hand relaxed and my nerves quieted. I let out a breath I didn't know I was holding. "She's been a leader from day one, competing in the Division Championships all six years and winning her events twice. She's also been to the State Championship meet twice and helped her team score in the top eight in several events. She is a co-captain and a leader with a bright future ahead of her no matter where she chooses to swim next. Tatiana Reese, please come to the podium and accept the award as Most Valuable Performer."

Tati made for the podium amid a standing ovation, Calvin Reese busting with pride. I joined the ovation too, knowing in my heart that Tati truly was the MVP.

Once all the congratulations were given, and the photographs taken, the banquet ended and people prepared to leave. Coach called for attention once more.

"We're not done," he said. "I have one more award, the first and last time anyone will receive it. I admit, I never thought I'd present this award until this year." He looked at Tati, and then at me. "Everyone knows Allison Singer has offered a challenge to the swimmer who breaks her record in the 500 free. No one has ever come close. This season, however, *two* swimmers vied for the challenge, and up until the last minute we had no idea if either of them would break it. Their efforts provided us with a lot of excitement, incentive, and motivation, and of course, pride, bringing national attention to our program. Both of these swimmers did break the record, but one of them was just a little bit faster, and that swimmer is the recipient of the Allison Singer Award, which, as you all know, comes with a fifty thousand dollar scholarship. Aerin Keane is that swimmer.

"Aerin came to our school as a senior, a young woman starting here as a stranger, an outsider, with a load of talent and a competitive streak I've never seen before. Over the course of the season, Aerin emerged not only as one of the greatest swimmers this school has ever seen, but also as a leader, and a friend, an exemplary student, a young woman we can all be proud of. Aerin, please come up to the podium and accept your award."

By the time he finished speaking, I was trembling and needed my father to help me get up and walk to the podium. Coach stood there beaming, a plaque in hand, but he was not alone.

Standing beside him was Allison Singer, also beaming, and holding a bouquet of roses. She handed them to me and shook my hand. "I'm glad it was you," she whispered. She turned to my father. "You've got quite a girl here."

"Don't I know it," he said. We walked back to our table with applause and congratulations coming from every corner of the room. My friends gathered around me - Mel, Erica, Charlie, Kelsey, Justin, and Tati – giving me hugs and exclaiming over the beautiful flowers and the plaque that read *Two Rivers Trailblazers Girls Varsity Swim and Dive Team RECORD-BREAKER - 500 freestyle - Aerin Keane - 4:46.49.*

"I bet it will take twenty years for someone to beat *that* record," Mel said.

"You might want to rethink your career choice," Justin said. At my puzzled expression, he explained. "You might need to come up with a scholarship of your own, and everyone knows coaches don't have that kind of money."

"I'm sure someone will break it someday soon," I said.

The party was ending. Parents grabbed their coats and kids.

Some of the younger team members had already left. Tati went to the front of the room and picked up the microphone. "Before we leave, the team has something for Coach."

The announcement caught everyone's attention. Coach turned back to the podium, surprised. The remaining girls clustered around him. Mel held a gift-wrapped box in her hand.

"Coach Dudash, you're the best coach we could have had," Tati said. "We can't say goodbye without giving you a little something to remember this season."

Mel handed him the gift.

"You girls didn't have to do this," he said as he unfurled the ribbon. He lifted the lid off the box and pulled out the timepiece we had selected. It was a superwatch and cost every cent we'd pooled together. The inscription on the back read *Best Coach, Two Rivers Girls Varsity Swim & Dive Team, 4x Champs!*

"I'm touched," he said as he fumbled to put it on. Mel helped him and when she had it secured, he raised his arm and showed it to everyone. "Thank you." The parents circled him to offer congratulations and check out his new watch.

The seniors wandered away from the admiring crowd.

"So what are we going to do now?" Erica asked as the excitement died down.

"My parents said we can hang out at our house," Mel said.

"That's not what I meant," Erica said. "What are we going to do now that swim season is over? It's our last one."

The realization cast a pall on the moment, and we grew hushed, looking at each other with sadness and uncertainty.

Mel broke the silence. "We're going to do what we always do. Take a break, enjoy the holidays, and get back in the water for club season after the first of the year. I, for one, am not done. I still have goals to meet and times to beat. And I'm still looking at colleges. What can I say? A swimmer's work is never done."

We all agreed and started talking at once, disclosing our plans and goals. As I shrugged into my coat before escaping into the winter night, Justin pulled me aside.

"Did I hear you say something about a goal?"

My cheeks flushed. I didn't think anyone could hear me amidst that rush of noise.

"Just a little one," I teased.

He cocked an eyebrow. "Care to share?"

"I was just thinking, wouldn't it be nice to break my own personal best as a freshman on a Division I team?"

"That *would* be nice," he agreed.

"It's going to take a lot of work."

"I've got time."

"So do I. I'll keep coming to morning practice and train with the club."

He broke out that megawatt smile. "Perfect," he said. "When my season ends, I'll train with you. Deal?"

"Deal." We shook on it.

We stood in the lobby of the banquet hall. Most everyone had left. My father was deep in conversation with Justin and Mel's parents. We joined them, and I took Dad's hand. We said goodnight to the Fords and headed for the door.

"What's the plan?" he asked as we stepped out into the cold December night.

"You know, Dad, I have a new plan. I'll tell you all about it on the way home."

THE END

About the Author

During swim season, you can find Marianne Sciucco, a dedicated Swim Mom for ten years, at one of many Skyline Conference swim meets, cheering for her daughter Allison and her team, the Mount Saint Mary College Knights.

Marianne is not a nurse who writes but a writer who happens to be a nurse. A lover of words and books, she dreamed of becoming an author when she grew up but became a nurse to avoid poverty. She later brought her two passions together and writes about the intricate lives of people struggling with health and family issues.

Her debut novel *Blue Hydrangeas, an Alzheimer's love story*, is a Kindle bestseller, IndieReader Approved, a BookWorks featured book, and a Library Journal Self-e Selection. It is available on Amazon, iBooks, Barnes and Noble, Kobo, Audible, iTunes, and other retailers. Her short stories *Ino's Love* and *Collection* (winner of the 2007 Tom Howard/John H. Reid Short Story Contest, Honorable Mention) are available on Kindle and Audible.

A native Bostonian, Marianne lives in New York's Hudson Valley, and when not writing works as a campus nurse at a community college.

Follow Marianne on her website mariannesciucco.com, Twitter, and Facebook.

A Note from the Author

Thank you for reading *Swim Season.* This novel was truly a labor of love started in the fall of 2011, when my daughter, Allison, was a junior in high school and on the swim team. The story of the Two Rivers Trailblazers followed me throughout her college swimming career, and I completed it at the start of her final varsity swim season in 2016. From the beginning, my intention was to write a story that would speak to the dedication, commitment, hard work, and determination of these young athletes who inspire me and make me love this sport.

Along the way, I had tremendous support for this story from friends and family, as well as swim coaches and swimmers. At the top of the list, as always, are my husband, Lou, and my daughter, Allison. I doubt it was easy for them to listen to me think out loud about my characters and imaginary swim meets in and out of season, but they allowed me to explore the story and it's likely better because of it.

Big thanks go to the following coaches who allowed me to pick their brains and craft the finer details of the plot: Frank Woodward, Middletown High School, Middletown, New York; Justin Wright, Monroe Woodbury High School, Monroe, New York; Jeremy Cuebas, Minisink Valley High School, Minisink, New York; and Danielle Lindner, formerly of Mount Saint Mary College, Newburgh, New York.

As a nurse and an author I had many questions surrounding the storyline of Aerin's mom, Devon. Susan Corbett, RN, BS, CASAC, SUNY Orange Wellness Center, Middletown, New York; Barbara D. Nahmias, RN, NPP, PMHCNS, BC, Outreach Coordinator, Statewide Peer Assistance for Nurses (SPAN), New York State Nurses Association, Albany, New York; and Sheryl Pincus, RN, MS, JD all provided valuable knowledge, and I thank them for sharing their expertise.

Several students from Orange County Community College (SUNY Orange) assisted in the production of this book. Many thanks to the following interns from the Arts and Communications program: Shannon Dowd, Carl Arcilesi, Jorge Vidals, and Ian Bruno. Your eagerness to learn, great ideas, and hands-on help were a huge asset and helped bring Swim Season to life.

Several people rallied to my cause when I launched a Pubslush campaign to help fund publication of this book. I thank the following for their support and patience: Kim Butterworth Adler, Ann Anzini, Carl Arcilesi, Inang L. Aziz-Antal, Janet Beam, Carina Blon, Maria Blon, Marge Clairmont, Bernadette Colby, Gina Cote-Mielke, Beverly Guaraldi, Eleanor Sciucco, and Lou Sciucco.

Big thanks to Janet Beam for teaching me how to score the swim meets. And *merci beaucoup* to Geneviève Haines for the French translations.

Much appreciation goes out to my beta readers, Jean Lee, Vicki Tapia, and Kathryn Harrison, who helped find my typos and errors and pointed out inconsistencies in my manuscript.

Above all else, I thank the thousands of swimmers I've had the pleasure to watch over the last ten years. Follow your dreams.

A Request from the Author

Feedback from readers is very important and I welcome your comments.

Please feel free to send me an email at MarianneSciucco@gmail.com.

You may also leave a review on Amazon and Goodreads.

To be among the first to hear of my upcoming releases sign up for my newsletter at http://eepurl.com/balkyT and receive a free copy of my short story Collection.

Thank you.